Nick Walker, U.F. Marshal
Asteroid Outpost

by
John Bowers

For Kimberley
Happy reading!

John Bowers

Science Fiction that doesn't *taste* like science fiction

Asteroid Outpost

An AKW Books eBook
Published by Kalar/Wade Media

First Publication: December 2012

Cover by Ravven

ISBN: 978-1-7266-6645-9

John Bowers

For Byker Bob.
May the flatus be with you...always.

Don't miss these great books by John Bowers
Published by AKW Books and FTL Press

NICK WALKER, U.F. MARSHAL

Asteroid Outpost
Sirian Summer
Rebel Guns of Alpha Centauri
Victoria Cross: United Federation Attorney
Bounty Hunter at Binary Flats
Gunfight on the Alpha Centauri Express
Manhunt on Tau Ceti 4
Assassin on Centauri B
Revolt on Alpha 2
Return to Sirius
Victoria Cross: Colonial Defense Attorney
Ambush at Galaxy Gulch

STARPORT SERIES

Starport
Guerrilla Girl
Famine Planet
Prisoners of Eroak
Occupy Eroak!

THE FIGHTER QUEEN SAGA

A Vow to Sophia
The Fighter Queen
Star Marine!
The Fighter King
The Sword of Sophia

Nick Walker, U.F. Marshal
Series Recap

1. Asteroid Outpost
    After four years in the Star Marines and two in the
    UFM Academy, Nick Walker receives his first
    assignment as a U.F. Marshal. Posted to Ceres, which
    some consider the anus of the Solar System, Nick is
    confident that he is ready to kick some serious
    asteroid. Youth and idealism are wonderful things, but
    they don't prepare you for the real universe...it never
    occurs to Nick that the asteroid might kick back.

2. Sirian Summer
    After two years on Ceres, Nick is posted to a small town
    on Sirius 1 called Kline Corners. The resident marshal
    there has been murdered and Nick has a dual
    mandate—take over the local office and find the killer.
    Sounds simple enough, right? But within hours of his
    arrival, Nick discovers evidence of not just murder, but
    racism, slavery, and human trafficking. How can a lone
    lawman hope to survive all that, let alone complete his
    mission?

3. Rebel Guns of Alpha Centauri
    Eighteen months after his arrival on Sirius, Nick is
    reposted again, this time to Trimmer Springs, a small
    mountain town on Alpha Centauri 2. It should be a
    quiet posting with nothing much to do. But when his
    deputy is killed by a sniper who was gunning for Nick,
    things quickly turn anything but quiet.

4. Victoria Cross: United Federation Attorney
    Victoria Cross is Nick Walker's ex-girlfriend. They were
    in the Star Marines together, fell in love, then she

broke his heart. Nick has never forgiven her, nor can she forgive herself. Now a Federation prosecutor on Alpha Centauri 2, Victoria knows her path and Nick's will eventually cross...and that will be awkward. In the meantime, she has a job to do, prosecuting the people Nick has arrested. But it isn't as easy as it sounds...one of them may be innocent.

5. Bounty Hunter at Binary Flats
   Still posted at Trimmer Springs, Nick is called 2000 miles south to investigate a threat to a colonial senator who has received a wanted poster with his name on it. At first glance, the poster appears to be a hoax, but Nick can't put it to bed without proof. The evidence leads him into uncharted territory at a place called Binary Flats. Here he finds all the proof he needs, but the proof will do him no good unless he can get out alive.

6. Gunfight on the Alpha Centauri Express
   For nearly five years, Nick Walker has been enforcing the law on the Final Frontier, but in so doing has racked up an impressive body count. Now, assistant U.F. Attorney Brian Godney wants him investigated for using excessive force, and Nick finds himself in a courtroom facing not only Godney, but Godney's assistant, U.F. Attorney Victoria Cross—Nick's old girlfriend. The timing couldn't be worse—with his career on the line, Nick still has to hunt down an interstellar terrorist whose body count is in the thousands...before he strikes again. It will be a tossup which will get him first, Godney or the terrorist.

7. Manhunt on Tau Ceti 4
   Two years after the shootout on the Alpha Centauri Express, Nick Walker has hit bottom. He's lost his

fiancée, his best friend, and his job...and the terrorist got away. Nick hunted him across the galaxy, but came up empty. Now he's stuck in a dingy saloon in the Martian badlands, drinking himself into oblivion. But Victoria Cross hasn't given up on him. She tracks him down and tries to coax him back home. He isn't having it, but then she plays her hole card, the only thing likely to get his attention—she knows where to find the terrorist.

8. Assassin on Centauri B
   Barely six months after his return from Tau Ceti 4, Nick Walker is handed a mission that he seems unlikely to survive. Federation President Vivian White Wolf personally requests Nick to infiltrate the Rukranian mob on Alpha Centauri B. The mob controls the BC government, which is on the verge of allying with Sirius, which poses a deadly threat to the entire galaxy. It's Nick's first undercover job, and he's going in not only alone...but unarmed. Even if he survives, an assassin is waiting for him at home.

9. Revolt on Alpha 2
   Flash back thirteen years. Nick Walker is a Star Marine, just 20 years old. While he was in training, the cult revolution began on Alpha Centauri 2, steamrolled over the Colonial Defense Force, badly bloodied the Federation Infantry, and captured 80% of the planet. If anything is to be salvaged, it's up to the Star Marines, and Nick Walker is about to get his feet wet. The day after he arrives on the planet, he gets news that his father has died of a stroke. The timing couldn't be worse, because he needs every wit at his command just to stay alive...and things will only get worse.

10. Return to Sirius

Someone is hijacking starships. Four, so far, with no end in sight, and all the passengers have disappeared. Nick Walker is assigned to find out who is behind the attacks and, if possible, stop them. He learns that one man had booked passage on all the missing ships, and when the same man books a fifth ship, Nick does the same. He suspects, but can't prove, that Sirius is behind the attacks; his only hope is to remain flexible and somehow intercept the attackers before another 2000 passengers disappear into the black hole of slavery. If he succeeds, he'll be a hero, but if he fails...well, the Sirians have been hunting him for years. The ending won't be pretty.

11. Victoria Cross: Colonial Defense Attorney
Once a Federation prosecutor, Victoria Cross is now a defense attorney. When Nick Walker takes down a pair of bank robbers who claim they stole the money in self-defense, she faces the challenge of proving their claim. It won't be easy, but Nick believes in her and helps investigate the crime. The real culprit turns out to be a former Star Marine who has turned to the dark side...and has no intention of going to prison. Neither Nick, Victoria, nor her clients will be safe until this man is taken down. But he has cops on his payroll, and taking him down could be deadly.

12. Ambush at Galaxy Gulch
In nine years of law enforcement, Nick Walker has never taken a real vacation.
When his favorite western hero, Yancy West, invites him to visit a movie set, Nick takes thirty days off for rest and relaxation. Watching the actors record the vid is fun, and he might even be used as an extra. But things turn sour in a hurry when stuntmen begin using

real bullets. Someone is out to sabotage the flick, and
Nick suddenly finds himself back on the job.

Chapter 1

Sunday, August 4, 0440 (Colonial Calendar)
The A Terminal - Ceres

When he stepped out of the airlock, Nick Walker almost broke his neck. The ship's artificial gravity was six times that of the asteroid, and the transition threw him off balance. He stumbled and dropped his space bag.

A uniformed security guard who saw the whole thing smirked.

"Watch your step," he said.

Nick swayed as he regained his balance.

"Thanks for the warning. You might have said something sooner."

"More fun this way." The man was still smirking.

Nick picked up the space bag and glared at the guard, taking note of his shoulder patch for future reference: Farrington Security.

It was almost midnight local time and Nick had no idea where to go at such an hour. It was his first trip to Ceres and if anyone was expecting him, they hadn't bothered to meet the ship; he would have to wait until local morning to find his destination. He took the lift down to the underground and found the hatch leading out of the terminal.

The area was dark, with only an occasional overhead lamp to illuminate things. An electric taxi was parked at the curb and Nick walked toward it.

"Need a lift, mister?" The taxi pilot looked about seventy, gaunt and grey and alcoholic.

"Sure. Is there a hotel anywhere on this rock?" Nick tossed his space bag into the back of the taxi.

"Closest one is in Centerville, but they'll be closing the front desk about now. Nobody ever rents a room after midnight."

"Why not?"

"Nobody ever stops off here on the way to anywhere else. If you *are* here, then you *live* here, and if you live here, you already got a place to sleep. Leastways, that's the theory."

Nick sighed. Due to space lag, he wasn't sleepy anyway. His internal clock was still set for Bradbury City on Mars, where he'd boarded the ship. He had six hours to kill.

"Anyplace to get a drink, then?"

"Sure. Saloons are open all night. The Open Airlock is just a mile down the tunnel."

Nick climbed into the front seat and settled down.

"Take me there."

The Open Airlock - Ceres

The music was like a jackhammer inside his head—no melody, just a fast, hard, throbbing beat.

Nick had never been in a low-gravity bar, but it looked very much like every other pub he'd ever seen. Dim and smoky, crowded. Noisy. It could have been in any ghetto district on Terra, but most closely resembled a biker bar he'd once visited in SoCal. Pool tables in the center, gaming tables in the back, a postage-stamp dance floor; grungy men with scars, tattoos, and greasy hair. Beards made up for baldness, belligerence for missing teeth. Everyone with an attitude.

The women didn't look much better.

Nick strolled toward the bar, his eyes missing nothing. He rested an elbow on the surface and turned his attention to the bartender, who gazed at him with undisguised curiosity.

"You new here?"

"Why? Is this a private club?"

The bartender shrugged. "Not as long as you pay cash. What'll you have?"

"What've you got?"

"We don't serve wine."

Nick reached for his wallet. "Give me a beer."

The bartender reached into a cooler and produced a cold bottle, placed it in front of Nick.

"Twenty-five terros."

Nick's hand stopped halfway from his pocket.

"Twenty-five! That's starship piracy!"

"The beer's imported."

Nick stared at the bottle. "That's Bloodweiser! The cheapest beer in the Federation."

"Real popular around here."

"It's cold piss!"

The bartender eyed him coldly. "It's imported. All the way from St. Louis."

Nick heaved an exaggerated sigh and pulled two twenties from his wallet. He dropped them on the counter. The bartender replaced them with two fives, deducting his own tip. Nick ignored the money and took a swallow of the awful brew, thankful it was at least cold. He would limit himself to one.

He drank slowly and surveyed the patrons, wondering if he was the youngest person in the room. Maybe not, but he was probably the most recently bathed.

Nick was no fool. He'd known even before he walked in that an unfamiliar face was bound to draw attention. People were staring at him as soon as he passed through the door, and as he drank his beer the roar of conversation dulled gradually until every eye in the place was fixed on him. The only sound in the bar now was the thundering music, and after a moment that also stopped as someone pulled the plug. Just like that, the room was deadly silent.

A woman sidled along the bar toward him, her eyes openly curious; the set of her mouth told him she was part of whatever was coming. He watched her approach, but remained aware of the men along the far wall. The woman stopped a few feet away, smiling cautiously.

"I haven't seen you in here before," she said in a voice loud enough to be heard by all.

Nick grinned slightly. She was attractive enough in the available light, but the room was so dim he couldn't even guess at her age.

"My first time."

She smiled knowingly, taking a step closer. She leaned slightly toward him.

"First time, huh?" Her hand approached his face and she stuck out her finger, lifting his chin just an inch. "Does your...*mother*...know where you are?"

In spite of everything, Nick blushed. Annoyed with himself, he nevertheless played along.

"No, she doesn't. Please don't tell her."

That drew a guffaw from somewhere, and momentarily distracted the woman's attempt to provoke him. Her head tilted as she studied him, searching for another gambit. Nick heard a chair scrape, and from the corner of his eye saw a man rise to his feet. A big man, all beef and beard and bad attitude.

The woman tried again, her eyes taunting him. "Aren't you going to buy me a drink?"

Nick held her gaze, even as he measured the big man's approach. Another chair scraped, and a second man stood up.

"Bartender," Nick said calmly. "Pour the lady a drink and put it on my tab."

"You ain't got no tab."

Nick's lips curled slightly as he winked at the woman.

"Damn. I tried."

Her eyes hardened, but she took a step back as the big man planted his feet in front of Nick. Nick swiveled slowly to face him, his right elbow still resting on the bar, the beer bottle in his hand. The bruiser glared down at him from four inches of extra altitude. Nick smiled.

"Hi."

The finger that jabbed Nick's chest felt like iron.

"This here is an adult establishment," the big man declared gruffly. "You best get out. No minors allowed."

Nick shrugged. "I've never worked in the mines."

The florid face confronting him swelled and began to fuse with color. The second man had arrived and stood slightly behind the first, looking around his shoulder at Nick. The rest of the room stood still, waiting for the explosion.

"You makin' fun of me, boy?" the beef trust demanded.

"No, sir, not a bit. But I ain't leaving just because you want me to."

"You better pay attention, son. Leave now, or you might git hurt."

Nick shook his head resolutely.

"I don't think you understand. I'm not in any danger here."

The belligerent's eyes widened in surprise. "You don't think so?"

"No, I don't. In fact, you don't need to be afraid either."

"What!" The man looked less certain of himself, but was keenly aware that others were expecting him to keep command of the situation. "I ain't afraid! What the hell are you tryin' to say?"

Nick set his beer bottle down on the bar and settled squarely on both feet, relaxed and steady. He raised his voice slightly.

"What I mean is that you..." He stabbed his own finger into the monster's chest. "...are a lot *safer* as long as I'm here."

Not a soul breathed for the space of three seconds. The big man stared in shock, then took a step back and burst out laughing. He turned to the man behind him.

"Did you hear that! He said—"

Nick hadn't been born in a test tube. He could read the signs and he knew the drill. When the big man lunged he ducked the swing, and while his opponent was still off balance, swept his leg from under him and used the low gravity to hoist him over the bar in a flying arc that crashed him into the rear wall, smashing the mirror. The second man was a tad slow to react, but when he charged, Nick's beer bottle disintegrated against his cheekbone. He hit the floor with a scream.

It happened so quickly that no one else could move. The air turned blue with shouts and curses, but Nick stepped over the broken-cheeked assailant to keep his back to the wall, then surveyed the situation. The first man was rising from the floor behind the bar, glass shards in his beard, dazed but still angry. He shook his head briefly, his eyes focused on Nick, and took an angry step forward.

He stopped when Nick's laser pistol appeared an inch from his nose.

"Like I said," Nick told him evenly, "you're a lot safer with me in here. But not if you fuck with me."

"Hey!" the bartender protested from the safety of fifteen feet away. "This is Federation territory! No weapons allowed."

Nick ignored him, still staring down the big man.

"What about it? You still want to fight?"

"Who the hell *are* you, mister?"

"My name is Nick. You didn't answer my question."

The bearded man cleared his throat, absently began brushing glass out of his whiskers.

"Well...looks like you got the hole card, so I reckon I got no choice but to fold."

Nick nodded slowly, and lowered his weapon slightly. He glanced at the man on the floor, whose face was bleeding. The woman was kneeling over him.

"You ought to get him a doctor," Nick suggested. "Put his union benefits to work."

The shouting had stopped, but the room was abuzz with conversation. Nick scanned the crowd briefly but saw no immediate threats. The bartender had moved a few feet closer, still staring at Nick's pistol.

"Did you hear me, mister? I said no weapons allowed. You better leave or I'll call the law."

Nick holstered the weapon. His left hand came up with a leather case in it.

"Don't bother."

The bartender stared at the badge in the leather case.

"U.F. Marshal? Why didn't you say so?"

"Nobody asked me." Nick put the badge away and looked at the bearded man behind the bar. "Bartender, pour this man a beer. Put it on my tab."

Chapter 2

Monday, August 5, 0440 (CC)
Government Annex - Ceres

The following morning, Nick Walker stepped out of a taxi in front of a store and hoisted his space bag. The door facing him boasted a sign that declared:

United Federation Marshal

Nick opened the door and stepped inside. The first thing he noticed was the cigar smoke. The second thing was how small and cramped the office was.

The third thing he noticed was the aging man behind the simple wooden desk. He looked about sixty, his hair thin and white, his neatly trimmed beard thick and white. He was bent over a computer cascade, a lighted cigar clamped in his teeth. He didn't move as Nick stopped and set his space bag on the deck.

"Marshal Milligan?"

The old man looked up slowly, squinting as if near-sighted, then leaned back in his chair.

"You Nick Walker?"

"Yes, sir."

"What took you? I was just looking at your itinerary. You got in last night."

"Yes, sir, but I didn't expect you'd be in your office that late."

"Well, take a seat. You ain't in the Star Marines anymore."

Milligan shoved a chair toward him and Nick caught it, swinging it around. He hadn't realized he'd been standing nearly at attention. He sat down stiffly, suddenly uncomfortable. He laid an envelope on the desk that contained his transfer papers and data chip. Milligan ignored it. His eyes scanned Nick up and down.

"Twenty-four, huh? I thought they were sending someone a bit older. This your first assignment?"

"Yes, sir. I graduated from the Academy three weeks ago."

"Hm. Well, you'll have to do. If you live long enough, you'll get experience fast. This is a rugged assignment."

"Yes, sir."

"Stop calling me 'sir'. You ain't in the Star Marines anymore."

"Yes, s— Uh, okay."

Milligan didn't smile, but his eyes gleamed. "You smoke cigars?"

"No, s— Er, no, I don't."

"Too bad. You smoke cigars, you'll never get worms."

Nick blinked. "Are...worms a problem here?"

The old marshal waved a hand. "Not if you smoke cigars. Did anyone brief you on what you'll be doing?"

"Not really. The information was that you needed an assistant, and since it seemed like an interesting assignment, I volunteered."

Milligan's eyebrows rose. "Volunteered! No one ordered you here?"

"No, s— Well, I think if no one had volunteered someone would have been assigned, but I jumped at it. I didn't want to get stuck somewhere boring for my first posting."

"Well, you were right about that. Nothing boring about this place." Milligan crushed the stub of his cigar in a glass dish and slapped his hands together to brush off the ash. "How much do you know about Ceres?"

"Not a great deal. I did a little research on the SolarNet in transit, but it was mostly textbook stuff. Nothing that sounded useful."

"And the Academy...they didn't talk about it?"

"Not really. Just that it's a Federation territory, not much else."

"Figures." Milligan cracked his knuckles and stretched. "You may have guessed by now that this is no suburban residential community. Ceres is a frontier world, just about as gritty as any place in the Solar System. Very few families here, and families aren't recommended. The Belt is a mining community, and by default a lawless place. Probably half the people who work for the mining companies are fugitives from somewhere, but as long as they do their jobs the companies look the other way."

He reached for a cup of cold coffee and sipped it.

"For that matter, so do we. If we arrested every wanted man in the Belt, the mines would shut down."

Nick frowned. "Is that even a consideration? I mean, enforcing the law is our job. The consequences are not our responsibility."

Milligan eyed him with interest. "Do you believe in second chances?"

"Well...sure. But I also believe in the law. If someone commits a crime, and pays his debt, then I'm all for second chances. But not at the cost of evading responsibility."

Milligan grunted.

"Very idealistic. But consider this for a moment—say a man commits a crime on Mars or Terra and somehow eludes capture long enough to make it out here. What does he do? He gets work in the mines, slaving long hours in a deadly environment, separated from his friends and family back home. He gets paid well enough, but he can never go home, so what good does it do him? *But*...he's producing something for the system economy.

"Now take that same individual, and say he gets arrested after committing his crime, gets convicted, and goes to prison for life. He doesn't produce *anything*. He eats three squares a day at taxpayer expense, enjoys free medical care, and gets to see his family on visitors' day—maybe even conjugal visits. Which scenario is more beneficial to the public?"

Nick clenched his jaw, but didn't answer.

"Look, I know what they taught you. You got the textbook stuff, and it's all very noble and righteous in theory. But the real universe can be very different."

"A lot of what they taught me came from you. One of my classes consisted entirely of your video lectures."

Milligan waved a dismissive hand. "I taught there for a couple of years, thought my experience might be worth passing on to a new generation. Didn't work out so well. Too many Academy instructors have never worked in the field, and I was outnumbered. So I said screw it and went back to what I do best."

Nick shrugged. "For what it's worth, sir, I got more out of your lectures than any of the other courses."

The old man grinned humorlessly. "Kissing my ass isn't going to gain you any points."

"I wouldn't dream of it. I just don't want to repeat mistakes you've already made."

Milligan tilted his head, conceding Nick's point. Nick returned to the original conversation.

"So we just leave the fugitives alone?"

"I didn't say that. When a man with a past causes trouble out here and draws attention to himself, we take a look. If he has a warrant and it's serious enough to justify the expense of transport, we send him back. But a lot of these guys are petty criminals, and others are just deadbeats hiding from alimony and child support payments. When we run across those, we attach their wages and make sure those payments get deposited back home.

"It's no picnic out here, Walker. The men who work here, honest or otherwise, don't have much to look forward to. A hot bath, a microwaved meal, a few drinks, a place to sleep, and maybe a hooker now and then. That's pretty much all they can hope for. Nobody gets rich."

"Are there any *honest* men out here?"

"Sure, here and there."

"Why would they even come here?"

"Who knows. Some people just thrive on danger, or a sense of adventure. Whatever it is, they keep on coming. Enough show up every year to replace those who were killed.

"You want some coffee?" Milligan pointed to an automatic brewer on top of a file cabinet.

"Sure." Nick stood, poured himself a cup into a foam container, and sat down again. Milligan unwrapped another cigar, searched his desktop for a lighter, and soon filled the room with a haze of blue smoke. He leaned back in his chair.

"Questions?"

Nick's head spun—he had so many.

"What's our primary duty here? You said we're the only law enforcement."

"We're the only *official* law enforcement. The mining companies have their own security, and they do a lot of the work that would normally fall to us. They detain people for theft, assault, drugs—stuff like that. We usually handle the heavy stuff, like murder and rape, human rights violations...

"There are four major mining corporations in the Belt. The biggest is Farrington Industries, which pretty much dominates the entire mining community around here."

"How many Marshals do we have?"

Milligan peered at him. "Now that you're here? Four."

Nick's mouth dropped open an inch. "*Four!* To police how many people?"

"Oh, maybe seventy-five, eighty thousand on Ceres, another twenty or thirty thousand on the outlying rocks. We're talking a few billion miles of space, mining outposts strung all the way around the sun. The asteroids are endless."

"How much of that is our jurisdiction?"

"All of it. The U.F. Marshal has jurisdiction in all Federation territory across the galaxy."

"That sounds like an impossible job."

"More or less." Milligan sucked at his cigar and squinted through the smoke. "We have seventeen marshals altogether, most of them posted elsewhere. This is the biggest population center, but the others are located strategically around the belt. If they were all in one place we could never respond to anything.

"Each mining company has its own jail system, and we turn our prisoners over to them for safekeeping when we make an arrest. The Federation pays them for their trouble, and they cooperate to some degree. Felons convicted of major crimes are sent to Terra or Mars to serve their sentences."

"How much juice do the company cops have? I assume they're subject to U.F. Marshal authority?"

Milligan nodded. "Glorified security guards, nothing more. But with the shortage of law enforcement out here, they wield a lot of power. They serve the same function as city cops back home. But if they try to bully you—and they will—put a stop to that shit right away."

"Anyone in particular I should watch out for?"

"I'll let you decide that for yourself. Don't want to project my own prejudice onto you."

"I saw something on the SolarNet about a judge?"

"Yep. We even have a courthouse of sorts, though it doesn't look much like one. One judge, two prosecutors, half a dozen defense attorneys. You should probably look them up and get acquainted, at least the good guys. Make sure they know you're on their team."

"Good guys?"

"The judge and prosecutors. The rest of that crowd doesn't impress me much. I was never a fan of lawyers anyway, and any defense lawyer that voluntarily practices in this place has to have skeletons hidden away somewhere."

Nick sipped his coffee.

"You said we have four men. Where are the others?"

"Out and around. You'll meet them eventually."

"How do you want me to proceed? Any open cases I should be working on?"

"Oh, we have a few of those. But I think the best thing for you right now is to move around and get a feel for the layout. You have a pocket 'puter?"

"Yes, sir. Academy standard issue."

"Good. Log on to the SolarNet and download a map of Ceres. Use it to get familiarized. Explore the rock, meet people, let them know you're in town." Milligan reached into his desk and withdrew a key card. He tossed it to Nick. "You have a permanent room at the Centerville Hotel, fourth floor. Stow your gear and clip on your badge. What kind of hardware did you bring?"

Nick reached into his space bag and pulled out his laser pistol. He laid it on the desk, and Milligan picked it up.

"I also brought this."

Nick handed him his other weapon and Milligan's eyes widened as he hefted the heavy revolver with the six-inch barrel.

"Ru-Hawk .44! Christ, I haven't seen one of these in ages!" He glanced at Nick. "That's pretty heavy artillery for this environment. You could blow a hole right through an airlock."

Nick shrugged. "I probably won't ever use it, but it's my favorite weapon, so I packed it. Maybe for my next assignment, if I get posted on a planet somewhere. By the way, is there some kind of uniform that goes with the job?"

"What do you want, a goddamn cowboy hat? This ain't the Ancient West, son. What you're wearing is just fine."

Milligan handed the guns back, then took a deep breath.

"Okay. Your desk is right over there..." He pointed. "...but you'll probably be out of the office most of the time. I'm here if you need me, but I want to be clear on a couple of things. First, you report to me, but you work for the people of the Federation, and nobody else. I'm here to guide you and help you stay out of trouble. I may hand you an assignment now and then, but otherwise you're on your own. Don't be afraid to ask questions, but make your own decisions—you don't have accept my opinion on everything."

"Yes, sir."

"You know how to drive an E-car?"

Nick looked blank. "Umm…"

"Easiest goddamn thing in the galaxy. We have a couple parked on the street—they'll take you anywhere you need to go as long as you stay on Ceres. If you need to travel off the rock, you'll have to rent a jalopy. But clear that with me first."

"Yes, sir. Do we have radios?"

"We do, but we never use them. The signals don't carry very well through solid rock, so use your porta-phone if you need to contact the office. The phone signals connect to a circuit system that always gets through."

"Got it."

"Another thing…that badge will be a red flag to certain people. You're a new face in town, so you can expect to be challenged. Watch your back."

Chapter 3

Centerville - Ceres

The hotel room was small, but Nick was used to tight quarters. In the Star Marines he'd lived in barracks on Terra with forty other men, and in much tighter spaces when on Luna or in space. His dorm room at the Academy had also been small, and during the trip out to the Belt his cabin had been only slightly larger than a coffin. The vast, wide-open vistas of his native San Joaquin Valley were but a childhood memory.

At least this room had a view.

The hotel was located in Centerville, barely a mile from the U.F. Marshal's office. Everything on Ceres was underground; Ceres was the largest asteroid in the Solar System, but it *was* an asteroid, surrounded by millions of other asteroids, and the danger of astral impact was always high. According to the map Nick downloaded from the SolarNet, the settlement consisted of a series of habitats carved out of the rock, some as much as half a mile across, each with self-contained life support. Each habitat was a sort of biosphere—or more correctly, a bio*hemisphere*—sealed with a double-airlock system that prevented decompression in one area from affecting other areas. The habitats were connected by monorail and road tubes, and each had at least two exits in case of catastrophe.

Centerville was the largest habitat on Ceres; more than twenty thousand people lived there.

From his fourth-floor hotel window Nick looked down on a small park. In the distance he saw other buildings, lots of them, and beyond them a wall of solid rock. Small electric vehicles moved along a network of streets. Artificial sunshine made everything gleam, but did nothing to detract from the claustrophobic sense that one was living just up the street from Hell.

Nick stowed his clothing and gear and stripped down for a shower. To his great delight, the shower actually boasted hot water, which he hadn't expected; his only other non-terrestrial home with such a luxury had been Luna when he was in the Star Marines...and Alpha Centauri during the war. As a general rule, military starships, freighters, and even some passenger liners offered sonic showers as the only option. He donned a fresh set of clothing, stuck his laser pistol into a shoulder holster, and pinned his badge to the front of his belt. After checking himself in the mirror, he locked his room and took the stairs down to the hotel lobby.

Government Annex - Ceres

The courthouse was a joke. Located in the Government Annex habitat just three blocks from the U.F. Marshal's office, much of the building was taken up by office space housing the judge, prosecutors, and defense attorneys. The actual courtroom was located on the third floor, and it was tiny—Nick had actually seen bigger cargo containers.

Court was in session. He stepped inside the double doors and took a seat; the gallery only had thirty chairs and when he sat down twenty-nine remained empty. The judge, an attractive black woman in her thirties, faced the courtroom from her bench against the far wall. The bench was low but wide, offering a measure of protection should an unruly defendant try anything. Two attorney tables faced the bench and a witness chair sat on the left side of the courtroom, facing a jury box on the right. The chair and the jury box were empty at the moment. A man in a striped jumpsuit was sitting at one of the attorney tables while a tall, blond prosecutor argued a point of law. The defense attorney looked even younger than Nick; like the judge, she was also black, but even prettier. Two security guards in dark uniforms flanked the room; their shoulder patches bore the words FARRINGTON SECURITY.

Nick settled in to watch. He had no idea what the case was about or who any of the players were, but wanted to get a sense of justice on Ceres. He quickly realized this was not a trial but an arraignment—the defendant had already entered a Not Guilty plea and the prosecutor was arguing against bail. Nick couldn't see the defendant's face, but could tell he was an older man, probably in his early fifties. He was pasty white, short and heavy-set; most of his head was bare scalp, with just a few strands of brown hair stringing down over his ears. He sat silently while the prosecutor talked, his hands chained to his belt. The judge stared in stony silence, her face unreadable.

"—has a history of alcoholism, your Honor, and is therefore a danger to himself and others. He operates a very dangerous piece of equipment, and allowing him to return to work while awaiting trial is only inviting another tragedy. One dead man is enough."

The prosecutor sat down; the judge glanced at the defense attorney.

"Miss Allen?"

The young beauty stood quickly.

"Your Honor, this is Mr. Rowan's first offense of any kind. Since coming to Ceres four years ago he has never been in trouble with the law and no evidence has been presented that he was drinking when the accident occurred. The defense requests he be released on his own recognizance until trial."

The judge compressed her lips.

"You say Mr. Rowan has a clean record on Ceres, but you overlook the reason he came to Ceres in the first place. I checked Mr. Rowan's record and discovered that he is a fugitive from justice in Dublin, Ireland. The Irish are sitting on a manslaughter warrant following a drunk-driving incident in which two people were killed...and that was *not* his first offense!"

"Your Honor, Mr. Rowan is not a flight risk. Ceres is an isolated rock—he has no place to go. As for Mr. Tarpington's concern about another accident, you can order him to accept unpaid leave until this case is settled, and he won't be operating any dangerous equipment."

The gavel banged like a gunshot in the courtroom.

"Defendant is remanded to the Farrington Facility until trial. We are adjourned."

The defendant stood shakily, looking around in bewilderment. The Farrington Security guards moved in like vultures, one grabbing each elbow.

"You said I wouldn't have to be locked up!" Rowan complained to his attorney. "You said I'd be out on bail!"

The pretty young lawyer stared at him with guilty eyes. "I'm sorry. I tried my best—"

"You *lied* to me!"

"Shut up, asshole!" One of the guards gave Rowan a shove; Rowan's heel caught on the table leg and he lost his balance, stumbling backward two steps where he plowed into the prosecutor, whose back was turned as he stuffed papers into his document case. The prosecutor, Tarpington, spun in surprise, alarm on his face. He pushed Rowan away reflexively.

The guards closed in again, but Rowan's eyes were wide.

"I need to talk to my lawyer! I'm not finished talking to my lawyer!"

"Yes you are!" The same guard who had shoved him now elbowed him in the chin, then grabbed the front of his jumpsuit.

"Get your hands off me!" Rowan bellowed in panic. "I need to t—"

The guard drove a fist into his face and Rowan hit the floor, blood spurting from his nose. Nick, seated ten feet away, was over the railing an instant later. He seized the security man's arm and spun him around.

"That was uncalled for! The man is shackled! He's no threat to you."

"Who the fuck're you!" The guard drew his fist back again. Nick drove a short jab into his belly with his left fist and grabbed his head with the other, slamming it into the defense table. The second guard hit Nick with a nightstick from behind, but it was a glancing blow. Nick spun quickly and kneed him in the groin, then flung him over the railing into the empty spectator chairs.

It was all over in three seconds.

"Order in the court!"

The gavel was banging loudly. The judge, who had been about to leave the courtroom, stood glaring at the commotion, her dark eyes blazing.

"Order in the court!" she repeated. "I will have order in this courtroom!"

She pointed the gavel directly at Nick's face.

"Who the *hell* are you?"

Nick stood still and stared back. Barely breathing hard, he pointed at himself.

"Me?"

"Yes, you! What is your name?"

"Nick Walker, your Honor. United Federation Marshal."

Silence reigned for ten seconds. Everyone seemed to be staring at him.

"You're a U.F. Marshal?" The judge's tone was a little less threatening.

"That's right, your Honor." He tapped the badge on his belt.

"How come I've never heard of you?"

"I just got in last night. I've only been on the job a couple of hours."

She stared at him for long seconds. Behind him, the security guards were picking themselves up and groaning as they brushed themselves off. Defendant Rowan still sat on the courtroom floor, bleeding from the nose. The judge took it all in, then spoke again.

"The security officers will take the defendant back to Farrington lockup. Make sure he gets medical attention. Everyone else...my chambers. *Now.*"

She turned and strode through a door behind the bench. Nick frowned as the meaner of the two Farrington guards brushed him aside to get to the prisoner. Tarpington and the defense attorney headed for the judge's door, and Nick followed at a slower pace. He stopped as one of the guards hauled Rowan to his feet and pushed him roughly toward another door behind the witness chair.

"If I catch you mistreating that prisoner again," Nick said, "I will arrest you." He glared at the man to make sure he understood the threat was not a joke.

The guard sneered. "You and whose army? Fuck you, tinhorn."

The prisoner and two guards left the courtroom before Nick could reply.

*

The judge's chambers were tight, barely big enough for a desk and two chairs. The Federation flag dangled from one wall, the Federation Seal was displayed on another. A name plate on the desk identified the owner as The HON. MONICA MAYNARD.

As Nick and the two lawyers crowded in, the judge removed her dark robe and hung it on a wall peg. She turned to face her visitors, giving Nick a good look at her for the first time. She was much better looking than he'd first realized— although ten or twelve years his senior, she had a figure teenage girls would kill for. But her gaze was stern and direct, and she pinned him to the spot with her glare.

"Marshal Walker, I don't appreciate scuffles in my courtroom. Not even from a Federation officer. What do you have to say for yourself?"

Nick was startled. He blinked once or twice before he replied.

"With respect, your Honor, maybe you had your back turned and didn't see that those guards were abusing the prisoner—"

"They weren't abusing him!" Tarpington interjected. "He was out of order and they were merely gaining control of the situation."

"By breaking his nose?" Nick met Tarpington's eyes and stared him down.

The defense attorney jumped in. "Your Honor, you *did* have your back turned and you didn't see what they did. My client was trying to talk to me and the guards began pushing him around. Marshal Walker intervened to keep the situation from getting any worse!"

"Ex*cuse* me..." The judge scowled at the defense lawyer. "...I was talking to Marshal Walker. When I want to hear from the rest of you, I will invite you to speak."

She turned her eyes back to Nick. He waited for her to continue, but she didn't. He spread his hands in surrender.

"I apologize for the scuffle, but I believe it was necessary. In the same circumstances, I'd do it again."

She stared at him for twenty seconds, and he stared back. He'd never come up against a judge before, but was confident of his position and his duty. He refused to be intimidated. Finally Judge Maynard sighed as if it were all too complicated to think about.

"Fine," she said. "We won't speak of it again." She pulled out her desk chair and sat down; the rest of them remained standing. "Marshal Walker, to your left is Federation Attorney David Tarpington..."

The tall blond man dredged up a grin and reached for Nick's hand. He shook it firmly and cracked half the bones in Nick's hand with his grip.

"...and to your right is defense attorney Misery Allen."

The young woman smiled as Nick nodded to her. She really was very young, he decided—she didn't look a day over nineteen.

"My name is Monica Maynard," the judge concluded, "but you can call me 'your Honor'."

For the first time, her iron exterior cracked and Nick detected a heartbeat. The corners of her lips curled in what was almost a smile.

"Back to my original question," she said. "How badly did you have to screw up to get this assignment?"

"I volunteered for it."

"You're kidding!"

"Nope."

"Did you have any idea what you were getting into?"

"Nope. Maybe I still don't."

She laughed, sincere and friendly.

"I really don't think you do. This is the armpit of the Solar System. It really is."

Nick was smiling. "And how did *you* end up here? You and those two attorneys look much too intelligent to get stuck in the armpit."

Maynard's smile faded somewhat and her eyes drifted back to her drink.

"I can't speak for the other two, but I did screw up. Big time."

"Yeah?" He wasn't sure if he should ask the next question, but she seemed in a candid mood, so he did. "How's that?"

"I came out here for love." Her eyes rose to meet his, and for just a moment she looked as young and vulnerable as a schoolgirl. "Stupid, huh?"

Nick didn't quite know what to say, but some response seemed indicated.

"You expected to find Mister Right on Ceres?"

She laughed and shook her head.

"Not quite *that* stupid. I was married to a good man. My husband got himself in some financial trouble...bad investments...and decided to run away from it all. He left me high and dry, but I was crazy in love with him, so I followed." She shook her head in self deprecation. "Biggest mistake I ever made."

Nick squirmed inwardly. This was getting awfully personal, and he'd first laid eyes on the woman barely thirty minutes ago. He sat silent.

"Long story short," she said, "by the time I got out here he was already dead. Mining accident. I'd spent everything I had on transportation and I was stuck. I had a law degree and there was plenty of legal work here, so I was able to support myself. Before too long the judge retired and I was offered this position."

She smiled.

"End of story."

Nick made the correct facial expression for the occasion, but he wasn't buying it. If it was truly "end of story" she wouldn't have told it to a complete stranger.

"With your courtroom experience," he suggested, "you should be able to find a position back home. Space fare paid by whatever jurisdiction hired you."

She shook her head slowly. "Not quite that simple, but I won't bore you with the why. What we need to establish now is...what about you? Are you married?"

"Nope."

"Girlfriend?"

"Nope." *Not anymore.*

She studied him for a long moment. "Do you...find me attractive?"

Yes, definitely.

"Jesus Christ, your Honor! Are you propositioning me?"

She laughed, maybe a little uncomfortably.

"Marshal Walker...may I call you Nick?" He nodded. "Nick, it's damn lonely out here on this rock, and I'm a little desperate. It's been a long time since I've felt a man's arms around me, so...yes, I guess I am. Propositioning you, I mean."

Nick felt his heart trip a little faster.

"Your Honor—"

"Monica."

"Monica, there must be five men on this asteroid for every woman—"

"Fifteen," she corrected. "It's fifteen to one."

"That's a pretty wide-open playing field. Surely, with that many single men... I mean, why me?"

She leaned forward, her eyes earnest.

"You're young and fresh and you look healthy. Nick, have you *seen* the men on this rock? I wouldn't sleep with most of them even at gunpoint! They're carrying microbes that haven't even been discovered yet."

"What about Tarpington? He doesn't look that old, and he definitely looks healthy."

Monica Maynard laughed, but not in a mean way.

"Dave Tarpington is every woman's dream. Unfortunately, he *does* sleep with the men out here, microbes and all."

"Oh." Nick felt a flush creep up from his collar—nothing about Tarpington's bearing had suggested his orientation.

"Listen, I'm not looking for love. No strings. Just two consenting adults occasionally coming together, that's all I'm saying. You think about it, and I'll leave it at that. Okay?"

He shrugged, then nodded.

"Okay. But doesn't that constitute a conflict of interest?"

"No. If it were Tarpington, then it would be improper, because he argues cases in my courtroom. But you're a law enforcement officer, not an officer of the court. Big difference."

Nick smiled easily, but his blood was racing. Now he was looking at her differently, and liked what he saw. She might be a decade older, but she was all woman, and he hadn't been laid in over a year.

"I'm glad we had this little talk," he said.

She laughed again, suddenly more relaxed.

"Me, too. Sorry to hit you like a meteor at our first meeting, but I wanted to get to you before someone else did. With your looks and that badge, you'll be a hot property among the women out here. Desperation makes us all a little forward."

* * *

Artificial sunlight flooded the atrium that formed the central core of the courthouse. As Nick left the courtroom he took the stairs down to the second floor where he found the prosecutor's office. Marshal Milligan had told him he should introduce himself to the "good guys" and get to know them, so...what the hell.

Somewhere in his imagination he expected to find an office bustling with sexy young women and harried prosecutors, but it was nothing like that. Like everything else he'd seen on Ceres, the office was cramped and overflowing, desks jammed together, paper stacked everywhere. One old man, probably a law clerk, manned the outer office, but glanced up at Nick and without a word returned to whatever he was doing.

"Excuse me." Nick rapped his knuckles on a desk top. "Is Mr. Tarpington around?"

The old man looked up again. "Whatcha want him for?"

Nick smiled to hide his irritation. "I just saw him upstairs in the courtroom. Thought he looked lonely, wanted to offer my shoulder to cry on."

The elderly gentleman glared for a moment, not sure if he was being mocked.

"Mr. Tarpington, if you don't mind," Nick repeated.

"Marshal Walker!"

The voice came from behind him and Nick turned. David Tarpington had stepped out of an office and extended his hand. This time Nick squeezed hard as they shook, to avoid injury.

"Come on inside." Tarpington gestured toward his office. "I was hoping you'd drop by. We should get acquainted."

"That's what I was thinking." Nick took the chair Tarpington offered and glanced around. The office was small, but neat—neater than anything he'd seen yet on the asteroid.

Tarpington walked around his desk and sat down. He pushed a wooden box across the desk. "You smoke cigars?"

"No, I don't. But thanks."

Tarpington grinned. "Neither do I, but I keep them for visitors. Marshal Milligan, for instance."

Nick nodded. "To prevent worms."

David Tarpington laughed hard. "Did he lay that line on you, too? Funniest damn thing I ever heard."

Nick smiled. His natural tendency, reinforced by Academy training, was never to take people at face value, but he was already starting to like this guy. Tarpington looked about twenty-eight, tall and fit and disgustingly handsome. Monica Maynard had described him as "every woman's dream", and Nick could see why. He stood about six feet four, obviously worked out, and had an engaging grin—with perfect teeth— that would captivate anyone, male or female. His wavy blond hair didn't hurt, either, and that deep baritone voice was also an asset.

"Is there anything I can offer you? Coffee?"

"I'm good, thanks. Had breakfast just before heading over here."

Tarpington nodded and sat back, relaxing in his chair.

"Well, it's good to see some fresh blood once in a while. Ceres doesn't offer much in the way of civilization, but for a young lawman itching to cut his teeth, it should be a golden opportunity. I hope you'll find the experience rewarding."

"I'm sure I will. I've already met some of the local wildlife."

"Really?"

"Yep. Went into a bar last night and got into a fight before I even finished my beer. Hadn't been off the starship an hour."

Tarpington laughed. "You must have gone to the Open Airlock."

"I think that's what it was called."

"It's one of the seedier joints on Ceres. There are a few pubs that are more...upscale. You picked a miner's bar."

"Must have been. First one I saw, so I went in."

They chatted for half an hour, measuring each other. Tarpington asked about Nick's background and Nick told him. Nick's opinion didn't change—he still liked the man.

"Now that you know my life story," Nick said, "what about you? You look well enough educated that you could find work in any major city on Terra. Why are you hanging around this place?"

Tarpington's grin faded slightly, his eyes took on a guarded look.

"To be absolutely honest? I'm a narcissist. I like to be the biggest fish in the pond, and the pond here is pretty small."

Nick nodded, slightly taken aback. He hadn't expected quite *that* much honesty.

"I also get an ego boost from living on a frontier world. Terra has gotten too civilized for its own good...and I say 'civilized' in quotes.

"And before somebody beats me to it," Tarpington concluded, "I'll also tell you that I'm a gay man. I'm perfectly content to live in a society that is ninety percent male." Tarpington watched him closely for several seconds, then his lips curled into a grin. "Too bad you're not gay."

Nick's eyebrows arched. "How do you know that?"

"You're a homophobe."

"The hell I am! I don't hate anybody because of—"

"I didn't say anything about hate. The term 'homophobe' simply means *fear* of gay people, not necessarily hatred. Of course, fear can lead to hatred, which can lead to violence."

Nick stared at him and felt his face flush.

"You probably have a tattoo on your tailbone that says DO NOT ENTER."

Nick squirmed. "Actually, it says EXIT ONLY."

Tarpington laughed. "All kidding aside, it's in the body language. Relax, Nick, I'm not going to try to kiss you."

Embarrassed, Nick nodded. "Fair enough. Not to get too personal, but is it safe to be gay in a place like this? You know...microbes?"

Tarpington laughed again, this time until the tears came.

"Judge Maynard," he said. "Right? That's her line. She's terrified of catching something, has no love life at all. She probably ambushed you, didn't she? She figures you haven't been here long enough to get infected."

Nick felt his face turn red again, but couldn't help laughing.

"Like I said, I don't want to get too personal."

Tarpington wiped his eyes.

"Well, you could do a lot worse than Judge Maynard. She's a very hot woman, even if she is thirty-six. If I wasn't gay, I'd be all over that."

"So tell me, what kind of crime do we get here?"

"You name it. Anything you can think of. Most of the people in the 'roids—probably two-thirds or better—are either on the run or hiding out from something, so they already have a criminal mentality...and the criminal imagination has no limit. Imagine it and they'll do it, everything from extortion to murder, and lots of shit in between."

"That guy upstairs in the courtroom...Rowan. What was his problem?"

"Drinking on the job and causing a man's death. He operates an ice crusher, a really nasty piece of machinery with lots of lethal moving parts. Rowan was impaired and let it get away from him. Killed a man."

"Allegedly?"

"Everything is 'allegedly' until the final verdict, but he's guilty."

"And what about Farrington Security?"

"What about them?"

"Are they always that rough with prisoners?"

Tarpington was silent a moment, then shrugged.

"I didn't see what you saw," he admitted. "As you said, my back was turned."

"Mine wasn't. Rowan was agitated, for sure, but the situation could have been handled a lot better than it was. So I was wondering if brutality is standard procedure for those guards or if that was an isolated incident."

Tarpington sighed. "We depend on the mining company security forces to house prisoners. Given the nature of the general population on Ceres, I won't claim that some of those security people aren't less than ideal. There have been complaints of brutality, but prisoners always charge brutality if they think it will give them some advantage. You'll hear charges of police brutality on Terra, too."

"Have you investigated those complaints?"

"Some of them. We've never been able to substantiate anything. If you're concerned about it, you might want to look into it yourself."

"Maybe I will. Are you the top man here, or do you work for someone else?"

"I do most of the courtroom work, but the chief prosecutor is Gary Fraites. He's on Mars at the moment, attending a conference. Should be back in a couple of weeks."

"How big is your staff?"

"Except for Howard in the other room, whom you've already met, you're looking at it."

"Wow. Must be a big job for one man."

Tarpington grinned again. "Like I said, I'm a narcissist. Right now, I'm the only fish in the pond, which makes me happier than a pig in shit."

Nick stood up.

"I won't take any more of your time. It was good meeting you. I'm sure we'll cross paths again."

They shook hands again.

"Be careful out there, Marshal. It ain't a big world, but it's a mean one."

Chapter 5

Although Marshal Milligan hadn't insisted on it, Nick decided, since he was already in the building, to drop in on the defense attorneys as well. He found their office on the same floor as the prosecutor's, but on the other side of the building. This suite was quite a bit larger, with two female law clerks in the outer office and several doors opening off it. Misery Allen was huddled with one of the clerks when he came in, and looked up. Her face quickly lit with a smile.

"Marshal Walker! I was hoping you'd drop by!"

"Really?" Nick rested his elbows on the counter and returned the smile. "I was hoping you'd be here when I did."

"Everybody, this is Marshal Nick Walker. He just arrived on Ceres last night. Marshal, this is Angie and that's Carla."

Nick nodded to the clerks, both of whom were watching him with interest. They looked older than Allen, but not by much—both were still in their twenties. Misery Allen swept across the room toward an open door.

"My office is this way," she said. "Come on in."

Nick followed her through the door and she closed it behind him. Like Tarpington, her space was small, but immaculate. She took a seat and reached into a small nitro-cooler for a cold drink, placing it before him.

"We're not terribly formal here, but that's the best water on four worlds. It's native to Ceres."

Nick picked up the bottle, which was so cold it almost burned his hand.

"Water? Native to Ceres?"

"Of course. That's our primary export. Water." She settled into her chair and sat admiring him.

"I thought Ceres was a mining world."

"It is. This whole asteroid is just one giant chunk of permafrost. We mine the ice and supply water to most of the

Outer Worlds." She smiled. "You were probably thinking of metal mining, weren't you?"

He nodded. "Yeah. I figured it was all iron and nickel and stuff like that."

"There's plenty of that, too, in the Belt. Thousands of mining operations all the way around the sun, but right here it's water."

Nick popped the top on the bottle and took a swallow. To his delight, it was delicious, better than anything he'd ever tasted, even on Terra. It was also painfully cold and refreshing.

"That's good stuff." He set the bottle on the edge of her desk.

She clasped her hands together.

"I really want to thank you for what you did. It's the first time I've ever seen anybody stand up to those Farrington thugs."

"I wanted to ask you about that. Is it common practice here to punch prisoners around?"

"Entirely too common. Farrington Security is the worst. They're the biggest operation on Ceres, and they have the largest lockup. They don't screen their people very well. What you saw today was fairly minor compared to some I've seen. Prisoners show up in court with bruises all over them, eyes swollen shut, missing teeth, and sometimes broken bones. It's disgraceful."

"And no one does anything about it?"

"Not so far. I've filed several complaints—we all have—but it never goes anywhere. The PO says they've looked into the allegations but can't substantiate them."

"The PO?"

"Prosecutor's Office."

"So what's the story on Rowan? Is he guilty of the charges against him?"

Misery Allen lowered her eyes.

"Probably. He does have an outstanding warrant back on Terra, and he does have a drinking problem."

"I heard you say in the courtroom that there was no proof."

She stared at him a moment, as if disappointed at the question. She sighed and explained.

"Marshal, my job is to represent the defendant, to give him the best defense I'm capable of. His guilt or innocence will be determined by the court, not by me. Part of giving the best possible defense is making sure the evidence is strong enough to back up the charges, and in this case the evidence hasn't been presented yet. You'll notice I never said he didn't do it, just that no evidence had been presented to prove his guilt. I operate on a presumption of innocence, as mandated by the Federation Constitution."

Nick nodded, impressed by her passion.

"So if he's guilty—"

"Let them prove it. Tarpington is good at his job, but he works only as hard as he has to. If someone doesn't hold his feet to the fire, he'll convict my client with little or no evidence."

"When the man was arrested, didn't they take a blood alcohol?"

"I haven't seen one. If they did, let them present it in court. Without it there's no concrete proof that he was drunk, and therefore no crime."

"What about the warrant from Ireland?"

Misery Allen smiled. "I can't help him on that. Whichever way this case goes, he'll be extradited to face those charges. We'll fight the extradition, of course—"

"Why?"

"Because that's what the defendant wants. If he's convicted in Ireland he's looking at thirty years, which at his age is a life sentence."

Nick frowned. "Two people in Ireland are dead."

"I didn't create the legal system, Marshal. I just work within it, and I use whatever tools it provides me. Fighting extradition is one of them. In any case, if he's convicted here, he'll be heading back to Terra anyway, for incarceration. He won't be able to escape the warrant then."

Nick shook his head and spread his hands in surrender.

"Sounds like your job is a lot more complicated than mine. And you can call me Nick."

Her smile beamed at him. For a moment his attention was arrested by how beautiful she was.

"And you can call me Misery."

"Is that really your name?"

"I'm afraid so. My mother was a bit of a pessimist, and just a little superstitious. She was so miserable when I was born that she thought naming me that might break whatever jinx was at work in her life."

"Did it work?"

She laughed. "You mean, am I miserable? No, I'm not, so I guess it might have worked. At least maybe it helped."

"Why was your mother so unhappy?"

"We lived on Ganymede. It's a harsh world, even after terraforming, and it was even worse back then."

"Ganymede! God, I've heard about that place. One of the reasons I volunteered for this assignment was because I didn't want to get sent there."

"You made a better choice. They're still terraforming the place. It gets a little better every year, but it has a long way to go. Growing up was tough—have you ever tried to play dodge ball in a pressure suit?"

Nick shook his head. "I've spent plenty of time in pressure suits, when I was in the Star Marines, but no dodge ball."

"It isn't easy."

"How long have you been away from there?"

"About four months."

Nick was startled. "Didn't you go to law school?"

"Yes, of course. On the SolarNet. After I passed the bar, I couldn't find a law firm that would hire me, so I came here. Ceres needed a lawyer and they weren't picky about experience."

"So you've never been to Terra?"

"I've never even been to Mars. Ganymede and Ceres, that's it."

He stared at her a moment, in wonder. "Wow."

"Pretty sheltered, huh?"

"Well, I'm not sure. Given the environments you've had to live in, I'm not sure 'sheltered' is the appropriate term. By contrast, I think people who've never seen those places are more sheltered than you were."

She tilted her head. "That's an interesting perspective. I will say that, except for the people, Ceres is the more comfortable place to live. Better than Ganymede, for sure."

"Ganymede has better people?"

"Oh, absolutely. They're not sophisticated, but the majority of them are hard-working and honest. That's more than you can say for this place. My mother used to read the Bible to me, and the term that sticks in my mind is 'den of iniquity'. I think that pretty well sums up Ceres."

"And yet you're defending the iniquitors."

She laughed. "Yeah, I guess I am. But I hope I won't be here forever. Some day I'd like to set foot on a planet with a real atmosphere and a warm star overhead. Just to see what it's like."

"I'm sure you will. What's the name of the law firm? I didn't see it on the door."

"Skinflint and Crony," she said with a straight face. Nick blinked and she burst out laughing. "I'm kidding. That was my dad's joke, that all lawyers were skinflints and good old boys. He warned me not to be like that.

"This office is actually a government firm, like the PO. No legitimate law firm wants to practice here, so the Federation formed its own public defender's office. I get paid the same way Tarpington does, and from the same people."

"Who runs this office?"

"Geraldine Gabbard. She's on Mars right now, attending a conference with Mr. Fraites. We also have three other attorneys. I'm the most junior."

"So you get the dirtiest cases."

She pointed a finger at him. "You're quick."

"Shit rolls downhill," he said. "Always has, always will. Are all your attorneys female?"

"No, we have one man. He's the sole, lonely representative of his gender."

"From what I've been hearing there are only about five thousand women in this place, yet nearly all the defense attorneys are female."

"Ironic, isn't it? And both prosecutors are male. It gets really ironic when the charge is rape."

"How do you handle that?"

"I haven't had one yet. Rape and murder are too big for me right now—the senior people like to handle those. But I've sat in on a couple, and they can get pretty nasty. The good news—if you can call it that—is that with so few women available the rape stats aren't nearly as high as you'd expect them to be, given the scum that inhabit this rock. The vast majority of women around here engage in prostitution at least part of the time. It's the only way most women can make a living, and while it may not be ideal, there is a need for it."

Nick nodded somberly. "Keeps the rape stats down."

"Well...rape is less about sex than it is about power. But point taken."

"Can I ask you a personal question?"

Her eyes narrowed to slits with her smile. "You can ask."

"How old are you? You look nineteen, but you must be older, with college and law school and all."

"Actually I'm twenty-one. The nice thing about SolarNet classes is that you can proceed at your own pace. I blew through about six years of classes in three years. Then it took a few months to find this job, and the rest is history."

"History."

"The last four months."

Nick took another swallow of cold water and gazed at the young defense attorney, enjoying the view. Not only was she gorgeous, she also had a sense of humor. He was liking her more every minute.

"Tell me about those security guards," he said. "Especially the one who punched your client. Do you know his name?"

Her smile faded.

"Benny Silva. He's one of the supervisors at Farrington Security, a real asshole. I've seen him hit prisoners before. The other one isn't quite as bad, except when he's with Silva. His name is Hooley." She cocked her head to the side. "What are you going to do?"

Nick chewed his lip thoughtfully.

"I told Silva that if I ever saw him hit another prisoner I was going to arrest him. I don't think he was impressed. Maybe I'll pay him a visit on his own turf. We might find any number of things to talk about."

Her eyes widened slightly.

"You be careful, Nick. Farrington Industries is the biggest special interest on Ceres. If you rock the boat too much..."

Nick grinned and shook his head.

"Nothing to worry about, just a friendly visit. But there is one more thing I need to ask you, and you have to be absolutely honest with me."

Her expression turned serious and she nodded. "Of course."

He leaned forward slightly and lowered his voice. "If you lie to me, I'll know it."

Her eyebrows popped up and she swallowed. "I won't lie. I swear it!"

He held her gaze for a long moment, then glanced over his shoulder to make sure the door was closed.

"Would you be at all interested in having dinner with me this evening?"

Chapter 6

Nick walked the three blocks back to the Marshal's office and stepped inside. Milligan was peering at his holo-monitor through narrowed eyes, a cloud of smoke hanging about his head. Nick sat down at his own desk and logged onto the computer. He hadn't used the equipment yet but found a user profile already set up. He created a password and waited for the system to log him onto the SolarNet.

"How'd it go?" Milligan asked without looking around.

"Interesting morning," Nick replied. "I stopped at the courthouse like you suggested and started getting acquainted. I met Misery Allen, Judge Maynard, and Dave Tarpington."

"Did Tarpington try to suck your cock?" Milligan was still staring at his monitor.

Nick laughed. "No."

"Did Judge Maynard?"

Nick was silent a moment, and Milligan looked around.

"Not exactly," Nick said.

"She will. She already put the screws to you, didn't she?"

He nodded, unable to suppress a grin. "Yes, sir, she explained it all to me."

Milligan puffed his cigar a moment, then turned back to his monitor.

"Well, if she rings your bell then go right ahead. But don't fall in love with her."

"No, sir. Falling in love isn't part of my career plan."

*

Nick ran a SolarNet search for Farrington Industries and got quite an eyeful. Farrington was the largest of four companies mining permafrost on Ceres and had its own fleet of freighters to transport the water to Mars and the Outer Worlds. It also hauled water for the smaller companies for a substantial fee. The company had been founded by two

Centerville - Ceres

Nick had seen the two E-cars parked in front of the office and used one to get to his hotel, which was in a different habitat than Government Annex. The cars were old and battered, nothing fancy about them, and ran on battery power. The only distinguishing features were the stencils on the doors that identified them as belonging to the U.F. Marshal's office; they had a top speed of about ten knots.

Nick left the office for the second time that morning and climbed into the pilot's seat of the newer looking car. He turned onto the street that led to the south tunnel and tooled along at a snail's pace until he reached the edge of the habitat. Each habitat was connected to the next by one or more tunnels; to enter or leave the tunnels one passed through a double airlock system. The locks were open most of the time, but would close under emergency depressurization to minimize loss of atmosphere and life. For Nick, entering the tunnel was no different than driving across a bridge back on Terra, and mere minutes later he emerged into the Centerville habitat.

On an impulse, he stopped at the hotel and went up to his room. Rummaging through his space bag, he drew out the Ru-Hawk .44 and hefted it lovingly. Marshal Milligan was right, of course—such a weapon was far too powerful to use in a controlled environment in space, or even on Ceres...but for some reason Nick felt compelled to carry it. He couldn't explain the feeling, but four years in the Star Marines and fifteen months in combat had taught him to trust his instincts. Right now he had a gut feeling, nothing more than that, but he refused to ignore it. He pulled the laser pistol out of his shoulder holster and replaced it with the .44, though it barely fit. Then he strapped on a conventional gunbelt and placed the laser in the belt holster. People might laugh, or people might sneer, but fuck 'em—with his badge on his belt and his laser on his hip, they would know he was a lawman.

Nick locked his room and headed down the stairs. In the hotel lobby he was halfway to the front door when someone called to him.

"Marshal Walker?"

Nick stopped and spun to his left, senses alert. The person who'd called him was a young fellow about his own age, tall and gangly and painfully thin. He was carrying a tool kit and looked nervous; he glanced about uneasily as Nick strode toward him.

"Are you Marshal Walker?"

"Yes, I am. Who are you?"

The skinny guy tried on a smile, but it looked forced and unnatural. He stuck out his hand.

"I'm Fred Ferguson. I, uh...came here to find you."

Nick nodded, looking him up and down. Ferguson's hair, barbered in back, was too long in front, long strands covering half his face. His skin seemed greasy and unhealthy, as if he hadn't bathed in a while, and he was pale...no surprise considering the lack of real sunlight in this place. Nick accepted his hand and shook it.

"What can I do for you?"

Ferguson glanced around again, as if fearing he might have been followed.

"Look, maybe it's none of my business, but I thought I ought to warn you."

"Okay. About what?"

Ferguson blinked several times.

"I was there last night. In the Open Airlock."

Nick's eyes narrowed. The joint had been packed with scruffy, unwashed bodies, too many faces to remember. He didn't recognize this one.

"Okay. Go on."

"The guy you beat up last night...the big one?"

"They were both pretty big."

"Yeah, but the first one, the one who challenged you..."

"What about him?"

This time Ferguson turned almost in a complete circle, looking for threats. Then he lowered his voice.

"He says he's gonna kill you. I just—thought you might want to know."

Nick felt his pulse spike a little; he hadn't been on the asteroid a whole day yet and he already had a death threat. He must be doing something right.

"He wants to kill me over a bar fight?"

"You humiliated him. Nobody's ever beaten him in a fight before, and now his reputation is on the line. Only way he can save it is to kill you."

Nick's tongue traced his top lip as he considered that.

"How come you're warning me, Fred? What's in it for you?"

For just a moment a flash of life brightened Ferguson's eyes. "Because I really enjoyed seeing you kick the shit out of him. He fucks with everybody, browbeats everybody. He thought you would be a pushover, but you surprised him."

Nick grinned slowly and Fred Ferguson actually smiled.

"Okay, Fred. Thanks for the warning. What's this guy's name?"

"Turd Murdoch."

Nick stared at him in disbelief.

"His name is Turd?"

"Yeah. Turd Murdoch. He's an ice drill supervisor, works for—"

"His mother actually named him *Turd?*"

Ferguson's smile died.

"Well—I don't know about his mother, if he even has one. But that's his name. Turd."

"What else did he say? Did he say when or how?"

"No. But after you left, he started telling everybody that you were a dead man. Said no two-bit pussy lawman could do what you did and live to brag about it."

"Two-bit pussy lawman."

"Yessir. That's what he called you."

"And he comes to the bar every night?"

"Yes, sir, Marshal. He's there every night. He gets off shift at 1600 and he's there by 1630. Stays till about 0100."

"What about the other people in the bar? Are they loyal to...*Turd?*"

Ferguson shrugged. "I'd say most of them are loyal to whoever proves to be the baddest ass. We're all survivors out here, Marshal. Nobody much stands on principle, we just do what we can to stay alive. If that means kissing Turd's ass then we kiss his ass. If somebody else comes along and beats him out, we'll start kissing a new ass."

Like you're kissing mine right now? Nick didn't ask.

"How many of them would be happy to see Turd go?" he said instead.

"Probably most of 'em. At one time or another Turd has dumped on everybody, so nobody's gonna shed too many tears if he gets his ass whooped." Ferguson cleared his throat. "You seem like a nice guy, Marshal. I figured if anybody can whoop Turd, you can. But not if he ambushes you first."

"Does Turd carry any weapons?"

"I think he has a knife. Just about everybody on Ceres carries a weapon of some kind."

Nick nodded slowly and stared thoughtfully through the front window of the lobby. He turned back to Ferguson.

"Okay, Fred, thanks. And if I see you in the Open Airlock, we've never met. Right?"

Ferguson grinned in relief. "Yes, sir, Marshal! I was just about to suggest that."

On the move - Ceres

Nick left the hotel and headed south out of Centerville. He figured to spend a few hours touring the entire settlement; so far he'd seen only a fraction of it, and his job demanded he become familiar with the terrain. The pressure tunnel leading out of Centerville brought him to an industrial area with a sign that read FARRINGTON SOUTH.

Only a quarter the size of Centerville, Farrington South looked like a factory complex, the entire area crammed with buildings, girders, and storage tanks. Nick drove around the periphery to see what he could see, but had little idea what he was looking at. Cranes, girders, and catwalks jutted above the buildings, giant pipes connected buildings with tanks, and electric vehicles moved to and fro, both on the ground and in the air. Hardhat workers bustled about, operating equipment or overseeing each other; harsh floodlights cast a glare over the entire scene, and the noise was horrific.

Nick was able to circle the entire complex by staying on the narrow road outside the forcefence, but when he'd made a complete circuit he turned into the main gate and stopped at the guard shack. A grim looking security guard leaned into his E-car and glowered at him. He looked about thirty, hard-muscled, with a thick but neatly trimmed beard.

"I'm new in town," Nick told him casually. "What is this place?"

The guard glanced at the badge on his belt and his scowl deepened.

"New in town, huh? How new are you?"

"Got in eighteen hours ago. I'm making a tour of the asteroid, thought I'd start here."

The guard grunted and straightened up. He glanced over his shoulder as if to see whether anyone was watching him.

"Is there a problem?" Nick asked, keeping his tone even. "Maybe something you want to tell me?"

The guard stared at him a moment, then leaned into the car again.

"You know a man named Turd Murdoch?"

Nick's eyebrows lifted a fraction. "I think I met him last night. Can't say I *know* him."

The guard studied him a moment, then inclined his head toward the factory.

"This here is Farrington South," he said. "Water crusher."

Nick showed his surprise. "Water *crusher?*"

"Yeah."

"I didn't know you could crush water."

"You can't, but you can crush ice. That's what this place does."

"So why don't you call it an ice crusher?"

"Because I didn't name the goddamn thing!"

"Where do you get the ice from?"

"That comes from Farrington North." The guard pointed. "That would be—"

"North," Nick finished for him.

"Right. They mine the ice, we crush it. Then we melt it—"

"And store it in those tanks," Nick guessed.

"You're good."

"How do you get the ice from North to South? I don't see any trucks coming this way."

"Underground conveyers. We also crush ice for the other mining companies, then pipe the water back to their tanks."

"And where does all this water end up?"

"Outer Worlds, mostly. None of the worlds outside the Belt have reliable water supplies, so they buy from us. Mars buys a lot of it, too, although they do have permafrost of their own."

Nick nodded thoughtfully. The guard seemed to know an awful lot about the operation for a guy who just watched the gate. On an impulse, he stuck out his hand.

"Nick Walker. United Federation Marshal."

"Yeah, I know."

"You do!"

"Yeah. Like I said, Turd Murdoch."

The guard ignored his hand, so Nick lowered it.

"What's your name?"

"You don't need to know my name."

Nick shrugged. "Fair enough. How long you been out here?"

"Too goddamn long."

Nick smiled and narrowed his eyes.

"What're you hiding from?"

The guard's eyes hardened and his lips compressed. He didn't answer.

"From what I hear," Nick went on, "just about everybody on this rock is running from or hiding from something, so it's not like I'm trying to single you out."

"What the fuck, are you tryin' to be my buddy?"

"Anything wrong with that?"

"Yeah. You're wearing a badge."

Nick nodded slowly, heaved a deep sigh, and reached for the throttle.

"Thanks for the guided tour. Maybe I'll see you around."

The guard stepped back as Nick turned the car. Just as he was about to drive away, the guard slapped the vehicle roof with his hand, and Nick stopped. The guard leaned in again.

"Statutory rape," he said.

Nick gazed at him without a reply, and the guard's eyes took on a tortured look.

"I was nineteen, she was seventeen. We were gonna get married. But then she got pregnant."

Nick's lips compressed as he began to suspect the rest.

"Even her parents vouched for me," the man said, "but the goddamn district attorney filed felony charges and demanded a life sentence."

"A *life* sentence!"

"Yeah. For making love to the girl I was gonna marry."

"The jury went for it?"

"They did. The way the DA set it up, they didn't have much choice. The law didn't make exceptions, he said. Love didn't enter into it, he said. The road to hell was paved with good intentions, he said. It all boiled down to whether we had sex and whether she was under age. Period. Obviously we'd had sex because she was pregnant—and I never denied it. And obviously she was under age because she was seventeen. So it was open and shut."

"Where was this?"

"Boston, North America's hotbed of religious fundamentalist insanity. Goddamn freaks, all of them!"

Nick shook his head sympathetically. "How the hell did you get out here? I would have thought they'd lock you up until sentencing."

"They did. Thank god the judge had a conscience. He gave me a choice of hard time or exile to the asteroids. Wasn't much of a choice."

"I guess not."

"So you see, Marshal, I'm not hiding from anything. I can leave here any time I want to, but when I do I go straight into lockup, and I won't ever be getting out." The guard smiled bitterly. "And I was gonna be a school teacher."

"What happened to your girlfriend and the baby?"

"I dunno. She wrote to me for a couple of years, but I told her to get on with her life. I ain't ever going home, so there was no point in her hanging on to me. She finally stopped communicating, and I try not to think about."

Nick was silent a moment. If the guard was telling the truth, it was a story too terrible to think about. He stuck his hand out the window again.

"That's a horrible story," he said. "I wish there was something I could do."

The guard shook his hand this time. "My name is Tim Barron. Nice to meet you, Marshal."

"Glad I met you, too."

"One more thing—you watch out for Turd Murdoch. I'm not much of a fan of law enforcement types, but I'd hate to see you get hurt."

Chapter 7

Turning east from Farrington South, Nick followed the pressure tunnel through a small habitat housing another mining operation, Astral Fountains, and continued until he reached another residential habitat. This was Ghetto Gardens, and looked very similar to Centerville, but was only half the size. From there he had no option but to travel north, the route taking him through East Village and Ceres North, also residential habitats. All three habitats were nearly identical, featuring several square blocks of compact housing structures, a small park with artificial sunlight, two or three markets, a dozen or more bars, a building that resembled a fire station, and a Farrington security office. He had seen a school in Centerville—a very small one—but none here. Very few people were on the streets and he only saw two women, both in the company of armed guards.

The tunnel out of Ceres North was a long one that ended at a freight terminal, known locally as a B-terminal.

According to the information he had downloaded earlier, Ceres had three B-terminals with access to surface transportation. Here, piped water from the ice crushers was loaded into tanks for shipping; the tanks were lifted to the surface and loaded onto cargo ships. The water froze again as soon as it reached the surface and was shipped to final destination as a solid.

Nick circled the terminal slowly and looked the operation over, but like Farrington South, entry was restricted by a security barrier. He could see portable tanks being shifted onto a cargo lift and others being filled with water. Literally thousands of shipping tanks were stacked about waiting to be filled, and men in hard hats bustled about. Once again he saw overhead cranes and catwalks, much like a shipyard on a planet.

Moving west from the terminal Nick entered Farrington North, another crushing operation, and turned south again. Passing through System Springs, another mining operation, he finally returned to Government Annex. In a little over an hour he had toured eighty percent of Ceres, and had seen the general layout. What he missed, according to his map, lay just west and a little north of Government Annex—Farrington Industries headquarters—and south of that, Colonial Waters. Nick was anxious to visit the Farrington facility, but not just yet. For some reason he couldn't yet explain, he had an uneasy feeling about FI, and before he dropped in it would be prudent to have as much information as possible. There was no rush.

Government Annex - Ceres

Nick walked into the office to find a ceiling fan sucking cigar smoke out of the air. Marshal Milligan was still at his desk, looking grumpy, but two other men were also present, both of them wearing U.F. Marshal badges. They turned curious eyes on Nick as he came to a stop in the middle of the room.

"This the new kid?" one of them asked. He was younger than Milligan, but not by much. He looked at least fifty, closer to fifty-five. Like most of the men Nick had seen so far, he had a hard look about him; he was about six feet three and a few pounds heavier than Nick, and wore an old fashioned gunbelt strapped around his waist, the holster hanging low so his hand didn't have to reach far for the laser pistol tucked inside. His most prominent feature was a beak-like nose.

Milligan cleared his throat.

"Russ Murray, meet Nick Walker. "

Nick smiled and extended his hand. Murray shook it, but didn't smile.

"I hear you're fresh out of the Academy," Murray said, making it sound like an accusation.

"That's what they tell me." Nick was fully prepared to accept a little hazing, even expected it, but it was still annoying to be called the "new kid". He kept the smile in place as a gesture of good will...no point making enemies until he had to, especially if they were wearing a badge.

Murray was looking him up and down.

"You seem physically fit."

"I try to be."

Milligan interrupted by gesturing to the fourth man in the room, a sturdy specimen who looked like a solarball lineman, all chest and shoulders and shaven head. He looked about thirty.

"And this is Sandy Beech."

Nick's grin widened as Beech reached to shake hands. "Sandy Beech? As in—"

"Don't even think about it," Beech said, his white teeth gleaming in his black face, "or I'll have to break your jaw."

Nick shook hands and laughed. "I wouldn't blame you."

"Welcome to Ceres, Walker."

"Thanks."

But Murray wasn't finished with him. Leaning back against a desk, he crossed his arms and peered narrowly at him.

"Ever killed a man, Walker?"

Nick stared at him for just a moment, feeling his throat turn dry and adrenaline surge into his blood. The smile died on his lips and he regarded Murray for a moment. A feeling of despair flooded him briefly, and he took a deep breath to fight it off—but he couldn't stop the faint tremble in his hands.

"Yes."

Murray's eyebrows tilted in surprise.

"Really! Tell us about it! Somebody try to steal your ice cream?"

Nick's annoyance faded, replaced by real anger. Good-natured hazing was one thing, but outright hostility was quite another. He glanced at Beech, but Beech appeared neutral; he turned to Milligan, but the old Marshal merely raised his eyebrows, as if to say, *You must have known this was coming, so deal with it.*

He looked at Murray again, whose expression had changed from feigned surprise to contempt—he clearly thought Nick was lying.

"No," Nick said finally. "It wasn't my ice cream. It was a little mountain town called Trimmer Springs."

"What?" Murray frowned in confusion.

Nick shrugged, his jaws clenched. "It's not important."

"Go ahead," Marshal Milligan urged. "Tell him. I'd like to hear it, too."

Nick stared at the old man for a moment, then lowered his head, feeling suddenly cold. He didn't speak for nearly thirty seconds; they all stared at him, waiting.

But he shook his head again.

"I don't like to talk about it."

Milligan nodded knowingly. He cleared his throat and spoke to the others.

"Walker's unit was bottled up in that little town, surrounded, outnumbered, and under bombardment. Most of the outfit was killed or wounded by artillery, but when the rebels tried to move in, Walker got up in a church tower with a sniper rifle and killed fifty-one men. The rebel attack stalled long enough for help to arrive. Walker sustained multiple wounds and was awarded the Crimson Cross *and* the Galaxy Cross. Federation Star Marines, Battle of Trimmer Springs, Alpha Centauri, November 19, 0436, Colonial Calendar."

Nick glanced at Milligan in surprise—none of that was in his U.F. Marshal packet.

"I looked you up," Milligan said. "I like to do my own background checks."

Murray stood up straight and stared at his feet, then turned to face Milligan.

"Maybe you should send Walker on that little errand we were talking about," he said. "A man with his background should be able to handle a couple of kidnappers, don't you think?"

Milligan smiled. "I have a better idea...why don't you *both* go."

*

Nick used his porta-phone to call Misery Allen and cancel their dinner date. She accepted his apology graciously but he felt bad about it— he had no intention of becoming involved with her, but canceling a first date was bad form. Unfortunately, he had no choice; Murray had told him they would be leaving Ceres and when they might return was anyone's guess.

"Where exactly is this place?" Nick asked as Murray piloted the E-car toward one of the A-terminals, which accessed surface transportation and the spaceport.

"Place called Caribou Lake."

"What?" Nick stared at him. Murray grimaced, possibly intending it as a smile.

"Out here in the 'roids, people get positively stupid when it comes to naming their rocks. They come up with all kinds of poetic shit, usually something nostalgic about where they came from. The place we're going is an empty rock with a few hundred people stuck to it, everybody living in pressure cubicles and garbage all over the fucking place, but hey, it's Caribou Lake." He shook his head grimly. "Sentimental fools."

Nick didn't reply. He was finding Murray's cynicism a bit unsettling.

"I've seen places called Mystic River, Shifting Sands, Rudolph's Rainbow, and Thundercloud City. There's a thousand more just like that, stretched all the way around the sun. The only ones that make any sense are the whorehouse 'roids—Sally's Secret, Heidi's Hideout, Jackson's Hole...when you hear a name like that you *know* what to expect. The rest of those fancy handles are just *sad*."

They passed through the Colonial Waters industrial habitat and arrived at the same A-terminal where Nick had arrived the night before. Murray parked the E-car and began hauling gear out of the back.

"How far is it?" Nick asked.

"'Bout thirty thousand miles. We'll be there in four or five hours."

Nick grabbed his space bag with his toothbrush and a change of clothes and followed Murray to the lift. Two minutes later they arrived at the surface station and Nick gazed through heavy Solarglas at the barren wasteland outside. The station was a sturdy starcrete building, reinforced against meteoroid strikes, and stretched a hundred yards in each direction. At one end was the access tunnel to the spaceport, at the other a terminus for surface transportation. He followed Murray toward the latter. As they walked he saw a coffee shop, souvenir stand, and a row of sleeping cubicles for rent. There was also a lounge with video entertainment and comm equipment for anyone who wanted to chat with the universe.

"Does anyone actually live up here?"

"Not many. I think some of the maintenance people have quarters here."

"I don't think I'd care for it. That Solarglas looks pretty thick, but if there was an astral impact..."

"We usually get plenty of warning when that happens," Murray said. "There's a couple of scientific stations on the surface and they track the other asteroids in the area. You can see them coming for days before they hit."

"Ever have any real disasters?"

"Occasionally."

Murray didn't elaborate but it didn't matter—they had reached their destination.

Murray handled the datawork and within minutes they were ushered into a chamber similar to an airlock where a long, torpedo-like vehicle sat waiting. Nick had seen similar vehicles in the military, but never at a civilian installation. It was about eight feet wide and sixty long; the rounded nose was festooned with maneuvering jets. The last ten feet of the tail was a rocket engine, and two fuel tanks hung on either side. It had no wings because it wasn't designed for atmosphere.

"This is called a jalopy," Murray told him. "Ever used one before?"

"No. I've never even seen one this small. How far will it go?"

"Depends on your fuel. I ordered enough to get us there and back, with a little to spare."

Murray opened a cargo hatch and tossed his gear inside. Nick added his space bag and Murray closed the compartment. The passenger cabin was immediately in front of the cargo space and quite a bit larger. Murray opened the hatch and crawled inside, Nick following.

"Shouldn't we be wearing pressure suits?"

"Don't need 'em."

It was tight. The passenger space was about ten or twelve feet long, with three fairly comfortable seats on each side separated by a narrow aisle. Except for the two forward seats, the cabin was covered, a small window port beside each seat. Murray took the left-hand seat forward and Nick sat across from him. The Solarglas canopy extended above the vehicle body, giving them a good view outside; Murray went to work powering things up, checking airtight integrity and life support, then activated the radio. He talked briefly to the controller, and outside the jalopy red lights began to flash.

After a thirty-second warning the chamber was depressurized and the outer door began to spiral open. Nick felt his stomach squirm just a little—he could see straight out into space. He sat silent while Murray activated the controls; the jalopy lifted a couple of feet to clear its cradle and Murray applied a tiny amount of power, nudging the thing through the airlock door until they were clear of the station.

"It may look complicated," Murray told him, "but it's about as hard as driving a boat. Once you get the feel of it, the rest becomes instinct."

Nick nodded and watched as Murray piloted the craft. He applied a little more power and Nick felt a nudge of acceleration that started the jalopy moving. Nick expected him to rotate the nose upward and climb, but instead he kept it level and gradually increased the thrust. The horizon was so close it appeared only a few hundred yards away, and gravity was so light that escape velocity was virtually nil. Within minutes the jalopy was moving away from the asteroid, leaving the surface of Ceres behind.

"That looked easy," Nick said. "I can't wait to see how you land it."

Murray gave him a blank stare.

"Who said I know how to land it?"

Chapter 8

In transit - The Asteroid Belt

Nick wasn't sure how fast they were traveling, but he could at least tell they were moving. No matter which way he looked he saw chunks of rock, none of them very close, but close enough to be visible. They seemed stationary, just hanging in space, and ranged in size from small boulders to several thousand feet across. He had always thought of the Asteroid Belt as being thick enough to walk on, but the pieces he could see were often several miles apart.

There were smaller asteroids, too, small enough to be invisible until one was right on top of them, and these constituted the real danger to travel. Fortunately, the jalopy's radar detected them in time to avoid collision, using the maneuvering jets in the nose. From time to time Nick heard a *tick* as a bit of gravel struck the jalopy, but the little rocket was tough and none of them penetrated.

It was hard to believe that people actually lived out here; for most of the trip he saw nothing but black space, distant stars, and the floating debris of what might have once been the makings of a planet that never formed. Once, on a larger rock in the distance, he thought he saw artificial lights flashing red and blue. He pointed it out to Murray.

"Dick's Drive In," Murray grunted.

"What?"

"It's a whorehouse."

Nick left it at that.

"What's this about a kidnapping? Maybe you'd better brief me before we get there."

Murray grimaced. "I wondered when you were gonna ask."

Nick glanced sharply at him. "I wondered when you were gonna tell me."

Their eyes locked for a moment; Nick saw suspicion and mistrust, though he couldn't imagine why. But Murray looked away with another grimace.

"Seems this missionary team ran into some trouble," he said.

"*Missionary!*"

Murray nodded. "Some preacher named Reverend Sledge. Has a church on Mars. I guess the Jesus business isn't doing too well on the Red Planet, so he decided to come out here and scare up some extra cash. He's been going from one mining 'roid to another preaching the Word, holding revivals, stuff like that."

"Did he know what he was getting into?"

"Apparently not. He brought his two daughters with him. Seventeen and nineteen."

Nick frowned. "Don't tell me—someone took one of the girls?"

"Both of 'em."

"When did this happen?"

"The call came in last night. The girls have been missing for a couple of weeks."

"Two weeks! And we're just now hearing about it?"

Murray shrugged. "That's not so unusual out here. People are used to solving their own problems if they can, and a lot of them don't want anything to do with law enforcement under any circumstances. So they might delay for quite a while before reporting something. In this case, the reverend called the local security cops first, since they have an office at Caribou Lake."

"And the security guys—"

"Aren't real cops," Murray finished for him. "A lot of them are no better than the people they arrest. Some take their job seriously, but others just get off on the prestige they think it gives them."

"So who called us? The reverend or the security company?"

"The security boys, at the reverend's insistence. I guess he finally realized they weren't gonna get his girls back, so he dug in his heels."

Nick felt a knot in the pit of his stomach. If the girls had been missing for two weeks, it might be impossible to locate them. In that time they could have been moved anywhere within the Belt, or even to a different world.

"Does this sort of thing happen often?"

"What, kidnapping?"

"Kidnapping women."

"Not all that often. First of all, there aren't very many women around to steal, and second of all, most of the women out here can be had for a price. It's not a nice thing to say, but it's true—as a general rule, what you might call 'proper' women just don't come out here."

"But a missionary's daughters might be an exception?"

"One would think so."

Nick fell silent, thinking. Finally he glanced at Murray.

"What you said about the security cops..."

"What about it?"

"How many security companies are there around here?"

"Half a dozen. Each of the major mining companies has its own cops—Astral Fountains, Colonial Waters, System Springs...and Farrington. Then you have a couple of independent security firms. They provide personal protection for individuals and security for businesses—"

"Earlier today I saw a couple of women on the street with armed escorts."

"That would be one of the independents. Certain ladies are afraid to venture out too far without guards, to prevent the very thing we're talking about."

"So that's six security firms on Ceres. What about the outlying rocks?"

Murray nodded. "Farrington is the biggest outfit for a billion miles. They not only mine water, they also run a casino and a string of whorehouses." He nodded over his shoulder.

"Dick's Drive In is one of theirs. *And...*" Murray dipped his head to make his point. "...they provide security on most of the smaller settlements. They have a small army scattered around the Belt."

"Including Caribou Lake?"

"Yep."

Nick glanced at him. "How would you rate their personnel?"

"Are you kidding? Like I said, a few of them take their job seriously—but only a few. Most of those I've seen are just thugs. If the U.F. Marshal ran background checks on them and arrested the felons, Farrington Security wouldn't have enough men left to guard a birthday party."

*

Nick was dozing when he felt the jalopy lurch suddenly. He jerked awake as he felt himself pressed into his seat under mild acceleration. It took him a moment to realize the jalopy had rotated and was traveling backward; the rocket burn was actually *de*celeration.

"We there already?" he asked with a yawn.

"Just about."

Murray was watching his cockpit display, and Nick could see the asteroid in the schematic. Glancing over his shoulder and looking out, he could see part of the rock looming just a few miles away.

"The trickiest part of conning one of these things is slowing down. The nose jets aren't nearly powerful enough, so you have to fly backwards for a while."

Fifteen minutes later Murray rotated again, and Nick saw the asteroid dead ahead, like a mountain peak with lights. Dead in the center of the asteroid sat what looked like a cavern surrounded by flashing amber beacons. A ripple of lighted arrows pointed the way in, and an automated voice from the cockpit speakers began issuing landing instructions, including trajectory and speed limitations. Murray began firing the nose jets to decelerate further, and soon the jalopy was barely moving as it drifted into the landing tunnel. At the end of the tunnel a large sign flashed CAUTION – SLOW in rapid succession.

Then the sign flashed, in large red letters, the word STOP.

Murray fired a final braking thrust and the jalopy came to a halt, hanging three feet above a landing cradle. Nick wondered how they would get out—they weren't wearing pressure suits and the tunnel was still open to space. Then he realized they were sinking slowly, and a moment later felt a jolt as the vehicle settled onto the cradle.

"What happens now?" Nick asked. "How do we get out?"

"Watch and learn."

A new graphic appeared on the display and Murray keyed instructions. The cradle began to sink below the tunnel floor into an airlock. They waited nearly a minute for the lock to pressurize, then a door opened and the cradle conveyed them forward, through a narrow tunnel, and finally emerged in a large, well-lit space that looked like a parking bay. Nick saw five or six other vehicles there, and the conveyer delivered them to a parking spot not far from an exit door. A message flashed on the console display and Murray began powering down.

"That's it. You can unstrap."

Nick followed Murray's lead, letting him exit the vehicle first. When he crawled out of the hatch he was surprised how cold it was—his breath was frosting—but he was breathing real air and was able to stretch his legs. He hadn't realized how cramped the cockpit had been.

"Bring all your gear," Murray advised. "Rule number one— never trust anybody out here, even if they're wearing a badge. You just never know."

Nick retrieved his space bag, wishing he'd also packed a heavy jacket.

"What's rule number two?"

"There is no rule number two. Let's go."

Caribou Lake

The hatch from the parking bay opened into a short corridor with two elevators. Nick and Murray took one that rose for nearly a minute before stopping. They emerged into another corridor that branched off in two directions. No signs were posted offering directions, but Murray seemed to know where to go, and Nick followed as he turned left. The corridor was narrow, lined with metallic siding, and felt very much like being on a spaceship. It opened into some kind of lounge with chairs, couches, and scattered vending machines. Three more corridors opened off in three directions, none of them marked, and Murray made another turn as they continued walking.

"Place isn't exactly designed for tourists, is it?"

"Nope."

"Where's the lake?"

"What?" Murray spun around in surprise.

"Caribou Lake," Nick deadpanned. "I was just wondering."

"Shit!" Murray resumed his stride and Nick followed, shaking his head. The man had no sense of humor.

Two or three turns later they came to their destination. This door actually had a sign—FARRINGTON SECURITY. Murray plowed through without knocking and they found themselves in the lobby of what looked like a police station. An elderly woman behind a counter was talking on a radio and didn't bother to look up. Several desks cluttered the small office space, but only one had an occupant. He was about Murray's age, Nick guessed, and didn't look any more pleasant. He regarded the newcomers with a scowl and got up slowly, as if stiff from sitting too long. He was wearing a faded uniform with the word FARRINGTON on a shoulder patch.

"Looks like the motherfuckers have landed," he said gruffly. "One motherfucker in particular."

Still scowling, he limped toward the counter, his eyes sweeping the two U.F. Marshals as if they carried the plague. Russ Murray leaned his elbows on the counter and stared right back at him.

"If it weren't for the motherfuckers," he said evenly, "the assholes would have become extinct a long time ago."

The other man shook his head. "That's not true. The cocksuckers are our allies now. And we can always recruit extra slapdicks if we need them."

Murray broke into a grin and extended his hand. The other man grabbed it and they both burst into laughter.

"Russ Murray! How long's it been, motherfucker?"

"Too goddamn long, asshole. How've you been?"

"All things considered, not too bad." The other man slapped his leg, and Nick heard the clink of metal. So that was the reason for the limp—he had a prosthetic leg. "Could have been a whole lot worse."

Murray nodded and stepped to one side to include Nick.

"Jim Keating, meet Nick Walker, United Federation Marshal."

Keating stared at Nick a moment, his smile fading.

"Jesus Christ!" he exclaimed. "They're robbing the day-cares now! Is he old enough to wear that gun?"

"Damn right he is! Ex Star Marine. This kid's a certified war hero."

Keating smiled and took Nick's hand. His grip was strong and warm.

"Just fucking with you, Nick. Not much entertainment out here, so we pick on each other."

Still amazed at Murray's introduction, Nick grinned and accepted the handshake.

"No problem. Just call me slapdick."

"You guys want some coffee?" Keating opened a wing gate for them to pass through. "I think we have a fresh pot, not more than five or six hours old."

He led them through the office into a lunchroom with a table and six chairs. The coffee smelled strong and bitter, but Nick accepted a cup anyway. He took a chair at the table with Murray and Keating, carefully sipping the scalding brew. Murray turned to Nick.

"Before we start," he said, "remember what I told you about rule number one? Well, this guy is the only exception to that on this entire asteroid. Just so you know."

Nick nodded and Murray explained to Keating.

"I was telling him about the high standards Farrington Security sets on its hiring practices. Just in case he wanted to apply."

Keating grinned, but without humor. "From the look of him, I don't think he would qualify. Too much integrity."

Nick, though enjoying the deadpan banter, tilted his head. "So why do you work for them?"

Keating shrugged. "At my age, with my disability, not too many jobs available. When I first took the position I thought it was honest work. By the time I figured it all out, it was too late."

"Your disability…"

Keating slapped his artificial leg. "Lost it in an airlock accident."

Nick raised an eyebrow. "Airlock accident?"

Keating shrugged. "Actually it was *bitten* off, but Farrington didn't want to pay for hazardous duty so they falsified the accident report."

Nick glanced at Murray, who nodded with a straight face. Clearly both men were screwing with him, but he didn't press the point. He pretended to go along.

"If it's not too personal, how come you didn't get a bio-regen? I've heard they're as good as the real thing."

Keating nodded. "I heard that too, but they're damn expensive. Company wouldn't spring for it."

He turned back to Murray.

"You got here pretty quick. You here about the missionary kids?"

Murray nodded. "Doesn't take us two weeks like it does some people."

Keating scowled angrily. "I would've called you ten days ago. I'm pretty sure those girls are no longer at Caribou Lake. But you know my captain."

"Yes, unfortunately."

"Enough said, then."

"You think the girls are even alive?"

"Oh, yeah. You oughta see them, Russ—they are two gorgeous kids. Young, fresh, innocent—nothing like that has been seen around here for years. Maybe not ever. Girls like that are worth a fortune in this environment."

"Forced prostitution?"

"Exactly. Men out here will pay huge for ten minutes with one of them. I suspect they're very much alive somewhere, but..."

He compressed his lips and cleared his throat, as if the rest of the thought was too painful to speak.

"No longer in pristine condition?" Murray offered.

Keating nodded. "Yeah, that pretty well sums it up."

"You've checked the whorehouses?"

"First thing. Turned them inside out, but the girls weren't there. We've also been all over this asteroid. Only so many places you could hide someone, and they all came up clean."

"What about private quarters?"

"Everything. We practically declared martial law, violated privacy rights, everything. Searched all vehicles, personal and commercial. No girls."

"Where's the father?"

"Holed up in his quarters. He was a royal pain in the ass for the first few days—understandably—but I think he's just about given up on finding his daughters alive. Spends his time praying and reading his Bible. We have a medic checking on him every few hours to make sure he eats."

"We'll want to talk to him."

Nick had been listening, but now interrupted with another question.

"You said you checked everyone's private quarters. Does that include security personnel, too?"

Keating stared at him in surprise, then his eyes glinted with humor as he glanced at Murray.

"Kid learns fast." He looked at Nick again and nodded. "Yeah. Everybody."

"How many people are there on this asteroid?"

"Couple of thousand. There's a small mining operation here, but mostly this is a community center for other operations in the area. Only about half the people here are miners; the rest work for the resort."

Nick's eyebrows shot up. "You call this a *resort?*"

Keating nodded. "Caribou Lake Enterprises. To the people out here it's Aspen and Vegas and Coney Island all rolled into one."

"How many women are here?"

"Maybe a hundred. They all have day jobs, but most of them also moonlight."

"Moonlight?"

"Yeah." Keating's eyes bored into him. "Do I need to explain what 'moonlight' means?"

Nick had the grace to blush and shook his head.

"How long were the girls missing before you started investigating?"

Keating sighed. "We're not absolutely sure. The reverend came to us and said he couldn't find his girls, but he wasn't clear about when he'd seen them last. So it could have been a few hours."

"Was there any space traffic around that time?"

"Couple of arrivals, but no departures."

"Where you going with this, Walker?" Murray demanded. "You have something on your mind?"

Nick nodded, gazing from one man to the other.

"The girls are still on the asteroid."

Chapter 9

The man who walked into the lunchroom ten minutes later was about thirty-five, slender and fit. His uniform looked new, more expensive than Keating's. Bars on his shoulder designated his rank and he sported a late model laser pistol that looked twice as powerful as Nick's. Nick figured it must have cost a fortune, considering import costs and the fact that the design was less than two years old.

Keating got stiffly to his feet as the man came in, and the two marshals also stood.

"Captain Guthrie, you remember Marshal Murray."

Guthrie nodded abruptly, but didn't smile or offer to shake hands.

"And this is Nick Walker, also a U.F. Marshal."

Nick nodded deferentially, but Guthrie's eyes narrowed slightly.

"Nick Walker? I've heard that name before. You the one that got the best of Turd Murdoch?"

Hairs prickled on the back of Nick's neck—word surely traveled quickly in the Asteroid Belt!

"Yes, sir."

"Better watch your back. I hear Turd is gunning for you."

Nick nodded solemnly. "Thanks for the heads-up."

Guthrie poured himself a cup of the greasy coffee, then turned to face the visitors again. He was a thin man, almost gaunt. His nose was bony and his eyes sat too close together; he wore a perpetual scowl that didn't improve his appearance one bit. His thinness made him look taller than he actually was.

"You're here about the girls."

"That's right," Murray said.

"I'm afraid you've wasted a trip. We've turned this rock upside down and they're not here." Guthrie pulled out a chair and sat down, placing his coffee cup on the table. "I figure they were dead within hours of the kidnap. Probably a rape-murder. They were lookers, both of them, and we don't get many of those out here. Some of the local scum probably grabbed them, fucked them, and pushed them out of an airlock." He shook his head sadly. "Most likely, if they ever do turn up, they'll be floating in space a few hundred miles from here."

Murray asked a few benign questions, but received the same answers Keating had already provided. Guthrie sipped his coffee, and five minutes later glanced at his watch.

"Well, good luck, Marshal," he said to Murray. "I've told you everything I know, but you can work with Keating if you think he can help. I have another commitment, so I'll say good-bye."

He got to his feet, nodded briefly, and left.

Silence hung in the room for twenty seconds after the door closed, and the three men at the table looked at one another.

"Bullshit," Nick muttered.

Keating burst into laughter.

"What's his story?"

Keating shrugged. "Company man. Started out on Ceres, worked his way up breaking heads in lockup, and got promoted to captain. They sent him here to run the Caribou Lake office and he ain't done a lick of work since."

"Pretty cushy job."

"Well...ain't nothing cushy about living here, but...relatively speaking? Yes."

* * *

The Reverend Crawford Sledge was in his late fifties, rotund and bulbous, with a tangled set of Old Testament whiskers that, had he not been wearing a clerical collar, would have distinguished him as one more besotted miner taking refuge in the Asteroid Belt. When Keating knocked, Sledge opened the door and let the three of them into his quarters. Nick glanced about with a lawman's eye and noted the tiny apartment's disheveled appearance; Sledge himself looked completely sleepless and strung out; his eyes were red and puffy, as if he'd been crying, and his white collar was stained. Sledge cleared a couple of chairs of religious pamphlets and pushed them toward his guests. Murray and Keating took the chairs, Nick leaned against the bulkhead. He was alert for the smell of alcohol, but didn't detect any.

Keating made the introductions and Sledge nodded listlessly.

"Reverend," Murray began, "what can you tell us about what happened? When was the last time you saw your daughters?"

Sledge stared at the floor, his thick grey hair bushy and tangled. He rubbed his nose with a finger and battled his emotions as he tried to remember.

"We held a gospel service that evening," he said. "Martha and Mary were assisting me. Mary played the pneumo and Martha led the singing."

He peered anxiously into Murray's eyes.

"Please find them for me, Marshal! They're all I have left in the 'verse!"

"That's why we're here, Reverend," Murray said with a gentleness Nick hadn't expected. "How long did the service last?"

"Hour, hour and a half. I usually like to keep the sermons around thirty minutes, long enough to deliver the message without boring everyone. Then we have the song service and personal testimonies...and altar calls. All that takes about an hour."

"Where were the girls during the sermon?"

"They were moving around. I encourage visitors to follow along in the Bible, you see, and most of them don't know how to find the scriptures, so the girls help them. I find the men are more attentive if the girls pay them a little attention."

"And when the service was over? Where were they then?"

Sledge frowned, his eyes narrowed in thought.

"That's where my memory fails me. The men were standing for the final hymns, and I lost sight of the girls."

"How many men were present?"

"Oh, Lord, I'm not sure—the hall was full, so...maybe a hundred, hundred and fifty."

"Were they all miners?"

"I'm sure I don't know that, sir. They looked like local men, but some of them were probably employees here on the asteroid."

"At what point did you notice the girls were missing?"

Sledge cleared his throat and took a deep breath.

"It was during the cleanup. I was picking up songbooks and Bibles—we have to provide both, you know—and I realized I was all alone. Usually the girls are helping me, but they just weren't there."

"And what time was this?"

Sledge shook his head slowly, calculating.

"The service started about seven-thirty, so...nine o'clock? Maybe a little later?"

Murray glanced at Keating, then back to Sledge.

"How long did you wait before reporting their disappearance?"

"I'm not sure. It was a couple of hours, at least. First I came back here, thinking maybe one of them was taken ill—their room is right next door—and then I hunted all over the asteroid for them...at least the places I was allowed to go."

"Do you have any holos of your daughters?"

"No, sir, but I have some flat photos." Sledge stood and crossed to a dresser, where he pulled open a drawer and extracted some glossy digitals. He handed copies to Murray and Nick.

Nick gazed at the photos without expression, but his heart began to pound in his chest. One girl was blond, the other brunette, and both were absolutely stunning. The photos were studio portraits, carefully posed; each girl was in semi-profile, facing slightly away from the cam and looking back over her shoulder—not at the camera, but at Heaven. Each had a beatific smile on her face, presumably reflecting the joy in her heart—perfect complexion, perfect white teeth, long hair brushed and gleaming.

The longer Nick stared at the photos the angrier he got.

"Reverend," he said, his voice edgy, "how old are these girls?"

"Seventeen and nineteen," the man told him. "Martha—she's the blonde—is nineteen. Mary is the brunette."

"And I assume they're both virgins?"

Keating and Murray spun to look at him, shock in their eyes. Sledge jerked upright as if he'd been shot.

"I should certainly think so!" he sputtered. "What kind of question is that?"

"What's your problem, Walker!" Murray demanded. "What difference does that make?"

Nick took a step forward and tossed the photos on the bed.

"Because anyone who would bring two innocent girls to a place like this is either out of his mind, or he's a goddamned fool!" Nick paused to let the shock sink in. "Unless...he was planning to rent them out."

Sledge stared at him in horror, turned two shades of pink and then three shades of red. Murray's mouth hung at half-mast and Keating's eyes glazed in disbelief. Nick didn't wait for them to recover.

"So which is it, Reverend—are you spreading the Word of God or just sending men to heaven a little early—for a price?"

For a moment Nick thought he'd gone too far. Sledge trembled and sank onto the bed, clutching his chest and gasping. Finally, shaking with emotion, tears flooded down his cheeks and he began to sob. Murray quickly got him a glass of water while Keating glared lasers at Nick. Nick leaned back against the bulkhead and watched, his face throbbing. As soon as Sledge was calm, Murray turned and took Nick by the arm.

"I want to have a word with you!"

*

"What is your fucking problem!" Murray rasped as soon as they were alone in the corridor.

Nick glared right back at him. "Two things—first, if those girls are what they appear to be, it's incredibly stupid to parade them around a mining camp without an armed escort. And second, I wanted to know if Sledge was being up front with us."

"Why wouldn't he be?"

"Look, we don't even know for sure that he's their father. For all you or I know he could be a pimp passing himself off as a preacher. What better cover for a traveling pussy festival?"

"That makes no sense! Why would he need a cover? Prostitution is legal."

"Not if those girls are captives."

"And what makes you think that?"

"I don't think that, *yet*. But you can't deny that it's a possibility. They both look fairly intelligent, which means they should be reluctant to expose themselves to this kind of environment. I've known a lot of girls who would never be caught dead in places a lot nicer than this."

Murray stared at him, the rage fading from his eyes.

"So what do you think now?"

"I'm still not sure. His reaction to what I said looked genuine, but he could be a very good actor."

"Well, the girls are still missing, so I'm not sure I see the relevance in your theory."

Nick shrugged. "It could be the girls went missing willingly. Maybe they chose the lesser of two evils."

Murray frowned.

"Aw, Christ, you're not suggesting that Sledge—"

"I'm not suggesting anything. I'm just keeping an open mind."

Murray turned in a circle, thinking.

"Okay, I don't want you to go back in there. I'll finish the interview, you can wait here."

He reached for the door but Nick caught his sleeve.

"I have a better idea. Why don't we split up?"

Murray frowned. "Why?"

"You've been out here before, so people recognize you. I'm a new face, and if people don't know who I am I might get someone to talk."

Murray was hesitant. "I dunno..."

"Marshal Milligan told me I would be working mostly alone. And *you* were going to send me out here by myself. So let me work."

"Undercover, huh?"

"For a few hours. I'll meet up with you back at Farrington Security."

Murray still seemed less than convinced, but finally shrugged.

"Well, you got yourself a Galaxy Cross, so I guess you don't need me to hold your hand. Just watch your ass. Do you have an implant?"

"No."

Murray reached into a pocket and pulled out what looked like a large button. He placed it in Nick's hand.

"Just squeeze it and talk. It's a dedicated freq."

Nick nodded. He pulled his badge off his belt and put it in his pocket along with the transmitter. Without another word he turned and walked away.

Government Annex - Ceres

"The witness may step down."

As the man with the wired jaw and splinted arm worked himself laboriously out of the witness chair and hobbled across the courtroom to take a seat, Judge Monica Maynard turned to David Tarpington.

"Call your next witness, Counselor."

Tarpington glanced up at the bench. "Your Honor, the Federation rests."

Monica glanced at Misery Allen. "Is the Defense ready to proceed?"

Misery Allen, trim and sexy in a tight pantsuit, stood.

"Your Honor, the Defense renews its request to dismiss all charges."

Monica's dark brows knitted in annoyance.

"Denied," she said flatly. "Again."

"Your Honor—"

"How many witnesses are you prepared to call?"

"Just one, your Honor. The defendant."

"And how long do you expect his testimony to take?"

"A few minutes, no more."

"Wonderful. Summarize it for me—what's he going to say?"

Misery's eyes widened a fraction in surprise.

"Just that he believed he was acting in self-defense, your Honor. Mr. Garrigus provoked him by constant taunting and was making threats."

"Self-defense." Monica stared at the burly, bearded defendant in disbelief. "The defendant will rise. I will question him myself."

The greasy looking man lumbered to his feet, his scarred face twisted in contempt. He was wearing work clothes and wasn't shackled.

"Mr. Murdoch, you are claiming self-defense?"

"Yeah."

Monica glowered. "By 'yeah' I take it you mean 'yes, your Honor'?"

"Yeah."

Monica leaned forward, her irritation rising. It was after eight o'clock and she had already missed her dinner. A hot bath was waiting...and waiting...and waiting.

"Well, I gotta tell you, Mr. Murdoch, I'm looking at Mr. Garrigus over there and he has a broken jaw, a broken arm, one eye is swollen shut, several teeth are missing, and I find it hard to believe that *you* are the victim here."

Murdoch said nothing.

"Explain it to me, Mr. Murdoch—how were you in any danger from the victim?"

"I was defendin' my reputation."

"Your reputation!"

"Yeah."

"And what was Mr. Garrigus doing to your reputation?"

"He was talkin' shit."

Monica Maynard heaved a deep sigh of frustration. David Tarpington was writing on a legal pad, grinning hugely. Misery Allen raised her eyes to the ceiling in hopelessness.

Monica leaned forward again.

"Mr. Murdoch...isn't your first name...*Turd?*"

"Yeah."

She studied him a moment, questioning her own sanity. What the *hell* was she doing holding court on Ceres?

"Your first name is *Turd*," she said slowly, "and you were offended because someone was *talking shit?*"

Barely able to hold it, Tarpington couldn't suppress a snicker. Tears were forming in his eyes.

"Yeah," Turd Murdoch said.

Monica tilted her head toward Misery Allen.

"Miss Allen, unless you have anything to add, I'm ready to render a verdict."

Defeated, Misery shook her head.

"The Defense rests, your Honor."

"Fantastic." Judge Maynard lifted a stack of papers and dropped them on their edge to align them. She looked at the defendant again.

"Mr. Murdoch, this court finds you guilty of aggravated assault. You are hereby sentenced to the following: you will pay all of Mr. Garrigus' medical bills, you will pay him one thousand terros for pain and suffering, and you will either pay a one thousand terro fine *or* spend ninety days in lockup. Which will it be?"

Murdoch's expression hardened as he glared at her.

"I didn't do nothin' wrong," he insisted.

"We're already past that phase, Mr. Murdoch. The court says you are guilty. The question now is, do you want to pay the fine or do the time?"

Murdoch glanced hatefully at Misery Allen, then glared hatefully at the judge.

"Fuck it, I'll pay the fine."

"Wonderful. Add another fifty terros for saying 'fuck' in my courtroom." She banged her gavel. "This court is adjourned."

Chapter 10

The Outer Orbit – Caribou Lake

Twenty minutes later, Nick walked into the only bar at Caribou Lake. He had taken a few minutes to study a map of the asteroid and get the lay of the "land", then slipped into a men's room. He still wore his gunbelt with the laser pistol—that seemed fairly common in the 'roids—but took the .44 out of the shoulder holster and tucked it into his boot, pulling his pants leg down over it; he buried the shoulder holster at the bottom of a waste can. He wetted his hair and used liquid soap to make it stick out in all directions, smudged his face and neck with dirt from the floor, and ripped the sleeve on his shirt so the tear was noticeable. By the time he reached the Outer Orbit he looked reasonably disheveled.

As expected, the bar was dim and smoky, so dark he could barely see the floor, but unlike the Open Airlock, Outer Orbit had no dance floor and the music wasn't nearly as loud. Neither did he see any pool tables, but there were some gaming machines in the back, black holes into which miners could watch their hard-earned wages disappear. The tables were lit by radium candles, which threw barely enough light that patrons could see each other's faces. The place was about half full, maybe thirty people, but conversation was muted. Nick wound his way carefully to the bar and leaned against it.

"Haven't seen you in here before."

The bartender was a woman, the only female he could see. She was trim and petite, even sexy, but the light was so bad he couldn't tell if she was pretty. He did see lines in her face that suggested she was a bit older than he was.

"My first time," he admitted with a wry grin. He slapped down ten terros. "Can I get a beer?"

She produced a bottle from a cooler and set it in front of him, took the ten and kept it. The beer was good, a Colorado brand he'd always liked...and a hell of a lot cheaper than the Missouri swill he'd bought at the Open Airlock. He twisted the top and drank deeply. The bartender was still looking at him.

"New to the 'roids?"

"Naw, I been out here a couple a years. Got me a small claim over on the Jupiter side, place called Sulphur Stones."

The woman whistled. "That's a fur piece from here. Couple of million miles."

Nick nodded and swigged his beer again.

"So what brings you to Caribou Lake? They don't have any watering holes out there?"

"Sure, they do. But I didn't come here for the booze."

Intrigued, she leaned her elbows on the bar, making sure her cleavage was visible.

"And what *did* you come here for?"

Nick gazed at her frankly for a moment, not missing the signals.

"To get laid."

Unfazed, she let her smile widen as she nodded slowly. This close, he could see her more clearly; she was at least fifty, but a very pleasant fifty.

"I'm willing to pay," he added.

She maintained eye contact with him, unblinking. Her smile didn't waver.

"Not too many women on this rock," she said casually.

"What time do *you* get off?"

She straightened up to her full five feet four and grabbed a towel, wiping the bar where his beer had dripped.

"In about four hours. But what makes you think I'm interested?"

"Why would I think you weren't?"

She laughed and swatted him with the towel. "Now you be nice."

In lieu of a reply, he reached out and placed his hand on the back of her neck, drawing her toward him. He bent over the bar and kissed her hard, holding her for long seconds. She made no effort to get free.

At a nearby table, two miners saw what was happening and stopped talking, staring in amusement.

"Careful, Bobbie!" one of them called out. "He looks an awful lot like that holo you showed me of your son!"

Without breaking the kiss, Bobbie the bartender extended her middle finger toward the table. Nick took a fresh grip on her, with both hands this time, and kissed her again, even harder. When he released her mouth he pressed his forehead against hers.

"You sure you can't get off work any sooner?"

"My, you *are* a horny one, aren't you!"

He nodded jerkily. "I'm young, too. You know what that means...staying power."

She pulled back from him and smoothed her hair with her fingers.

"It'll cost you fifty terros for as long as you want. I usually charge a hundred a pop, so that's a bargain."

He nodded and reached for his wallet. She quickly put out a hand.

"Not now." She smiled. "Later."

"How much later?" He looked desperate.

"Four hours. Sorry, I can't change that."

Nick gazed at her in disappointment, then sighed in resignation. "Okay, give me another beer. I'll be over in the corner."

With two beers in hand, he found a corner table and settled down, openly ignoring the room at large but quietly observing everything that moved. He was pretty new at this and had no idea if his ploy would work, but it was the only thing he could think of. He was halfway through the first beer when he sensed movement coming in his direction, and spotted a shadow looming over his table.

"Mind if I sit down?" The voice was gruff, middle aged, but not unfriendly. The face was in shadow but he could see a beard...and a hat, which seemed odd in this environment. With a casual wave of his hand he indicated the chair opposite.

"Not a bit. Have a seat."

The other man settled into the chair and rested his elbows on the table. He glanced around as if to make sure no one nearby was close enough to hear.

"I couldn't help overhearing your conversation with the barkeep."

Nick looked at the man more closely. In the radium light he could make out features now, and realized this was the man who'd teased the bartender about Nick looking like her son. The man stuck out his hand.

"My name is Willoughby."

"Nick Jones." Nick shook hands.

"So, what kind of claim you got at Sulphur Stones?"

"Just a small one. I move to a new spot every few months."

"Is that right? What're you looking for?"

"Trace minerals. The stuff they use in warp drives. They're pretty rare, so there are no big deposits. Pick up a few grams here and a few more there."

"That's a lot of work."

"Yeah, but the payoff is huge. Sell ten kilos and you can retire."

"How much you sold so far?"

"A few ounces." Nick shrugged. "I'm young, I got time."

Willoughby had brought his own beer and sipped it slowly, staring at Nick as if weighing a decision.

"What brought you out here in the first place?" he asked.

Nick frowned in annoyance. "Why do you want to know that? You some kind of cop?"

Willoughby laughed and shook his head. "No."

"U.F. Marshal, maybe?"

Willoughby shook his head more emphatically.

"Not me, my friend. I stay as far away from the law as possible."

"You runnin' from something?"

"Aren't you?"

Nick took a deep breath and sighed. He tipped his beer bottle again.

"I guess we all are."

Willoughby's beer bottle was empty and he shoved it to the side of the table. He leaned forward confidentially.

"What really brings you to Caribou Lake?" he demanded. "You didn't come here to fuck Bobbie, that's for sure. She's over sixty and has grandkids your age."

Nick gazed straight back at him. "Right now, in my present state, she looks damn good."

"They don't have whorehouses out on the Jupiter side?"

"Yeah, they do. But I've been through all the merchandise six times and I'm looking for something new. Variety is the key to happiness, my mother used to say."

"Your *mother* said that?"

"I dunno. I heard it somewhere."

Willoughby grinned and lowered his voice.

"How old are you, Nick?"

"Twenty-four."

"When was the last time you screwed someone younger than yourself?"

Nick stared at the table and scratched his head. Finally he looked up.

"I don't remember," he said. "Maybe never. I started pretty young, and it was always easier to get older women."

"Then you're overdue. What if I told you that I know where you can get a seventeen year-old girl who looks better than anything you've ever seen in a holoporn vid?"

Nick blinked and swallowed. "A virgin?"

"Not quite, but damn close. A virgin would cost you a hell of a lot more, and virginity is overrated anyway."

Nick swallowed again, his breathing becoming labored.

"How much?"

"Five hundred."

"Blonde or brunette?"

"Take your pick."

Nick gaped in surprise. "You've got *two* of 'em?"

Willoughby laughed and placed a hand on his arm.

"Easy, boy. One at a time. You interested?"

"Mister, I ain't only interested, I'm in love. Just tell me where they are!"

*

Nick had no opportunity to give Murray a heads-up; he and Willoughby left the bar as soon as Nick had finished his beer, stopped in the men's room to empty their bladders, then Willoughby led him on a round-about tour of the asteroid that was obviously designed to confuse him. He didn't complain; intent on finding one or both of the missing girls, he was willing to take whatever chances necessary, and had no illusions that Willoughby was his friend.

They walked for twenty minutes, long enough to tour the entire asteroid twice. They went down ladders, up a lift, through a section of private quarters, into a storage bay and out the other side, down another lift, through a narrow tunnel, all the while passing through barriers marked NO ADMITTANCE – AUTHORIZED PERSONNEL ONLY. They finally arrived at what appeared to be an external pod on the outside of the asteroid, and if Nick's sense of direction meant anything, it was at the opposite end of the habitat from the parking bay.

They stood in a narrow corridor with two doors on the right, about ten feet apart. On the left was a recess leading to a small airlock—Nick could look through the double windows and see empty space outside. He looked expectantly at Willoughby, whom he could see more clearly now, though the corridor was dim. The man was actually fat, though it was a hard fat and he looked as tough as he needed to be.

"Where the fuck are we?" Nick demanded suspiciously

"We," Willoughby grinned at him, "are *here*." He pointed at one of the doors on Nick's right, then the other. "Take your pick—blonde or brunette."

Nick's brow knitted in thought. "They both good looking?"

"Angels from heaven."

"Both seventeen?"

"Near enough."

Nick rubbed his crotch and considered.

"How about let me look at 'em first. Easier to pick that way."

"Nope. Cost you five hundred apiece just to look, even if you don't do nothin' else."

Nick's eyes narrowed in suspicion. "You better not be shittin' me, Willoughby! If you try to cheat me—"

"Easy, Jones, easy. Just protecting my investment, that's all. These girls are top of the line. You won't find another like them anywhere in the 'roids, and that's a fact. I'll need the money up front."

Nick shook his head. "Uh-uh, I don't think so. Not until I see the goods."

Willoughby's cheek twitched as he measured Nick's resolve. Finally he nodded.

"Awright, half now, half later. But you better have five hundred."

Nick pulled out his wallet and removed a wad of bills. It was everything he'd brought with him to Ceres—he hadn't had time to visit a bank yet. He peeled off five fifties and handed them to Willoughby, peeled off five more and let him look at them. Willoughby nodded in satisfaction.

"Okay. Make your choice, then."

"The blonde, I guess." Nick put his wallet away.

"I'll need your gunbelt, too."

"Whoa!" Nick took a step back, hands out at his side. "No way. The first thing I learned out here is never go anywhere without my gun. You just back the fuck off!"

Willoughby sighed patiently, as if Nick were being unreasonable.

"It's just a precaution, okay? I don't want any weapons anywhere near those girls."

"What, you think I'm gonna *shoot* one of 'em? I would never do that!"

"No, of course you wouldn't, but what if you get distracted and she gets her hands on your gun? She could kill you and try to make a break for it. It's like keepin' a gun away from a child, you just can't take the chance."

Nick looked startled. "What are you talking about? Are these girls *prisoners!*"

"Of course they are. Why do you think they're way the fuck down here, instead of a regular room in the resort?"

"Aw, man, I dunno...I don't need no more trouble with the law."

"Ain't no law around here, son. Just Farrington Security, and they don't give a shit."

Nick was still hesitant. "I ain't never raped nobody before."

"And you ain't raping nobody now. This is a business transaction, all right? Nothing more than that."

Nick took his time thinking about that, letting Willoughby wait. He never broke eye contact. Finally, with great reluctance, he unbuckled the gunbelt and handed it over.

"I swear to god, if you fuck me over...!"

But Willoughby grinned and shook his head. He hung the gunbelt on a hook bolted to the bulkhead.

"It'll be right there when you come out."

He turned and produced a key, the old fashioned kind, and unlocked the first door. It was a pressure door—he pushed the control lever and it slid into the wall with a pneumatic hiss. Grinning, he nodded at Nick and waved toward the door.

"Enjoy yourself. You've got one hour."

* * *

"I think Walker is right," Russ Murray said as he and Jim Keating headed back to the security office. Rev. Sledge had told them everything he could remember but added nothing much that was new.

"Right about what?"

"The girls are still on the asteroid. Based on the traffic pattern you described earlier, they couldn't have been taken off before their disappearance was reported, and you've been monitoring everything since."

"Okay, but where the hell are they?"

Murray sighed wearily. It was almost 2200 hours.

"That's the sixty-four megabyte question. You're positive every inch of the asteroid has been searched?"

"Every millimeter." Keating looked around. "Where *is* Walker, anyway?"

"He went to prowl around a little on his own. Thinks he might uncover something."

"Is he any good?"

"I have no idea. He just arrived on Ceres last night. He's a rookie, too, no experience whatsoever. I'm not expecting too much from him at this juncture."

"Seems like a nice enough kid."

"I guess."

They entered the security office and retired to the lunchroom again. A fresh pot of coffee sat waiting for them.

"What kind of security staff do you have here?" Murray asked.

"About twenty men altogether, five or six to a shift. And, of course, Macy on the radio. She's the only female on the crew."

Murray nodded. "How many of them do you trust?"

Keating smiled, as if they had already settled that point. "One," he said. "Me."

"How did the search go down?"

"What do you mean?"

"How was it conducted? Who was in charge? Was it done in teams or all at once?"

Keating frowned as he thought back two weeks.

"Captain Guthrie organized everyone into teams," he said slowly. "Four teams, I think. Sent each team to search a different part of the rock."

"All at the same time? Or in shifts?"

Keating's eyes narrowed. "What are you thinking, Russ?"

"I'm wondering how much overlap there was. You know, search one section, move the girls into it, then search the section where the girls were but no longer are."

Keating's jaw tightened. "You think some of our people were involved in this?"

Murray shrugged again. "To quote Walker a little while ago, I'm keeping an open mind. Think about it, Jim—if every inch of this rock was truly searched, then the only way the girls could have remained undiscovered would be if at least one of the searchers knew where they were and searched around them."

"But what would be their motive?"

Murray's mouth crinkled in irony as he stared at his friend.

"Do you really have to ask that?"

But Keating was shaking his head.

"I dunno, Russ—some of these people leave a lot to be desired, but kidnap and rape..."

"How well does Farrington Security pay these guys?"

Keating snorted. "Are you kidding? You could make more working for the U.F. Marshal."

"That bad, huh? You said yourself these girls are worth a fortune in a whorehouse. Maybe that's an incentive."

Keating thought about it. His mouth became a grim line.

"Hide them out, wait for the heat to blow over, then quietly move them off the rock?"

"Makes sense, doesn't it? Guthrie has already given up on finding the girls alive. Now Walker and I are here, but we won't be here forever. Soon as we're gone, the coast will be clear. Wait a couple more days for insurance, until you lift the traffic restriction, and it would be safe to move the girls. Send them halfway around the Belt, turn them over to a qualified pimp, and take fifty percent."

"Wow! That's downright scary. So the question is, which security men do we need to be looking at?"

"More to the point, who was in charge of those teams? If the team leader wasn't in on the plot, it would be tough to pull that off."

Keating nodded and stood up. In two stiff strides he reached a data board on the wall covered with a diagram of the asteroid and markings made by the search teams.

"Team A," he said slowly, pointing, "was led by Ted Hiromoto. Team B was Wilbur Barrett—" He pointed again. "—team C was run by Calvin Best, and Team D..."

He pointed at the section of the asteroid farthest from where they were standing. He turned and looked at Russ Murray.

"Team D was Walter Willoughby."

* * *

Willoughby closed the door behind Nick and locked it. The room was tiny, barely six feet by eight—and *cold*. It had originally been used as a storage space for EVA construction crews, probably when the asteroid was first being drilled out for habitation. The insulation was thin and Nick's breath suddenly frosted in front of his face; goose bumps appeared on his arms.

He stood over a thick mattress that rested on the deck and gazed down at the girl lying there. She was awake, staring right back, and she was everything Willoughby had said she was— absolutely stunning. Her long yellow hair lay in a pile beside her face and she had snuggled her cheek into it for warmth. She was covered by a heavy insulated blanket, but her breath also frosted the air and her cheeks were blue.

Tears slid down her cheeks as she stared at Nick in terror.

"Please!" she whispered. "Please, don't!"

Nick knelt quickly beside her and put a finger to his lips. His heart pounded with anger at her condition, but he would think about that later. Right now he had more important things to consider.

"You don't have to be afraid of me," he whispered. "I'm not here to hurt you. I'm a United Federation Marshal, and I've come to get you out of here."

"A m-marshal?"

"Shh! Don't talk out loud. Someone is right outside."

She blinked and swallowed, daring to temper her fear with hope.

"Are you Martha?" he asked quietly. She nodded. "And where is Mary?"

"I-I'm not sure. Right next door, I think."

Nick nodded. That agreed with what Willoughby had told him. "Have you been able to talk to her?"

"No. But...I hear her crying sometimes. When the—men come in."

Nick's gut twisted. "How many men?"

She shook her head helplessly, fresh tears flowing.

"I don't know. Six, maybe seven. Policemen."

"*Policemen!*" Nick was shocked.

"I think so. They have uniforms. H-How did you find me?"

Nick pulled the blanket up a little higher and tucked it around her chin.

"I'll tell you all about it later. I don't have time right now. Just keep quiet for a minute, okay?"

Nick stood up and turned to the door. It had no window, so he couldn't see out, but neither could anyone look in. The room might be wired for sound or surveillance, but he'd seen nothing that might hide a camera, though a micro-cam could be planted in one of the vents. If Willoughby *was* watching, and Nick didn't do anything with the girl, he might become suspicious and come in. He didn't have a lot of time.

He ran a hand over the door. Most pressure doors had controls on both sides, and this one was no different, but he suspected the control on the inside was disabled to keep the girl from letting herself out. When Willoughby had locked him in, he had effectively trapped Nick until he returned. He'd said Nick had an hour, but Nick had no intention of waiting that long. He'd found the girl and it was a fairly safe bet the other one was right next door. All he really needed to do now was get out of the room and take Willoughby down.

How hard could that be?

He reached into his boot and withdrew the Ru-Hawk .44. The gun was freezing cold, but when he cocked it the cylinder rotated. He lowered the hammer and took a deep breath. With the gun behind his back he pounded on the door with his left hand.

"Willoughby!"

Willoughby's voice was muffled as he answered. "Goddamn, Jones! You finished already?"

"Let me out! I want my money back! This girl is dead!"

For just a moment there was total silence, then he could hear someone fiddling with the pressure door. It slid open with a hiss of compressed air and Nick took a step back, expecting Willoughby to rush inside to see for himself. But it didn't quite happen that way.

"Nice try, Marshal Walker," Willoughby said smugly. His fat face was twisted in a grin and he was holding a laser pistol in his hand. To his right, a smirk on his face, stood Capt. Guthrie.

Chapter 11

"Where's Willoughby now?" Russ Murray asked.

"Off duty. He could be anywhere."

"Can you page him?"

"Sure. But he might not answer. He's about as uncooperative as Captain Guthrie when he wants to be. What makes you think he's the one we're looking for?"

Murray pointed to the diagram.

"This area right here—it's the farthest place on the asteroid from here, and farther from the rest of the inhabited spaces. If I was going to hide a kidnap victim, that's where I'd do it. You said his team searched that area, so that makes him my prime suspect."

"Okay. I can page him—what do I say?"

"Just ask him to come to the office, that the U.F. Marshal needs his help."

Keating shrugged, as if he didn't think it would do any good. He walked into the outer office and picked up a radio.

* * *

"Did you think you were fooling anyone, Marshal?" Capt. Guthrie asked with a wry grin. "With that clumsy attempt at undercover snooping?"

Nick nodded ruefully. "Yeah, I did. At least, I was hoping I was."

Guthrie snorted. "I've been watching you since the minute you landed. When you split off from Murray, I sent Willoughby to keep an eye on you."

"He didn't do a very good job of it. He led me straight to the girls. I wasn't even getting close until he showed up."

"You would have found them sooner or later. I know Murray—he would have searched the asteroid all over again, especially this end because there's nobody down here. But now he won't have to, because you've already done that and you didn't find anything."

"You expect me to tell him that?"

"No. But when this section decompresses, it will be obvious there's no one alive down here. And you won't be around to tell him what you found."

Nick laughed in spite of the situation.

"You think killing a U.F. Marshal is going to take the heat *off?*"

"Oh, I'm not going to kill you. You're going to have an accident. You know, eager-beaver rookie from Terra, doesn't know shit about how to work an airlock...pushes the wrong button."

"Well aren't you just the criminal genius?"

Guthrie shook his head. "It's not about that."

"And now...you're going to tell me what it *is* about?"

"It's about money. It's about retirement. I'm sick to death of living on the ass end of the Solar System. Once I get those girls into circulation, in six months I'll have enough cash to get to Mars or Titan and settle down. I ain't looking for much, don't need to get rich—I just want to get a planet or a moon under my feet. No more deep space, no more low-gravity habitats, no more microwaved food. Just a few creature comforts. I don't think that's too much to ask, do you?"

"No, I don't. I just think it's too bad you're willing to sacrifice two innocent young women to fulfill that need."

Guthrie's lip twisted into a sneer.

"I'm sorry for them," he said. "I really am. But they had no business coming out here in the first place. I heard what you said to their old man—that habitat is wired—and you were right. He was a goddamn fool to bring them here. So it's on him, not me."

"How do you figure that? *He* isn't the one selling his daughters into prostitution."

"Simple logic, Walker—if I don't do it, someone else will. Those two will never get out of the 'roids intact, no matter what, so it might as well be me."

"What about Willoughby here? Sounds like you're going to take all the money...what does he get out of it?"

"Once I get mine, all the cash goes to him."

He took a step to his right.

"Now come on out here, like Willoughby said, and raise your hands."

Nick took a step forward, through the pressure hatch; the toe of his boot snagged on the coaming and he tripped. Both men started involuntarily as he fell; he caught himself and straightened up. When he did, his .44 was pointed directly at Willoughby's chest.

"May I suggest...that you drop your pistol very slowly."

Willoughby turned pale as he gazed at the cannon in Nick's hand. Even Guthrie showed some emotion as his eyes widened.

"Walker, if you pull that trigger you'll blow this habitat all to hell," he said in a tight voice. "You'll kill all of us!"

Nick's nerves were humming, but he kept his voice even.

"In that case, I'm guessing you don't want me to pull the trigger. So tell the fat man to lower his weapon. If I let you keep these girls they'll both die a slow and painful death. I'd much rather kill them now than let that happen."

"Don't be a fool, Walker!"

Nick raised the .44 and aimed it at Willoughby's heart.

"If you shoot first, my trigger finger will jerk by reflex. Even if I miss you, I won't miss that bulkhead. And we all know it can't stand up to a .44 Magnum. So what are you going to do?"

Willoughby swallowed in indecision, glanced at Guthrie, then back at Nick. His breathing had become labored. Slowly, reluctantly, he lowered the weapon.

"Drop it," Nick said. "Kick it over to me."

Willoughby let the pistol tumble from his fingers, then gently nudged it forward with his boot. Nick watched him carefully, tense as a coiled spring.

Willoughby's radio shrilled sharply, filling the space with a piercing tone. Willoughby jerked as if he'd been shot, and Nick was so startled he almost fired. Guthrie seized the moment and went for his expensive new laser pistol. He cleared leather almost before Nick saw the motion.

Nick spun but was too late—Guthrie had him cold. The only thing that saved him was Guthrie himself, who hurried his shot. The bolt flashed off the bulkhead inches from Nick's head, and he fell away to the right. Guthrie fired again, missed, and tried to track him for a third shot. Falling on his right side, Nick's elbow hit the deck painfully; he couldn't seem to get Guthrie in his sight, so he pulled the trigger anyway. The .44 roared like a Howitzer and blue smoke boiled into the room. The slug exploded through both airlock doors and the sudden shriek of escaping air drowned out every other sound.

The habitat didn't decompress all at once, but air was screaming out at a terrifying rate; within seconds Nick found it hard to breathe, and his two opponents staggered as suction drew them toward the breach. But Guthrie still had his sidearm, and was determined to finish it. Struggling to regain his balance, he took aim at Nick once more, but in those few seconds Nick's situation had stabilized—he was down on the deck, the .44 was up, and he fired first.

The shot slammed Guthrie against the bulkhead and opened a second breach. Nick staggered to his feet, gasping, and saw that Willoughby was also down, sucking air like a fish out of water. Only seconds remained if anyone was to survive, and Nick dived back through the pressure door into the room with the girl, slapping the door control as he did so. The door swished shut behind him.

Martha Sledge was sitting upright, panic in her eyes, choking for air. Her mouth was moving but no words came out. Nick dropped to his knees beside her, fishing in his pocket for the communicator Murray had given him. His ears popped painfully and his eyeballs seemed to bulge—the air pressure was down by half, but didn't seem to be getting any lower. If they could keep breathing until help arrived...

He squeezed the button and tried to talk, but couldn't seem to form any words. Blackness edged his peripheral vision. He dropped the button and lifted his chin, trying to enlarge his airway. His vision was fading, his thoughts were tumbling...and the girl was already unconscious. *Christ,* he thought, *I sure as hell blew it this time.*

Seconds before he passed out, he heard the click of a relay switch. From a duct in the floor and another in the ceiling, high-pressure air flooded into the room.

* * *

"He isn't answering," Keating said, gazing at Murray. "Doesn't really surprise me—he's an arrogant son of a bitch."

Murray shrugged. "Do you know where his quarters are? Maybe we can find him there."

Keating put the radio down in its cradle.

"It's getting late. My suggestion is we all get some sleep and come at this again in the morning. Willoughby's on duty then and he'll come here before—"

The lights began flashing insanely, alternating red with white. From speakers in the ceiling an alarm bleated loudly, insistently, chilling the blood. Both men looked up, startled.

"Is that what I think it is?" Murray asked breathlessly.

"Atmospheric breach," Keating said.

* * *

Every habitat in space—ship, space station, or asteroid—depends on atmospheric integrity for survival. A breach is always life threatening and of the highest priority. When Nick's first bullet punched out the airlock, section pressure doors slammed shut all over Caribou Lake and alarms blazed automatically. Everyone except emergency personnel headed for pressure chambers which, like bomb shelters, were provided for just such an event. Emergency crews quickly identified the location of the breach and swung into action; within twenty minutes the threat was contained.

Nick Walker could hear damage control people outside his pressure door, their magnetic boots clanging on the steel deck, but could not communicate with them. He'd tried several times to contact Murray with the communicator button, but perhaps the signal couldn't get through the rock, because Murray never answered. The girl on the mattress was awake again, her color returning to normal, though she still looked traumatized. The air that had surged into the room when the pressure dropped was much warmer than the air that escaped, and she had stopped shivering. Though it was gradually getting colder, for the moment they were almost comfortable.

But next door, the other sister was sobbing loudly. Nick dimly remembered hearing her scream when the guns were firing, but hadn't had time to think about it. Now Martha Sledge was calling out to her, assuring her they would be all right.

But Nick wasn't one hundred percent sure that was true; though they must have found bodies in the corridor, the emergency workers had no way of knowing, and perhaps no reason to suspect, that anyone was alive behind the pressure doors. If they opened those doors before repressurizing the corridor, it would mean disaster. Nick tried calling out without success; he pounded on the door with the butt of his .44, but they were probably wearing space suits, and until air filled the corridor again, would be unable to hear him.

* * *

Jim Keating turned pale as he listened to the voice on the other end of the comm link. Russ Murray could see the shock in his eyes, but didn't dare ask questions until the conversation ended.

"You're sure it's Captain Guthrie?" Keating said.

Murray couldn't hear the answer, but Keating nodded.

"What about those storage rooms? Is anyone alive inside them?"

Another pause.

"Well, don't open them until you get the atmosphere back. You got that? If there's anyone—goddammit, *listen* to me! Stop talking! *Do not* open those doors until atmosphere is restored! Did you hear me?" He rolled his eyes at Murray. "Repeat it back to me!" He nodded once, twice, and once more. "Yes, that's right. In fact, don't open those doors at all until I get there. I'm headed your way."

He hung up the comm and sighed in exasperation.

"What is it?"

"We've located Willoughby," Keating said. "He's dead."

Murray blinked in surprise, but Keating wasn't finished.

"Guthrie is dead, too. Someone blew him open with a very big gun."

* * *

Nick stayed by the door, sweating, as work in the corridor continued. He could hear men moving about, could hear their equipment, but couldn't hear what they were saying. It was a little over an hour before he heard high-pressure air flooding the corridor outside his door. Only then did his tension begin to ease. Using the butt of his .44, he banged on the door again, but it was still ten minutes before it opened.

The first person he saw was Russ Murray.

Chapter 12

Wednesday, August 7, 0440 (CC) — In transit, the Asteroid Belt

Nick stared out the canopy as Russ Murray piloted the jalopy back toward Ceres on Wednesday morning. He and Murray had spent all day Tuesday clearing things up at Caribou Lake, and it had been quite a snarl. Murray and Keating, each with a report to write, had questioned him closely about the shootings. Nick would also have to write a report but at the moment he didn't care—he felt unbelievably light-hearted. Not since Alpha Centauri had he experienced such a heady joy at just being alive.

Three of the rear seats were occupied by Rev. Sledge and his two daughters. Murray had suggested, and Sledge agreed, that it might be wise to get his girls out of the Asteroid Belt as quickly as possible. Both girls had been raped and were suffering mild medical and severe emotional trauma. From Ceres they could arrange transport back to Mars, where Sledge had his church.

The girls' rescue had been followed by a great deal of drama, everything from tears of joy to wails of despair. They had been captive for two weeks and both claimed that multiple men, all wearing Farrington Security uniforms, had abused them. Certainly Willoughby had been one, and probably Guthrie, but the girls couldn't categorically identify anyone, so any other men would never be called to account. Sledge and his girls said they didn't want revenge, just escape, but in Nick Walker's mind the matter was far from settled.

"How much farther is it to Ceres?" Sledge asked as he peered through the forward screen at the endless vastness of black space.

"Three hours, more or less," Murray replied with a yawn.

"Thank the Good Lord." Sledge leaned back in his seat.

Nick turned to face him. "I got a question."

"Yes? How can I help you?"

Nick studied him a moment, then let his tongue slide over his lips.

"First of all, I want to apologize for what I said to you the other night. I may have been a little too harsh under the circumstances."

Sledge's eyes crinkled and his dingy teeth showed through his beard.

"Young man, you saved my children. I bear no grudge toward you."

Not yet, you don't. You haven't heard what I'm about to say.

"I just want to know what the hell *missionaries* are doing in the Asteroid Belt? Can you tell me that?"

Sledge looked surprised, if not exactly offended.

"Why, preaching the Word of God, of course. That's what missionaries do."

"Yeah, I know that, but historically I thought they went to places where the Word hadn't been heard before. Pagan cultures, things like that."

"Yes, that's true. But you saw for yourself the decadence of that place! Those people need salvation. They need the good news of the sacrifice Jesus made for them!"

"I won't argue that. But don't you think they've already heard that message? Ninety percent of the people out here come from the Western Hemisphere of Terra. Christianity has been prevalent in the Americas for centuries."

Sledge smiled. "Of course they've *heard* it, but how many of them *believe* it? The very fact that they're here at all is ample proof that they've lost their way. Most of the people out here are fugitives of one kind or another. They've lost their souls. They're depraved! They need redemption."

Nick nodded slowly, as if Sledge had just made his point.

"Yes they are. 'Depraved' is the perfect description for most of them." He pointed at the two girls huddling together in the rear seats. "And you took those two gorgeous, innocent girls into that environment! You led them straight into the lion's den! What the hell were you *thinking?*"

Sledge's smile evaporated and he swelled slowly in indignation.

"Marshal, you may not believe this, but there is no higher calling than the service of the Lord. No sacrifice is too great—"

"Are you sure about that?" Nick pointed at the girls again. "Was *their* sacrifice worth it?"

"They wanted to come. They volunteered."

"Did they? You didn't pressure them?"

"Of course not! They're fine Christian girls, with hearts of gold. Their hearts ached for the sinners on that rock. They went in there with the love of Jesus in their hearts, and those men responded."

Christ! The girls were raped!

Nick sighed.

"Reverend, forgive me for being cynical, but don't you think it's just possible that those men came to see the girls and didn't give a shit about your *message?*"

"Well—I'm sure some of them did, but—"

"And now that you're gone, they'll go right back to their sinful ways and never think about the message again?"

Sledge huffed impatiently. "What is your point, young man?"

"You damn near got your kids killed, Reverend!"

"I admit," Sledge said reasonably, "that it was a calculated risk. But all things worthwhile carry some measure of risk. Christians have been martyred for millennia while spreading the Word. We count it an honor to be persecuted for His name's sake."

Nick closed his eyes and rubbed a hand across his forehead.

"All I'm saying is that sometimes you can bring persecution on yourself. If you want to risk your own neck, fine. But if I were you I'd think twice before putting those girls in danger again."

Nick turned around and faced forward again, suddenly depressed. He felt Murray nudge his knee and glanced in his direction.

"Save your breath," Murray said quietly.

No one spoke the rest of the way back to Ceres.

Government Annex - Ceres

Marshal Milligan was just lighting a fresh cigar as Nick and Murray came into the office. He glanced at them as if they were just returning from lunch, then turned back to his computer and finished the task he was working on. Nick walked over to his own desk and dropped his space bag on it, then rummaged for a cup and filled it with bitter coffee. Murray dropped into a chair with a sigh, and a moment later Milligan swung around to face them.

"Well?"

"Walker found the missing missionaries. Case closed."

Milligan remained silent, but shifted his gaze to Nick.

"The case is not closed," Nick said.

Milligan's eyes returned to Murray, who looked at Nick in surprise.

"What the hell are you talking about? Here I am bragging on you and you make me look stupid."

Nick saw his expression and faltered.

"Sorry, I didn't mean it like that." He spoke to Milligan. "Yes, we did find the missing girls. They're alive and safe, and they're here on Ceres."

"What do you mean the case isn't closed?"

"Well...that case is solved, but I think there's a bigger issue. We brought back two dead men who worked for Farrington Security. One or both of them were the kidnappers, and they also raped those girls."

"Farrington Security?" Milligan's shaggy brows lowered.

"That's right. Remember the other day I was asking you about prisoner abuse? Well now I think the problem may be a lot bigger than that."

"How much bigger?"

"I don't know yet, but I'm starting to think that Farrington Industries is corrupt through and through. Certainly their security branch is, from everything I've seen."

Milligan peered at him through a haze of smoke. "What are you gonna do?"

"Nothing...yet. But if I had a gut feeling before, now it's a full-blown suspicion. I'm gonna investigate. I'll let you know what I find."

Milligan sniffed and laid the cigar down.

"Before you go running off anywhere, go see Judge Maynard. She's looking for you."

"Did she say what she wanted?"

"No, and I didn't ask. But you might want to shave your armpits."

*

Court was in session when Nick walked in, so he took a chair and watched the proceedings. Monica Maynard spotted him and fifteen minutes later called a recess. As she left the bench she made eye contact and inclined her head toward her chambers. Barely a minute later they were alone behind closed doors.

"I hear you made a trip to Caribou Lake," she said as he settled into a chair.

"Yes, your Honor."

She smiled. "Nick, when we're alone, you can call me Monica."

He grinned. "Yes, Monica."

"How did it go? Kidnapping, wasn't it?"

"Suspected kidnapping. In fact, that's exactly what it was. We were able to recover both victims alive."

"Really! That was fast."

"We were lucky."

"Who is 'we'?"

"Marshal Murray and myself."

"Mm. Russ Murray. Arrogant bastard, isn't he?"

Nick dipped his head, but didn't answer. Monica smiled again.

"And what about the perp?"

"Perps—there were two of them that we know of. They're both dead."

She tilted her head. "Dead how?"

He cleared his throat. "I killed them."

"In...self-defense?"

"Yes."

"Good. I'm sorry I won't get them into my courtroom, but at least they didn't get away with it."

"Your courtroom? Does your jurisdiction extend to Caribou Lake?"

"This is a Federation court. My jurisdiction extends all the way around the sun."

He nodded. "I guess that makes sense. I just hadn't thought about it."

She sat smiling at him, and the silence stretched for several seconds. He began to feel a little uneasy.

"The reason I wanted to see you," she said, "is that while you were gone I had a defendant in here name Murdoch."

Nick blinked at her. "*Turd* Murdoch?"

"You know him."

"Met him once, the night I arrived on Ceres."

She nodded. "Mr. Murdoch is no stranger to this courtroom. I've had him in front of my bench six or seven times for a variety of offenses, mostly involving assault and personal injury. The case in question this week stems from a beating he delivered a couple of weeks back in which he severely injured a man who dared to stand up to his bullying."

Nick frowned. "That was before I met him."

"Yes."

"Why wasn't he in jail awaiting trial?"

"He's an ice drill supervisor, apparently a very good one. His employer posted his bail."

"Who's his employer?"

"Farrington Industries."

Nick said nothing, but mentally filed that item in his Farrington collection.

"Nick, while he was in the courtroom waiting for his case to be heard, the bailiff heard him mention your name."

"*My* name?"

"Yes." She stared at him a moment, concern in her lovely dark eyes. "Exactly what happened the night you met him?"

"I walked into a bar called the Open Airlock, ordered a beer, and was minding my own business when he approached me and ordered me to leave. I declined his invitation and he attacked me."

"Did he hurt you?"

"He never laid a hand on me. I threw him over the bar and into the mirror. That's about all there was to it."

Monica's eyes widened. "You *threw* him over the bar? He's twice your size!"

Nick shrugged. "Low gravity. It's all in the leverage."

"I wish I could have seen that!" She smiled with pleasure. "So you embarrassed him in front of his friends."

"Yeah, if that's what they are. I'm not sure he has any real friends. People are just afraid of him."

"As well they should be." She took a deep breath and let it out in a sigh. "He's threatening to kill you, Nick."

*

After leaving Judge Maynard's office, Nick saw Misery Allen sitting at the defense table studying a brief. He stopped next to her and she glanced up.

"Marshal Walker!"

"Hi. Listen, I'm sorry about canceling dinner on you. I had to leave the asteroid on a case, and it came up all at once."

"I understand, Marshal. It's the nature of law enforcement."

"Let me make it up to you?"

"Of course."

"Thanks. When I figure out what I'm doing, I'll call you."

She laughed and swatted at him. He winked and walked out of the courtroom.

System Springs - Ceres

The habitat just north of Government Annex was a small one, roughly the size of Farrington South. System Springs, one of the four water corporations, had its facility there, both the mine and the office. Nick identified himself at the gate and asked for the head of security. After a short wait the guard pointed to a long, low building fifty yards inside the gate and let him through. Almost before Nick could park his E-car a door opened and a man stepped outside to wait for him.

"Are you Marshal Walker?" The other man was around thirty, medium height and clean cut, with a perpetual gleam in his eye. He looked very dapper in slacks and a white shirt with a carefully knotted necktie, something Nick hadn't seen since leaving Terra.

"That's right." Nick offered his hand and the other man shook it.

"Milo Zima. Come on inside."

The office was clean, efficient, and businesslike. Nick saw four people working at desks, two of them attractive women. Zima led him to a glassed cubicle on one side of the main room and closed the door behind him. He gestured to a chair and Nick sat down.

"Can I get you anything? Coffee? Water?"

"Not right now, thanks."

"Are you sure? I make the best coffee on Ceres."

Nick's eyebrow lifted a fraction and he grinned. "I'll take that bet. I haven't had a decent cup since I landed."

Zima laughed and poured him coffee from a brewer on a corner table. Nick sipped it and closed his eyes briefly as the roasted flavor penetrated his sinuses. When he opened them again Zima was grinning at him.

"Well?"

"Mr. Zima, I think I may have just found the first honest man on Ceres. This is heavenly!"

Zima laughed again and sat down behind his desk. He regarded Nick with frank but friendly eyes.

"I've been looking forward to meeting you, Marshal. I didn't expect it to be this soon."

"I'm surprised you've even heard of me."

"Don't be. By now everyone on Ceres has heard of you."

Nick sipped the coffee again and set the cup down. His surprise was evident.

"You're the man who broke the kidnapping case at Caribou Lake," Zima told him. "You're the man who roughed up a pair of Farrington goons in the courtroom, and you're the man Turd Murdoch wants to kill."

Nick gazed at him in astonishment, his head spinning.

"Jesus Christ! I did all that?"

Zima laughed delightedly. "Word travels fast here. Ceres is like a microchip—electricity doesn't have to travel very far and it takes very little to get the job done. Substitute 'gossip' for 'electricity' and you get the analogy."

Nick nodded slowly. "Wow."

"So how can I help you?"

Nick shook off his surprise and screwed his mind down to business.

"You said something about 'Farrington goons'."

"Did I say 'goons'?" Zima's eyes twinkled. "Maybe I was being too generous."

"I'd like you to elaborate on that, if you don't mind."

Zima leaned back in the chair and clasped his hands behind his head. His smile faded and his eyes became serious.

"Are you sure you want to travel down that path?"

Nick studied his eyes, trying to decipher the warning.

"Yeah. Why wouldn't I?"

"Because right now, the only person trying to kill you is Turd Murdoch."

Chapter 13

"I think you better explain that."

Nick picked up the coffee cup and sipped it. Milo Zima didn't reply immediately, his eyes still locked on Nick's face.

"Why did you come to me?" he asked finally.

"You're just the first on my list. I plan to visit all the security offices, and you were the closest."

Zima nodded. "Fair enough. What is it you want to know?"

"I picked up a rumor about prisoner abuse. So far the only suspect I have is Farrington Security, but it occurred to me that it might be more widespread than that."

"You were wondering if System Springs Security is also guilty."

"Are you?"

The gleam returned to Zima's eyes.

"I guess it depends on your definition of the word 'abuse'. It also depends on which side you're on. A prisoner who gets whacked over the head is likely to scream abuse, but the guard who whacked him might have just been protecting himself. You see, Marshal, when a man's life is threatened, it isn't difficult to overreact. One whack turns into two, and sometimes ten."

For just an instant, Nick's mind flashed back three years, to a cratered hilltop on Alpha Centauri 2...a terrified young Star Marine, already bleeding from shrapnel wounds, smashing an unconscious rebel's head with a rifle butt. He took a deep breath and set the coffee down.

"I can understand that. Force is sometimes necessary. But I saw a guard rough up a man in a courtroom when there was no call for it."

"You won't find that in my facility. I won't say it hasn't happened, but when I find out about it I get rid of the offender. I've had to fire seven men since I've been here."

"How long have you been here?"

"A little over five years."

"You didn't prosecute the offenders?"

For just a second Zima's features clouded. "There isn't much interest here for prosecuting that sort of thing. When I fired them they just went to another security firm."

"Which one?"

"Take a guess."

Nick sat back in the chair and crossed his legs. He spread his arms, as if blessing a congregation.

"Talk to me."

"About what?"

"About whatever is on your mind. You're dying to tell me something, but I don't know which questions to ask. So you take the lead."

Zima grinned broadly. "Am I that transparent?"

"I wouldn't say transparent, just anxious. You're practically jumping from one foot to the other."

"Well." Zima was still grinning. "I suppose I can trust you?"

"I think you already know the answer to that."

Zima's smile faded again, his eyes turned serious.

"There are," he began, "four detention facilities on Ceres, one at each of the mining security firms. Ours is one of the smallest, Farrington has the largest. Most prisoners are detained at Farrington, both long and short term incarceration. Other firms, such as ours, send them overflow when our facilities are full."

"How many can you house here?"

"Only about fifty. Astral Fountains is the same—Colonial Waters can hold about a hundred."

"And Farrington?"

"Three thousand. They have a real prison over there, and it's full most of the time."

"Are there that many prisoners on Ceres? I thought the population was only eighty thousand."

Zima nodded. "That's right, but this 'roid is packed with felons. We have twice as many men on probation as locked up, probably more."

Nick was silent and Zima continued.

"The staff over there, with very few exceptions, are no better than the people they incarcerate. In some cases they're much worse. What you saw in the courtroom was not an anomaly, but neither was it typical. The usual treatment of prisoners is much worse."

"How much worse?"

"People die, Marshal. Women are raped. Farrington is the only place with facilities for women, and some of the guards over there are sex offenders."

"Jesus!"

"And that's not all." Zima leaned forward. "Some of the guards pimp the females to the male prisoners."

Nick stared at him in shock. "You can prove this?"

Zima sat back and shook his head grimly. "I have evidence, but it's not conclusive."

"What kind of evidence?"

"Circumstantial, most of it. A few case histories, a few statistics...you have to put the pieces together."

"What about eyewitness testimony? *Victim* testimony."

"Several, but none who are willing to take the stand. They barely got out of there alive, and they'd like to stay that way."

"Has any of this been reported to the U.F. Marshal? Before now, I mean."

Zima shrugged. "Marshal Milligan is a good guy, but he's very pragmatic. He isn't going to make a Federation case without hard evidence, and so far I just don't have enough to satisfy him. I'm not blaming him—he has a big enough job already, with the whole damn Asteroid Belt to police. That, plus the fact that he isn't a young man any more..."

Nick waited for Zima to complete the thought, but he didn't.

"I'm a little younger than Milligan," he said.

Zima's smile returned. "I was thinking the same thing. This is much too big for a private security firm to take on, but you're a real, honest to god U.F. Marshal."

"What about Russ Murray? Have you told him all this?"

"Some of it, but Murray's an asshole. And that other guy, Beech—he's a good guy, but he's afraid of Murray. Won't take a shit unless Murray okays it."

"So that leaves me."

"Yes it does. A rookie marshal, trained and tested, but without the institutional baggage that will eventually stick to your ass like the barnacles on a sea ship."

Nick had to laugh, partly because it was funny, but mostly because he needed the emotional relief. What Zima was alleging was already starting to depress him.

"What else do you have for me?"

Zima pulled open a desk drawer and reached inside. He pulled out a tiny data chip and tossed it over.

"There's a copy of what documentation I have on the situation in Farrington lockup. Study it on your own time and do with it what you will. I'm available if you need me."

He closed the desk drawer as Nick slipped the chip into his pocket.

"Anything else?"

"Isn't that enough?"

"Well, yeah, but I had the feeling you had a lot more to say."

"I do, but it's all speculation. Pure gossip."

"Gossip isn't a crime."

Zima laughed. "Look, Marshal, I've given you a heads-up on what I know for sure. Anything else I say might be misleading. I'd rather not steer you in the wrong direction just because of a gut feeling."

"A gut feeling about what?"

"I think Farrington is dirty. Top to bottom. Not just the security division, but the whole goddamn thing."

"What do you base that on?"

"Absolutely nothing. That's why I don't want to talk about it. I'm just a security cop, not a detective. I try to deal in visible facts and leave the blue-sky to those who are trained for it."

Slightly disappointed, Nick waited for him to continue, but he was done. Nick got to his feet and drained the coffee cup.

"Mr. Zima, thank you for the great cup of coffee and the information. It's been enlightening."

Zima rose and shook hands.

"Like I said, Marshal, if you need me, you can call. Day or night."

Government Annex - Ceres

Nick returned to the office to find it empty. Milligan had apparently gone to lunch, and neither Murray nor Sandy Beech was present. Nick took the data chip and plugged it into a player, slipped into a headset, and began to educate himself.

Zima's data contained medical records dating back four years, dozens of them, detailing injuries to prisoners that could only be the result of fights, beatings, or even torture. Nick knew that fights were common in lockup, and wouldn't have been surprised if the list had been limited to broken jaws, ribs, knocked-out teeth, or an occasional stabbing, but this list went much further than that. Some of the records indicated extensive burns, severed ears, mutilated eyes, even a couple of severed tongues. There were the inevitable inmate rapes, of course, but also genital mutilation, including evidence of electrode and acid burns. Many prisoners had lost fingers and toes, either severed or crushed, and nails had been pulled out. In at least thirty of the cases before him, the prisoners had died.

And that was just the male prisoners.

In the women's wing the abuse took on a more sado-sexual tone: penetration injuries, both vaginal and anal; circulation and soft-tissue injuries, possibly the result of bondage-type ligatures; severed nipples; severe bite marks on breasts and buttocks; petechial hemorrhaging caused by non-lethal strangulations...the list went on. And, again, there were fatalities—nearly one-sixth of all women who went into Farrington lockup never came out alive.

After an hour Nick leaned back and closed his eyes. Farrington lockup held nearly three thousand men, out of eighty thousand on the asteroid, but also over seven hundred women; with only five thousand females on Ceres, that meant fourteen percent were behind bars. Prostitution was legal, so what kinds of crimes did *women* commit in a place like this?

He rested his eyes for a few minutes—or maybe it was his heart that needed resting—then returned to the data. Several survivors had given statements to Zima describing their experiences in lockup, but none were willing to testify in court. After reading the transcripts Nick didn't blame them, and yet someone needed to do just that.

He shut off the chip reader and dropped it into a desk drawer. He sat in thought for several minutes, then opened his space bag and pulled out his .44, along with the holster he had hidden in the men's room at Caribou Lake. Before returning to Ceres he had retrieved everything, including the two hundred fifty terros he'd paid Willoughby. Now he put the .44 back in the shoulder holster and strapped it on, securing the gun under his left arm. He might never need it again—it was too powerful a weapon for this environment—but he wasn't willing to bet his life on it.

Grabbing the keys to the E-car, he walked out of the office.

Ceres North - Ceres

Nick found Jessica Garner at her apartment in Ceres North; the apartment building sat facing the west wall of the habitat. The apartment was on the top floor and Nick had to ring the bell four times before he got a response. The voice that came through the door speaker sounded tenuous and frightened.

"Who is it?"

"Nick Walker, Ma'am. United Federation Marshal."

"Nick Walker? I've never heard of you!"

"I'm new in town, Mrs. Garner. I just arrived on Ceres three days ago."

"What do you want?"

"I need to ask you some questions. About Farrington Industries."

He waited for her to reply, but it took several seconds.

"I don't work there anymore," she said finally. "Please go away."

"Sorry, Mrs. Garner, I can't do that. I'm investigating a case and I need your help."

She was silent for nearly a minute, and Nick knocked again.

"Mrs. Garner? I need to come inside."

"I don't *know* you! I've never heard of you!" Her voice was becoming ragged.

"I'm going to hold up my badge so you can see for yourself."

He pulled the badge off his belt and held it close to the camera. Nearly a minute passed before she spoke again.

"Are you carrying a gun?"

"Yes, Ma'am. Two of 'em. But they're for your protection as well as mine."

"Who do *you* need protection from?"

"Lots of people, Ma'am. Same as you."

After a moment he heard the snap of the lock, but the door didn't open.

"I have a gun, too," she said. "If you try to shoot me, I'll shoot you first."

Nick's eyebrows shot up. He hadn't expected that, but he couldn't fault her for being careful. He debated for a moment, then nodded.

"Okay, here's how we'll play it. I'm going to take my guns off and hold them up by the belt. You keep yours in your hand. When I come inside, I'll put mine down and you can keep yours. That way we can talk and you'll feel safer. Do we have a deal?"

"I guess that's okay. Take them off and let me see them."

Nick removed his gunbelt and shoulder holster, holding them up to the camera by the leather. She murmured something he couldn't quite make out, and the door slid open. He stood there a moment, hopelessly vulnerable, until he spotted her. She was ten feet inside the apartment, facing him, a small laser pistol in her hand. He nodded briefly, then took a step inside. As he approached, she backed away, keeping ten feet between them, and pointed her pistol toward a couch by the wall. Nick walked over to it and sat down, then placed both weapons on the floor at his feet. Jessica Garner closed the door, locked it, and took another chair facing him—still ten feet away. The pistol remained in her hand.

"What do you want with me?" she demanded in a strained voice.

He sat back against the couch cushion and placed both hands flat at his sides, trying for a nonthreatening pose. He smiled tentatively.

"I'm investigating possible prisoner abuse at Farrington lockup. I understand you were a prisoner there for a while."

She stared at him as if he were crazy. Her face twisted into a sneer.

"*Possible* prisoner abuse! Did you say *possible?*"

He nodded, watching her closely. The gun in her hand trembled slightly, but he was gratified to see that the charge light was amber, indicating standby mode—if she decided to fire, she would need to flick the safety off, which would give him about three seconds before the light turned green. But she made no move toward the safety; the look in her eyes fluctuated between normal and demented.

"That's right. I'm trying to build a case, but I need more information. I was hoping you might tell me about your experience."

She shook her head decisively.

"I'm not testifying! I already talked to Captain Zima; I told him and I'm telling you—*no way*. Those people almost killed me, and if I take the witness stand they *will* kill me!"

Nick held up both hands in a calming gesture.

"I'm not asking you to testify. Eyewitness testimony isn't enough. If you take the stand, they'll just call you a liar. I need hard evidence."

"Then what do you want from me?"

"Just tell me your story. Give me an idea of what I'm dealing with." He waited for her response, but all he got was tears sliding down her cheeks.

"Mrs. Garner, I'm sorry to have to involve you in this, but I'm pretty sure you've been through something no human being should ever have to endure, and I'd like to nail the bastards who did it to you. Maybe if we—"

"*Nail* them?" She laughed scornfully. "What are you going to do to them, all by yourself? You can't touch them! Nobody can touch them."

"What makes you say that?"

"They're all in on it! They have two hundred men, maybe more! They're all part of it."

"Can you give me some names?"

She shook her head again.

"No. I'm not accusing anyone. You can't use anything I say, or I'll be dead. You should never have come here!"

"Well," he said in a reasonable tone, "I am here, so it's too late to change that. Just tell me what you can, whatever you feel safe telling, and I'll take it from there. Your name will never come up, I promise."

She stared at him for a long time, her eyes searching his face, perhaps looking for clues to his integrity. He studied her as well, and was impressed with what he saw. She was in her late twenties, slender and brunette, with long silky hair down to her shoulders. She was quite pretty; compared to most of the women he'd seen on Ceres, she was an absolute beauty—but he saw madness in her eyes that shouldn't be there. From what he'd seen in her record, he had a pretty good idea where she'd acquired it.

"I was only supposed to be in there for three months," she said. "I was convicted of assault, a simple misdemeanor. The judge gave me a choice—pay a fine or spend three months in lockup. I didn't have three thousand terros, so I had no choice. I went to jail."

"Who did you assault?"

"Nobody! It was self-defense. My boss tried to rape me, and I fought him off."

"Who was your boss?"

She shook her head. "I told you, no names!"

"Okay. Where did you work?"

"Farrington Industries. In the corporate office. I was a file clerk there."

Nick nodded. He already knew part of the story, from the file Zima had given him. He just needed her to keep talking.

"You were sentenced to three months, but how long were you actually in there?"

"Two years and two months." Her eyes lost their focus as she gazed into space, remembering. "They sent me to the women's wing. It was supposed to be short time; they even assigned me a job, working in the laundry." She shook her head slowly. "The night I got there I went into a private cell. I figured it was only temporary, because I arrived after lights out. But they kept me in that cell for days. I was there a week before I ever saw the main cellblock."

"Jesus!" Nick felt his scalp tingle as he frowned at her.

Fresh tears coursed down her cheeks.

"They started in on me that first night. The two who locked me in there, and five or six others. The next day there were even more, and more after that. Every day—every goddamn day—"

"How many?"

She shook her head slowly from side to side, her long hair swinging. Tears sluiced down her cheeks.

"I don't know! *All* of them?" She phrased it as a question.

Nick sat silent for a time, giving her time to deal with the memory. He hated himself for putting her through this, but he needed to know.

"It got better," she said, "but it never stopped. Once they put me in the cellblock, someone came for me almost every day. And I wasn't the only one. They abused other women, too, but it seemed like I got special attention." She wiped her eyes. "Maybe they thought I was prettier than some of the others, I don't know."

"How did three months become two years? They had to have some kind of excuse to hold you past the term of your sentence."

She laid the laser pistol down and wiped her eyes with her wrists. Nick figured that was all he would get out of her, but now the dam had burst and she kept going.

"I tried to obey the rules at first. I did everything they told me to, hoping they would get tired and leave me alone. But nothing I did satisfied them. They weren't men, they were monsters. So finally...I tried to fight back. One of them forced himself into my mouth, and I bit down. I sent him to the hospital, but that didn't end it. They beat me half to death for that, and filed a criminal charge that I had assaulted a guard. That got me another year."

"Did you go to court on that charge?"

"No. They told the judge that I was incapacitated, that they had to beat me into submission to save the guard. So I was tried in absentia."

"You weren't allowed to testify in your own defense?"

"No."

"Did someone take a deposition?"

"No."

Nick frowned. He would have to check with Monica Maynard on that. He was no expert on legal matters, but that didn't sound quite kosher.

"Who was your defense attorney?"

"I don't think I had one."

"Who defended you against the original charge?"

"Geraldine Gabbard."

She wiped her eyes again, then gave him a slightly bizarre smile.

"You want to know the worst part? My old boss, the one who tried to rape me in the first place—he actually *did* rape me, after I was in lockup."

She emitted a short, half-insane laugh.

"The bastard came for me twice a week, like clockwork. They even tied me down so *I* couldn't hurt *him*."

Nick rubbed his face with both hands, wondering if it could get any worse.

"How did you finally get out of there?" he asked quietly.

She smiled again, half sad, half mad.

"My original sentence was three months. Then they added twelve more for assaulting a guard—that's fifteen. The end came and went, and I was still there. They no longer had any legal authority to hold me, but they did."

"Where was your husband? Why didn't he petition the court for your release?"

"Oh, didn't I tell you? They murdered him while I was in prison. It was listed as an industrial accident, but they killed him."

"How do you know this?"

"Read the accident report. You'll see for yourself."

Nick nodded, letting it go at that. She continued her story.

"Eleven months after I was supposed to be released, they brought in another woman, younger and prettier than me.

They needed my cell, so they said they would release me if I signed a document attesting to fair and equal treatment while in lockup."

"And you signed it?"

"Goddamn right I did. I was out of there the next day. Homeless, jobless, single, and broke. I weighed eighty-nine Terra pounds, but I was alive."

"And when was that?"

"A little over two years ago."

"Where do you work now?"

"I *don't* work. I hide out here. Farrington owns this building and they offered me this apartment." She swept a hand toward the door. "That's why I have such a spectacular view—solid rock. But I'm not complaining. I haven't been outside this building for two years. I have groceries delivered; Farrington pays for that, too."

Nick stared at her for a moment, wondering... *Why would Farrington pay for her support? Were they saving her for something?*

"With no money and no job, how do you plan to get off the asteroid?"

"I don't know. I live from day to day, minute to minute. I have no plans, no future. Marshal, I went into that place a human being, but I came out a mutilated...*thing!* I'll probably die here in this apartment, but I don't know what else I can do."

* * *

Nick left Jessica Garner's apartment feeling sick, as if he'd eaten tainted food. Her story was bizarre, almost unbelievable. She was accusing prison guards of the worst kind of criminal behavior. She was talking about men who were supposed to be officers of the law. It wasn't too difficult to believe that one or two, or maybe a handful, of such men were capable of such behavior, but...*all* of them?

And yet...

Nick was a student of history. He remembered accounts in Terran history of entire governments being taken over by criminal elements and committing the worst kinds of atrocities against their own people. The Russian Revolution of 1917; Nazi Germany in the 1940s; Cambodia in the 1970s; and many others, all of them pre-Colonial Calendar.

Ceres, by its very nature, was a criminal enclave. Virtually every man on the asteroid had a criminal past or was running from the law. Was it so terribly hard to believe that some of those men would take jobs in a prison where they had access to prey that was already housed in steel cages?

The sickness in his stomach turned to anger, barely-controlled rage. Jessica Garner was telling the truth. One only had to look at the madness in her eyes to understand that. It was an intolerable situation that had to be corrected. *Someone* had to do *something*.

And if no one else was doing it, that left it up to him.

Chapter 14

Government Annex - Ceres

It was midafternoon when Nick headed back to the office, and he realized he hadn't eaten. He stopped at a sandwich shop in Ceres North and grabbed a hotdog, then drove back to Government Annex. Milligan glanced up from his computer cascade when he came in.

"Having a productive day?"

"Very."

"Have you slept since you've been here?"

Nick thought about that a moment. He hadn't spent a single night in his hotel room.

"I don't remember."

He dragged a chair into the middle of the room and sat down facing Milligan's desk. The aging marshal watched him without a word.

"Where's the morgue around here? I couldn't find it on my 'puter map."

Milligan looked surprised. "The morgue? You chasing dead bodies now?"

When Nick didn't answer, he pointed vaguely.

"Two blocks over, in the hospital basement."

"And who's the medical examiner?"

"Shirley Chin."

"Who pays her salary?"

"The Federation. What the hell is this about?"

"I'm not sure yet. Just running down some leads."

"What kind of leads?"

Nick shrugged. "I told you I was going to investigate—I'm investigating. If I find something, I'll let you know."

Milligan sniffed. "Before you get buried too deep, how about writing that report for Caribou Lake? Before you forget the details."

Nick groaned. He'd all but forgotten that report, and hated the idea of losing his momentum on this new angle, but he knew the old marshal was right. He nodded grimly.

"Okay. I'll have it to you by 1800."

*

He spent the rest of the afternoon working on the report. He was amazed at how many details were already fading, and had to think hard to get some of them back. He actually had the report done by five-thirty, sent a copy to Milligan's computer, and stood up to stretch. Milligan perused it on his cascade and nodded approvingly.

"Good job," he said. "That's more detail than I'm used to seeing."

"Is that bad? I can always summarize it in the future."

"If you do, I'll have to shoot you. Don't ever change a good habit, no matter what other people do."

Milligan continued reading, absorbed by the report. Finally he looked up.

"Whatever happened to Bobbie the bartender? Did you stand her up?"

Nick shook his head. "By the time her shift was over everything had gone to hell. I looked her up the next day and gave her fifty terros for lying to her."

"How did she take that...being lied to?"

"She didn't seem to care. I think she's used to being lied to by men."

Milligan smiled. "That was a pretty thin ruse, you know."

"What was?"

"The line you used about being horny. Did you seriously think she knew anything about the kidnapping?"

Nick shrugged. "She's a bartender. Bartenders hear things. She's also a woman, and women are generally sympathetic to other women, so if she knew about the girls, and felt sorry for them, she might tell me something."

Milligan frowned. "Why would she do that? She would have thought you wanted to fuck them."

Nick laughed. "I was gonna come clean with her," he said.

"Come clean?"

"About being a lawman. Later, in private."

"In the bedroom?" Milligan's eyes widened. "You were actually going to *sleep* with her?"

"Well...yeah, if it came down to that. Why not?"

"Walker, she was twice your age!"

"Well...if it would have got me closer to the girls... Hey, I'm not prejudiced. She's a good looking woman."

Milligan shook his head in wonder. "God! Walker, you have no scruples."

"Of course I do." Nick looked offended.

But Milligan was chuckling. "Don't get me wrong—that's a good thing. Sometimes you have to take a few steps on the dark side to get the job done. The trick is knowing how many steps to take, and when to step back."

Nick frowned as he tried to digest that. Before he got very far his porta-phone rang. He pulled it off his belt and answered it.

"Nick Walker."

"Nick, this is Judge Maynard."

Nick was a little surprised to hear her voice. His senses were instantly alert.

"Yes, Ma'am!" he said abruptly.

She laughed. "You can call me Monica, remember?

Nick glanced at Milligan, who was pretending not to listen. "Yes, Ma'am, I understand."

Maynard hesitated briefly. "Is someone there with you?"

"That's correct."

"Someone you don't want to overhear our conversation?"

"Yes, that's right."

She sighed. "Well, it's no big secret. I just wondered if you're open for dinner tonight."

"Of course. Just tell me the time and place."

"My suite in the Centerville Hotel. Room 419. Eight o'clock?"

"I'll be there."

Maynard hung up and Nick checked his watch. It wasn't quite six yet.

"What did Judge Maynard want?"

Nick's eyes snapped around; his mouth dropped open in surprise.

"How did you know?"

"I didn't. But now I do."

Nick blushed in spite of himself. He shook his head and laughed.

"You watch your ass, Nick. She's a very sexy lady, but she'll eat you alive."

The Open Airlock - Ceres

Nick walked into the Open Airlock at a quarter past six and looked around. The place was already jumping, though the music wasn't quite as loud as the first time he'd been there.

If Fred Ferguson's information was correct, Turd Murdoch should have been there almost two hours already, and hopefully was pleasantly plastered. Not that it mattered—men like Murdoch could drink the place dry and still function soberly. Some men had a tolerance for alcohol that defied belief.

This time Nick was wearing his badge on his belt, and as he walked slowly through the room people turned to stare. Conversation dwindled, then faded completely as those in his path made way, watching expectantly. Nick spotted Turd at a pool table toward the back and strolled directly toward him. Someone pulled the plug on the music generator and the room became silent except for the *click* of a few billiard balls and some heavy breathing.

Murdoch was bent over the velvet lining up a shot when he saw Nick's approach. He straightened up ominously, his beefy face flushing red. He stood there holding the cue stick with the handle resting on the floor. Nick stopped two feet in front of him, and placed both hands on his hips.

"I hear you've been looking for me," he said loudly enough for everyone in the joint to hear. "So here I am."

Turd gazed down at him as if contemplating a mouse, his shaggy face breaking into a contemptuous grin.

"Well, well, well. If it ain't the boy marshal and his toy laser pistol."

Nick didn't rise to the taunt.

"Are you looking for me, or not? Word around the 'roid is that you plan to kill me. Since I'd hate to give you a chance at an ambush, I'm making it easy for you. Here I am, right now, in front of God and everybody."

Turd's eyes betrayed surprise as he tried to maintain his overbearing demeanor. He stared at Nick a couple of seconds, then laughed derisively.

"Fuck you! You think I'm gonna kill you in front of fifty witnesses? You got your badge, you got your toy pistol...I ain't goin' down for killin' a U.F. Marshal."

Nick unbuckled the gunbelt, rolled it up, and handed it to the nearest bystander, who looked startled but took it. Nick never took his eyes off Murdoch. He unpinned the badge and threw it on the pool table, where it lay face up, shining like a jewel.

"No laser pistol. No badge—no U.F. Marshal. You think you're man enough to take me?"

Turd's eyes widened dramatically; his mouth dropped open, and he sucked a sharp breath. The challenge was clear, and no one in the room could miss it. In defiance of all the odds, Nick was calling him out, and if he didn't accept the challenge he would be labeled a coward. It took Turd two or three seconds to process all that, and then he swelled like a toad and drew back a massive fist.

"Why, you scrawny little motherf—"

He never finished. The second his fingers balled into a fist Nick's right hand snatched the .44 out of its shoulder holster and slammed it across Turd's skull, splitting his scalp and exposing white bone. Blood squirted in thirteen directions,

spattering onlookers who jerked in shock, and the big man crashed heavily to the floor like a broken skytower. It happened so quickly that no one moved, all eyes on the fallen giant.

Nick stood over him a moment to make sure he was out cold, then bent over and ripped a piece of fabric off the man's shirt. He used the fabric to wipe the blood off the .44, then shoved the gun back under his left arm. He picked up his badge, accepted the gunbelt which the bar patron returned to him, and turned in a slow circle while he reattached the badge and belt.

"If anyone here has a problem with what just happened," he said sharply, "then now is the time to speak up. You don't threaten a U.F. Marshal and walk away clean, and that's what this man tried to do.

"Anybody?" He scanned every face within view, male and female. They all looked back at him with stricken expressions.

"Nobody? All right. When this asshole wakes up, tell him his reign of terror is over. Throw his ass out and don't let him back in. Ever."

Nick swept them with his eyes once more, then turned and walked out of the bar.

Centerville Hotel - Ceres

Since arriving on Ceres, Nick hadn't spent a single night in his hotel room. When he located Monica Maynard's suite, he was surprised to discover it was across the hall from his own— she was in 419, he was in 420. But he had a very small room, and Monica actually had a real suite. A comfortable living room gave way to a bedroom on one side and a kitchen on the other. Her place was exquisitely decorated with paintings and ceramic artwork, two holovid screens, a hexaural sound system, and a holographic fireplace. She even had flowers.

He barely had the presence of mind to pick up a bottle of wine before ringing her bell, and when she let him in he was pleasantly shocked to see her wearing a thin, filmy...*something*...that barely concealed the curvy nude body beneath it. Her hair had been brushed out and spread across her shoulders, shiny black and gleaming, and she smelled heavenly of some perfume he had never encountered before, something exotic, erotic, and heady.

"Nick!" she breathed happily when she opened the door. "I was afraid you wouldn't make it."

"Why wouldn't I?" He was stunned at the sight of the room, his eyes wide with wonder. Was he still on Ceres?

She smiled seductively as she locked the door. "Oh, you know—lawmen are always being called out at all hours."

Not tonight, I hope.

Nick handed her the bottle of wine; she took it with a smile and set it on a nearby table. The next thing he knew her arms were around his neck and she was pressing a pair of full, warm breasts against him. Her lush lips found his mouth and locked on like magnets; she moaned with pleasure as she sucked at his mouth, and without a second thought he wrapped his arms around her, returning the kiss with interest. He hadn't been this close to a woman in at least a year, and every male instinct he had went on red alert.

"Oh, *god!*" she sighed as she broke the kiss and pressed her cheek against his chest. "You have no idea how badly I've been wanting to do that. It feels so good to have a real man in my arms again."

He pressed his face into her thick hair and kissed his way down her temple, past her ear, and buried his lips in her neck.

"It's been a long time for me, too," he murmured.

"Are you hungry? I mean...are you starving?"

"I could eat," he admitted, "but it doesn't have to be right now."

She smiled and kissed him again.

"I was hoping you'd say that. I have a roast in the oven, but it won't be ready for at least an hour."

He gazed into her sexy dark eyes with feigned innocence.

"A whole hour? Gosh, what in the world will we do until then?"

Monica laughed, seized his hand, and led him toward the bedroom. When they came out again, the roast was very, very well done.

*

The roast was slightly charred but only on the outside. The potato and vegetables had been cooked ahead of time and kept in a warmer, and Monica served him fresh sourdough bread with real butter. It was the best meal he'd eaten in years and even the wine was good. Monica chattered happily throughout the meal, laughing at his jokes even when they were lame. Nick enjoyed her company even though she was a dozen years older; he was certainly no virgin, but while at the Academy he'd had little social life, and before that had been the Star Marines, which was pretty much an all male experience. For a couple of hours, at least, he felt almost like a husband—or at least a lover—and it was a pleasant diversion.

After dinner he wasn't terribly surprised when she turned on the fireplace and pulled him into a love seat to cuddle while they finished the wine. Their conversation was aimless and silly, and when the wine was gone they were all over each other, kissing and groping like honeymooners. Quickly enough they were back in the bedroom; Nick had never been with such a passionate woman, and when she finally finished with him he was as wasted as if he'd just finished a ten-mile run, uphill, with full combat pack. She drew him into her arms and held him as if he were a child, kissing him repeatedly with sighs of contentment...

...and the next thing he knew, it was morning.

Chapter 15

Thursday, August 8, 0440 (CC) — Government Annex - Ceres

"Morning, Walker."

Marshal Milligan glanced up as Nick came in the door. He still looked dusty and rumpled, as if he hadn't moved since Nick left him. The cigar tray was overflowing with butts and ash.

"Morning, Marshal," Nick said cheerily as he headed for the coffee pot.

"You're awfully chipper this morning," the old man observed.

"I had a really good night's sleep. I feel ten pounds lighter."

Milligan smirked. "Ten gallons is more likely. You get laid last night?"

Nick almost poured coffee on his hand. He turned toward the old marshal with innocent eyes.

"Marshal, what kind of question is that! A gentleman doesn't kiss and tell."

"I got a feeling you did more than kiss," Milligan grunted. "Well, hell, good for you. Get it while you're young, before you figure out that the whole thing is overrated."

Nick stared at him in surprise.

"What's overrated?"

"Love. Sex. Marriage—all of it."

Nick laughed incredulously. "You think *sex* is overrated?"

"Absolutely."

Nick took a chair facing him, his coffee cup forgotten.

"How do you figure that?"

Milligan cleared his throat, as if about to begin a video lecture.

"I been studying the phenomenon since well before you were born, Walker, and I've come to the conclusive conclusion—" His eyes twinkled. "—that ninety-nine percent of the hysteria over sex is the result of advertising."

"Advertising!"

"That's right. Now I ain't saying sex isn't *necessary*—else the human race would die out—and I ain't saying it isn't *pleasant*—else the whorehouses would be out of business, thereby severely crippling our economy—but it's still overrated."

Nick's eyes glazed slightly as he tried to follow the logic, if one could call it that, and determine if Milligan was toying with him.

"I still don't get it."

"Of course you don't. At your age it seems the most important thing in the 'verse, but when you get right down to it—when you weigh the need for sex against the need for food, water, shelter, and air...it comes in a dismal dead last."

He raised his eyebrows in challenge.

"Right?"

"Uh...I guess so."

"Of course it does. When you were stuck in that pressure room at Caribou Lake, for example, and the air was escaping, and you were starting to ice up, were you thinking about sex?" He shook his head. "Absolutely not. You had a beautiful girl right there in front of you, but screwing her never entered your mind. Even if she hadn't already been raped, thereby rendering her an object of pity rather than an object of lust, you still had no interest in her loins. Did you?"

"Well...no."

"No, you did not." Milligan lifted his coffee cup and swigged the cold dark liquid down.

"But that's not—"

"I'm not finished!"

Milligan set the cup down and turned his eyes on Nick again.

"Sexual desire, by its very nature, is the result of pent-up physiological pressure, at least in the male. Have you ever noticed, for example, that immediately after having intercourse you are able to gaze upon the female form without the slightest biological interest? And, by contrast, when you haven't experienced a release of pressure in a while, you become increasingly enticed by the most unattractive of females? That the longer you go in between, the more attractive they all are?"

Nick blinked at him, still not sure if he was being jerked around.

"What the hell are you talking about?"

"I'm talking about sex being overrated. It's all in the advertising."

"But you just said it's physiological."

"And so it is, but not the hype, not the hysteria. For young men such as yourself, it's more about the ego than the actual need. Any boy or man, no matter how unattractive, can find a female to mate with, if biology is the only issue. But are you satisfied with that? Not usually. You want to bed the most beautiful, the most desirable, the most exotic female you can find. Why? Is the sex any better with the beauty than the beast? Of course not—everyone has the same equipment. You can have just as much fun with an ugly girl as with a holo queen, but you want to be able to brag to your friends that you were able to attract the cream of the crop, as it were.

"Now why would you care what your friends think? Because you and all of your buddies have been seduced by the advertising. All the titillation, no pun intended, about sex is about the hottest, sexiest, slinkiest, prettiest, gorgeousest of the gorgeous. You all think your lives will end in utter disaster if you can't attract and inseminate the finest of the fine, when a plain fat girl can do the job just as well."

Milligan leaned back and glared at him.

"Overrated."

Nick sat staring at him for fifteen seconds.

"Okay...maybe you're right. But you said love and marriage, too. What about that?"

Milligan shrugged. "Love is primarily a selfish emotion. Oh, I know the preachers tell you it's defined as 'outgoing concern', but when was a preacher ever right about anything? The only reason you fall in love with someone is because you want that person for yourself. That doesn't mean you don't care for them—you do, or you wouldn't want them for yourself—but your primary goal is to secure for yourself that person's love in return, along with whatever services they might have that you want."

"You're talking about sex again?"

Milligan's eyebrows lowered, as if Nick were simple. "How many people fall in love without sexual expectations? Of course I'm talking about sex!"

"Okay..."

"The only *true* examples of love are when you do something for someone without any expectations in return. Helping someone who is hurt, giving money to the needy, taking in an orphan, something like that. That's true love. Erotic love is entirely selfish, and therefore doesn't qualify as love at all.

"Marriage, in light of all that, is also overrated. The only advantage of marriage is if you want to raise children in a stable home. But once you take that step, you can kiss your sex life good-bye. The best sex you'll ever have will probably be with a complete stranger, a one- or two-night stand in which neither party expects anything of the other. The best sex is spontaneous, and married sex is *never* spontaneous. Again, it all boils down to advertising, the vanity of the young...the desire to prove to the 'verse that you can attract and capture the most desirable partner possible.

"But once you've done that, you've locked yourself in a cage. Women, by their very nature, are illogical, irrational, overemotional, and impossible to get along with. If you lock yourself in a cage with one for the rest of your life, you'll never have any peace of mind, because she will pick at you, and pick, and pick, and nag, and erode your confidence. You'll never be good enough, rich enough, clean enough, smart enough, and she'll never let you forget it. I ain't saying they aren't necessary—without them the human race would die out—but they exact a terrible price.

"Women are just like alcohol—they should only be taken in small doses and never more than once a week. Overrated."

Nick sat silent, with no idea what to say.

"I don't believe that," he said finally.

"That's because you've never been married. Your liaisons have been part of a mating ritual, in which each side continually tries to impress the other. If you aren't married, or at least in a committed relationship, she has no power over you...and she knows it. She will keep her claws sheathed until she nails you down, but once that happens, you'll discover that I'm right."

Milligan reached for a fresh cigar. "Now—what the hell did you do to Turd Murdoch?"

* * *

Shirley Chin was a slight woman, barely five feet tall, who might have weighed a hundred pounds on Terra but considerably less on Ceres. Nick guessed that she was around forty, petite and slender, with a twelve year-old body and short, shiny black hair which she wore in a cute flip that curled inward at chin level. When Nick introduced himself her already tentative smile froze a little and her almond-shaped eyes widened. She led him into her basement office beneath the hospital and offered him a chair. He sat down and gazed around briefly at the overstuffed room—anatomical charts decorated the walls and her desk was stacked with folders and forensics reports. She skipped the amenities and sat stiffly, her fingers interlocked beneath her chin, waiting for him to begin.

"How long have you been the M.E. here?" he asked.

"A little over seven years."

He nodded slowly. Her body language suggested resistance, so he tried for a charming smile.

"Lots of autopsies?"

"Yes. There is a lot of violent death here." Her expression remained guarded.

"I guess you've seen just about everything."

She nodded impatiently. "How can I help you, Marshal?"

Nick gave up on the charm—it wasn't going to work and he wasn't very good at it anyway. He leaned forward and placed a file folder on her desk.

"What can you tell me about these?"

She opened the folder and gazed at the contents. One by one, she began turning each document face down as she looked at the next.

"Where did you get these?"

"They came to my attention during the course of an investigation."

"What kind of investigation?"

"These are death certificates issued on twelve inmates at Farrington Security, accompanied by medical reports of injuries sustained prior to death."

"I can see what they are." She looked at him with a flat stare. "What would you like to know about them?"

Nick held her gaze until she looked away.

"These death certificates all bear your signature."

"Yes, that is correct."

"I'd like to know how you arrived at the cause of death in these cases."

She stacked the documents again and closed the folder.

"Are you investigating *me?*"

"Would you like to answer the question?"

"I don't think I appreciate your tone, Marshal." She shoved the folder across the desk toward him.

Nick leaned forward and dropped a second folder onto her desk. She only stared at it, without touching it.

"The people in that first folder were all men," he said evenly. "This one contains death certificates and medical reports for fifteen females. Once again, the cause of death doesn't seem to be supported by the other documentation. Would you care to take a look and perhaps explain them to me?"

Shirley Chin swallowed involuntarily. "I'm really very busy, Marshal. Perhaps we can do this another time?" She stood abruptly.

"I have a better idea. Let's do it now."

She sat down again, agitation in her eyes. Her breathing seemed suddenly labored, and Nick could practically see the goose bumps on her arms.

"I don't appreciate you questioning my integrity," she said, forcing calm into her voice.

"I haven't done that, at least not yet. Maybe, if you can answer my questions, I won't have to."

She closed her eyes briefly, as if summoning a prayer. When she opened them she looked directly at him.

"What would you like to know?"

Nick had studied the reports and recited from memory.

"Jasmine Jefferson, age nineteen, inmate at Farrington Security. She was brought in D.O.A. The physical examination reported a broken jaw, ligature strangulation marks, and severe vaginal and anal bruising consistent with forcible penetration. Her cause of death, signed by you, was heart failure."

"Inmates can be very cruel to each other," Shirley Chin said.

"Yes they can, but this girl was in a women's lockup, yet she was raped and sodomized."

"Rape with a foreign object is not uncommon in female detention. Obviously the girl had been badly traumatized and her heart just couldn't take it." She clasped her hands together, as if that settled it. "Heart failure."

"Semen was recovered."

"How does that change anything? It was still heart failure."

Nick stared at her until she looked away.

"There is a box on that medical exam sheet labeled 'suspicious', and another labeled 'homicide'. Neither of those boxes was checked."

He waited, but she didn't respond.

"I didn't see any indication that the semen was tested for DNA," he added.

"That would be your department, not mine."

"True, but the checkboxes are for *you* to fill out. Yet you didn't check them. Why not?"

"The cause of death was as I stated. It was heart failure, probably induced by extreme physical trauma. Inmates can be very cruel."

Nick mentally shifted files and recited another case.

"Renee Carmelletti, age forty-four, inmate at Farrington. Also came in D.O.A. Post-mortem X-rays revealed partially healed fractures of both arms, several ribs, and one foot. She had ligature marks that had partially faded, showed signs of genital trauma, and one eye was swollen shut. Cause of death—natural causes."

Shirley Chin sat rigidly at her desk, her face frozen. She began to tremble ever so slightly.

"Doctor Chin? Can you tell me about Mrs. Carmelletti?"

He stared accusingly at the woman behind the desk, and waited until she finally made eye contact with him. He saw the glitter of tears.

"No," she said so quietly he could barely hear. "I can't tell you anything." She took a shaky breath and swallowed hard. "Are we done?"

His demeanor relaxed a fraction as he realized what was really going on. His mounting anger began to fade—the woman was scared to death.

He stood up and retrieved the folders.

"Yes," he said quietly. "We're done."

* * *

The courtroom was packed with prisoners in jumpsuits when Nick walked in, so he sat down and watched the proceedings for awhile. Monica Maynard spotted him but tapped her watch, as if to tell him she couldn't take the time at the moment, so he waited. Most of the cases pending seemed to be arraignments and plea agreements, each taking only minutes to conclude, and forty minutes after he arrived, the last prisoner was escorted out. Monica called a recess and headed for her chambers. Nick knocked on her door a minute later.

"Come in."

Nick opened the door and stepped through. Monica was waiting and wrapped her arms around him, hugging him tight.

"Oh, god, I've *missed* you!" she said.

"It's only been three hours," he laughed.

In lieu of a reply, she hooked her arms around his neck and drew him down for a long, passionate kiss. He felt his body respond in spite of the beating it had taken the night before.

"You want to go for it right here on your desk?" he asked when she released him.

"I would love to, but if anyone came in it wouldn't look very dignified, would it?"

She walked around the desk and took her chair, leaning back and gazing at him as if he were an exotic painting. He sat facing her and heaved a sigh.

"So how're you feeling?"

"Like a new woman. And you?"

"I think I need an I.V."

She frowned in confusion.

"To replace lost fluids."

Monica burst into laughter. "Well, I can certainly believe that. So, how can I help you, Marshal? You didn't come over here just to kiss and make out, did you?"

"I'm afraid not, though that would be a lot more fun. I need to ask you a procedural question."

"Sure."

His brow knitted as he sought the proper way to phrase the question.

"Suppose you had a prisoner in lockup serving out a sentence, and that prisoner was suddenly charged with a crime committed while incarcerated."

She frowned and nodded, trying to follow.

"Now, let's say the prisoner had been injured during the commission of that crime and was unable to physically appear in court—"

"You mean, he attacked a guard, they beat the shit out of him, and he couldn't appear?"

Nick grinned. "You're quick."

"That happens sometimes. What's the question?"

"How does that prisoner defend himself?"

"Through his attorney."

"What if he doesn't have an attorney?"

"He has to have an attorney if he isn't physically able to appear. Someone has to represent him."

Nick nodded. "That's what I thought. But in the case I have in mind, the prisoner did *not* have an attorney, and wasn't even deposed."

Monica's lips pursed dramatically. "What case are you referring to?"

Nick hesitated; he was pretty sure he could trust Monica— she was a judge, after all—but he'd made a promise.

"I...would rather not say at this point."

She spread her hands. "If you're talking hypothetical, then the answer is, it couldn't happen. But if you have a specific case in mind, I can't help you without a name."

Nick sat silent for a moment, drumming his fingers on the chair arm.

"Let's keep it hypothetical. Suppose the prisoner was not represented by Geraldine Gabbard or any of her staff. Are there other attorneys who *might* represent him?"

Monica nodded. "There are other attorneys on Ceres, but they're privately employed."

"Really? How many?"

"Ten or twelve. But they're corporate; they don't handle criminal cases."

Nick's eyes widened slowly and his heart beat a little faster.

"Could a corporate attorney represent a person in a criminal proceeding?"

"Theoretically, yes. It doesn't happen very often, though."

"But it has happened?"

Still frowning, she tilted her head curiously. "Nick, what are you investigating?"

He shook his head. "I'm sorry; I don't feel comfortable telling you that right now."

"Nick, this is me. I fucked you last night. Remember?"

He nodded. "The first time we met, you said no strings. This could be a string."

She shrugged and spread her hands in surrender.

"Okay."

"Do you remember any cases where a corporate attorney represented a criminal defendant? In particular, someone in lockup who was physically unable to appear?"

She thought a moment, then nodded slowly.

"Yeah, I think that happened two or three times."

"Do you remember who the attorneys were?"

"It was the same attorney in each case. Stanley Cramer."

Nick let his breath out slowly, sensing victory.

"And where do I find Stanley Cramer?"

"Farrington Industries. He's head of their legal department."

Chapter 16

The outer office was empty when Nick walked into the public defender's office, but Misery Allen heard the door and popped her head out.

"Nick!" she exclaimed with a smile. "What a surprise!"

"Hi, Misery. How are things?"

"Busy, as always. Come on into my den."

He stepped into her office and took a seat.

"Can I get you anything?"

"I'm fine, thanks."

She scurried around her desk and settled into a chair, beaming at him.

"It's so good to see you again!"

He grinned. "Seems like a month since I was here. So much has been going on."

She nodded, her dark eyes sparkling. "You've been a busy boy. Rescued two missionary girls and I hear you cleaned that bully's clock yesterday."

"Bully...?"

"Turd Murdoch."

"Oh. Word travels fast."

"Like a virus. We don't need holonews here. So what brings you to this overworked, understaffed establishment?"

Nick grinned a little sheepishly. "I have a confession to make."

"A confession! Do you need representation?" Her eyes twinkled.

"I hope not. I was hoping to throw myself on the mercy of the court."

"And what is this great transgression of yours?"

"I feel like I cheated you. I cancelled our dinner date the other day, but last night I had dinner with Judge Maynard.

Somehow that seems unfair, but I swear she invited me and I couldn't really turn her down."

Misery sat back in her chair with a knowing smile.

"So *you're* the one!"

Nick's eyes widened in genuine surprise. "Huh?"

Misery laughed. "Everyone in court today swore she must have gotten laid last night. She's been positively civil all morning."

Nick couldn't stop the flush that swept up from his collarbone; he could feel his face burning.

"Can I invoke the right not to incriminate myself?" He spread his hands. "She's a judge. I didn't want to be held in contempt."

Misery laughed again. "Nick, don't be embarrassed. Everyone is thrilled that she's found someone. A happy judge makes for a happy courtroom."

Nick's eyebrows arched. *Found someone?*

"Don't misunderstand," he said, "she and I are not an item. I mean, we're not 'together'. It just happened."

"And it will happen again. Ever since you showed up she's been drooling over you, so don't think she won't come after you again."

You watch your ass, Nick. She's a very sexy lady, but she'll eat you alive.

"Thanks for the warning. Anyway—" He leaned forward. "Since I'm not sure when I'll be available for dinner, I was hoping I could interest you in an early lunch."

"You mean right now?" She glanced at her watch. "Well—sure. I don't have anything moon-shaking for the next couple of hours."

"Great! I'll let you pick the place...since I don't know of any."

She smiled and reached for her purse. "I know just the spot."

* * *

It was a small café just two blocks from the courthouse, certainly nothing fancy, but Nick could smell the kitchen as soon as they walked in the door. The floor was a black and white checkerboard, the tables small and bare. They were too early for the lunch crowd, so the place was empty. Misery ordered for both of them and Nick sat back with a cup of watery coffee while they waited for the food.

"I've been looking at records," he told her casually. "You guys really run a lot of cases through that place."

"Oh, I know. It gets insane sometimes."

"How do you keep up with it? Every time I go into the courtroom it seems like things are backed up."

Misery stirred her coffee. "Ninety-nine percent of it is boilerplate. You have assaults and fights and minor thefts; the PO pleads most of them out, offering standard deals, and the defendants usually accept them. If we had to hold an actual trial for every case we'd be here until eternity."

"Looks like a lot of people get probation."

She nodded. "There isn't enough room in the lockups to imprison everyone. Farrington lockup houses most of those incarcerated, and their facility is running near maximum all the time. The other lockups are completely full, even overcrowded."

She chatted on for several minutes and Nick didn't interrupt. The food came sooner than he expected and they began to eat.

"What the hell is this stuff?" he inquired as he stirred the soup.

Misery laughed. "You probably don't want to know."

Nick glanced up at her.

"It's hydroponic gruel," she said. "At least that's the standard joke. Probably a little meat in there, but nobody knows for sure."

Nick sipped it with his spoon and tested the flavor.

"Not too bad," he ventured.

"It's a little strange at first, but you'll acquire a taste for it. Some people actually like it."

Nick looked at the rest of the food and wasn't overly impressed. It bore a strange resemblance to military rations he'd eaten in combat, except it was hot.

"Is everything microwaved around here?"

"'Fraid so. Real food is obscenely expensive. Everything has to be imported from Mars, or even farther, so most of the population lives on hydroponic meals. It leaves a lot to be desired, but it's affordable and it's supposed to be nutritious." She smiled thinly. "Sorry."

He shrugged. "I've eaten a lot worse."

Once he started eating, he realized it was actually better than those military meals, and he was nothing if not flexible.

"The first time we met," he said, "you were telling me about problems with Farrington Security."

"I think I used the word 'thugs'." She smiled.

"Yes, you did. And since then I've heard the word 'goons'."

"I like that word even better."

"You've only been here a few months. And yet you have a decidedly low opinion of Farrington Security. For you to form such a firm opinion in such a short time, conditions over there must be really bad."

She locked gazes with him, all humor gone from her eyes.

"That wasn't a rhetorical statement, was it? What are you looking for?"

He glanced around involuntarily, but they were completely alone.

"I was wondering if you could pull some records for me. About one case in particular."

"I thought you were already looking at records."

"Yeah, but those were given to me by someone else."

"You can access court records yourself. It's all public information."

"I'd like to get inside this case without anyone knowing about it. I can't tell you why right this moment, but if certain people found out I was nosing around, it might put someone else in danger."

"Someone? Like who?"

He hesitated, then spoke slowly.

"I have to be able to trust you completely, Misery. I think I can, but I have to know for sure."

"What does that mean?"

"It means you can't tell a soul that I made this request, and certainly not the name of the party I'm inquiring about. You can't tell your staff, your boss, and certainly no one outside your office."

"Will I be in danger?"

"Probably not, but it's possible. But a defense attorney accessing old transcripts would be a lot less suspicious than a U.F. Marshal walking in off the street doing the same thing."

Misery glanced at her food, thinking it over, and took another bite. A moment later she looked into his eyes again.

"Okay."

"Are you sure?"

She nodded. "If this will contribute in any way to improving things at Farrington lockup, then yes. I'm sure."

Nick laid his hand over hers and squeezed it.

"Thank you, Misery. I've got your back if you need it."

She smiled. "I never doubted that, Nick. I may be a small-world girl, but I know an honest man when I see one. What records do you need?"

"I want to see the trial transcripts for one Jessica Garner. There should be two cases—the original assault charge and another filing a few months later for assaulting a prison guard." He gave her the approximate dates.

"Okay. I can have it for you later today."

"You be careful. And don't breathe a word of this to anyone."

"You don't need to worry about that."

*

Back at the U.F. Marshal's office, Nick dropped into his chair with a sigh. Milligan wasn't there, but Sandy Beech looked up from his desk opposite and grinned.

"Walker! Man, you really get around. I haven't seen you since the first day we met."

"I've been in and out. What do you do all day?"

"Boring shit, mostly. Unlike you, I haven't been in a fight for days."

Nick laughed. "Boring sounds pretty good. I could do with a little boring."

"I hear you laid out Turd Murdoch last night."

"I did. He threatened a U.F. Marshal, and I don't take that lightly. Does everybody on this rock know about that guy?"

"Oh, yeah, just about. He's in and out of court constantly."

"Sounds like he needs some serious jail time."

"No question about it. But his employer keeps paying his fines. They consider him an essential worker."

"Must be nice." Nick kicked his heels up on the desk and locked his fingers behind his head. "Tell me about Farrington Industries."

Beech looked blank. "What about them?"

"Are they legit?"

"I guess so. Why wouldn't they be?"

"I've been here four days and everywhere I turn I run into evidence that something really stinks over there. The men who kidnapped those missionary girls were Farrington employees, Turd Murdoch is Farrington—I've been hearing about prisoner abuse in Farrington lockup, inmates being tortured and killed, women being raped...that paints a pretty grim picture."

Beech looked surprised. "You've heard all that?"

Nick nodded. "In four days."

"Well...every company has a few bad apples. I mean, you can't really blame FI for what happened at Caribou Lake..."

Nick inclined his head to the side.

"In the Star Marines, we had a quarter million men on Alpha Centauri. There were bad apples there, too, but very few committed atrocities against civilians. I was there for fifteen months and I only heard of one rape and maybe a dozen other crimes. The men who did it were given star-courts and sent to prison, some of them for life."

Beech looked confused. "What's your point?"

"The organization conforms to the morality of whoever is at the top. If the man in charge is corrupt, his employees feel free to do whatever they want. Has anyone run background checks on Farrington's security people?"

"I dunno. That would be their responsibility, not ours."

Nick nodded. Beech was right, but it might be an interesting exercise.

"Anyway," Beech said, "I don't think there's much interest in taking on the Farrington corporation. If they closed their doors, or someone shut them down, this whole rock would dry up. Farrington runs eighty percent of the water mining on Ceres, and Ceres water is the lifeblood of the Outer Worlds. Titan, Europa, and Ganymede would literally die if they lost that water. Seriously, they wouldn't last more than a few weeks. Even Mars gets forty percent of its water from here."

Nick's eyes widened a fraction as he gazed back at Sandy Beech. *That was it!* That explained how Farrington Industries had become so powerful. No matter how corrupt they might be, too many people depended on them for anyone to stand up to them. Even Marshal Milligan wasn't too excited about the prospect.

Nick closed his eyes a moment, as if dozing, and Sandy Beech returned to his computer cascade. But Nick wasn't dozing, he was thinking. What were the risks of pursuing his investigation further? If literally millions of lives were at stake—dependent on Farrington water—what did it matter if the company was corrupt? Was the welfare of a few hundred more important than the lives of millions?

It was an imposing question, and not one to be taken lightly.

Nick found Scott Garner's accident report without help. It wasn't filed with court documents, but in the vital statistics database at the morgue. As he pulled it up on his computer cascade, he felt reasonably sure that no one would be able to trace his inquiry; no one should have any reason to even suspect it.

The accident report itself was pretty straightforward; Scott Garner had worked on a drill crew for Farrington Industries, one of the men who serviced the drill heads that bored into the permafrost and dug out the ice that would later be crushed and converted into water. According to the report, Garner had failed to set the locking brakes on the drill head before attempting to service it. During the course of maintenance the locking brakes had slipped and the head, which was six feet wide, had activated, chopping Garner into hamburger in a matter of seconds.

Read the accident report. You'll see for yourself.

Nick read the report twice, and then a third time. On the surface it seemed plausible enough—men who worked at dangerous jobs sometimes became numbed by the routine and got careless; but when viewed in the perspective of Garner trying to get his wife released from Farrington lockup, where she was being repeatedly raped and tortured, it took on a whole new look.

Nick scrolled down and read the eyewitness accounts, then the signatures attesting to the accuracy of those accounts. There were three signatures, including that of the crew chief.

His name was Turd Murdoch.

Chapter 17

Farrington Industries - Ceres

The habitat housing Farrington Industries was almost as big as Government Annex. Located outside the loop on the extreme north-west edge of excavated habitats, it was somewhat isolated from the rest of the Ceres community. As Nick came out of the tube he saw the monorail station where employees arrived and departed, and the pedestrian bridge that took them from the station into the facility itself. By following the paved road, he was obliged to stop at the main gate, where his ID was rigorously inspected.

"Federation Marshal, huh?" the guard grunted. "What's your business here?"

"I came to inspect your prison facility," Nick replied with a straight face.

The guard's mouth fell open as if he'd been slapped. He stared at Nick as if he were mad.

"Do you have a, uh, warrant?"

"Do I need one?"

"Well, I..."

"The only reason I should need a warrant would be if you have something to hide. I can get one, if you think that's the case."

The guard stood speechless, his tongue sliding across his lips.

"*Do* you have something to hide?"

"*I* don't."

"Then what's the problem?"

"I, um...let me make a call."

"Stop right there!" Nick shoved his door open and stepped out of the E-car. The guard, who looked about nineteen, took a step back. "What's going on in there?" Nick demanded.

"I, uh—look, sir, I don't work in there, okay? I just work the gate here."

"Then why are you suddenly scared? Is there something I should know?"

The kid shook his head, his eyes filled with dread.

"It's just that—I could lose my job."

"Why? Who told you that?"

The kid fidgeted, glancing to right and left as if looking for help.

"I asked you a question! Who said you would lose your job, and why?"

"I—sir, I need to make a call."

Nick glared at him, then nodded. "Fine. Put it on speaker and we'll both make the call."

Thoroughly intimidated, the young guard stepped into the gatehouse, Nick on his heels, and reached for the comm set. He punched three buttons, then the speaker button.

"Silva."

"Mr. Silva, there's a U.F. Marshal at the gate. He wants to inspect the lockup."

"Bullshit! Tell him to go to hell."

"I told him it was no dice, sir, but he's pretty insistent."

"Goddammit, Browning! Tell him it's private property. He has no authority here."

Nick shouldered the guard aside and bent over the comm unit.

"Benny Silva? How's your forehead? Still got a headache?"

Silence spilled from the speakers for five seconds.

"Who the hell is this!"

"I think you know who this is. We met in the courtroom the other day."

"What the hell do you want?"

"You know that, too. I want to inspect your facility."

"Well, that ain't gonna happen, asshole! You got a warrant?"

"Why do I need one?"

"Because this is private property, that's why."

Nick stared through the window and made a decision.

"Here's how we're going to do it, Silva—I'm coming in there, *without* a warrant, and you can sue me later. However...if I find what I'm pretty sure I'm gonna find, then *you* will be taking a one-way, all expenses paid trip to Mars where you will be sucking prison dick for a very long time. How does that sound?"

Nick glared at the young guard, Browning, while he waited for an answer. Browning paled and swallowed hard.

"You stay where you are, Marshal!" Benny Silva growled. "I'm coming out."

The connection was cut and Nick stepped out of the guard shack.

"Open the gate. I'm going to park my car before he gets here."

Browning nodded and the gate swung upward. Nick got back into his vehicle and guided it into the nearest parking space. As he exited the car again he saw a familiar face striding toward him from a long, five-story building on the north end of the compound. Silva was coming hard, and as he approached, Nick could see the fury that flushed his features red.

He was two inches shorter than Nick, but stockier, with a weathered brow and curly black hair. They weighed about the same, and Silva was wearing a laser pistol in a belt holster.

"Who the fuck do you think you are!" he snarled as they met in the middle of the parking lot.

"That's what I should be asking you. I'm a United Federation Marshal, duly authorized and sworn by Federation Authority in London. You're just a two-bit overpaid security guard on a rock in the middle of the Asteroid Belt. And you dare defy *my* authority?"

"*Fuck* you, Walker!"

Nick's eyes crinkled with amusement. He'd run into Silva's kind before, and when the chips were down they always resorted to the same refrain—*fuck you!*

"Would you like to give me a tour?" he asked conversationally, "or let me prowl around by myself? I can do it either way, but whichever way we do it, I *will* see what I came here to see."

"We ain't doing either one!" Silva inclined his head to the right. "Mr. Farrington wants to see you."

*

The Farrington compound consisted of several buildings, the prison being far and away the largest. The main office was more modest, a simple two-story stone structure with a tower in the center that stuck straight up like an obelisk. Seven rows of windows decorated the tower; Silva marched Nick toward the main entrance and led him past a security desk to the elevator, then used a round metal key to send the lift to the top floor. Silva stepped out before the doors closed, and Nick winked at him.

In spite of everything, his heart was beating faster. He had known that eventually he would face the Farrington brothers, but hadn't planned on doing it just yet; circumstances had dictated that now was the time, so he went with it. One benefit of Star Marine training was the ability to adapt to the situation.

Improvise!

The elevator opened into a private lobby with an elderly, white-haired woman sitting behind a desk. She peered at him through thick-lensed eyeglasses—a rarity these days—and spoke without smiling.

"Marshal Walker?"

"Yes."

"Mr. Farrington will see you immediately." She nodded toward the door behind her. "Go right in."

His nerves humming, Nick walked toward the heavy oaken door and pushed it open. As he stepped inside he saw at a glance that the entire office was paneled in oak, which must have cost a fortune to import from Terra. The office itself was huge, larger than most conference rooms, and decorated tastefully with various works of art. The floor was an intricately woven parquet of polished, multicolored wood and the broad window facing him displayed a magnificent mountain landscape—a stunningly clear lake flanked by evergreens, crowned by a towering snow-covered peak. Nick knew there was no such view outside the window—this was a holo-window, an expensive one, that offered the illusion of a terrestrial landscape where no such thing existed.

Nick strode slowly into the room, taking it all in, and his eyes came to rest on the man behind the wide mahogany desk. Harvey Farrington was slumped in his chair, his elbow resting lightly on the left arm, an amused look on his face. He didn't look much like a monster, Nick decided, just a funny little man with too much money and too much power. An aura of arrogance surrounded him like the vapor from a block of CO_2. As Nick stopped in front of the desk Farrington didn't take his eyes off him, and the eyes became more amused as the seconds ticked away.

Nick looked at the other man in the room, this one leaning against the wall a few feet away, a wine glass in his hand. He appeared taller, though it was hard to be sure because Farrington was sitting down. That they were brothers was obvious. Indeed, they were identical twins, though not exactly identical. The Farrington behind the desk had a rounder face, wavier hair, and his jaw seemed to shift from side to side as if he were chewing a nut between his front teeth. The Farrington standing by the wall was leaner, less comical, but the same amused arrogance reflected from his eyes. His lips curled up on one side in a cynical sneer.

Nick looked at the man seated behind the desk.

"Let me guess. Harvey Farrington." He nodded at the man standing. "Henry Farrington."

"Very *good*, Marshal Walker!" Harvey Farrington said. "You are obviously smarter than you look."

Nick gave him a wry smile, then settled into a chair without being invited. His senses were on high alert—he left plenty of room for his right hand in case he needed to draw his weapon.

"Too bad I can't say the same about you," he replied.

Harvey Farrington burst into laughter, a harsh braying that didn't sound quite human. After a second he subsided and sat staring at his visitor, his jaw still sliding about as if he had tectonic plates in his mouth.

"Nice view." Nick nodded at the holo-window. "Mt. Shasta, isn't it?"

Farrington's brows floated upward. "Mm, impressive. You've been to California?"

"Born and raised. Chowchilla."

"Ah, the state capital. My brother and I are from the old capital."

Nick nodded. "Sacramento. I've been there, too. Nice town."

"It used to be. Until the niggos ruined it."

Nick frowned. "The...*what?*"

"The niggos. You know about niggos, don't you, Marshal?"

It took Nick a second. He'd heard the word once, years ago...or maybe he'd read it in a history book. He couldn't remember for sure, but it was an archaic term, a racial epithet of some kind. He searched his memory, but came up empty.

"No," he said slowly, "I don't think I do."

"Oh, come on, Marshal! Sure you do. You slept with one last night."

Nick felt a chill ripple across his skin. The Farringtons had him under surveillance? He felt his face turn red and it annoyed him—Farrington saw it too, and his look of amusement deepened. Nick took a deep breath to fight back his adrenaline, consciously relaxed in the chair, and crossed his legs.

"I've been here four days," he said, "and you already know who I'm sleeping with? Why would you want to know that?"

"Why would you be investigating Farrington Industries?" Henry asked from his place against the wall. "Like you said, you've only been here four days."

Nick glanced at him and saw that the amusement in *his* eyes had faded. He looked positively angry.

"Who says I'm investigating you?"

"Do you deny it?"

"No. But if I've only been here four days, why would you know that already?"

Henry ignored the question. "Are you fucking that niggo defense attorney, too?"

"*What!*"

Harvey brayed with laughter again, then sat staring at him with undisguised contempt, more amused than ever.

"You can't keep any secrets on this asteroid, Marshal. Now why do you want to inspect our lockup?"

"Why do you want to keep me out?"

The brothers exchanged glances, as if communicating by telepathy. Harvey turned back to Nick.

"I would think the U.F. Marshal had better things to do than worry about the fate of the losers we have locked up."

"Is that what you would think?" Nick struggled to get his balance back—these were two very cagey characters, and the last thing he wanted was for them to think they owned him. He glanced at the brother by the wall. "What would *you* think, Henry?"

"'*Mister* Farrington', if you don't mind," Harvey said.

Nick glanced at Harvey, then back at Henry.

"What would you think, Henry?" he repeated.

Henry Farrington glared at him, hostility evident in every muscle.

"I think we need your interference like we need a hole in the head."

Nick didn't reply right away. He glanced from one brother to the other, then back again. Throughout the conversation, almost subliminally, he'd been picking up a sound, barely audible, that sounded like a *grunt*. Now he realized it was coming from Harvey Farrington, some kind of unconscious nervous exhalation that was barely noticeable.

There it was again...

Uh. Uh.

It seemed to coincide with Harvey's jaw movements.

"What kind of interference are you worried about?" Nick asked casually. "Your mining operation? How you run your office? Are you afraid I'll start making business decisions for you?"

Henry angrily drained his wine glass and slammed it down on the corner of the desk. Nick picked up a pungent scent as droplets spattered across the surface.

"Are you drinking *vinegar?*"

Harvey answered the question for his brother.

"We grew up poor," he said. "My brother always liked wine, but when we couldn't afford it he learned to sip watered-down vinegar as a substitute. He developed a taste for it."

Uh. Uh.

Nick shrugged. "Whatever circles your orb." He placed both hands on his knees. "So, do I get to inspect your lockup, or not?"

"Not," Henry said.

"Why? What are you hiding over there?"

"We're not hiding anything, but we don't appreciate heavy-handed government interference."

"Which you need like a hole in the head."

"Fuck you."

Nick winked at Harvey Farrington. "Your brother is very eloquent."

Harvey smiled. "He's coming along."

Uh. Uh.

"I understand you are the company president?"

"You understand correctly."

Uh. Uh.

"What does your brother do? His name doesn't seem to appear on any corporate documents."

"Do you understand 'need to know', Marshal? You don't need to know."

Nick grinned at him, as if they were sharing a private joke. Harvey grinned back.

Uh. Uh.

This was going in a circle. Nick took a moment to consider his position, then decided to go for broke.

"All right, Harvey—"

"Mister Farrington."

"All right...Harvey...tell me this—you said you grew up poor. How did you make your money?"

Harvey laughed again, hurting Nick's ears.

"Are you crazy, Marshal? Look around you! Farrington *dominates* the mining industry on Ceres!"

"Before that. You came here twelve years ago and started acquiring properties, which you then built into this huge industry. Where did you get your start-up capital?"

Harvey's eyes gleamed with enjoyment, his jaw worked from side to side.

"I don't see how that's any of your business."

Uh. Uh.

"Maybe it isn't, but what's the harm in telling me? Is there anything in there that you're ashamed of?"

"Me? Ashamed?" Harvey brayed again. "I've never done anything that I'm ashamed of, Marshal. Not once, not ever."

Watching the arrogance drip from his chin, Nick believed him.

"So you came here with nothing, no capital, and started acquiring properties. Is that how it happened?"

"It might have been. Or not."

"I can find out."

"I'm sure you can. But you won't find out from me."

Uh. Uh.

"We know our rights, Marshal," Henry Farrington said. His color had returned, his fury somewhat abated. Now he merely looked cynical again. "We're not doing anything illegal and we resent the implication that we are."

"Nothing illegal?" Nick asked innocently. "Nothing at all?"

"Nothing at all."

"So...you're not going to let me inspect your lockup?"

"Not without a warrant."

"Which you won't be able to get," Harvey added, "because you don't have any probable cause to apply for one."

"His niggo judge would probably give him one," Henry suggested.

Nick didn't rise to the bait.

"In any case," he said, "the time it would take me to get a warrant would give you time to hide anything that might be incriminating. I'll just have to find another avenue."

Harvey grinned at him. "Have fun with that."

Uh. Uh.

Nick nodded and got to his feet.

"Thanks for your time. I found it...interesting."

Both Farringtons watched him without comment, Harvey grinning, Henry glaring. Nick stood there a moment longer, then turned for the door. Just as he reached it, a thought occurred to him and he looked back.

"You want to know what I think, Harvey?"

Harvey Farrington clasped his hands above his desk and shook his head.

"Marshal, I couldn't care less what you think! About anything."

As Nick walked out the door, he heard Harvey Farrington braying behind him.

Chapter 18

Government Annex - Ceres

Driving back to Government Annex, Nick was feeling depressed. He'd handled the situation badly, no question about it. The Farringtons had buttfucked him, and done it without breaking a sweat.

First of all, there'd been two of them, which gave them numerical advantage. Secondly, they did know their rights—their lockup was private property, and without proper datawork he couldn't inspect it. But what galled him the most was that Harvey Farrington had laughed at him to his face. Nick was still young but had been around some, had learned quite a bit about people. He'd listened to people talk and observed their actions—had seen some pretty terrible things, in fact—and come to the conclusion that, of all the defects in human nature, arrogance was the absolute worst. It was bad enough when a man could make fun of you to your face and you had to take it, but when that same man was a criminal, flaunting his criminality, it was very near intolerable.

Nick vowed silently that, if it was the last thing he ever did, he would see both Farringtons in prison...or die trying.

The problem was how to do it. He had tipped his hand by going there. Well, that wasn't exactly true, was it? They had also tipped theirs; by their own admission they had followed his movements from the moment he arrived on Ceres. How, exactly, had they done that?

Well, that was pretty obvious, too—within an hour of his arrival he'd tangled with Turd Murdoch, who was a prize employee at Farrington Industries, as evidenced by the fact that they spent whatever necessary to keep him out of jail. Turd had probably reported the upstart U.F. Marshal that first night.

Then, of course, they would have been advised that Nick had killed Guthrie and Willoughby at Caribou Lake (funny they hadn't mentioned that), so that was three strikes against him. Clocking Turd with his .44 would have been the fourth strike, and sleeping with Monica Maynard was apparently also a strike. Damn! How did they know about *that?*

He shook his head slowly as the tunnel ended and he emerged into Government Annex. He'd tried to keep control with the Farringtons, so they wouldn't own him. But they'd apparently owned him long before he ever showed up in their office, so...maybe he was using the wrong strategy. Maybe the better strategy was to let them keep the upper hand—or at least *think* so—until he was ready to strike.

He nodded with satisfaction. He would let *them* pursue *him*...until he caught them.

*

Nick was gratified to find David Tarpington in his office instead of the courtroom. It was always a pain having to sit in court waiting for someone to be available, but he had timed it right. Tarpington seemed glad to see him and offered him coffee again, which he declined.

"You've been a busy marshal!" Tarpington grinned as he leaned back in his chair. "I heard about Caribou Lake."

"I was lucky."

"Don't complain, lucky is good."

Nick grinned. "Got a question for you."

"Shoot."

"The other day you gave me the impression that you can tell when a man is gay."

"Sometimes." Tarpington nodded. "Usually."

"I assume you've met Harvey Farrington?"

"I have."

"Is he gay?"

Tarpington laughed. "Definitely not. He is a little odd, but I think I can safely say he isn't gay. If anything, I'd say he was asexual."

Nick looked startled. "Really!"

"Yeah. In fact, I'm not even sure he has a dick."

This time it was Nick's turn to laugh. Tarpington had a definite talent with words.

"Why do you ask? Have you met him?"

"I just left his office. I've never met anyone quite like him."

"That's probably because there *is* no one quite like him. I've never met anyone with his level of arrogance, and I've encountered a few, let me tell you."

"So have I, and I have to agree with you. What about his brother?"

"Henry? Also not gay. Quite the opposite. He has enough dick for both of them. In fact, since they're twins, Henry may have gotten Harvey's endowment along with his own."

"Why do you say that?"

"Henry likes women. A little too much."

Nick's eyes narrowed as he tried to follow the meaning.

"Sex offender?"

"In spades. Can't catch him at it, though. I've got victims, but they won't testify."

"Too afraid?"

"Terrified."

"How many?"

"Six, that I know of. I'm sure that's just the tip of the asteroid."

"Got any names for me?"

Tarpington shook his head. "Won't do you any good, Marshal. Most of them have criminal records, so even if they did testify it would be tough to get a conviction. In any case, they've made it clear that they prefer to remain silent, and I've agreed not to pursue it."

Nick's eyes narrowed further.

"The women have criminal records?"

Tarpington nodded.

"Did these rapes take place in Farrington lockup?"

"Some of them. Some took place after the women were released. Henry seems to have an instinct for which women are the most vulnerable."

"The other day you and I were talking about prisoner abuse. You didn't mention this then."

"I thought we were talking about male prisoners."

"I guess we were, but this is worse."

Tarpington shrugged. "I didn't see any point in opening this particular vial of germs. It isn't going to go anywhere."

"It will if I can find a victim who will testify."

"You won't."

Nick didn't like that answer, but couldn't fault Tarpington for being honest. He changed the subject.

"When someone is convicted in court, they serve their time at Farrington?"

"If they're not major felonies. The other mining companies also have lockups but they're much smaller. The prisoners in those facilities are usually just awaiting trial. Once the trial is over, if they're to be incarcerated, they go to Farrington."

"And the Federation pays for their incarceration?"

"Correct."

"How much?"

"Twenty-five terros a day. Per prisoner."

Nick's eyes widened as he tried to do the math, but his multiplication skills couldn't go that high.

"Someone told me that the Farrington facility can hold about three thousand men," he said.

"Maximum. The average population is around twenty-five hundred, plus a few hundred women."

"So how much does Farrington bill the Federation?"

Tarpington turned to his computer.

"Twenty-five hundred prisoners...times twenty-five terros equals..." He whistled. "Sixty-two thousand, five hundred terros *per day!*"

"Jesus Christ! And how much does that calculate to per year?"

Tarpington worked the numbers and shook his head slowly.

"Almost twenty-three million."

Nick sat stunned. Why hadn't he thought of that before? Even without the mining operation, Farrington Industries could make a fortune off the lockup facility alone.

"Next question—I've been told there are only about five thousand women on Ceres. Yet something like fifteen percent of them are in prison. What kind of crimes are they convicted of?"

"Everything from assault to theft to murder."

Nick looked skeptical. "Murder, or self-defense?"

"They usually claim self-defense, and to be honest with you I'm often inclined to believe them, but the preponderance of evidence usually overrides that."

"What kind of evidence?"

"Eyewitness testimony. It's unreliable as hell, and prone to perjury, but it's still considered valid evidence, and juries buy it."

Nick sat in thought for a moment.

"So, if I had a grudge against a woman, I could accuse her of stealing something, bribe a few drunks to swear they saw her do it, and she would go away?"

Tarpington looked uncomfortable. "Theoretically."

"And if I were Henry Farrington and wanted to rape a woman without complications, I could do the same thing; once she was in prison she'd be all mine for as long as she was locked up."

"Tied up in a pretty pink ribbon."

Nick felt his face heating with anger. "How long has this been going on?"

"Since before I came here."

"And you can't do anything about it?"

"I wish I could, but you're familiar with the legal system. Rules have to be obeyed, procedure has to be followed."

"What about a Federation investigation? Has no one called for one?"

Tarpington, looking increasingly unhappy, shook his head.

"Nick, this is Ceres, the asshole of the Solar System. No one inside the orbit of Mars gives a shit what happens to the people out here because most of them are losers anyway, or fugitives of some kind. The only thing the Federation *does* give a shit about is the flow of potable water from this asteroid to Mars and the Outer Worlds. As long as that flow is uninterrupted, nothing is going to change. And god help anyone who interrupts it."

"That's a pretty grim statement."

"That's a pretty *true* statement."

"So if I wanted to put the Farringtons out of business—"

"You'd better have someone standing by to replace them."

*

Nick walked across the hall to the defense attorney's office and found Misery Allen at her desk. She smiled as he entered and ushered him to a chair. She closed her door before taking a seat.

"I pulled the transcripts you were asking about," she told him in a confidential tone. "You aren't going to *believe* what I found."

"I think I will. I already know that she worked for Farrington..."

"Yes. She was a file clerk, and claimed that her boss tried to rape her."

"And her boss was...?" Nick was pretty sure he already knew.

Misery's eyes were wide as saucers.

"Henry Farrington!"

Chapter 19

Silence hung in the room for thirty seconds. Misery was so excited she was almost dancing in her chair, her eyes bright, a big grin on her face.

Nick let his breath out slowly. "Interesting," he said in the understatement of the day.

"What does this mean, Nick?"

"I'm not sure at this point. I need to read the trial transcripts."

"I copied them to a chip for you." She pulled it out of a drawer and handed it to him.

"Thanks."

"Can I help?"

"You already have. This could be very important."

"Why are you investigating this case?"

He shook his head. "Don't ask me that. If and when you need to know, I'll share it with you. For the moment you don't know anything about this. For your own safety."

She smiled, a little disappointed.

"Okay, Nick, but you can't blame a girl for trying."

"And I don't."

He looked at the data chip she had given him, then met her eyes again.

"Do you know someone named Stan Cramer?"

"Of course. He's an attorney for Farrington."

"You've met him?"

"Sure. There are only about thirty lawyers on Ceres, so everyone knows everyone, or at least has met everyone."

"How well do you know him?"

"Not well. He isn't the warm and fuzzy type."

"What type is he?"

"Very cold and distant. He rarely comes into the courtroom except to see the clerk, mostly to file corporate documents."

"He doesn't try cases?"

"I've never seen him litigate, but—" She pointed to the chip in Nick's hand. "—he was Jessica Garner's attorney in that second action you were asking about. The one when she got the extra time added to her sentence."

"Does that seem in any way odd to you?"

Misery nodded decisively. "It seems *very* odd. He's head of Farrington's legal department and Mrs. Garner had been convicted of assaulting one of his bosses...yet he was *her* attorney of record?" She shook her pretty head. "Makes no sense."

Nick smiled at her earnestness. She noticed.

"Why are you smiling?"

"Everything makes sense when you know all the facts."

Misery stared at him a moment, then laughed.

"You sound like a philosopher. Did you come up with that yourself?"

"Nope. It's a quote from a video lecture I heard at the Academy. Wanna know who said it?"

"Who?"

"Marshal Milligan."

*

Nick spent the rest of the afternoon on his computer cascade reading Jessica Garner's trial transcripts. The original assault trial had been a clear case of he said/she said—"he" being Henry Farrington and "she" being Jessica Garner. Farrington testified that Garner attacked him with a writing stylus when he rebuffed her attempt to seduce him. Garner testified that Farrington had tried to rape her in his office, even ripping her dress in the process, and the only defense she had was a stylus lying on the desk. She had plunged it into his chest, a painful but non-lethal wound. Farrington's security guards had beaten her senseless, leaving her bruised and bloody, and charged her with assault with intent to commit grave bodily injury.

Given the injuries sustained by Jessica Garner, the case might have been dismissed as unwinnable, except that two female office workers at Farrington testified they had witnessed the whole thing. Garner, they swore under oath, had been stalking their boss for weeks, one of them characterizing her as "practically in heat".

It had still been a tossup that might have gone either way. It was a bench trial; the case was heard by Monica Maynard, and she had rendered a guilty verdict of simple assault, a misdemeanor. She had also handed down the lightest sentence possible short of probation—three months in lockup—to be served at...Farrington lockup.

As he read the judge's sentencing comments, Nick's eyes narrowed.

Judge Maynard:

Mrs. Garner, your actions in this matter are of grave concern to the Court; assault is a serious crime, and I feel we are fortunate that your attempt to injure Mr. Farrington did not result in a more serious injury. Taking into account that this is your first offense, I am giving you the lightest sentence I can.

It is my hope that you will take the time to reflect upon your crime and evaluate your motives. You are a married woman—I find it reprehensible that you would set your sights on an upstanding citizen like Mr. Farrington and continue to stalk him even after he clearly indicated a lack of interest in your advances. So dry your tears, desist with the objections, and take your medicine. I don't ever want to see you in this courtroom again.

Nick let his breath out slowly. It appalled him that the judge had taken a stance like that. It was bad enough she had handed down a guilty verdict, in view of the lack of solid evidence—at the very least there remained a reasonable doubt—but to admonish the defendant in that manner seemed a little over the top.

Of course, Nick reminded himself, he already had a bias in the matter. His interview with Jessica Garner had prejudiced him in her favor, and at the time of sentencing most of the events she had related to him hadn't happened yet. The judge had much less information then than Nick had now, but...

Still.

He turned his attention to the second trial, in which Jessica Garner had been charged with assaulting a guard. She had not been present in the courtroom, but was instead represented by Stan Cramer, a Farrington corporate attorney. (That, all by itself, seemed rather bizarre.)

It had been a short trial, less than a half hour. Flat photos had been entered into evidence showing the injuries sustained by the guard, and he had testified as to the events in question. His name was Donald Hooley—Nick remembered him as the man with Benny Silva the first time he'd visited the courtroom. Hooley had deep, bloody bite marks on his throat from the assault, and testified that Jessica Garner had tried several times to rip his pants off and have sex with him in the three months he'd been guarding her. He had always refused, of course, and each time he refused she threatened him with snarling obscenities. On the night in question, she had skipped the usual attempt at sex and gone for his throat with her teeth.

Nick felt his pulse throb as he read the testimony—Jessica Garner had told him she bit a man's penis when he tried to copulate her orally. Yet the photos entered into evidence were of bite marks on the throat. So either she was lying, or Don Hooley wasn't really the man she had injured.

The prosecution case had gone swiftly; Hooley and one other guard testified, then Medical Examiner Shirley Chin took the stand to confirm that the bite marks matched dental impressions taken from Jessica Garner.

Finally the defense got a turn.

Judge Maynard:
Mr. Cramer, you may call your first witness.

Mr. Cramer:
If it please the Court, we have no witnesses. Mrs. Garner is unable to appear due to injuries suffered when the guards pulled her off Mr. Hooley—she is currently receiving medical care—but I have consulted with her and she wishes to plead No Contest to this charge.

Judge Maynard:
Is your client aware that a No Contest plea is equivalent to a guilty plea?

Mr. Cramer:
She is, your Honor.

Judge Maynard:
And you have no evidence to present in mitigation?

Mr. Cramer:
We do not, your Honor. We merely ask the Court to recognize that Mrs. Garner has been despondent in lockup and to take into account the fact that her husband was recently killed in a mining accident. We ask the Court to show mercy.

Judge Maynard:
Does the prosecution have anything to add before I pass judgment?

Mr. Tarpington:
The Federation has nothing to add, your Honor.

Judge Maynard:

Very well. In the absence of mitigating defense testimony, I have no option but to find the defendant guilty as charged in Count 1 of the information. While it is regrettable that the defendant's husband met a tragic death, that in no way excuses the defendant's actions in this case. This is a second offense, of a similar nature to the first. The defendant is hereby sentenced to an additional twelve months in lockup, to be served consecutive to the original sentence.

Next case.

Nick leaned back in his chair with a weary sigh and rubbed a hand across his face. *Un-fucking-believable!* He was no courtroom expert, had yet to testify in a real proceeding, so he had a lot to learn, but everything he had just read screamed *foul!* His sense of right and wrong was severely bruised by the contents of those transcripts...

...not least of all by the words of Monica Maynard herself.

He made a mental note to check the hospital records for the date of the attack and find out if a prison guard other than Donald Hooley had been treated for bites on the genitalia.

And he needed to talk to David Tarpington, but was reluctant to do so. He had promised Jessica Garner to keep her name out of his investigation, and he couldn't do that if he went around asking questions of everyone in sight. What was painfully clear to him now was that the Farrington brothers were far more powerful than they had any right to be, and they were also corrupt. Clearly they had people in their pockets, but the question was...who and how many? Tarpington seemed like an upright guy, and probably was, but Nick couldn't gamble with Jessica Garner's life.

At the moment, aside from Misery Allen, he didn't know whom he could trust.

"You gonna stay here all night?"

Nick looked up in surprise. He'd been so intent on his musings that he'd forgot Marshal Milligan was still in the office. He glanced at the front door and noticed that it was getting dark outside—Ceres turned the "sunlight" down at five in the evening, and completely off at eight, to simulate the Terrestrial day-night cycle.

Milligan was on his feet, stretching. He grunted as his back popped and let out a sigh of satisfaction. He'd shut down his cascade and was looking at Nick.

"Can I talk to you about something?" Nick asked.

"That's what I'm here for."

Nick leaned back and gazed at his mentor a moment, wondering how best to present his thoughts.

"I think Farrington Industries is dirty."

Milligan's eyebrows shot up.

"Do you?"

"Yes, sir, I do."

"Dirty how?"

"In every way. Their security people are mostly goons, for one thing, and I've uncovered evidence of not only prisoner abuse but severe prisoner mistreatment as well. I'm looking at a case right now where I believe they framed one of their employees for a crime, and Dave Tarpington tells me that Henry Farrington is a rapist."

"Is that all you have?" Milligan's grin was ironic.

"The body count from their lockup facility is way too high, and the cause of death in many cases isn't consistent with the medical records for the dead. The M.E. is too scared to talk to me and I'm starting to think that Farrington is exerting more control over this asteroid than meets the eye."

Milligan's grin faded and he sat on the edge of Sandy Beech's desk, arms crossed.

"Go on."

Nick sighed wearily and rubbed his eyes.

"Right now that's all I feel safe telling you, but—"

"You're afraid to tell *me?*" Milligan showed real surprise for the first time since Nick had met him. "You don't seriously think *I'm* on their payroll, do you?"

"No, of course not. What I mean is that if I speak out of turn at the wrong moment I might get someone killed."

"Like who?"

"The employee that I told you had been framed? I've given my word to keep her name out of it, yet she pointed me toward what I believe is a serious problem."

Milligan nodded slowly. Protecting confidential informants was standard practice.

"Okay, I'll buy that for now. What else?"

"From people I've talked to today, including Sandy Beech, I'm getting the feeling that a lot more people than me know about this problem, but because Farrington is the prime mover of water to the Outer Worlds, nobody is willing to do anything about it."

"Good theory. What's your solution?"

Nick shook his head. "I don't have one."

"Yet."

"Right. I don't have one *yet*. But if I'm right about what's going on, then someone has to take action."

"What kind of action?"

"I don't know. That's why I need your help. You've been out here a while. You know things about this place that I don't."

Milligan studied him a moment, rubbing his chin.

"When I got here," he said, "Farrington was already king cock. Had been for several years."

"But how did they get that way? They came here with nothing, as far as I can tell. No money, no investment capital. And in two or three years they're running the whole goddamn asteroid."

"Why don't you ask them?"

"I did."

Milligan's eyes widened again, this time in near shock.

"You've been to Farrington?"

"Yes, sir, this afternoon. Sat in Harvey Farrington's office while he and his brother insulted me."

"You should have insulted them right back."

"I tried to." Nick grimaced. "They're a lot better at it than I am."

"They've had a lot more practice," Milligan grumbled.

Nick brightened a little. "What do you know about them?"

"Not a great deal. They rarely venture out of that cave they have over there, and they don't talk to the common folk...like law enforcement. Your interview with them is a rare and newsworthy event.

"From what I've observed, they represent everything that's wrong with capitalism. They're more like feudal lords than anything else. If they could legally use slave labor, they'd do it."

"Do you know how they got their start? The business, I mean."

"I don't. Word is they bought up two or three companies that were faltering, consolidated them, and moved forward from there."

Nick compressed his lips in frustration.

"But you can find out," Milligan told him. "All that stuff is a matter of public record. Farrington is a Mars corporation, so dig into the Martian databases and start looking at records. You should be able to find out which companies they purchased and the details of transaction. I'm not sure what good it will do you..."

"If I can find any evidence of foul play, then I'll have something to work with."

Milligan looked skeptical. "And what will you do with it?"

"If my suspicions pan out, I'd like to put them in prison—and out of business."

Milligan shook his head.

"Don't forget, they're the prime mover of water to the Outer Worlds. You said it yourself."

"Yes, sir, but why can't the Federation put them under receivership and continue operations until a buyer turns up?"

"Mm. That might work." The old man yawned and stood up. "You're biting off an awfully big chunk, Walker. I hope you can chew it." He started toward the door. "Good night."

"G'night, Marshal."

Chapter 20

Nick spent two more hours on the computer, until his eyes were burning. He checked the hospital database and found no record of a prison guard with bite injuries to his genitalia. Nor did he find any record of Donald Hooley's bite wounds on the neck. Curious—Hooley's injuries had not been life threatening and could have been carefully inflicted with the help of a female (or even male) employee—but the other guard should have received medical treatment, if for no other reason than to preserve his manhood. Jessica Garner hadn't told Nick the man's name, if she even knew it, so without interviewing her again there was no way to check further.

On a hunch, he pulled up the Farrington home page and discovered that Farrington Industries had its own infirmary. Records from that facility were private and unavailable...which meant that Jessica's story could not be verified one way or another. Nor could Donald Hooley's injuries.

Setting that question aside, he logged onto MarsNet and began a records search for corporations. Farrington Industries popped up after a simple search and he drilled down to see what he might learn. The records were clinical and detailed, including copies of original document filings and a list of transactions that left a clear trail of how the firm established.

Nick was no expert on business matters, but for what he was looking at he didn't need to be; Farrington Industries had been created effective January 1, 0431 (CC), just over nine years earlier. The company had come together quickly, it appeared, as the result of the buyouts of three other mining companies: Ceres Creek, the smallest of the three; Ceres Ice; and the largest, Agua Solar. Each had been purchased after filing bankruptcy—Farrington had paid nine cents on the terro for them.

Nick noted the names of the people who had owned those enterprises and searched for them as well. One appeared to be deceased, another had returned to Terra...but Esteban Castillo, CEO of Agua Solar, was living on Mars.

Refining his search, Nick pursued Castillo through MarsNet and sighed with disappointment; Castillo was alive, but barely. Less than a year after losing his mining operation he had suffered a stroke and was now living on an intensive-care satellite orbiting the Red Planet. His condition was so grim he couldn't even speak, so it seemed unlikely he would be of much help.

Nick returned to the Agua Solar page and tried looking for other corporate officers. His eyebrows lifted when he got to the Chief Financial Officer...her name was Carmen Castillo-Bernal—Castillo's daughter—and she lived on the same satellite as her father, which apparently provided quarters for patients' family members.

Nick glanced at his watch—it was almost six-thirty, but that meant nothing; Ceres time was simulated to match the orbital rotation of Terra, humanity's mother planet, but Mars had its own rotation and he had no idea what time it might be where Carmen lived. Only one way to find out...he would have to settle with Milligan later on the expense.

He placed a call.

* * *

Carmen Castillo-Bernal was an attractive, if somewhat severe looking woman in her late forties. Her thick black hair was streaked with grey and a few lines eroded her face, but she was still a striking woman. She peered at him through hard black eyes as he gazed at her face on the subspace comm screen.

"Did you say United Federation Marshal?" she demanded.

"Yes, Ma'am. I'm calling from the Ceres office."

Her eyes widened a fraction and her lips parted.

"Ceres!"

"Yes, Ma'am. I have no idea what time it is where you are, so I hope this call isn't an inconvenience."

Her momentary surprise vanished and her face hardened. "What do you want with me?"

Nick hesitated a brief moment—he had a lot to explain and she didn't seem terribly receptive. He would have to get her attention quickly or she might disconnect.

"How would you like to get Agua Solar back?"

* * *

"Is this connection secure?" Carmen Castillo asked.

Nick nodded. "It is on this end. Why do you ask?"

"Because that *cucaracha pendeja* threatened to kill me if I ever told anyone."

"*¿De cual cucaracha hablas?*"

Her eyes widened again, more pleasantly.

"*¿Tu eres latino?*"

"My mother is," he said with a friendly smile. "*Ella me enseñó el idioma.*"

"You don't look it."

"My dad was *gringo*. I look more like him."

"*Bueno.*" Her iron exterior seemed to relax a little. "To answer your question, the *cucaracha* I'm talking about is Harvey Farrington. He stole my father's company and laughed in our face while he did it."

"Can you prove that?"

"Not in a Ceres court, no."

"What does that mean?"

"It means there is no justice on Ceres. It means I shouldn't even be talking to you."

Nick tensed, sensing he might lose her.

"*Señora*, I just got here four days ago. I'm not part of whatever establishment you're familiar with. The reason I'm calling you is that I'm trying to figure out just what's going on around here, who's really running this place, and see if I can do something about it."

"How did you get my name?"

"I'm digging into Farrington to find out how they got to be so powerful. I went back to the beginning, found the name of your company, your father, and you."

She stared at him for long seconds, probably a hundred terros worth of transmission time. Finally she nodded slowly.

"What do you want to know?"

"Everything. I wish we could sit down face to face but I doubt if I could get authorization to travel to where you are."

"As long as the connection is secure, I'll talk to you."

He nodded. "Thank you. I understand that Farrington grew out of the ashes of three companies, yours being the largest. Can you tell me how that happened?"

She nodded, leaned forward, and spoke earnestly.

"Agua Solar was founded over a hundred years ago by my great grandfather. It's been in the family ever since, and we were publicly traded. Farrington came out of nowhere about twelve years ago and decided he wanted to buy us out. We were not for sale, and he had no money anyway, so we turned him down."

Nick's heart skipped as he realized this was what he'd been looking for. He made notes as she talked.

"Then things started to happen."

He frowned. "What kind of things?"

"Accidents. Suspicious deaths."

"Can you be more specific?"

She sighed. "Did you ever hear of the *Agua Express* disaster?"

He strained his memory, but the words didn't ring a bell.

"When did it happen?"

"In Four Twenty-nine."

"No, I'm sorry. I would have been about thirteen then, and I never listened to the news. What happened?"

"*Agua Express* was one of our water freighters carrying ice to Titan. It disappeared between the orbits of Jupiter and Saturn on an outbound voyage. At first it just went silent, and we hoped it was nothing more than a communication failure, but when it never arrived at Titan, an emergency was declared and the Space Force went looking for it. They found it drifting on past Saturn, toward the orbit of Neptune. It carried a crew of twelve, and they were all dead."

"Depressurization?"

"No. There was a time bomb on board, one that released a massive quantity of carbon monoxide. The explosive portion of the bomb destroyed the damage control computer, so when the gas was released there was no defense, no overrides, nothing. The crew died a quiet, painless death, but they still died."

Nick felt the hairs on his neck prickle.

"Let me guess—whoever placed the bomb was never caught?"

"That's right. But two days after the disaster hit the headlines, Harvey Farrington showed up again and renewed his offer to purchase Agua Solar."

"That looks suspicious," Nick said, "but it proves nothing. It's purely circumstantial."

"That's what we were told. The loss of that freighter was a blow, but it didn't put us under. It turned out to be a warning of things to come. Over the next few months we had several 'accidents' in our mining operation, everything from exploding drill heads to a malfunctioning ice crusher that flooded an offline storage tank undergoing maintenance. In every case people were killed, and before long our employees started bailing out. On top of that, Federation safety inspectors landed on our backs and started shutting things down until they could determine if we were criminally negligent."

Nick's mouth compressed as he began to detect a pattern. He continued to scribble while she talked.

"In the meantime, the Solar Press was trumpeting our misfortunes and one of the Outer Worlds was threatening lawsuits because their population needed the water and we were unable to fulfill our contracts. How could we, with the inspectors all over us?"

Nick glanced at the screen in time to see a glitter of tears in her eyes.

"All of that went on for the better part of a year," she said, "but what really finished us was when the investors began pulling out. Stock prices took a nosedive, but nobody was buying."

"And Farrington came to see you again?"

She nodded. "He brought his lawyer. They already had the papers drawn up, and all we had to do was sign."

"For nine cents on the terro."

"Yes." She brushed at her eyes and cleared her throat, her voice turning hard again. "The other two companies had similar experiences, and they caved even before we did. By the time we walked away Farrington had control of all three, including all real property and fixed assets. They took over our fleet and our contracts and the accidents miraculously stopped. You tell me, Marshal—was all of that a coincidence?"

"Sure doesn't sound like it."

"No. It doesn't."

"You said Harvey had no money."

"Not when he first showed up. But when he came to see us the last time he did."

"How did that happen?"

"I have no idea."

"What was it you said earlier, about no justice on Ceres? What were you referring to?"

"Two years after we were forced out, Farrington filed suit against us, claiming that we had hidden some liquid assets during the sale. It was ridiculous, of course, because we were deep in debt and barely got off that rock with the clothes we were wearing. But they wanted ninety million terros they claimed we had held back from them, and they had auditors on the case trying to find out where we had hidden the cash.

"My father was already ill, so he couldn't do anything about it, but I went back to Ceres to see what could be done. Judge Boxner had always been fair, and I was sure he would hear our petition, but when I got there I found out he was dead. His replacement acted like *I* was a criminal for even filing the petition!"

Dead! Monica had told him the old judge retired.

"What was the petition for?"

"I was asking for an injunction of relief against Farrington and requesting an investigation of their business practices. I also wanted an independent audit of our books."

"So what happened?"

"The judge called a hearing of all parties to settle the matter. Harvey Farrington showed up with his lawyer and laughed at me and mocked me and sneered at my father's illness, and then threatened me with further lawsuits unless I coughed up the money. And the judge did nothing about it. Did nothing, said nothing, and in the end denied my petition."

Nick rubbed his face wearily.

"Jesus! What was the outcome?"

"The auditors never found any money—because there isn't any—and I had to go even further into debt to defend us against that monster. We had a few thousand a year income from an insurance policy but that all got sucked up and left us with nothing. We're now living on welfare from the Martian state and I have to work in the office here on the satellite just to keep my apartment, such as it is."

"Did Farrington drop the lawsuit?"

"Temporarily. I live day to day with the threat that he'll renew it. He still claims we owe him money."

Nick sat back in his chair, anger churning in his guts. Carmen Castillo could be feeding him a line, but he didn't think so. He'd always been pretty good at reading people and her body language told him she was truly distressed by the whole thing.

"Marshal, did you mean what you said in the beginning? About us getting our company back?" Her dark eyes were tense with hope.

"I don't know, *señora*. But from everything I've learned so far, Farrington has got to go. Somebody has to take over when they do, and it would only be proper if that someone was you."

"I don't have any money, if that's what is required."

"I can't make you any promises, but if I get my way, you won't need any."

She stared at him for a moment, then sagged slightly, as if it were too much to hope for.

"I want to thank you for talking to me," he said. "I'll keep you up to date if I can accomplish anything on this end."

"Thank you." She smiled briefly. She was a very pretty woman when she smiled.

"One more question, if you don't mind?"

"Of course."

"You mentioned Farrington's lawyer. What was his name?"

"Stanley Cramer."

Nick nodded, not at all surprised. He was going to have to meet Mr. Cramer one of these days.

Soon.

"Oh—and the judge who treated you so poorly? What was his name?"

Carmen Castillo's face twisted with anger.

"It was a woman. Judge Monica Maynard."

Chapter 21

Centerville - Ceres

For the first time since arriving on Ceres, Nick Walker slept in his own bed in his own hotel room. He'd hardly spent any time there, just dropping in for a quick change of clothes. But tonight, weary beyond belief, he slid between the sheets and closed his eyes, vaguely comforted by the tight quarters, as if in all the universe he had only this one tiny space to call his own.

In a very real sense, that was true. He'd left home at eighteen, going straight into the Star Marines, and while serving had owned practically nothing; from there to the U.F. Marshal Academy, where again he lived a dormitory life...and now, a rented room provided by the Federation as a perq to his salary. It wasn't really "his", but he could pretend it was, at least for the moment.

Tired as he was, sleep was slow in coming. In four days he'd been through a whirlwind of events and conversations, had killed two men, beaten a couple of others, and been threatened with death. One thing for sure—life as a U.F. Marshal hadn't been boring. He had a vague sense that he was in over his head, in really deep water, but one lesson he'd learned in the Star Marines was to keep moving forward, present your face to the enemy, and never give up. Right or wrong, he wouldn't give up now, either—it simply wasn't in his nature.

But as he lay staring into the darkness, he began to have serious doubts whether he could accomplish all that lay before him. The problems he'd uncovered, if his assessments were correct, had been around for years; other men, like Marshal Milligan and David Tarpington, had either never recognized them or never dealt with them. Nick had been here four days— did he seriously think he could accomplish what they had not?

He didn't know. He was a rookie marshal, after all—maybe he hadn't discovered his limitations yet, and everything would come crashing down when he did...but for the moment he knew only one course of action—keep moving forward.

Improvise!

Friday, August 9, 0440 (CC) — Government Annex - Ceres

The coffee was fresh when he arrived at the office on Friday, and so was the cigar smoke. Beech and Murray were both there, chatting about solarball scores, and greeted Nick when he arrived. Nick had never been a sports fan, so didn't join the conversation until he had a hot cup in his hand, and changed the subject abruptly.

"I hate to break up all this auto-eroticism, but I have a question."

Murray grimaced in annoyance but Beech laughed. Milligan merely stared at him.

"Whatever happened to Judge Boxner?" Nick asked.

A moment of silence followed the question, and everyone looked away, as if the subject were taboo.

"I'm sorry," Nick said, "I didn't think the question was that hard."

Milligan cleared his throat with a growl, but Murray spoke up.

"He's dead."

"I heard he retired."

"Nope." Sandy Beech shook his head. "Shot in the back. Laser pistol, late at night, no witnesses."

"You're telling me the case was never solved?"

"Remains open to this day," Murray said. "It was a class 3 laser, the kind that everyone carries if they carry at all. You can't do ballistics on a laser beam."

Nick considered that a moment. "When did it happen?"

"Eight, nine years ago. The crime report's in the database, if you want to look it up."

Nick nodded. "Thanks. I will."

"How come you're asking about him?" Milligan asked.

"I heard the name last night. Wondered why he stepped down."

"Well...he didn't."

* * *

After finishing their coffee, Beech and Murray left to do whatever they did all day and Nick sat down at his desk again. Milligan waited until he was deep in the database and spun around to face him.

"You making any headway on the Farrington thing?"

Nick looked up. "Do you need me on something else?"

"No, not at the moment. If you can do any good on this, then keep going. But I'd like to stay up on your progress."

Nick told him about the call to Carmen Castillo-Bernal, causing Milligan to frown as he anticipated the subspace charges.

"That's why I asked about Judge Boxner," Nick said when he finished his tale. "I hadn't heard the name before and was just curious. Mrs. Castillo said Boxner was a fair man, but she wasn't so generous with Judge Maynard."

"Well, I told you to watch out for Maynard. She runs hot and cold, and you never know from one day to the next which it's going to be." He got up and walked to the coffee pot, refilling his cup.

"What do you know about Stanley Cramer?"

Milligan turned in surprise.

"Cramer! Shit, he's worse than Harvey Farrington. Slick son of a bitch—arrogant, conniving, merciless."

"Crooked?"

"Undoubtedly. Trouble with lawyers is, they know the law better than we do, so they can operate on the dark side of it for years and never get caught. If we try to get something on them we usually run into starcrete walls."

"What do you know about his background?"

"Not much. He came out here with Harvey Farrington, or maybe a little later, and sort of took over the pond. No one likes him but he doesn't seem to give a shit. He takes care of his client and, apparently, his client takes care of him."

"How important is he to the Farrington operation?"

"Hm. Don't know for sure, but if I had to guess, I'd say he's the real brains of the outfit. For all his in-your-face snobbery, Harvey is about as intelligent as a rock crab. He has absolutely nothing on the ball except a gift for talking shit, and I suspect Cramer even has to hold classes on that so Harvey doesn't get confused."

"What about Henry?"

"The dangerous one. Harvey takes point on everything, but he's completely transparent. Henry is the scorpion in your shoe."

Nick poured more coffee and returned to his computer cascade. He looked up the crime reports on Judge Boxner's death. As the others had stated, it was a cold case, completely unsolved, with no witnesses and not even a suspect.

Nick moved on to news reports of the incident and learned that the Ceres court had remained closed for six days after the killing, until a Federation court on Mars had appointed a local attorney to the bench. That appointment, of course, was Monica Maynard, but what surprised Nick was the glowing recommendation she received from another prominent local attorney. It was this endorsement which apparently convinced the Martian Judiciary to confirm her; his name was Stanley Cramer.

* * *

By midmorning Nick felt he was at a crossroad, with no idea which direction to take. He was accumulating evidence at a staggering rate, to the point that he was starting to suffer information overload. Some of it was little more than gossip, yet he was convinced it was all important...somehow. The question was, what could he do with it?

More to the point, what did he *want* to do?

Frowning as he narrowed his focus, he opened a text document and started making a list. Included in the list were a corrupt corporation and its crooked lawyer, prisoner abuse by Farrington Security, a space freighter with a murdered crew, falsification of death certificates, probable sabotage in the interest of affecting a hostile takeover, an unspecified number of deaths as a result of that sabotage, a murdered judge...

He was starting to lose track. Some of these events had happened several years apart, so were they even connected? But how could they *not* be connected? Everything seemed to be centered around, or pointed to, Farrington Industries. Looking at Ceres through the unobstructed eyes of a newcomer, Nick was seeing a cancer...a cancer that was slowly eating away at the legal and social stability of the entire asteroid, and that cancer was Farrington Industries. Yet not a single person who had been here any length of time—not Milligan, not Tarpington, not Monica—had done a thing about it as far as he could tell. Could they not see the nebula for the stars?

At the bottom of the list he added two more names— Jessica Garner and her husband Scott. Below that he added the word "solution:", and sat in thought for several minutes. Finally, he completed the phrase: "shut down Farrington".

The only question remaining was...*how?*

* * *

When Nick reached the second floor of the courthouse he saw David Tarpington coming down the stairs from the floor above. The tall blond prosecutor grinned with pleasure and halted at the foot of the steps.

"Howdy, Marshal! What are you up to this morning?"

Nick returned the smile but nodded up the steps, where Misery Allen was making her way down.

"I need to have a few words with your opponent."

Tarpington glanced up with a grin, then turned back to Nick, leaning in confidentially.

"Don't noise this around, but I think she has the hots for you."

"Really! You think so?"

Tarpington nodded. "Trust me, I'm a trained observer."

Nick laughed and started to turn away. Tarpington caught his sleeve.

"Hey, if you aren't doing anything tonight, I'd like to invite you to have a drink with me. I'll show you a tavern that's a lot nicer than the Open Airlock."

Nick gazed at him a moment. "Do I have to wear leather or anything?"

Tarpington hooted with laughter.

"Well, that's up to you. There will be a few leather freaks in attendance."

Nick shrugged. "Sure, why not? Can I bring a date?"

"You mean, like a *female* date?"

"Yeah. My favorite defense attorney, for example."

Tarpington's eyes gleamed with suppressed laughter.

"If you can convince her to go in there, you bet. She'll be a lot safer than you will."

"Okay. I'll drop by around five o'clock."

Nick left Tarpington and joined Misery Allen, who had stopped to wait for him. She smiled brightly and Nick realized that Tarpington was right—she was practically glowing.

"Hi, Nick! What're you doing here?"

"I came to see you."

"Well, you timed it perfectly. Court just let out for the morning. Come on to my office."

Two minutes later they entered her office and she closed the door. As she turned toward her desk she bumped into him, thinking he'd taken a chair when he hadn't.

"Oops! I'm sorry."

"Don't be." Nick took the document case from her hand and set it on the floor, then put his hands on her shoulders. She looked up at him expectantly, almost breathless, her eyes suddenly wide. "I don't want you to take this the wrong way," he said, "because it means absolutely nothing."

"Okay...take what the wrong way?"

"This."

He wrapped both arms around her and pulled her against him, kissing her firmly. He felt her tremble for a few seconds, then she relaxed and slid her arms around his neck, returning the kiss with passion. He held her for several seconds, then pulled back slowly.

"This doesn't mean we're engaged or anything," he said. "But I've been wanting to do that since the first time I saw you."

She teetered slightly, breathing hard.

"You have?"

"Yeah. Sorry if I've sexually harassed you or anything."

Misery laughed, more a release of tension than humor, and pulled him back down, resuming the kiss for another ten seconds.

"And I've been wanting to do *that*," she said. "Not very professional, I'm afraid."

"Not for me either."

She walked on around the desk and sat down. He took a chair facing her. She still had a glow in her eyes as she smiled at him.

"So, Nick, other than getting that out of the way, what's up?"

He leaned back in the chair and stretched, then cracked his knuckles.

"I need to get inside Farrington lockup."

Her smile faded slowly. "You'll need to see Judge Maynard for that. I doubt if they'll let you in without a warrant."

"They won't, but I don't think Maynard is going to give me one. I don't have enough probable cause, at least not that I can reveal to the judge."

Misery nodded. "You haven't told her about Mrs. Garner?"

"I haven't told anyone except you. And I have to keep it that way for the time being."

"I don't see how I can help you."

"Well, I was wondering...do you ever visit clients out there? You know, defense prep, pretrial stuff, things like that?"

"Sure, sometimes."

"Do you have any interviews planned for today?"

"No, I don't have anything immediately pending."

Nick grimaced, drumming his fingers on the chair arm.

"Can you invent something? Maybe ask some redundant questions just to clarify a point of evidence?"

Misery nodded, looking slightly confused. "Sure, I guess I could do that. But how would that help you?"

Nick grinned. "I can't get in to inspect the place without a warrant, but I don't think they can keep me out if you need a bodyguard."

Her eyebrows arched. "A bodyguard!"

"Of course. Hasn't anyone threatened your life lately?"

She laughed and shook her head. "No!"

He twisted his face into a comic caricature of a villain and lowered his voice to a growl. "If you don't hire me as your bodyguard, I'll *kill* you!"

Misery laughed delightedly.

"Okay, now my life has been threatened! Will you please protect me from...yourself?"

"Of course I will. I will follow you all over Ceres."

"When do you want to do this?"

"Whenever you have the time. I know you're busy."

She glanced at her watch. "I have about two and a half hours right now. Court resumes at one o'clock." She glanced up. "You aren't going to see much, you know. The interview rooms are near the visitor's entrance. You'll never get near a cellblock."

He shrugged. "I'll take whatever I can get."

"They'll take your gun."

He snorted. "They'll try."

"No, I'm serious—they will."

He considered that a moment, then spread his hands. "Whatever it takes."

Farrington Industries - Ceres

Browning, the young guard at Farrington Industries, gazed warily at Nick when Misery Allen drove up to the gate and announced her intent to interview a client.

"What's he doing here?" Browning pointed at Nick.

The pretty lawyer glanced at Nick as if surprised to see him sitting beside her.

"Oh, this is Marshal Walker. He's here to protect me."

Browning looked even less thrilled. "Protect you from what?"

"I had a death threat this morning. I asked Marshal Walker to accompany me just in case it came from someone at the lockup."

Browning stood a moment in indecision.

"I have to make a call."

Three minutes later Benny Silva was at the gate, looking like a thundercloud.

"What the fuck are you doing back here?" he asked Nick.

"The lady needs protection," Nick said with a smile. "Someone threatened to kill her, and I can't let that happen."

"The call didn't come from here!"

"Who said it was a call? It could have been a letter or a courier message. How did you know it was a call?"

Silva's face darkened another shade. "You can't come in here without a warrant."

Nick pushed the door open and stepped out of the E-car. Now he was staring down at Silva from two inches of altitude.

"You said I need a warrant to inspect the place. Well, I'm not here to inspect, I'm here to protect. I don't need a warrant for that."

Silva seemed to swell. "I can't let you in."

"You can't stop me. If you try, I'll arrest you for obstruction." Nick leaned toward him and lowered his voice. "And I'll lock you up at one of your competitors' facilities."

Silva glared at him, blinked several times, and glanced over his shoulder.

"Goddammit!" he hissed, "you're gonna get me fired!"

"Awww." Nick looked sad. "I'd hate to do that. You might have to find *honest* work."

Silva's face fused beet red, his fists clenched and unclenched.

"Don't even think about it," Nick said. "If you try it, you won't even be able to crawl away."

Silva took a slow step back, took a deep breath, and let it out slowly.

"I'll have to accompany you."

Nick shrugged. "Fine."

"And I'll need your weapon."

Nick shook his head. "No, you won't. Nobody needs my weapon except me."

"It's policy."

"Fuck policy. You're not even a real cop. You will *not* dictate terms to a Federation Marshal."

Silva's expression hardened again, his breathing seemed labored.

"Then I can't let you in."

Nick sighed and shook his head. "We're going in circles here. Go back to the part where you said you would accompany me."

"Can't do it."

"Browning!" Nick glanced at the young guard. "Open the goddamn gate before I decide to kill your supervisor here."

"Don't do it, Browning!" Silva shouted.

Browning's eyes sprang wide as he stared from one man to the other.

Nick's gaze focused on Silva, his eyes narrowed.

"Ten seconds, Browning! Before I put out both of his eyes."

Browning faltered. Even Misery Allen looked suddenly scared.

"Nine!" Nick counted. "Eight! Seven!"

Browning spun to open the gate.

"Browning!"

Silva lunged at Nick. Nick's left fist crashed into his temple and he staggered sideways. Silva turned and tried to renew his attack, but Nick hit him again. Silva stopped, shaking his head, looking dazed.

"You're under arrest," Nick told him, "for assaulting a Federation Marshal. Place your hands behind your back." Nick reached for his E-cuffs.

Silva was not a large man, only medium height with a stocky build. His power was mostly in his attitude, so Nick was taken off guard when he roared like a bull and charged again, driving Nick straight into the side of the E-car. Nick's back slammed into the metal vehicle with bruising force, and pain shot up his spine into his neck. All the air whooshed out of his lungs and for a second he thought he might pass out. The only thing that saved him was that Silva had used a solarball tackle, which put him too close to do further injury without taking a step back, and he was off balance. They were practically hugging, so Nick had time to grip his laser pistol before Silva stumbled back.

Silva swung his right fist into Nick's jaw, but before he could draw back for a second blow Nick shot him through the foot. Silva howled and toppled sideways, giving Nick time to spring forward and cuff him.

Silva was still yelling in pain, though the laser wound wasn't even bleeding. The shot had burned through the side of his foot, cauterizing as it went, and probably broken a bone or two, but that was all. It was debilitating, but hardly life threatening. Nick searched him for weapons but found only his company laser pistol. Spotting the key ring on Silva's belt, he recognized the large round key that Silva had used to send the elevator to the top floor of the Farrington tower, and plucked it off the ring. Taking it was probably illegal, but Silva had attacked him, so he would worry about that later. He put the key in his pocket and hauled Silva to his feet.

"Do you still need to see that client?" he asked Misery.

"No, it can wait."

"Let's head over to System Springs."

He shoved Silva into the back seat of the E-car.

Chapter 22

Government Annex - Ceres

Judge Monica Maynard was sitting at her desk finishing her lunch. As she ate she was studying briefs pertaining to the trial that was to start at one o'clock. It was another assault case, this one complicated by the fact that three combatants were accusing each other of starting it, with conflicting eyewitness testimony. It was all bullshit anyway, she thought, because most of the men on this rock were just wild animals with prehistoric mentalities; trying to keep the peace was futile. Justice would be much better served if Natural Selection just took its course and allowed the weaker ones to be eliminated, exponentially reducing the threat to society.

But...the law was the law, and she had her duty to perform. She took another bite of sandwich and flipped a page, still reading.

Her desk comm chimed.

"Yes?"

"Call for you, your Honor. Line Ten."

Monica's sandwich stuck in her throat. There was no "line Ten"—Ceres was too small for that much comm traffic; she only had three active lines for normal chatter—but there was one other line, a dedicated number that only one person ever used. It was dubbed Line Ten.

"Thank you."

Monica wiped her fingers on a napkin, then wiped her mouth. Taking a deep breath, she slipped on a headset and activated the call. This line had no video, and she was thankful for that.

"This is Monica."

The voice on the other end was harsh, male, and as usual, angry.

"Are you alone?"

"Yes. What do you want?"

"I understand you're screwing that new marshal."

Monica's blood ran cold; she had to swallow hard.

"How do you know about that?"

A cynical laugh filled her ears. "There isn't anything about you that I *don't* know, your Honor. You should know that by now."

She closed her eyes, dread flowing into her bloodstream.

"What do you want?"

"I want you to get even closer to the young prick."

"Why? What's he doing?"

"He's making himself a liability. You know where that leads, so if you care anything about him, find out what he's up to and make him stop, or send him off in another direction."

Monica swallowed again, to control her nerves.

"I'm not sure I can do that. He's young and ambitious—and smart. If I try to steer him he'll see right through it."

"He's also horny, and he likes niggo women."

Monica's hands clenched into fists. "Goddamn you—"

"*Fuck* you, your Honor. Don't forget who put you where you are! And don't *ever* forget what life is like in lockup." A grim chuckle followed that statement. "You have your orders. Make it happen."

* * *

"You never did get into the lockup," Misery said as she pulled into the courthouse parking lot. She and Nick exited the car and walked toward the building.

"Maybe I don't need to," he said. "At least not right now."

"Then what did you accomplish?"

He shrugged. "I got myself a stellar headache, for one. And my back hurts."

She smiled and slid a hand up his back, rubbing gently. "Poor baby."

"Don't get too mushy on me, counselor. I told you that kiss meant absolutely nothing."

"A girl can dream, can't she?"

He slid an arm around her and gave her a squeeze. "Sorry, but I'm off the market."

"For how long?"

"Until further notice. However..." He stopped walking and turned to face her. "Tarpington invited me for a drink this evening. I'd like you to come with me."

Her dark eyes searched his face. "As your attorney?" she asked, only half kidding.

"No. As my date."

Her smile returned and her eyes sparkled. "You're asking me out on a date?"

"Yeah. To a gay bar."

Misery laughed and swatted at him. "You're unbelievable, do you know that?"

He grinned. "So what do you say?"

"I say yes. You may need me to fend off some of David's horny friends."

"That's what I was thinking. Just don't let go of my hand."

"And what happens after the drink?"

His eyes twinkled. "Oh, I was thinking we might do something a little more...hetero."

She laughed again. "You should be so lucky."

"Yeah, I should. That's what they called me in the Star Marines—Lucky Nick."

"Really?"

"No."

*

They parted company in the parking lot and Nick returned to his office. He sat down and did the datawork on Benny Silva's arrest, then walked back to the courthouse to see Dave Tarpington. Tarpington wasn't available, as court was in session, so Nick filed a copy of the datawork with Howard, the old law clerk, then went upstairs and took a seat in the courtroom. His back was aching and his head still throbbed, so it felt good to just sit still for a little while. He had nothing immediately pending and could afford the time.

The trial was proceeding smoothly, with a witness on the stand giving testimony. Half a dozen spectators sat to one side, the first time Nick had seen anyone in the spectator seats, but he paid little attention. He didn't know what the trial was about and didn't care, but hoped for a recess so he could talk to Tarpington. Twice he caught Judge Maynard gazing in his direction but her expression never changed. He wondered absently if she would be upset when she found out he was taking Misery out on a date, but pushed it out of his mind. Monica had thrown herself at him, and though he found it pleasant, she in no way had any claim on him. Neither did Misery, which he had tried to make clear this morning.

Forty minutes later, testimony halted while the attorneys began arguing over a point of law. Nick sensed a recess in the making and left the courtroom before it was called, pacing about in the hallway and stretching to ease his aches. Barely two minutes later the front door opened and Tarpington came out.

"Got a minute?" Nick asked as he started for the stairs.

"Sure, but court reconvenes in ten. What's up?"

Nick followed him down to his office and handed him a copy of the arrest report.

"I know I don't dictate to you," he said, "but I'd like this man charged with obstruction, interfering with an investigation, and assault on a Federation officer. Hit him as hard as you can."

Tarpington scanned the arrest report, then looked up with clear blue eyes.

"The assault seems clear enough, but I can't make the other charges stick. There's nothing here to back them up. Maynard will throw them out."

"They don't have to stick. I just want to turn up the heat a little."

Tarpington's half grin showed a mixture of mystery and mischief. "What the hell are you up to, Nick? This is going to ignite a firestorm over there."

"That's what I'm hoping. They sit over there in that goddamn fortress like a cage of coiled snakes and I want to flush them out."

Tarpington handed the report back to him. "You may not like it when they flush."

Nick grinned and stuck the copy into his pocket.

"Oh, I think I will." He got to his feet. "But they won't."

*

The Marshal's office was empty when he returned. Milligan had gone somewhere and he had no idea where the other two went or what they did. He sat down at his desk and tried to organize his thoughts. Things had been happening swiftly for several days and he felt he ought to be doing something, but when he looked at the situation he realized he had probably done enough—locking up Benny Silva at the System Springs facility was likely to force the opposition's hand. Tarpington was right—Farrington Industries would take some kind of action, and the smart thing for him to do now was give them a little time to take it.

He twisted his neck around to try and relieve the headache, and sat thinking back over what he knew. A ton of information had landed on him in the past couple of days and he sifted it in his mind, looking for things he might have overlooked. As he thought back, his thoughts drifted to Jessica Garner. Something she had said still gnawed at him, something he should follow up on, but for several minutes it eluded him. Then...

...they brought in another woman, younger and prettier than me. They needed my cell...

Nick jerked upright in his chair. *Jesus Christ!* He lunged for his cascade and began digging into the courthouse database. How had he let that get past him? Who was the other woman? What had she done? Where was she now?

Jessica Garner had been out of lockup for two years, she said, and he knew the approximate date of her release. He began searching arrest records for cases involving female defendants during that time, and came up with six. One had been acquitted, two had pled out, and three others were convicted. All had been charged with one form of assault or another, and as he quickly read the information his jaw tightened with anger. Tarpington had been right again—most of these charges looked trumped up, men charging women with assault after having sexual advances refused. "Assault" in these cases seemed to be defined as "scratching a man in the face while fighting off an attempted rape"; the two who pled out had taken probation and a fine in exchange for freedom, but neither had done any serious physical harm to their "victims". The other three had fought harder.

Nick saw three names. All had caused injuries that required medical treatment, and all had been sentenced to time in lockup. But which one had taken Jessica Garner's cell?

...younger and prettier than me.

Nick checked the ages on all three women and settled on the youngest. Her name was Nikki Green, age twenty-two. His scalp prickled as he pulled up her file and gazed at the flat photo on his cascade. Nikki Green was a black girl who looked like a fashion model. Slender, willowy, gorgeous. Even her mug shot, which showed her in a state of disarray, revealed her innate beauty. Long hair, lush lips—she had the whole package, the kind of face that would generate instant lust in most of the denizens who inhabited Ceres.

Nick read the file carefully, starting with her profile. Nikki Green was a recent college graduate with a degree in Humanitarian Studies, a liberal-minded young woman concerned about improving the lives of the downtrodden and underprivileged. She had come to Ceres to do research for a doctoral thesis, and had aspirations toward "making a difference". She had been on Ceres less than three weeks when she was charged with biting the ear off a man who had "asked her for a date". According to her own statement, the biting had only occurred *after* the man raped her. Three others had held her down and it was the first chance she had to defend herself.

Other witnesses, however, declared that no rape had occurred, the sex was consensual, and she had simply "gone nuts" when it was all over.

Nick didn't have access to the courtroom testimony, but the file was marked CONVICTED – CASE CLOSED. The preponderance of evidence must have gone against her—four men against one girl—and she had been judged guilty. Because of the grievous nature of the injury, she received the minimum sentence for a felony, one year and one day, to be served at Farrington lockup. On a hunch, Nick looked up the one-eared "victim" and discovered—no surprise—that he was a Farrington employee.

Nick sat back in his chair, his headache forgotten. Nikki Green had been locked up just over two years ago, yet her sentence had only been for one year. He quickly searched court records again but found no evidence that she had ever been released. Another search, this one in the Airlock Authority database, showed no sign that she had left the asteroid. So...dead or alive, she was apparently still on Ceres.

But where?

*

Nick left the office and walked back over to the courthouse, stopping along the way to pick up a sandwich. Court was back in session and Misery Allen wasn't in her office. It was almost four o'clock so he decided to wait, chatting with Angie and Carla in the outer office. Misery came in twenty minutes later, smiled in surprise, and ushered him into her office. She closed the door and sat down.

"I didn't expect to see you just yet. What time is our date?"

"About an hour from now. But I have another question for you."

"Another Farrington question? How many does that make now?"

"I've lost track."

"If I get them all right, do I win a prize?"

"Of course."

"Good! Ask away."

"I need information on another case, this one about two years ago. Similar to the Garner case, only this girl didn't work for Farrington. Her name was Nikki Green."

"'Was'? Is she dead?"

"I don't know. It looks like another frame job. She tried to fight off a rape and bit a man's ear off in the process. It got her a year and a day in lockup. What I want to know is, was she ever released."

"That information should be in the court records database."

"It isn't. She was sent away but, as far as I can find, never came out."

Misery looked shocked. "Jesus, Nick, this is bad!"

"Yes, it is. I need transcripts, if you can find them. I have the arrest records but I need to see what went on in the courtroom. Also, see if you can find out if there were any subsequent hearings, like in the Garner case. If they're still holding her a year after her scheduled release, then I've got the bastards."

"I'm not going to get to it this afternoon," she said. "I simply don't have time."

He shrugged. "Tomorrow is soon enough."

"Nick, I don't work tomorrow. It's Saturday."

"Is it?" He glanced at his watch. "Oh."

She smiled. "But if I have a really good time tonight, I might log in remotely and do it anyway."

"Where do you live?"

"Same place you do. The Centerville Hotel. Almost everyone who works in Government Annex lives there."

Nick stared stupidly. "I didn't know that. No one ever told me that."

She laughed. "Don't worry about it. This isn't a game show, and it isn't going to be on any civil service test. I'm in room 515, just in case you need to know."

He winked. "I do need to know."

*

Misery still had work to do and their date wasn't for another hour, so he returned to the office to keep out of the way. At five minutes to five, his porta-phone rang.

"Nick Walker."

"Hi, Nick, it's me." Monica Maynard sounded breathless and sexy in his ear.

"Hi, Judge."

"Nick, I need to see you."

"Right now?"

"No, not here. Tonight, at my place. Can you come for dinner?"

"Is it important? I already have plans."

"Oh." She sounded crestfallen. "What about tomorrow? Can you come over then?"

"Sure. What time?"

"Just whenever you wake up. I'll have a pot of coffee waiting."

"Okay. See you then."

Chapter 23

East Village - Ceres

The tavern was called The Blue Nebula.

The music was almost as loud as the Open Airlock, but much more tasteful. It carried a definite beat, but didn't explode inside the head, and Nick could detect a distinct melody in the music itself. The light was dim but the haze in the air came from incense, not drugs or tobacco; a spinning glitter ball near the ceiling scattered bright points of light around the room, giving the atmosphere a certain magical quality. The place wasn't terribly crowded, but it was noisy.

The joint was already jumping when Nick arrived with Tarpington and Misery. Most of the patrons were male—in fact, Misery was the only woman in sight. Tarpington led them past a group of dancing men to a corner table near the back, out of the main traffic path. They settled in and ordered drinks from the RoBarTender at their table, then Tarpington lifted his glass with a smile.

"To liberty and justice for all."

"Hear-hear," Misery said.

Nick didn't comment, but clinked glasses with them and sipped his drink.

"You guys hungry?" Tarpington asked. "They have a pretty decent microwave here."

Misery laughed. Nick didn't.

Tarpington signaled to a waiter who brought them a menu. Nick studied it briefly, found nothing remarkable, and ordered cheese enchiladas.

"I've never tried those," Misery said. "I'll have the same."

"What the hell," Tarpington said. "Me, too."

After the waiter had gone, Tarpington leaned across the table.

"I invited a friend to join us. Hope you don't mind." His eyes twinkled. "My own date for the evening."

Nick shrugged uncomfortably. Misery glanced up at him and giggled.

"What's good for the goose, huh?"

"Sure. Whatever."

They chatted for ten minutes before the food came. The enchiladas were preprocessed, but steaming not. Misery tried hers and exclaimed over the flavor. Nick wasn't quite as thrilled but admitted that they were better than he expected.

Sitting with his back to the wall, Nick spotted a familiar figure winding his way toward them through the crowd. Milo Zima slid into the seat next to Tarpington and stuck his hand across the table.

"Marshal Walker." He smiled. "Good to see you again."

"Same here." Nick shook hands and watched in astonishment as Zima kissed Tarpington on the lips. Tarpington glanced at him.

"Milo's the date I was telling you about. I didn't realize you two had met."

Nick nodded awkwardly. "Yeah. Couple days ago and again this afternoon."

Tarpington noted his expression and burst out laughing.

"What's wrong, Nick? Never seen two dudes kiss before?"

Nick started, aware that he must look like a fool.

"Yeah, actually I have. I just..."

"Freaks you out, does it?"

He nodded miserably, embarrassed to admit it. "I guess so."

"Well, don't worry about it. Some of us feel the same way when we see a man kissing a woman. What's natural to one side seems unnatural to the other." He lifted his glass again. "To diversity!"

Still blushing, Nick clicked his glass. "Hear-hear."

Zima belatedly ordered the same meal as the others and soon the conversation became more relaxed.

"Without revealing any names," Milo Zima said presently, "how's your investigation going, Nick?"

"To be truthful, I'm not sure. I'm still waiting for the blowback on that arrest this afternoon."

"You won't have to wait long. Farrington is already pressuring my office to release Silva. They said they would guarantee his appearance at arraignment."

"Don't do it," Tarpington told Zima. "The charges are too serious."

"Don't worry, Silva's not going anywhere without a court order."

"Which reminds me," Nick said to Tarpington, "I have another question for you."

"Sure."

"I've asked Misery to check on this, but since you're here, you might remember—does the name Nikki Green mean anything to you?"

David Tarpington stared at him in thought for a moment, his eyes glazing.

"That name does ring a bell. Give me a hint."

"Sentenced to a year and a day for biting a man's ear off. She claimed she'd been raped but four others refuted her statement."

"Ah, yes, couple of years back. College student, wasn't she?"

"Graduate student. Working on her Ph.D."

"I do remember. It was another one of those cases where he said/she said, and the 'he's' won. What about it?"

"Did you prosecute her?"

Tarpington nodded unhappily. "Yeah, afraid so. But I think she was telling the truth. The medical exam revealed vaginal bruising, but of course the 'victim' and his friends claimed it was consensual. Said she took them all on." He saw Nick's expression and grimaced. "My boss said push the case, so I pushed it. I hoped I would lose."

Nick nodded. He wasn't blaming Tarpington. "My question is, where is that girl now? It was over two years ago, but I've seen no record that she was ever released from lockup."

Tarpington stared at him a moment, thinking. He shook his head slowly.

"I don't know. Once the verdict is in, our files are closed. We don't usually follow up on prison releases, unless there's something out of the ordinary involved."

"Who would know?"

"Judge Maynard, probably. Farrington Security, certainly."

"Farrington Security isn't going to tell me anything." Nick took another bite of his enchilada. "But they might tell you."

Tarpington nodded decisively. "I'll call them first thing in the morning."

"You're working tomorrow?" Zima asked in surprise.

"No, but this is important." To Nick, "I'll call you as soon as I learn something."

*

Nick and Misery Allen spent a pleasant two hours with Tarpington and Zima, visiting happily and even taking a turn on the dance floor. When they left the bar the habitat was dark, and Misery snuggled up against him.

"Where to now, Nick? You said something earlier about…"

"Hetero." He grinned and pulled open the passenger door on the E-car. "Would you be interested in something like that?"

"Sure, I think so. Why wouldn't I?" Her smile dazzled him in the dim light from a street light.

"Because it has to be no strings. I hope I've been clear about that."

"Yes, you have. But there isn't much on this rock for a girl like me, Nick. I'll take whatever you have to offer."

He gazed into her lovely dark eyes for a moment, then leaned in and kissed her. She was warm and soft, her perfume intoxicating. She responded hungrily, her hand grasping the back of his head. His blood began to race with excitement.

"We'd better stop this," he murmured. "Right now."

She pulled back, disappointment in her eyes. "Why?"

"Because if we don't, I'm never gonna make it to the hotel."

Centerville - Ceres

Ten minutes later they were inside his tiny hotel room, embracing and kissing passionately. Nick buried his face in her thick, silken hair, panting like a dog.

"What's that *perfume* you're wearing?" he gasped. "I've never smelled anything like it."

"It's something I've been saving," she said, nibbling his neck. "Very expensive. This is the first time I've ever worn it."

"It's hitting me like a drug."

"That's what it's supposed to do. It's from Vega 3." She sucked at his lips for a moment. "They're supposed to have the most beautiful women in the 'verse. At least, that's the rumor."

Nick didn't care. At the moment he was more turned on than he could ever remember being, and he fumbled for the clasp on the back of Misery's dress. Releasing it, he peeled her like a banana, then ran his hands down her warm, smooth back and over the swell of her bottom. She clung to him, gasping, as he lifted her onto the bed, then laid her down and tugged off her skirt. To his surprise, she was wearing nothing underneath, and in the dim glow from the window he could see her entire form stretched out before him, feminine and sexy and glorious.

"Oh, god!" he whispered. "I had no idea you were so beautiful!"

He got rid of his own clothing in record time and joined her on the bed. Panting with desire, she wrapped her arms around him and drew him against her, then he was inside her; her back arched and her chin lifted as she moaned with pleasure. Nick wrapped his arms around her and held her firmly, forcing himself to slow down. This was too exquisite to rush. Misery's head rolled from side to side as her ecstasy mounted, breathing hard, her hands gripping his shoulders. The realization filtered into his mind that she wasn't very experienced, but she had plenty of passion, and that was all that mattered. He took his time, stretching it out, and brought her to a climax. Her body convulsed under him like a snake on hot pavement and her cry rattled the window. Every muscle in her body was rigid and she labored for breath as the moans continued to escape her.

Finally Nick could stand it no longer—his own climax followed and then he lay heavily on top of her, too weak to move, his face buried in her dark hair. For several minutes they remained like that, completely wasted, their bodies slowly cooling. When she had regained her oxygen, Misery began to kiss him, slowly walking her full lips across his face, her fingers playing with his hair.

"Oh, Nick! I've never had anything like that. Not ever."

He lifted his head weakly and pushed his forehead against hers.

"You weren't a virgin, were you?"

"No. Why, did I disappoint you?"

"Mm-um." He shook his head. "Nothing about that was disappointing, believe me. I just wondered. You said you were a small-world girl, and you are pretty young, so..."

"I had a boyfriend back on Ganymede. We dated less than a year, and we only did it a few times." She squirmed to a more comfortable position. "Since I came here I've never run across a man that I wanted. Until now."

"Microbes?"

She laughed. "No, that's Monica's phobia, not mine. I just don't care for felons or other assorted smelly men."

Nick disengaged and lay down beside her, pulling her into his arms.

"You're saying I don't stink?"

"You definitely don't stink. I wouldn't be here if you did."
She kissed his nose. "How long are you going to be on Ceres?"

"I don't know. The average assignment is two years, I think."

She smiled. "So...can we do this again?"

He adjusted the pillow under his head, giving him a better view of her face.

"As long as you don't fall in love with me."

"And what if *you* fall in love with *me?*" Her glittering eyes teased him.

"That won't happen."

"How do you know? Am I that unattractive?"

"I think you know better than that."

"Maybe I'm not your type?"

"I don't have a 'type'. I'm just not in the market."

She gazed at him a moment, stroking his cheek.

"Someone hurt you, didn't they? Tell me about it."

But he shook his head. "Nothing to tell. I'm career oriented, that's all. My line of work isn't conducive to domestic life. I'll be going too many places, and some of them will be very alien, not the kind of place to take a wife and family, and not fair to leave them at home for years at a time. It's as simple as that."

He closed his eyes, suddenly tired. Misery stared at him in the faint light for several minutes, then rolled on top of him, kissing him again.

"What was her name?"

He lay silent for nearly a minute, breathing evenly.

"Victoria Cross. And that's the end of the discussion."

"All right," she said softly. "If this is all we have, then this is all we have. I'll take it."

He reached up with both hands and seized her face, pulling her down for a deep, satisfying kiss.

"I was hoping you'd say that."

Saturday, August 10, 0440 (CC) — Centerville - Ceres

"What are all those scars?"

Misery Allen was sitting up in bed, completely nude, watching Nick brew a pot of coffee. Artificial sunlight filled the room from the window, casting a bright glare over everything, including the old wounds on his bare back. He glanced around at her, his eyes resting on her sexy, dark-chocolate body.

"Bad memories," he said.

"Were you in an accident?"

He shook his head. "Alpha Centauri 2. These came compliments of the Rebel Coalition."

Her eyes grew wide. "Oh, my god! You were in the war?"

He nodded, pouring water into the brewer and setting the timer. He strolled back to the bed and sat down on the edge.

"Did you follow the war?"

"Not really. I was pretty young then."

"Alpha 2 has petitioned for independence, but until they establish a stable government they're still a Federation colony. The problem is, there are about six factions that want to be in charge, and some of them are willing to fight to do it. Two of them banded together to form the Coalition and take the planet by force, so the Star Marines were sent in to stop them. The Federation doesn't want to turn the planet over to any government that's willing to go to war that easily."

"How long were you there?"

"Year and a half, more or less."

"You probably saw a lot of bad things."

He nodded. "You can't believe what ordinary people are capable of in situations like that."

She leaned forward and pulled him against her, resting her chin on his shoulder.

"I'm sorry, Nick."

He held her a moment, then kissed her on the temple.

"I found out what *I'm* capable of," he said quietly. "It was a sobering revelation. That's why I decided to become a U.F.

Marshal, to make sure that whatever bad things I do will be for the right reasons."

"But you're not a bad person, Nick. If you did bad things, it was because you had to."

He nodded again. "Trouble is, it got to the point that I *enjoyed* doing them. That's what scared me."

She looked into his eyes, her lips parted with wonder.

"Do you *still* enjoy it?" she dared to ask.

Nick hesitated, then thought back to recent events—shooting Capt. Guthrie, shooting Benny Silva, laying Turd Murdoch out with his .44. He blinked once and met her open gaze with trepidation in his eyes. He nodded slowly.

"Yeah. I do."

Chapter 24

Nick made love to Misery again, then they shared coffee and conversation for an hour.

"How long will you be gone?" she asked as he strapped on his gunbelt and snugged the .44 under his shoulder.

"Couple of hours, maybe. After I see Maynard I want to run by the office for a little bit. If you want to hang around it wouldn't break my heart. I'm sure we could find something to do for the rest of the day."

She giggled and bit him on the ear.

"Maybe I'll grab a nap and charge up my batteries. I feel like electricity already."

He took her head in both hands and they mated mouths, exploring with their tongues, then he let her go. He was already becoming aroused.

"Two hours," he said. "Tops."

He went out the door.

Nick stepped across the hall and knocked on Judge Maynard's door; she let him in with a smile.

"Good morning, Nick! Enjoy your night out?"

He stepped inside and she locked the door behind him. "Who said I had a night out?"

"Well, you said you had plans, it was Friday night—I took a wild guess. Ready for some coffee?"

He wasn't—he was all coffee'd out—but he said yes. Monica poured him a cup and set it on her dining table, ushering him into a chair across from her. She was wearing a white bathrobe that contrasted nicely with her dark skin, and showed him more skin than was necessary. She had apparently also put on some perfume, and smelled magnificent.

"How's your investigation going?"

He shot her a blank look. "Which investigation?"

"Whichever one you're afraid to talk about. Farrington Industries, isn't it?" She locked gazes with him, an open challenge. Nick's eyes narrowed minutely.

"What do you want to know?"

"I'd like to know what you're investigating. Maybe I can help."

"You invited me over on a Saturday morning to ask me that?"

She waved a careless hand. "It's too hectic through the week. You've seen how it is."

"Yeah, it does look pretty wild."

"I sensed your urgency the other day; I could tell it was important to you, and I thought, well, maybe it would be easier if you could talk to someone who was around when it happened. Whatever *it* was."

Nick nodded slowly, turning his coffee cup with his fingers.

"You've been a judge how long?"

"Almost nine years. I've sat on hundreds of cases. Thousands."

"You can't possibly remember them all."

"Of course not. Most of them are routine plead-outs and no contests, but a lot of others stand out. And I have records."

Nick pursed his lips briefly, then made a show of coming to a decision.

"Do you remember a defendant named Nikki Green?"

Monica blinked once, then frowned in thought.

"Nikki Green. That does sound familiar. About two years ago?"

Nick nodded. "She bit a man's ear off."

Monica snapped her fingers and pointed at him. "That was it. I remember now."

"Whatever happened to her?"

"She went to lockup. I think I gave her a year."

"She said she was defending herself from rape, but you convicted her."

Monica looked surprised at his accusing tone. "Nick, she bit off a man's ear! That's a pretty serious injury."

"Not life threatening."

"It's disfigurement! In a Terrestrial court she might have gotten more than a year."

"She said she'd been raped. The medical report seems to back that up. You didn't believe her?"

"The testimony was four to one, Nick. It wouldn't be the first time a woman cried rape just because things got a little too rough."

"You think that's what happened?"

"I don't know! Maybe she agreed to do one of them and he brought his friends. Maybe she agreed to do *three* of them and they brought a fourth. In some of these cases it's impossible to tell who's lying and who isn't. In a lot of cases everyone involved is lying, so good luck at getting the truth."

Nick sipped his coffee, giving her a moment.

"What about reasonable doubt? I saw a picture of that girl. She had vid-star looks. She could get any man in the Solar System with the wink of an eye. Why would she voluntarily fuck four microbe-infested creeps from Ceres?"

Monica's eyes widened and her mouth dropped open.

"Nick...are you accusing *me* of something?"

He shrugged. "You said you wanted to help. Help me understand this."

She stood up and turned away, tightening her bathrobe at the throat. She took a few steps across the room, then turned back.

"It isn't easy being a judge, Nick. Sometimes you can rely on your instincts, but other times your instinct is dead wrong. I've made a couple of serious errors that I regret making, but all I can do is move forward and try not to repeat them. As much as possible, I rely on the evidence presented in court, the same as a jury would do—"

"But you have better resources than a jury. You can rule to exclude evidence, which means you get to see the evidence beforehand. You can't be one hundred percent impartial all the time."

"That's true. I am human and prone to mistakes, but the good news is that I only sit in judgment of the minor cases. Big stuff always goes to a jury."

"By 'big stuff' you mean murder and rape?"

"Yes, felonies that draw long sentences. In the smaller cases, like assault and minor theft, we're talking about short sentences, so if I get it wrong I'm not stealing someone's entire lifetime."

"What's the average sentence for something like that?"

"Three months to a year, sometimes even less."

"You gave her a year and a day—"

"Because it was a felony. That's the minimum I could give."

"But where is she now?"

Monica blinked. "What do you mean?"

"That was two years ago. I checked the records, at least the ones I can access, and I found no indication that she was ever released. According to Airlock Authority records she never left the asteroid, and there's no death certificate on file."

Monica was frowning in alarm.

"What are you saying, Nick?"

"I think she's still a prisoner in lockup."

"But—that's impossible! Her time would have been served a year ago."

"Exactly. Where is she now?"

Monica took her chair again, a little unsteadily. "You're sure she wasn't released?"

"No, I'm not sure. That's why I'm asking. There's no record of her release in the courthouse database."

"But—why would Farrington Security keep her if her time was up? What's in it for them?"

"Twenty-five terros a day." *And another year of good-ole-boy rape and torture,* he didn't add. "Can you find out?"

"Yes, of course. I'll do it right away." She stood again and headed for the comm set.

"Monica, wait."

She turned back. "What?"

"Don't call just yet. I'm waiting to hear from Dave Tarpington."

"About what?"

"About this, what we're talking about."

"You told Tarpington? Why didn't you come to me first?"

"I saw him last night in a bar. He was there, so I asked him. He promised to look into it this morning."

Monica stood there a moment, looking indecisive. He saw her swallow involuntarily, and his scalp tingled in sudden awareness. *Jesus Christ! She's scared!*

"Well..." She sat down again. "If he doesn't get any answers, then I'll look into it."

"Fair enough. In the meantime, I need a favor."

"Sure. What is it?"

"I need a warrant. To inspect the Farrington lockup."

Her eyes narrowed. "What for?"

"I think they're abusing prisoners there."

"Based on what?"

"Based on several things—my own observation of how they treat prisoners in the courtroom; information I received from a CI; and the fact that when I requested permission to look around they got downright hostile. That makes me real suspicious."

She considered that for a moment, looking, he thought, indecisive...again.

"I'm afraid that's not enough, Nick. What you saw in the courtroom happened in the courtroom—"

"Exactly! If they did that in the courtroom where they could be observed, how much worse is it behind stone walls where no one can see?"

"—testimony from a CI is always hearsay," she continued, "and their hostility toward you could be interpreted any number of ways."

"Like what?"

"Personality clash, for one. Their perception of your attitude when you requested permission...they could argue any number of scenarios. I need something more definitive."

"Okay, how about this—if Nikki Green is still in lockup a year past her release date, does that qualify?"

She gazed at him for a long moment, breathing slowly.

"It could be just a clerical error," she said finally.

"Yes, it could. It could also be something a whole lot worse! Christ, Monica, doesn't anything make you suspicious!"

"As a matter of fact, yes! I'm starting to wonder why you're so hell-bent on getting inside Farrington! You've been after them since the day you got here! What the hell do you expect to find?"

Nick was silent a moment, watching her, judging her demeanor. Her pulse had increased, as evidenced by her heavy breathing, and her hands were trembling slightly. The gleam was gone from her eyes as she glared at him. So far he'd told her only a little of what he suspected, and her reaction surprised him. She actually seemed to be *defending* Farrington Industries, and that was out of character for the woman he thought he knew. His skin tingled at the possible implications and he hoped he was wrong. There was one way to find out.

"I think Farrington is dirty," he said quietly.

"You th—*what!* What do you mean, dirty? Dirty how? What the hell are you talking about!"

"Dirty," he repeated. "Inside and out, top to bottom. Dirty, rotten, putrid, starting with the Farrington brothers themselves. I think they acquired their holdings illegally and hurt a lot of people along the way."

Her mouth had dropped open and she stared at him as if he had two heads.

"Nick, what—where did you get this idea? What kind of...*evidence* do you have?"

He reached across the table and seized her wrist, squeezing it lightly.

"You give me that warrant and I'll find out for sure. I'll either hang them or I'll clear them. And if I'm wrong I will not only leave them alone, I will publicly apologize in the Solar System press. *And* pay restitution for any harm I've caused."

He leaned back and held her gaze while an array of emotions danced across her face.

"So, can I have the warrant?"

She looked away finally, then glanced back.

"Let's see what Tarpington finds out. If that girl is still there, then you can have the warrant."

Nick smiled and relaxed a little. If she had said anything other than what she'd just said, he would have been forced to add her to his list of suspects. It felt really good to be wrong.

"Nick." She was staring across the room at the holo-fireplace. "Do you have any idea what would happen if Farrington got shut down? How many lives would be affected?"

"You're talking about the water supply to the Outer Worlds?"

"Yes." She turned to face him again. "And Mars, and every settlement in the Belt. Not to mention the jobs that would be lost here on Ceres. This asteroid would dry up."

"There are three other companies."

"Yes, but all three combined don't produce a fraction of the water that Farrington does. It may titillate your moral fancy to shut them down over a few technical issues, but if you did that it would harm literally millions of people."

Her gaze intensified, her brow tightened.

"You do understand that, I hope. Don't you?"

He nodded again.

"Yes, I am aware of all that. I hope all that can be avoided. But one thing you need to understand about me, Monica, is that I would do it anyway. In the Star Marines we had a policy—leave no one behind. Call me youthful or idealistic or whatever clichés you care to apply, but I am not prepared to sacrifice one innocent person for the so-called 'greater good'."

His jaw clenched firmly.

"You can take that to the ATM."

Government Annex - Ceres

He had just parked the E-car in Government Annex when his porta-phone rang.

"Nick Walker."

"Nick, it's Dave. I just talked to someone in Farrington lockup."

Nick's pulse quickened. He stood in the artificial sunlight and felt it warm his skin.

"What did you find out?"

"Nothing."

"They wouldn't talk to you?"

"Oh, they did talk to me, but there was nothing to report."

Nick frowned. "I don't get it."

"My friend works in prison records. She did several searches and did not find any indication that Nikki Green was ever released."

Nick's heart surged with adrenaline. "Then we've got 'em!"

"Not so fast, there, Solarman, that's not all."

"I'm listening."

"There's also no record she was ever locked up. Her name didn't come up anywhere, past or present."

Nick turned in a circle, staring at the ground.

"Whoa-whoa-whoa, what are you talking about! We *know* she was sent there!"

"Yeah, well, we thought we did. According to court records she was sent there for incarceration, but she was never logged in as a prisoner."

"That doesn't make any sense!"

"Maybe it does. If she was never logged in, she wouldn't have to be logged out. You said she was a hot body, didn't you?"

"Yeah, from the flat photo in her file."

"And didn't you just kill two Farrington Security guys for trying to steal a pair of other hot bodies a few days ago?"

Nick felt suddenly weak, and leaned back against the E-car.

"Oh, Jesus Christ! You think they're pimping her?"

"I dunno, but it would seem to fit. I think you need to get inside that lockup, my friend. And I'll tell you something else—when you do, I'm going with you."

Centerville - Ceres

"Hello?"

"How did it go with Walker?"

"Not well."

"Explain."

"He's idealistic and single minded."

"What's his agenda?"

"He found out about Nikki Green."

"How much does he know?"

"He knows she should have been released a year ago. And he's pretty sure she wasn't."

"Can you head him off?"

"I tried. I gave him the song and dance about the greater good, but he isn't buying it. He sees this as some kind of moral crusade."

"Sell it to him."

"I can't! If I try, he'll suspect *me!*"

"You better figure something out. You have a lot at stake here, and killing a U.F. Marshal has got to be the absolute last resort."

"*Goddammit!* I'm a Federation *judge!* I'm too high profile to do what you want! I can only do so much."

"Do more. Charley's counting on you."

Click.

Tears. Sobs.
The comm rang again.

Chapter 25

Government Annex - Ceres

Nick unlocked the office and stepped inside, turning on the lights. The coffee pot was on, which indicated that someone had been there, but whoever was working wasn't here now. Nick sat down at his desk, his head spinning. He briefly ran through things he had to do and prioritized them in his mind, then reached for the comm and punched in a number. It rang six times.

"Hello?"

Her video was off, but Monica Maynard sounded weak and subdued, as if she'd just woke up...or been crying.

"Monica, this is Nick. I need that search warrant."

He heard a cough, then she blew her nose. She coughed again.

"Sorry about that, Nick. My allergies are flaring up, I guess."

Allergies? On Ceres?

"Maybe you're allergic to me," he said. "I just left there."

Her laugh sounded strained. "I don't think that's it. So..."

"Search warrant."

"You found the girl? She's still there?"

"No, she *isn't* there...well, she may be, but I won't know until I go over there and look for myself."

"I don't understand. You still need probable cause, and this isn't it."

"I think it is. The girl was never logged in as an inmate—"

"*What!*"

"That's right. For the last two years she's been in limbo somewhere. I need to find her."

"Well...if she wasn't logged in, then she isn't there."

"Why would you say that?"

"It only makes sense. Inmates have to be logged in. How else could they keep records?"

"Maybe they didn't want to keep records. Maybe they had something else in mind."

"Like what? Nick, you're not suggesting they *killed* her?"

"Anything is possible, but this girl was a looker, so I doubt it. More likely she's in a whorehouse somewhere. But I need to get inside that lockup."

She was silent for a long time. Too long, it seemed to Nick. "Monica?"

"Yeah...I'm here. Just thinking."

"What's to think about! Just give me the goddamn warrant!" He was losing patience.

"Okay, okay. No need to get angry. Meet me at my office in...oh, give me an hour. I'll have the guard let you in."

She rang off and Nick sat back, feeling numb. Monica didn't sound like herself, had been edgy all morning. What the hell was going on?

The front door opened and a young man Nick had never seen walked in. He was wearing slacks and a white shirt open at the collar. He stopped in front of Nick's desk and smiled.

"Are you Marshal Walker?"

"Yes, I am. Can I help you?"

The young man extended an envelope and Nick took it.

"What's this?"

"You've been served. Have a nice day, Marshal."

The visitor walked out the door and Nick popped the envelope. For just a moment he couldn't believe his eyes, then he threw the document on his desk and tilted his head back with a sigh.

"Jesus jumping Christ!"

After a moment he reached for the comm again and called Dave Tarpington.

"What's up, Nick?"

"Are you in your office?"

"Yeah. Why?"

"Don't go anywhere. I'll be there in five minutes."

Centerville - Ceres

Misery Allen dozed contentedly in Nick's bed, happier than she had been in years, maybe happier than she had been in her life. She drifted in and out of slumber, sensuous dreams flitting through her head like vids projected just behind her eyelids. It was warm here, the bed firm but soft. Just outside the window she heard an occasional E-car, or a voice calling out. People in the park, Centerville on a Saturday morning—a pleasant reprieve from the weekday grind.

Sex with Nick had been great, the best she ever had. She rolled over leisurely, stretching, her nude body relaxed and content, her blood flowing smoothly. Her eyes opened and then closed, then opened again. She should get up, she thought, then closed her eyes again. Drowsing, that delicious state between sleep and waking, when she was no longer tired but enjoying sleep too much to stop. She took a deep breath and let it out as a sigh, twisting her head to the left, her thick hair bunching up on that side, her opposite breast flattening out as the muscles pulled the other way. Mmmm. She could smell him, on his pillow. He wore a light, very basic aftershave, and she could just detect a trace of it, enough to make her heart beat a little faster. She couldn't wait for him to return so they could make love again.

She should get up, she reminded herself. He would be back soon. He'd said a couple of hours, and that was...how long ago?

She sat up abruptly, letting the sheet drop away. She should get a shower, then start a fresh pot of coffee. Have it ready when he got here. She wanted to please him. He'd been very clear that he wasn't looking for a permanent relationship, but she was only twenty-one, so she had plenty of time for that. Right now, if they could have two years together, she would take it. And who was to say he wouldn't change his mind? Especially if she made him happy.

She yawned, sighed again, and twisted her neck around to work the kinks out of it. Mmmm. Felt good. She rubbed her eyes and kicked her feet over the side of the bed.

The bathroom was tiny, even smaller than the one in her apartment on the fifth floor. She found soap and a fresh towel in the linen compartment and slid the shower door aside. She set the thermometer and gave it a minute to prep, then stepped inside and turned the water on. It was cool at first, gradually warming, as it was supposed to do, in case she had set the temp too high and needed time to turn it down. The modern showers were amazing. She turned in a complete circle, soaking her body from every angle, then broke open the soap and poured it into the massager. The massager went to work, scrubbing her with soft, gentle brushes, and the water reached the desired temperature. She closed her eyes and turned slowly, letting the massager at her from every angle. She began to think about what she and Nick should do for lunch.

Misery turned again, lifted her arms, and the brushes moved in, scrubbing briskly. The hot water felt good, but she had set it a little too high—it was starting to sting. She turned to the thermostat and bent down to look at the screen. It was fogged by steam and she had to wipe it with her finger to read the setting, but it looked okay—just what she had programmed. But the water was getting hotter still, and it was starting to burn. She frowned slightly and reached for the override, to turn up the cold.

The minute she touched it, the override came off in her hand—she stared at it in surprise. Surprise turned to fear when the blue thermostat setting began to spiral downward, indicating a reduction in the cold water; the red was still at the same setting, but started spinning up higher. Steam clouded her vision and suddenly the water spraying her skin was scalding. Misery screamed and grabbed for the door, but the door was jammed. She jerked it frantically, breaking a nail, but it wouldn't budge—

Something exploded; it was just a small thing, part of the thermostat, but the shower went to full force, blasting the tiny space with near-boiling water. Misery Allen's terror turned to horror and her scream became a shriek. She lunged against the door, again, and again, thrashing helplessly in the tiny space. Agony washed over her, like nothing she had ever imagined. Within seconds consciousness faded as her mind began to shut down and shield her from further trauma; she slumped against the wall, gasping as she slid down to the shower floor, where she finally, mercifully, passed out.

The shower continued to rage for six more minutes, then shut itself off. Just that suddenly, the bathroom was silent; except for the trickling water draining out, there wasn't a single sound.

Not even a heartbeat.

Government Annex - Ceres

"Is this a joke?" David Tarpington stared at the document in his hand in disbelief.

"Doesn't look like one. Farrington Industries is suing me for harassment."

"Jesus Christ!" Tarpington's blue eyes met Nick's brown ones. "What're you gonna do?"

"I'm gonna make them work for it. If they think I've harassed them before, they haven't seen anything yet."

Tarpington handed the document back. "So what's the next step?"

"Judge Maynard said to meet her upstairs and she'll give me that warrant. You want to come along?"

"Hell, yes. I have nothing better to do today."

They left Tarpington's office and headed up the stairs to the courtroom.

"Question," Nick said thoughtfully. "Were you here when Monica became judge?"

"No. I came a couple of years later. Why?"

"I was just wondering. She told me she was working as an attorney when she got the appointment."

"That's my understanding, too."

"Was she a prosecutor or a defense attorney?"

"Neither. She was privately employed."

Nick glanced at him. "Yeah? Employed where?"

"Farrington Industries."

*

Monica had said she would have a security guard let Nick in, but Tarpington had his own key and they strode through the courtroom toward the judge's chambers in the back. Nick knocked once and she called out to enter. He and Tarpington stepped inside and stared in surprise at another man who was already there.

Monica was seated at her desk but, Nick thought, looked a little ill at ease.

"Marshal Walker," she said, "I don't believe you've met Mr. Cramer."

Nick's eyes narrowed as he sized up the man before him. Five feet ten, slender, athletic, forty-five, curly brown hair, slightly balding, expensive suit, immaculate grooming, pencil mustache. Stanley Cramer's eyes were hidden behind dark shades which were hardly needed anywhere on Ceres and certainly not in this dim office; his face held no hint of a smile or any other emotion. He exuded all the charisma of an android.

Nick extended a hand just to see what would happen; Cramer gave it a perfunctory shake and released it.

"Mr. Cramer is the head of Farrington Industry's—"

"Legal department," Nick finished for her. "I've heard the name."

Cramer tilted his head. "Indeed? Where?" His voice was surprisingly soft.

Nick shrugged. "Oh, I don't remember. Important men get talked about. It was probably in a bar somewhere." He turned to Monica, who looked at him uncertainly. "I didn't realize Mr. Cramer was invited to our meeting."

She smiled weakly. "I didn't realize Mr. Tarpington was invited."

"*Touché.*" Nick pulled out a chair and sat down.

Monica kept her voice even. "Mr. Cramer came by to seek a restraining order."

"Against...?"

"Against you."

Nick nodded as if he'd expected it. He threw the document he was carrying onto her desk.

"I guess that goes hand in hand with this." He glanced at Cramer, who was still standing. "Right?"

"No. That's a separate matter entirely," Cramer told him.

Monica picked up the document and studied it, then turned wide eyes on Stanley Cramer.

"You're suing Marshal Walker?"

"For one million terros," Cramer said. Nick detected no emotion in his voice, neither smugness nor anger. The man was an android.

"For harassment?" Monica was still trying to wrap her mind around it.

"He tried to bully his way into Farrington lockup two days ago. He tried to browbeat Messrs. Farrington and Farrington, and when Mr. Silva refused to let him carry weapons into the lockup yesterday he shot him in the foot."

Monica turned questioning eyes on Nick.

"That's one version," Nick said. "Then there's the truth."

"I just told you the truth," Cramer said.

Monica held up both hands. "Hold on! This is not a hearing, so let's stop this right now before you start shouting at each other."

"I'm not shouting," Nick said.

"Not yet. Look, we have a situation here—"

"*I* don't have a situation. I just want that search warrant. You said I could have it."

Monica looked flustered. "Y...es, I did, but now Mr. Cramer is seeking a restraining order, so...that puts a whole new light on things." She studied her desk as she spoke.

Cramer started talking, but Nick didn't hear him. As he stared at Monica something clicked and he felt a peculiar sensation ripple across his skin. Things began to jell in his mind, pieces coming together...pieces that formed a picture he didn't like very much.

"Did you call him over here?" he asked suddenly, cutting Cramer off.

"*What!*" Monica spun on him in shock. "What did you say?"

Nick's eyes bored into her like radar.

"You didn't need an hour to get over here. When I was at your place earlier you had already showered and groomed. All you had to do was change clothes, but you wanted an hour."

She shook her head in irritation. "Nick...what the *hell* are you talking about?"

Nick glanced at Cramer, who still stood there like an android.

"For a man who's suing me for harassment, and someone seeking a restraining order, you're awfully calm. Things like harassment and protection orders usually tend to raise the blood pressure a little, but you're standing there like a goddamn robot."

"I resent that remark," Cramer said quietly.

Nick swung back to Monica, whose eyes had gone wider than ever, her mouth hanging half open.

"Ever since I started talking about a warrant you've been trying to talk me out of it. But once I told you about the girl you knew you couldn't sidestep it, so you stalled me to give *him*—" Nick inclined his head toward Cramer. "—time to file an injunction."

Monica's mouth closed and her already dark skin darkened further with rage.

"You are skating awfully close to a contempt charge, Mister!"

"No I'm not. Do I get the warrant or not?"

"*Not* if you continue to speak to me in that tone! I am a Federation judge—"

"Which *he* bought and paid for!" Nick stood suddenly and kicked his chair back against the wall, freeing his hands for action.

"That's *it!*" Monica shouted, leaping to her feet. "You are in contempt! Five hundred terros or five days in lockup!"

"Take it out of my paycheck!" Nick turned to face Cramer squarely. "Where is Nikki Green?"

If Cramer was frightened, his shades concealed it; not a muscle in his face so much as twitched.

"Excuse me?"

"Nikki Green. Female, African ancestry, beauty-pageant gorgeous; she would be about twenty-four by now, if she's still alive. Where is she?"

"I'm afraid you have me confused with someone else. That name means nothing to me."

Monica's head swiveled from one man to the other; behind Nick, David Tarpington still stood by the door, rooted with astonishment. Nick saw Cramer's expression and realized conventional methods weren't going to work. Cramer was supremely confident—he had the power and knew it. Nothing Nick could do legally would get past the starcrete wall in front of him. He considered for all of five seconds, and two thoughts came to mind:

Sometimes you have to take a few steps on the dark side to get the job done.

And the other was:

Improvise!

He drew his laser pistol.

Chapter 26

"*Jesus Christ!*" Monica Maynard screamed. "Put that away!"

"Nick, for god's sake!" Tarpington started forward, but stopped when Nick held up his left hand. Nick's eyes never left Cramer's face.

"I'm going to ask you one more time," he told Cramer in a low, dangerous voice. "You tell me where that girl is, *right now*, or I swear—"

"You're going to shoot me?" Cramer clasped his hands together, as if preparing to deliver an invocation. "Is that how you solve your problems, Marshal? With violence?"

Nick hesitated only a second, then took one quick step forward and grabbed Cramer by the coat collar with his left hand. He spun him around and slammed his forehead into the wall, then spun him back and held him by the throat. A trickle of blood streamed from Cramer's forehead.

"That's right, asshole! I *will* use violence if I need to. When I'm dealing with the scum of the galaxy I'll do whatever it takes. You've used plenty of violence yourself, haven't you?"

"I don't know what you're talking about," Cramer wheezed.

"Oh, yes you do! You asteroided Jessica Garner for an assault she didn't commit, locked her up in that dungeon you call a lockup, and had her systematically raped for two years."

"She tried to kill Mr. F—"

Nick jerked him forward and slammed him back into the wall again, cutting off his words.

"You had her husband murdered in the bottom of an ice mine because he was trying to get her released from your torture chamber. You've got the medical examiner terrified of her own shadow so you can get medical reports and death certificates altered to cover the hundreds of cripples and dead bodies that come out of that place. You sabotaged Agua Solar's space freighter and killed the crew, *and* you sabotaged their drilling equipment to cause accidents that would cast doubt on their safety procedures, forcing their stock into the toilet and putting them out of business...all so your Farrington pals could get control of the entire ice mining industry on this rock."

"You're delusional!" Cramer grunted, showing a little emotion at last. "I'll have you—"

Nick slammed his head into the wall again.

"I'm not finished, shithead!" He glanced at Monica, then back to Cramer. "You also had Judge Boxner murdered so you could install your own pet judge in the only courtroom on Ceres. I can't imagine why she went for it, but I'm going to find out."

"You're insane! Certifiably *insane!*"

"And you're under arrest."

Nick holstered his pistol and spun Cramer around, wrested his arms together, and E-cuffed him. He shoved him to the floor and turned on Monica. She was staring at him in horror, showing more fear than anger.

"Nick! Have you lost your fucking *mind?* Where did all that come from? You can't prove any of that!"

"I will, by the end of the day."

"If you think I'm going to give you a search warrant now—"

"I won't be needing it," he said, taking a step toward her. "Turn around."

Her eyes couldn't get any wider—but they did.

"*WHAT?!?* Jesus, what do you—"

"You're under arrest." He grabbed her wrists and spun her around, carefully but firmly. She twisted her head around to make eye contact, but he was snapping a second set of cuffs on her wrists.

"Oh what charge?" she demanded, her voice wavering.

"Conspiracy to commit murder. Don't fight those cuffs, you'll electrocute yourself."

He released her arms and she stumbled back against the wall. Tears streamed down her cheeks as she stared at him, her whole body rigid.

"*Murder!* Have you gone *insane?*"

Nick turned to David Tarpington, who stood on the balls of his feet, as if ready to run. His expression suggested he also thought Nick might have suffered a mental episode.

"Is Milo working today?"

"I—no, I don't think so."

"Call him. Tell him to meet us at his facility. I have two prisoners for him."

"*What murder?*" Monica screamed. "Nick! What murder?"

"Judge Boxner. You replaced him."

"Yes, but I didn't *kill* him!"

"You had to be a party to it. Cramer had him killed and it was Cramer's recommendation to the Martian Judiciary that assured your appointment. You were working for Cramer then and you're working for him now."

She stood in shock—trembling, breathing hard, but she didn't deny it. Instead she wheeled on Tarpington.

"David! Are you just going to stand there? *Do* something!"

Tarpington was clearly conflicted. "What do you expect me to do?"

"*Help* me, goddammit! He's gone insane! I'm a Federation *judge!*"

"And he's a Federation marshal."

She stared at him in desperation, but Nick took her arm and pulled her close.

"Why did you do it, Monica? What was in it for you?"

Shaking hard, she seemed unable to speak. They locked gazes for twenty seconds.

"Why, Monica? Just tell me why."

"I have nothing to say to you! That badge has gone to your head!"

"You'll have to tell me eventually."

"No, I won't," she said. "I have the right to remain silent."

System Springs - Ceres

"I want both Cramer and the judge isolated," Nick told Milo Zima. "Nobody talks to them and they don't communicate with anyone, especially not each other."

"I don't have any facilities for women," Zima said. "This is a male lockup only."

He stared at Monica Maynard in disbelief. She stood forlornly to one side, wrists E-cuffed behind her back, refusing to meet anyone's eyes. She cut a pitiful figure, the Federation judge no longer in authority, now just another inmate.

"What do you do when your people have to arrest a female?" Nick asked with a frown.

"We send them to Farrington for holding. They have a special wing for women."

Nick grunted. "No way she's going to Farrington. At least not yet." He glanced up and down the cellblock. "I suggest you clear out the cell farthest from the rest of the population and put her in it. Put up some screens or something so she can have some privacy. She doesn't need to be humiliated."

Zima thought for a moment, then nodded.

"Okay, I'll figure something out. How long does she stay locked up?"

"Until I come for her." Nick hesitated. "Or any other U.F. Marshal. She is *not* to be released to anyone else. Understood?"

Zima, still slightly in shock, looked at Tarpington, and Tarpington nodded.

"Let's go with the marshal on this. It's complicated, but I think he's on the right track."

"Okay. I'll see to it personally."

Nick nodded grimly and shook Zima's hand.

"Shouldn't be more than a day or two."

He and Tarpington walked out into the parking lot. Nick's mind was racing.

"Where to now?" Tarpington asked.

"Farrington Industries."

Tarpington squinted. "Are you sure that's a good idea?"

"No, but it's got to be done." They reached the E-car and Nick pulled the door open, but didn't get in. He stared across the roof at Tarpington. "Are you going with me?"

Tarpington nodded decisively. "I don't want you going in there alone. Besides—" He ventured a smile to ease the tension. "—if you do something illegal, it will be easier for me to prosecute you."

"It could be dangerous."

"Even more dangerous for one man alone. What about backup?"

Nick's eyes narrowed. "Tell you the truth? I'm not sure Milligan will back me on this one. I need to get something solid to make sure he comes on board. Once I have that, we can take that place down."

"So this is a fishing expedition?"

"No, it's more than that. You were there in the judge's chambers. What did you think?"

"I have to admit I was a little surprised she caved as easily as she did."

"Which tells you what?"

"She's hiding something." Tarpington rested his elbows on the roof of the car. "I've known her a long time, Nick, and I'm having trouble picturing her as complicit in all this, but—well, it looks really bad."

Nick's porta-phone rang.

It was probably Misery, he thought, wondering where he was. He'd told her he would be back in a couple of hours, and forgot to update her.

"Nick Walker."

The voice on the other end wasn't Misery Allen. It was Marshal Milligan.

"Walker, where are you?"

"System Springs. What's up?"

"Get over to your hotel right away."

Nick felt a jolt of dread—something in Milligan's voice...

"Why? What's happened?"

"I'll brief you when you get here. Move it!"

Milligan hung up.

Nick stared at the phone for a second, then stared at Tarpington.

"What's wrong?"

Nick stared at him a few more seconds and his heart came to a quick freeze.

"Misery!" he whispered.

Centerville - Ceres

She was still lying in the bottom of the shower, curled into a fetal position, forearms over her face in a pitiful final attempt to ward off the horror that had literally engulfed her. She was absolutely naked. Blisters covered her body, large red welts that obscured her pigmentation and called to mind the image of a boiled hot dog. Clear fluids mingled with traces of blood on the shower floor, leakage that occurred after the water shut itself off. The smell wasn't bad yet, because she hadn't been there long, but neither was it pleasant.

Nick stared in absolute horror, shaken down to his core. Tears sprang to his eyes and slid unnoticed down his cheeks. For several minutes he had trouble breathing. Sandy Beech pulled him out of the room and led him down to the lobby, which had been sealed off to all but emergency traffic; Beech settled him onto a sofa near the doors leading into the hotel garden. Nick sat with a hand over his face, too shaken to speak. A few minutes later Milligan joined them, taking a padded chair nearby.

"Nick, I have to ask you a few questions. You up to it?"

With a supreme effort of will, Nick raised his chin. His face was wet with tears, but he cleared his throat and forced himself to breathe, reminding himself that he had seen worse. Alpha Centauri had been a lot worse, but the difference was that this kind of thing wasn't supposed to happen here; not like this—not to a *girl*.

"Yeah," he croaked. "I can talk."

Milligan eyed him closely, scowling.

"Did you know she was in your room?"

"Yeah. I left her just a couple of hours ago."

"She was okay then?"

He nodded. "She spent the night, and I told her to go back to sleep. I had a couple of things to take care of, and I was gonna be back."

"That's the last time you saw her?"

"Yeah."

Milligan made some notes, then looked closely into his face.

"You've been on Ceres, what—six days?"

"I think so."

"I know part of that time you were out with Murray, so how many nights have you actually spent in your room?"

"Two, I think." He shrugged. "Maybe three. I'm not sure."

"How many times did you use the shower?"

Nick thought for a moment, then shook his head.

"Only once, I think."

"When was that?"

"The day I met you. The first time I went into the room. After that I was usually in a hurry—I would just do a quick sponge bath." He frowned, his eyes focusing. "What are you saying, Marshal? What happened?"

Milligan peered at him for a moment, but didn't answer.

"The shower was booby-trapped," Beech told him.

Nick spun on him. "*What!*"

"Some kind of device had been installed," Milligan said, "attached to the thermostat. As soon as the water hit a certain temperature, it blew. It shut off the cold water and cranked the hot up to maximum."

Nick stared in disbelief, unable to grasp the enormity of it.

"What's worse," Milligan added, "the door was rigged. The minute it closed it was permanently jammed. Anyone inside would be unable to get out."

"Jesus!" Nick buried his head in both hands and sat shaking it from side to side. "Why would anyone *do* that! She was a *defense* attorney! She tried to *help* those bastards!"

Nick sat rocking back and forth for several minutes, trying to fight his tears, failing. The other two leaned back and waited him out. Finally he got it under control and sat wiping his eyes, breathing hard.

"Who found her?" he managed to ask.

"Hotel maintenance. When the gadget blew it triggered a leak alarm in the hotel plumbing. It was the maintenance guy's day off, so it took a little bit for him to respond, and he shut off the water supply to the hotel. When he figured out the leak was in your room he went there to fix it, but nobody answered, so he let himself in. The shower door was jammed but he could see her through the glass, and that's when he called us."

"Murray talked to the desk clerk," Beech told him. "He said you had a plumber come up to your room a few days ago. You want to tell us about that?"

Nick stared at him in fresh surprise, shaking his head slowly.

"I never called a plumber! When was this?"

Milligan's eyes pinned him to the chair. "The day you got here. The clerk saw you talking to him right here in the lobby."

"Why would I call a plumber? That would be the hotel's job."

"The guy you were talking to told the desk clerk you wanted a custom enhancement in your bathroom."

Nick stared back at Milligan and felt his heart begin to beat again. Blood flowed through his veins.

"Jesus Christ!" he whispered.

"What?"

"That was no plumber. It was just a guy warning me about Turd Murdoch. He said Turd was threatening to kill me." He shook his head slowly. "He was carrying a tool kit, but I didn't even pay attention."

Beech and Milligan exchanged glances.

"Do you remember his name?" Beech asked.

"Yeah. I do."

Chapter 27

System Springs - Ceres

Monica Maynard gripped the bars of her cell as Milo Zima placed the last privacy screen to shield her from the eyes of other prisoners.

"Milo!" she whispered hoarsely, trying to keep emotion out of her voice. "I need to make a comm call."

Zima stood perfectly still for a second and gazed at her. She implored him with her eyes, even tried a smile.

"I'm sorry, your Honor, but I have my orders. Marshal Walker—"

"Is out of his mind! For god's sake, Milo, we've known each other for years! You can't possibly believe I'm some sort of criminal!"

"It doesn't matter what I think, your Honor. If you're innocent you'll be cleared."

"Not if Walker asteroids me!"

"I don't believe he would do that. In any case, I can't defy him—he's a Federation marshal."

"And I'm a Federation judge! Milo, the Constitution guarantees every prisoner one comm call. You know that!"

"But it doesn't say *when* you get the call. I'm sure you'll get one. But Marshal Walker specifically said no calls until he gets back."

"That's illegal and you know it! Do you want to be complicit when the law catches up to him?"

Zima stared at her in indecision.

"Look, you're Federation, *he's* Federation—this is a family argument. I don't want to get caught in the middle of it."

"I've been a judge for nearly a decade. He's been a marshal for about a month. I clearly have seniority, if that's what's troubling you, and the only reason I'm in here and he's out there is because he has a gun. Milo, I'm not asking you to release me. One comm call! That's all!"

Zima stared at her another moment, conflict in his eyes. She was right—the call was standard procedure after an arrest. But Walker had been adamant, and David Tarpington had been leaning toward Walker's side of the street.

"Who do you want to call?"

"That's privileged information. You have no right to ask me that."

Zima sighed in frustration. "Goddammit, you're going to get me in so much trouble!"

"No I'm not. I'm trying to save you from more trouble than you can ever hope to want. You know the law, Milo. You've been doing this too long not to know it."

"Jesus Christ!" Zima shook his head and headed for his office. "I'll be back."

Monica Maynard settled in to wait, confident she had just made her case.

Government Annex - Ceres

Back at the U.F. Marshal's office, Milligan poured Nick a shot of brandy. Beech sat watching him while he drank it, and Milligan pulled his own chair around. Tarpington leaned against the wall, looking out of place.

Nick felt the fruity liquor slide into his stomach and spread its heat through his body, but it did nothing to sooth the ache in his heart. He was thinking a little more clearly now, but his former urgency was even more pronounced.

"I've got to get inside Farrington lockup," he told Milligan bluntly.

"What for?"

Nick had never given Milligan or Beech the whole story behind what he was working on. Now he took fifteen minutes and laid it all out, starting with prisoner abuse, falsified death certificates, Jessica Garner, Agua Solar, Nikki Green, and his new-found suspicions about Stan Cramer and Monica Maynard.

"You arrested the *judge?*" Milligan looked truly shocked.

Nick nodded. "She's dirty. As dirty as Farrington."

Milligan exchanged glances with Beech, who looked just as stunned.

"What proof do you have?"

"I already told you."

"That isn't proof! It's suspicion. Everything you told me is circumstantial."

Milligan leaned back and rubbed his face.

"Christ! You've just ended your own career before it started."

But Nick was shaking his head. "I can prove it," he insisted. "I just need to get inside Farrington."

"Well, good luck with that! You just arrested the only person who can get you inside. You need a warrant."

Nick lifted his eyes to meet Milligan's. "What about the Martian Judiciary? There must be some way to get a warrant from them. I mean, if the judge on Ceres dies, there has to be some kind of backup."

"I doubt if you'll be able to convince them on what you've got. In any case, it's Saturday—they won't be open again for at least forty hours."

"Then I'll go without a warrant."

"No you won't. I can't authorize it."

"The day I got here you said I would be working mostly alone. You said I report to you but I work for the Federation. So I don't need your authorization."

"I also told you I'm here to keep you out of trouble. This is trouble, more trouble than you need."

"What about the Garner woman?" Beech asked. "Would she be willing to testify?"

"I don't think so. She's convinced that no one can bring the Farringtons down, and as long as they're in place she feels her life is in danger."

"What if we guarantee her safety?"

"She would never believe it. Once we have the Farringtons behind bars, she might be persuaded, but not until then."

The room fell silent. Nick looked up at Tarpington.

"What about you, Dave? You can get inside, can't you?"

"What, the lockup?" Tarpington looked startled. "Sure, if I have business there."

"Find some."

"Like what?"

"I don't know! Interview a prisoner! Anything."

"And then what? I can't just take a self-guided tour when I'm there. I have to respect their privacy rights."

"Oh, come on, Dave, help me out here. You said yourself the judge looks fishy. Get inside, then find an excuse. Look for the men's room and get lost or something. You're a resourceful fellow."

Tarpington stood there in thought for a moment, looking uncertain. Finally he sighed.

"What sort of thing should I look for?"

"Look for Nikki Green, or anyone else who looks like they might be mistreated."

"You think she's actually over there?"

"I hope to god she is. If she isn't, we may never find her."

Tarpington straightened up slowly, almost reluctantly.

"There is one prisoner I could probably interview. In the women's wing." He glanced at Milligan, then back at Nick. "I'll see what I can find out. Where will you be?"

"At the hotel. I need to lie down. Call my porta-phone."

Farrington Industries - Ceres

"Hello?"

"Hello. It's me."

"What do you want? I'm very busy right now."

"I just wanted to tell you—I've been arrested."

"*What!*"

"Cramer, too. Marshal Walker is starting to figure things out."

"Goddammit! I told you to keep him under control!"

"I did my best."

"Then what went wrong?"

"Nothing! I told you, he's smart and ambitious."

"Who else knows?"

"Tarpington. He stood there and let it happen, didn't even try to stop it."

"Where are you?"

"System Springs lockup."

Long silence.

"Never send a niggo to do a man's job."

"*Fuck you!*"

"Oh, no, you're the one who's fucked. This is not a good thing for Charley, not a good thing at all."

"Leave Charley out of it! There was nothing I could do to prevent it. It was nobody's fault."

"Oh, I think it's clearly your fault."

"Listen, instead of throwing accusations back and forth, maybe we should be talking about how to fix this."

"Don't worry, I'm on top of it. You'll be out by tomorrow. Then we're going to sit down and have a long talk."

"About what?"

"Your future. We're going to renegotiate your contract."

Government Annex - Ceres

Nick had said he was going to his hotel to lie down, but that was a lie—he had things to do and didn't want Milligan hanging over his shoulder while he did them.

He arrived at the Medical Examiner's office just as she was preparing for an autopsy. Shirley Chin was wearing a gown and gloves but hadn't donned her mask. She scowled when she saw him.

"I can't talk to you right now, Marshal. I have a post mortem waiting."

She turned to leave but he blocked her path.

"I won't keep you," he said, "but I need two minutes of your time. In private."

She led him into her office and closed the door, pulling off her gloves.

"I have nothing to report yet. The body just arrived."

He looked blank for a second, then it hit him.

"Oh!"

"I understand she was a friend of yours?"

He nodded. "Yes."

"Then you probably want to know the cause of death. I can't tell you that unless you let me do my job." Shirley Chin sounded angry.

Nick, off balance, merely nodded. Then he cleared his throat.

"Actually, I didn't come here about that. I just wanted to let you know that Stanley Cramer is in custody. So is Judge Maynard."

"What!" Shirley Chin looked shocked.

"Before the weekend is over I'm going to have the whole Farrington superstructure at my feet. So you can stop being afraid and start cooperating with me."

Her lips parted and she sank into her chair, staring at him.

"You can tell me the truth about those cases I spoke to you about," he continued. "You and I both know the cause of death was falsified in most of them. I can only assume you were working under duress, that either you or someone close to you has been threatened. The sooner you come clean with me, the sooner I can eliminate that threat."

She clasped her hands together and stared at them, her jaws clenched, for nearly a minute.

"Jessica Garner didn't really bite Donald Hooley on the neck, did she?"

Her eyes flicked to his face, but she didn't reply.

"There was no record of Hooley being treated at this facility. You didn't even examine him, did you?"

"I don't examine live patients," she said calmly. "I only deal with the dead."

"Then why were you called to testify?"

She stared into his eyes for a long time, then stared at her hands again.

"Doctor Chin?"

"I think you know why," she said quietly.

"I think I do, too. But I need to be certain. I need you to tell me."

She shook her head slowly. "I can't tell you anything. I'm not even supposed to talk to you."

"Who told you not to talk to me?"

Her lips pursed, her cheek twitched, but she didn't answer. Nick tried another tack.

"You do know who Stanley Cramer is, don't you?"

"Yes."

"He's behind bars at this very moment. I can keep him there until tomorrow, but if I don't come up with some solid evidence by then, I'll have to release him."

"You won't find anything."

"I won't find anything if someone doesn't *start talking!*"

She met his eyes again. "Judge Maynard is locked up, too?"

"That's right. I believe she's working for Cramer. With a judge on the payroll, Farrington Industries has a blank check."

"So...if you find evidence against them, who will you give it to?"

"David Tarpington will file indictments with the Martian Judiciary. They'll have to send someone out to hear the evidence, or we'll have to take the prisoners to them. Either way, it won't be Judge Maynard's courtroom."

She sat like a statue for another minute, trembling slightly. Finally she stirred and pushed her chair back.

"I really must get on with that autopsy. Come back tonight, and I'll give you a report."

His eyes widened slightly in hope.

"A report about...?"

"Whatever I have to report. I need time to think."

Farrington Industries - Ceres

David Tarpington was less than thrilled when he drove up to the guard shack at Farrington Industries. He loved being the big fish in a small pond, but his pond of choice was a courtroom, not a cellblock. His normal self-assurance came from the fact that he was very good at what he did and always knew when he was on firm ground; today none of that was true, and he wasn't even sure it was safe. He didn't really think he would be in danger, but given the variables involved, any mistakes he made might cause harm to someone else.

The guard at the gate passed him through without question—his face was well known—and he parked near the entrance to the lockup and strode in the front door with his document case. The guard in the office opened the document case and inspected it, then nodded curtly. Tarpington signed in with his thumbprint and was passed through the electronic gate. At the next stop he came face to face with the day supervisor; since it was a Saturday, the weekend shift was working, and a pleasant surprise awaited him.

"Hey-hey! Counselor!" The man grinning at him was Tim Spencer, a frequent patron at the Blue Nebula. "Haven't seen you since last night."

Spencer offered his hand and Tarpington took it with a grin.

"What brings you out on the weekend?"

"You know how it is, Tim. The cause of justice knows no holiday."

Spencer guffawed. "Yeah, right! Who do you need to see?"

"Lubov Kalashnikova. I think she was brought in Thursday night."

"Yeah, she was, and she hasn't stopped bitching since. Please tell me you're gonna offer her a deal, so I can cut her loose."

Tarpington smiled and winked. "I'll see what I can do."

Spencer grabbed a fistful of E-keys and came out the door, leading the way down a long corridor flanked with holding cells. He chatted nonstop and Tarpington replied in monosyllables, his heart pounding as his head swiveled in case he might see anything that would help Nick. Presently they arrived at an interview room and Spencer held the door.

"Take a seat inside and I'll fetch the prisoner."

Tarpington took a seat at the table and opened his document case. He wouldn't learn anything here, but at least he was inside. He would go through the motions with the prisoner and hope for inspiration.

"Don't believe a word this bitch says," Spencer grinned as he shoved a woman through the door. "She's likely to tell you anything."

Lubov Kalashnikova was a Rukranian woman of indeterminate age; she was probably around forty, but looked sixty. She was a stout woman with Slavic features, not ugly but badly weathered. Her bleached hair was short and spiky, sticking out in every direction; her face had the leathery look of hard living, and her eyes were mere slits that gazed back at Tarpington like blue crystals. Her lip was curled in a permanent sneer, but her single most prominent feature seemed to be her attitude.

"Wot the fuck you want!" she demanded. Her accent was overpowering.

Tarpington smiled. "I was looking over your arrest report," he said, studying a document in his hand. "I thought you might answer a few questions for me."

"*Fuck* you. I got nothing to say."

He shrugged. "Well, you might want to reconsider; according to another witness—"

"*Fuck* you."

Tarpington stared at her a moment, his grin still in place.

"As I was saying, the woman who is accusing you might be—"

"*Fuck* you. I got nothing to say."

He let the smile die and stared at her a moment.

"Are you pleading guilty, then? If you are, you'll probably get—"

"*Fuck* you. The bitch deserved it. I don't mind lockup. I been here before."

"You enjoy being locked up?"

She shrugged. "I don't mind it. I don't gotta work, I get fed, I get to fuck."

Tarpington's eyes widened a fraction. "Who do you get to fuck?"

Lubov's heavy lips curled into a grin. "Anybody I want! Maybe I fuck *you* before you go, eh?" She cackled madly, and Tarpington fought back an involuntary gulp.

"Uh, well, I'm certainly tempted, but I don't think they'll allow it."

"The fuck you talking about? Sure they allow it! They allow it alla time."

Tarpington's heart beat a little faster.

"Where did you hear that?" he asked, lowering his voice.

"I don't hear nothing! I *do* it. Every time I come here, I fuck whoever I want."

"Who do you fuck?"

"I tol' you—anybody I want!"

"Really?" He barely remembered to smile encouragement at her. "Where does this take place?"

"Inna men's lockup. Poor horny bastards, they get no pussy, they take anything."

Tarpington stared at her in amazement, hardly daring to believe her.

"What about the guards? You fuck them, too?"

"Yeah, sure. Not so many women on Ceres, *da?* Alla men are horny." Her eyes crinkled and almost disappeared as she smiled. To his amazement, she had perfect white teeth. "Maybe you horny too, eh?"

His tongue slid over his lips. "Uh, yeah, most of the time. But...I already got laid last night." *Thank god*, he didn't add.

"*Fuck* las' night. Las' night is las' night—today is today." She beamed at him.

Tarpington closed the document case and pushed it to one side. His heart hammered as he rested elbows on the table, leaning in confidentially—he might have just found that inspiration he'd been hoping for. He had picked her name because it was familiar; he'd prosecuted her at least a dozen times, always for minor assault, always with the same result— she refused every plea agreement and served her time, usually ninety days in lockup. This had been going on for years.

"How many times have you been in here?" he asked, just to confirm his memory.

"Plenty. Ten times, twenty times...who's counting?"

"How come you never take the plea agreement?"

Lubov shrugged. "I get horny, I start a fight. I get locked up, I get to fuck. I take plea, I got to work." She shrugged again.

"Do other women in here fuck the guards, too?" He tried to look titillated.

"Yeah, sure. Some of 'em."

"Which ones?"

"I dunno names. The pretty ones."

He opened his document case again and pulled out a flat photo.

"What about this one?"

Lubov peered at the photo a second and nodded.

"I see her before."

"Do you remember when?"

"No. Maybe two year, maybe three."

"And you saw her fucking the guards?"

"Naw, she not fucking them, they fucking her."

Tarpington's mouth turned dry. He swallowed to moisten it.

"How many men?"

"I dunno. Different every time. Two this time, four next time, ten after that. Day after day. Night after night. She cry, she scream, nobody care. I say, 'Hey, wot about me?', but they not listen. They like the pretty one."

"Did she see you?"

"Naw, I don't think so. She cry, she scream, she pass out. They shock her awake and start again."

Tarpington sat there a moment, rigid, his blood surging with adrenaline. Everything Jessica Garner had told Nick was true! This woman had seen it.

"So wot about you, now?" Lubov grinned, trying to get him back on track. "You wanna do it?"

He blinked and forced a smile.

"Maybe not today, Lubov, but it's been fun talking with you. Have you seen other women like that one? Pretty ones like that one?"

"Yeah, always one or two around. Guards like to play."

"Are there any here now?"

She looked thoughtful, then shrugged. "I not see, but I hear."

"You heard what?"

"Crying. Screaming."

"When?"

"Las' night. This morning."

"Do you know where?"

"Other end of lockup. Maybe far cell, maybe cross corridor. Not sure."

Tarpington put the photos away and locked his document case. He stood.

"Okay, Lubov. I think we're done here. Hope everything works out for you."

"You come to my cell now, *da?*"

"Sorry, I don't have time today." He winked. "Maybe I can come back."

He moved to the door and rang the bell. A moment later Spencer came in to escort the prisoner back to her cell. Tarpington waited in the hallway.

"Mind if I tag along?"

Spencer looked surprised, then a little apprehensive.

"No need. You're done with her, aren't you?"

"Yeah." Tarpington felt his heart beat a little faster. "But I can't leave until you let me out, and I'm not in a hurry."

Spencer had Lubov Kalashnikova by the arm and was escorting her down the corridor; now he stopped.

"I don't think it's a good idea, David. It's against the rules."

Tarpington grinned his most engaging. "What's the harm? I'm not armed." He held both arms away from his body as proof. "I'm not going to break anybody out. Hell, I'm the prosecutor—it's my job to put people in."

Spencer wavered. Tarpington read him perfectly.

"I'll make it worth your while."

"Yeah?" Spencer's eyes glittered slightly.

Tarpington slid a hand behind his head and kissed him firmly, sliding his tongue deep, then released him and sucked briefly at his ear.

"I promise," he murmured.

Lubov cackled. "Ah, you not come to my cell now. You like him better, *da?*"

Tarpington winked at her. Spencer swallowed hard, his eyes filled with lust. Before he could arrive at a decision Tarpington strode on ahead, leaving Spencer to bring his prisoner and catch up.

"I swear to god, David! You're gonna get me fired!"

"It'll be worth it!"

Chapter 28

The Open Airlock - Ceres

Nick returned to the Open Airlock in search of Turd Murdoch, but he wasn't there. Apparently the bar's patrons had taken Nick at his word and barred Turd from drinking there anymore. He realized he had no idea where to find the man, especially on a Saturday. He ordered a beer from the bartender and stood there a moment drinking it.

The beer had little effect on him; he was operating in that narrow space between Life and Limbo—his mind was working at full speed, but he was feeling nothing at all. That changed a moment later as he gazed at the patrons, inspecting them one by one as his view shifted around the room. At a table in the far corner, the dimmest part of the room, three men were drinking together, talking...laughing. Nick saw two of them clearly, but the other's face was hidden in the gloom. He seemed to be keeping his head down, as if to avoid being noticed.

Nick felt his skin tingle...something about that man!

He set his beer on the bar and began winding his way through the crowd. The patrons parted to let him pass, but he was hardly aware of them. He came to a halt by the corner table, three feet away, and stood there, glaring down at the three drinkers. Two of them looked up with surprised expressions, innocent expressions. The third man sat facing him, gazing at the tabletop, idly running his finger through the water that sweated from his beer bottle, his face obscured by long hair hanging over it.

"Fred Ferguson," Nick said slowly. "Stand up."

The room fell silent. The two men flanking Ferguson shifted their gaze to him, more surprised than ever, and one of them pushed his chair back. The third man didn't move, didn't look up, but began to tremble ever so slightly.

"You heard me, Ferguson! Goddammit, *stand up!*"

Finally, the youth whose hair was too long in front lifted his face, pale as a ghost. Tears glimmered on his cheeks.

"I'm sorry, Marshal!" he said weakly. "I never would have hurt her. It was meant for you!"

Both his drinking buddies were now on their feet, shock in their eyes. They looked from Nick to Ferguson and back. Nick drew his laser pistol and pointed it at Ferguson's face.

"I'm not telling you again, Ferguson. Stand up. You're under arrest for the murder of Misery Allen."

Centerville - Ceres

"What are we doing here?" Fred Ferguson glanced around fearfully as Nick pulled the E-car behind a stone wall in the Centerville public park. Nick stepped out of the car and walked around to the passenger side, then hauled Ferguson out and slammed him against the wall. From where they stood they were largely hidden from view in any direction. Only the top floor of Nick's hotel was visible above the wall, and in the other direction only the naked rock of the habitat wall. None of the people in the park could see them.

"I have several options here," Nick said slowly, checking Ferguson's E-cuffs to make sure they were secure. "I can take you to lockup, where you can get a lawyer and plead Not Guilty to murder, then take your chances with a jury. Or, I can beat the shit out of you and make you wish you were lying on a slab next to Misery Allen. *Or*...I can just shoot you in your fucking head."

He glared at the prisoner with cold hatred in his eyes, reaching for his laser pistol. Fred Ferguson trembled with terror.

"Right now," Nick said quietly, "I'm leaning toward option number three."

"You can't do that!" Ferguson pleaded. "I'm supposed to get a trial!"

"Well, yeah, you are *supposed* to get a trial. And Misery Allen is *supposed* to be alive. But, gee whiz, guess what—*SHE ISN'T!*"

Nick pushed the laser muzzle against the prisoner's throat and thumbed the charge switch. After a brief whining sound, the charge light turned green. Ferguson closed his eyes and began to blubber.

"I swear to god, Marshal! It wasn't meant for her! I would never have harmed her! She was a beautiful girl."

"Yeah, and she would have given you the best possible defense in this situation. But she can't. She'll never defend anyone again."

"I'm sorry! I'm *sorry!*"

"I'm sure you are, but that doesn't do her a hell of a lot of good, now does it?"

Ferguson's eyes looked desperate, panicked.

"What do you want from me? What do you want me to say? I did it! I wish I hadn't, but I did!"

"You didn't do it on your own. Who hired you?"

Ferguson shook his head, his face slick with tears.

"Oh, Christ, I can't tell you that! I'll be a dead man."

"You're already a dead man. Unless you start talking."

"Marshal, *please!*"

"Was it Turd Murdoch?"

Ferguson shook his head rapidly.

"No. Turd wanted to kill you himself. He would never pay someone else to do it."

"Then who?"

Sobbing, Ferguson shook his head from side to side. "*Please!*"

Nick thumbed the pistol, setting the beam spread to needlepoint, and shot him through the left ear. It made a tiny hole, more of a burn than a wound, but blood sprayed across his collar. Ferguson screamed.

"Last chance, Fred. The next one goes through your dick."

Ferguson was lunging up and down; Nick had to push him back against the wall and hold him with his left hand.

"Stan Cramer!" he shouted. "It was Cramer!"

Nick's eyes widened with surprise. "How do you know Cramer?"

"I work for Farrington. I'm a plumber. I've done plumbing in his office."

Nick's eyes narrowed in thought. He had really thought the mastermind behind the shower bomb was Turd Murdoch, but this put a whole different spin on things.

"Why did Cramer want me killed? I hadn't even been on the asteroid a whole day."

"When you jacked Turd up that first night, the news spread like a solar flare. It was all over Ceres before morning. Cramer heard about it, and it upset him."

"Upset him why? What was Turd to him?"

"Turd is a drill supervisor, a good one. He's also a maniac, and Cramer uses him sometimes to take care of people."

"What people?"

Ferguson swallowed, panting with pain.

"Troublesome people. Turd is good at arranging accidents. Nobody ever challenged Turd before, but you did, and that worried Cramer. He said we didn't need any U.F. Mavericks running around on Ceres."

"U.F. *Maverick?*"

"That's what Cramer called you."

Nick frowned again. "So why didn't Cramer send Turd after me, instead of you?"

"Cramer knew that Turd couldn't kill a U.F. Marshal and get away with it. He also knew Turd would do it anyway, sooner or later, so he wanted you dead before Turd got a chance to kill you. To protect Turd."

"So...if I got boiled in the shower, it would just be a plumbing problem. Nobody to blame."

"Yeah. Exactly."

Nick thumbed his pistol back to standby and stuck it in his holster.

"Why did you warn me about Turd that day?"

"I was hoping you'd kill him. Then I could warn you about the shower. I didn't want to set that device, Marshal, but I had to. If I didn't, Cramer would have sent Turd to kill me."

Fresh tears coursed down Ferguson's cheeks.

"I'm not a violent man, Marshal. I'm just trying to survive."

Nick stood still for a minute, breathing hard. He still had an animal desire to hurt Fred Ferguson, and hurt him bad. Maybe it was the murder instinct that had plagued him for years after the war, or maybe it was just his natural desire for retribution; whatever it was, he dared not give in to it. Ferguson had done a terrible thing, but Nick would have to let the legal system deal with it. He took Ferguson's arm and shoved him toward the car.

"I'm glad we had this little talk, Fred. I don't hate you quite as much as I did a minute ago."

Ferguson said nothing as Nick shoved him into the front seat. Then Nick had another thought and hauled him out again.

"You said Turd is good at arranging accidents. Did Turd arrange for Scott Garner's accident?"

Ferguson looked blank, and Nick gave him a shake.

"You're doing real good, Fred—don't clam up on me now!"

"Who's Scott Garner?"

Nick sighed. It had been nearly four years ago, so Ferguson might not remember.

"Do you do plumbing in the Farrington lockup?"

"Yeah. That's where I work most of the time."

Nick hauled him back to the stone wall and pushed him against it.

"Good. I need some more information, and if you lie to me, I'll shoot your other ear."

Farrington Industries - Ceres

David Tarpington had been to the Farrington lockup literally dozens of times, interviewing inmates, offering deals, doing his job. He had never been this far into the building, and found it more than a little depressing. This was the women's wing, the smallest of all the cellblocks, but he saw hundreds of women sitting in cells. The place carried a powerful smell of bad food, strong urine, and shit. Of those who spotted him, with his wavy blond hair, sexy good looks, and muscular body, a few sneered and two or three cursed, but the overwhelming majority hooted and cat-called him.

"Hey, there, sweetie! You lonely?"

"Baby, oh baby! Where the fuck you been all my life?"

"You sleepy, hon? I got a place you can rest, dark and deep."

Tarpington ignored them. They reached Lubov's cell and Spencer, getting more nervous by the minute, pushed her inside with her three cellmates. Tarpington kept walking, heading for a cross corridor just ahead.

"Where does this lead?" he asked as Spencer trotted to catch up to him.

"You can't go down there." Spencer took him by the arm. "Come on, man, you have to leave now."

Tarpington shook him off. "What's your problem, Tim? I'm just looking around."

But Spencer's expression was pained.

"Look, this isn't a Federation facility. It's private property. You need permission to look around."

Tarpington spun around and grabbed him, kissed him again, and patted his cheek.

"I don't need permission, Tim. I'm with you."

"I don't have the authority—"

But Tarpington was already gone, striding quickly down the cross corridor. The far end was dim, but he saw handrails and steps leading down. The image of a dungeon flashed through his mind, and his heart beat a little faster. Just before he reached it he stopped and turned to his left, his jaw dropping and his eyes growing wide. His heart hammered harder than ever.

Spencer bumped into him, then turned and looked as well. Before them, clearly visible behind a wide window, was a brightly lit room. A woman was suspended from the ceiling by the wrists, completely nude, her head hanging as if she were dead or unconscious. She was no kid—she was at least thirty-five, maybe older; she looked slightly emaciated but her bare breasts were full and heavy. Her hair was cut short in a style fancied by many housewives. She rotated slowly as if in a light breeze, her feet dangling barely a foot above the tiled floor. Tarpington stared in complete shock as he gazed upon the cuts, bruises, bites, and burns on her pale skin. Sitting to one side on the floor was a generator with coiled cables and alligator clips.

"Jesus Christ!" he whispered. "Who is she?"

Spencer was so agitated he was almost sobbing.

"I dunno, man. I *told* you not to come down here! You should've listened to me!"

But Tarpington pressed his hands against the window. He stared at the woman closely, trying to recognize her.

"I've never seen her before. What's she doing here? She was never processed through the court."

Spencer took his arm and literally tried to pull him away.

"Get out of here, David! Get the fuck out of here right now!"

Tarpington took a step back, his eyes still glued to the woman. Who was she? Why was she here? Who had authorized...*this?*

He heard a footstep behind him, the solid click of hard leather on the starcrete floor.

"Oh, Christ!" Spencer gasped.

Tarpington turned. He clearly recognized the third man, and opened his mouth to speak.

"You should listen to your lover boy, faggot!" the other man said.

Tarpington didn't see the sap until it crashed into his skull. Pain flashed through his head and then he was falling. Everything was black before he hit the floor.

Chapter 29

Farrington Industries - Ceres

Nick arrived at the security shack at a few minutes before eight in the evening on Saturday. The artificial sunlight was still bright—Farrington didn't conform to the rest of the asteroid on day/night cycles. He stopped in a small parking lot outside the gate and studied the layout for a moment; the administration building looked quiet, as it should on a weekend, with very few cars in the parking lot. The parking area near the prison building was more populated, but not as heavily as a few days earlier. The lockup was running a skeleton staff for the weekend.

He picked up his porta-phone and called Marshal Milligan.

"I need you to round up Murray and Beech and meet me at Farrington Industries," Nick told him.

"Walker? What the hell, I thought you went back to the hotel!"

"Change of plan, sir. I've got the goods on these bastards and I'm going in."

"Not till we get there! Give me thirty minutes."

Nick hesitated only briefly. He knew Milligan was right—going in without backup was foolhardy. But then he thought of Misery, her pitiful body curled up naked in the bottom of that shower. He shook his head, too deep-down angry to care about procedure.

"Sorry, sir, I'm going in now. I'll see you when you get here."

"Walker—!"

Nick shut the phone off and hung it on his belt. He got out of the E-car and slammed the door, then strode briskly toward the gate.

The man at the gate was one Nick had never seen before; Browning must have weekends off. Well, maybe that was for the better—this guy didn't know him and wouldn't be unduly alert. Nick saw his eyes flicker briefly toward the badge and saw his expression tighten, but that was probably just a standard reaction to law enforcement of any type, not necessarily directed toward Nick personally.

He stepped away from the guard shack as Nick approached.

"Can I help you, Marshal?"

Nick walked right up to him and nailed him with a right hook, dropping him like a stone. The guard's hat flew off as he fell and Nick dragged him inside the shack, then E-cuffed his hands behind his back. He turned to the control panel and opened the gate, locking it so it would stay open. That would aid Milligan's entry when he arrived.

The guard had a small E-car parked near the gate, just inside the fence, and Nick took it. The car was clearly marked with Farrington's logo, so anyone seeing it traverse the parking lot wouldn't be suspicious. Nick headed straight for the main entrance to the Admin building, and when he reached it, left the car where it was and walked inside. The broad lobby was empty except for another security guard. This one looked up in surprise as Nick approached, but again didn't seem unduly concerned. He even smiled.

"Can I help you?"

"Yeah..." Nick pointed out the front door. "Do you know anything about E-cars? I think my battery is dead, and I don't know where to charge it."

The guard stepped out from behind his desk, staring at the front door. As soon as he was clear of his console and out of position to trigger an alarm, Nick drew his laser pistol and jammed it against the man's head.

"If you make one sound," he said coldly, "I'll fry your brain like an egg. Drop your gunbelt and radio."

The guard's eyes sprang wide as they met Nick's, and he gulped in fear.

"What's this about?" His hands fumbled for his gunbelt.

"I don't remember telling you to talk! I won't warn you again."

The gunbelt hit the floor, the radio with it. Without taking his eyes off him, Nick knelt quickly and retrieved the guard's E-cuffs, then pushed him against the wall.

"Hands behind your back," he said quietly.

Seconds later he had the man cuffed. He threw the gunbelt behind the desk and then shoved his prisoner toward the elevators.

"Let's go for a ride."

Nick pushed the guard to the floor and used the key he had taken from Benny Silva to send the elevator to the top floor. When it arrived he swept the lobby with his laser pistol, but as he'd hoped, the lobby was empty. Without a word he pushed a button to send the car down again, then stepped out, leaving the guard inside. Even if the man freed himself, Nick would have two or three minutes before he could send help. He didn't expect he would need much more than that.

He holstered his pistol and pushed open the heavy oaken door into Harvey Farrington's office.

System Springs - Ceres

Milo Zima had gone home; he didn't normally work weekends.

The man in charge on Saturday evening was Lewis Williams, a beefy monster who would have weighed three hundred pounds on Terra, and only part of it was fat. Williams had just unwrapped a sandwich and was going over the daily logs as he began to eat. At the moment all twenty-five cells were full, or nearly full—forty-eight men and one woman. Another prisoner had just been brought in an hour ago, leaving only two beds available for men and one empty bed in the woman's cell. Williams frowned as he recognized the woman's name...*Judge Maynard?* What the hell was that about?

"Can I have a bite of that?"

Williams glanced up at the man who'd just come in the outer door. Chewing slowly, he lowered his heavy lids to look as intimidating as possible.

"After the fight."

The visitor, almost as big as Williams but more muscular, laughed. He wore a thick, shaggy beard and his stringy hair was tied in the back. His arms were scarred and tattooed, his teeth grey and grungy. Williams knew the visitor well, had known him for years. Had seen him in the lockup on several occasions, but never as a visitor.

"The fuck you doing here, Murdoch?" he demanded. "Only time I ever see you here is when you're under arrest."

Turd Murdoch grinned. "Yeah, but I never stay long, do I?"

"I noticed that. You must be sucking some mighty big dick."

Murdoch grinned even wider and nodded. "Mighty big."

Williams stared at him, waiting for an answer to his original question.

"I came to spring a couple of your prisoners," Murdoch said.

"Yeah? Which couple?"

"Stanley Cramer and Judge Maynard."

Williams' eyes narrowed and he shook his head. "Can't have 'em. They don't go anywhere without specific orders from the U.F. Marshal."

"You talkin' about Walker? He's the one sent me over here, did I forget to mention that?"

"Funny he didn't say anything when he was here."

"When was he here?"

"Less than an hour ago. He brought in another prisoner."

Murdoch's smile faded. "Who'd he bring in?"

Williams glanced at the log, then back at Murdoch. "Fred Ferguson."

Murdoch shrugged. "Well, he told me to get them two out and bring 'em to his office. I guess he did forget to mention it to you."

Williams crossed his arms and glared. "Seems like he would've took them when he was here."

Murdoch hesitated, then spread his hands in defeat.

"Well, fuck, it's not my problem. I just do what I'm told."

"Since when are you and Walker such big buddies? Last I heard, you were aiming to kill him."

"Aw, that was just a misunderstanding. We kissed and made up since then." Murdoch winked. "Sorta like your faggot supervisor."

Williams didn't smile. He wasn't gay himself, but he liked Milo Zima and didn't appreciate hearing him slurred.

"That kind of talk won't get you anything," he said, "except my boot up your ass. If Walker wants those prisoners released, have him call me. Until he does, they don't go anywhere."

Turd Murdoch grimaced and glanced down the corridor toward the cellblock. He looked back at Williams and shrugged.

"Like I said, no skin off my ass."

He turned toward the outer door. Williams picked up his sandwich and took another bite, returning to his logs. Murdoch stopped and turned back.

"By the way, I forgot to tell you—"

Williams looked up.

Turd Murdoch held a laser pistol in his right hand; he shot Williams straight through the eye.

Farrington Industries - Ceres

Harvey Farrington was sitting at his desk. Even though it was a Saturday evening, Nick wasn't surprised. From everything he knew about the man, Farrington had no private life, no personal interests. He lived for his business and nothing else—business was his mistress. Farrington looked up as Nick approached, amusement springing to his eyes.

"Marshal Walker! What a pleasant surprise! I was just thinking about you."

Uh. Uh.

Nick stopped in front of the desk, his eyes on the holo-window behind Farrington. The gorgeous splendor of Mt. Shasta was still displayed in all its glory.

"How much does something like that cost?" Nick nodded at the picture.

Farrington smiled smugly. "Seven million terros, including transportation and installation. There isn't another one anywhere in the Asteroid Belt or the Outer Worlds, and only two on all of Mars."

Uh. Uh.

Nick nodded. "Very impressive."

Without another word, he reached under his left arm and drew the Ru-Hawk .44 Magnum. Taking deliberate aim, as Harvey Farrington's eyes widened in dawning horror, he fired one round into the holo-window. The display exploded in a flash of electronics and compressed gas; smoke boiled along the wall and flame flickered around the edges. Farrington gaped in shock, all the condescension gone from his eyes. He stared at the smoking wall for ten seconds, then turned back to Nick, his face flushed with fury.

"You *motherfucker!* Have you lost your goddamn *mind?*"

Nick drew back the hammer on the .44 and took a step closer to the desk. Without a word he carefully laid the pistol on the desk, hammer cocked, the barrel pointing at Farrington's chest.

"I wouldn't make any sudden moves," he said casually. "That thing has a hair trigger. Almost blew my own foot off before I got used to it. So...if you even bump that desk..."

Farrington's mouth clamped shut. He stared at the .44 and swallowed hard, all the flush fading from his cheeks. Nick drew his laser pistol, pulled up a chair, and sat down. He took a deep breath and let it out slowly.

"Let's talk about Agua Solar."

Farrington looked stunned. "What about Agua Solar?"

"You acquired their operation by fraudulent means. Same with Ceres Creek and Ceres Ice. You arranged accidents. People were killed."

"That's a lie! I never did any such thing."

"I've been talking to Stanley Cramer. He told me everything."

"You're lying! Stan would never—"

"Tell the truth?" Nick grinned. "Do you honestly think he's loyal to you? For all his apparent sophistication, Cramer is just another felon. Just like you. He'll do or say anything to save his own skin."

Farrington sat staring at him, blinking uncertainly, his jaw rotating rapidly back and forth.

Uh. Uh.

Nick continued. "For example, it was Cramer who provided the startup capital for your takeover. Once he drove their stock prices into the sewer, it didn't take that much cash to purchase those companies, because they were already ruined. You got the operations and all their assets for nine cents on the terro, all of it for just a few million terros. Quite a bargain, I have to admit."

Nick was fishing, but Farrington's expression said he had guessed right.

"You're delusional, Marshal. You've been here less than a week and you know all this already?"

Nick shrugged. "They say the eye is attracted to motion. If you don't move, you don't get noticed. But since I've been here all I've seen is Farrington Industries in fast forward, everything from kidnapping to prisoner abuse to murder."

"Murder! What the fuck are you talking about?"

Uh. Uh.

"Oh, didn't Cramer tell you? He ordered me killed. But he missed me and got Misery Allen instead."

Farrington looked truly surprised. He shifted in his chair, but Nick held up a hand.

"*Don't*...make any sudden moves."

Farrington froze, his eyes snapping back toward the pistol on the desk, which still pointed at him. His tongue snaked across his lips.

"I don't know anything about any murder," he said slowly.

"We can come back to that. We have a lot of other things to discuss."

Farrington's eyes returned to meet Nick's. "Like what?"

"How did you manage to persuade Monica Maynard to work for you?"

"I don't know what you're talking about."

"Did you order Judge Boxner to be shot in the back, or was that Cramer's doing?"

"I was as shocked as anyone when Boxner was killed."

"Were you? Was Cramer shocked, too?"

"I didn't talk to Cramer about it."

"Well, I find it very interesting that Monica Maynard was a member of your legal department before the killing, and jumped straight to Federation judge afterward. On Cramer's very influential recommendation, I might add."

Farrington shrugged. "You'll have to talk to him about that."

"Where's your brother?"

"He's not here."

"I can see that. Where is he?"

"I'm not my brother's keeper."

Uh. Uh.

"Tell me about Nikki Green."

"Who?"

"Nikki Green. Where is she?"

"I have no idea who that is."

"No? How about Jessica Garner?"

"Are these people prisoners? You'll have to talk to my brother about that; he oversees the lockup."

"So he *does* have a function. What's his title?"

"He doesn't need a title. He's my business partner."

"You run the business, he runs the prison?"

"Something like that."

"And you give him a free hand?"

"Why not? He's my brother. I trust him."

"That lockup generates twenty-three million terros a year. I would think you'd want to know what goes on down there."

"I'm touched that you're so concerned about our operation." Farrington's eyes glimmered with returning humor; he was starting to enjoy himself again.

"It doesn't concern you that Henry rapes and tortures women in lockup?"

"If such a thing were true, it wouldn't concern me a bit. I have my appetites, Henry has his."

Uh. Uh.

Nick smiled. That sounded suspiciously close to an admission, though it fell far short of admissible evidence.

A door opened at the far end of the room and Henry Farrington stepped through, a wine glass in his hand. Nick swiveled toward him, covering him with the laser pistol; Henry walked unconcernedly toward his brother's desk, showing no surprise at Nick's presence. One eyebrow was elevated, his cynical sneer stamped across his face. Then he saw the ruined holo-window and his eyes widened in shock.

"*Ghastly!*" he breathed. "What the fuck...?"

"Marshal Walker decided to do a little redecorating," Harvey said with a smirk.

Uh. Uh.

"You goddamn bastard! That's going to cost you!"

"Don't worry," Harvey said, "when we finish suing the Federation, we'll attach Walker's wages. He should have it paid off by, oh, the end of his life." He looked at Nick again and burst into a bray. Nick winced as the decibels washed over him.

"Take a seat, Henry." Nick waved his pistol at a chair. "You can join our little chat."

"I need a chat with you like I need a hole in the head." But Henry pulled up the chair and sat down. Nick shifted his own chair slightly to keep them both covered. He caught a whiff of vinegar from Henry's wine glass.

"Harvey doesn't know anything about Nikki Green," Nick told Henry, "but I'll bet you do."

Henry didn't even blink. "What about her?"

"Where is she now?"

"How the hell should I know? She did her time and was released."

"Wrong answer."

Henry shrugged, his lip curling in a sneer. He sipped his vinegar. "If you already know the answers, why did you ask?"

"She was never logged in as an inmate. Which tells me you kept her off the radar."

"Why would I do that?"

"So you wouldn't have to release her when her sentence was served. She's a real looker, isn't she? You like them young and hot, don't you?"

Henry smirked, arrogance and amusement in one easy expression.

"I don't fuck niggos."

Nick shook his head in reproach. *Tch tch tch.* You're such a racist, Henry. To your way of thinking, people who aren't white aren't really people, are they?"

The twins exchanged glances, sharing their amusement. Nick could almost see the data stream that passed between them.

"Where are you headed with all this, Marshal? What do you hope to gain here?"

Nick smiled again. "Oh, that's easy. I'm going to put you out of business. I have enough hard evidence and eye-witness testimony to lock you both up forever and ever."

Harvey Farrington brayed loudly.

"Good luck with that, Marshal! The Federation Colonial Commission will never let that happen. If we go out of business, twelve million people on the Outer Worlds will die within a matter of weeks. We are an essential industry."

Nick shook his head. "I've already been in contact with the FCC. They've dispatched a receiver to take over your operation. He left Mars yesterday."

The brothers exchanged looks again, this time with considerably less amusement.

"And Carmen Castillo is with them," Nick finished, completing the lie. "She will take the reins and make sure the water shipments continue...until the receivership is lifted and she regains control of Farrington Industries."

Henry's face turned ugly. "That wetback bitch!"

Nick shrugged. "Seems only right, doesn't it? You stole the company from her father, so she's the perfect candidate to return it to."

Henry's eyes were blazing, but suddenly Harvey brayed loudly again.

"Relax, Henry! He's bluffing. If there really was a receiver on the way, Walker wouldn't tell us about it until he got here. It's all bullshit."

Nick felt a flush creep into his cheeks and was annoyed with himself. He was searching for another gambit when he heard the oaken doors creak behind him.

"Keep telling yourself that, Harvey," he said. "You two can discuss it in your jail cell. Looks like my backup is here."

He stood up and turned to look, fully expecting Marshals Milligan, Murray and Beech. Instead he saw Turd Murdoch, followed by Monica Maynard and Stanley Cramer. Murdoch was grinning; he held a laser pistol pointed straight at Nick's heart.

Chapter 30

No one spoke for a long moment. Nick stared at Turd's pistol, his own still aimed generally toward Henry Farrington. Turd was grinning. Monica Maynard appeared to be in minor shock, eyes wide and mouth open. Stan Cramer skirted the room to keep himself out of the line of fire while he flanked Nick.

Fred Ferguson came in the door, almost reluctantly, and stood a few feet behind Turd. His ear wound had been sprayed with LiquiSkin, which left it an orange color.

Nick's mind was racing. He tried to calculate whether Turd would shoot or wait for orders. He slowly turned to face him, bringing his own laser around.

"You better put it down, Marshal," Turd said, his eyes bright. He snapped his fingers at Ferguson. "Get his gun, Fred."

Nick lowered the weapon but still held on to it. He shifted his eyes toward Ferguson, who came slowly forward.

"Looks like you got bailed out, Fred. How's your ear?"

Ferguson's cheek twitched as he made eye contact and then broke it. He reached for the pistol and Nick handed it to him. He backed away, holding it awkwardly.

"Be careful with that," Nick said. "It has a sensitive trigger. You could kill some girl with it very easily."

Pain registered in Ferguson's eyes. It occurred to Nick that Ferguson really did regret Misery's death. He decided to push the needle a little.

"Killing a girl is bad enough, but killing a U.F. Marshal is a whole lot worse, legally speaking."

Ferguson's tongue flicked across his lips. "I didn't want to kill anybody. I just did what I had to."

"Shut up, Fred!" Cramer bellowed. "Nobody needs to hear from you right now."

"Oh, I don't know." Nick raised his arms half way. "I know that Fred only set that shower bomb because he was afraid of *you*, Cramer. He knew you'd have Turd kill him if he didn't follow orders. I think a jury will take that into account, when the time comes."

"You don't know what the fuck you're talking about!" Cramer glanced at his watch. "I have something to take care of. Turd, you know what to do."

With a meaningful glare at the grungy gunman, he turned and went out the door.

Nick turned to Turd. "Well, there goes the party. I guess this is the part where the killing starts, huh?"

Turd Murdoch grinned malevolently. "Yeah, this is the part. But it ain't gonna take very long, since there's only one person to kill."

"So...you go from committing life-in-prison crimes to death penalty crimes. Sure you're up for that?"

Turd frowned; his eyes clouded. "Shut the fuck up!"

"It's like I was telling Fred," Nick continued. "No jury in the system will let him skate for killing a lawman. On the other hand—" He smiled. "—if he were to kill someone while *defending* a lawman, that would be justifiable homicide."

Turd Murdoch's eyes turned flat with confusion; he glanced at Ferguson. Ferguson stared back at him, then at Nick; his eyes were wide with comprehension and not a little fear. Nick merely smiled.

"It might even make up for killing Misery Allen."

Monica Maynard gasped in horror. "Misery Allen is *dead?*"

Ferguson's eyes sprang even wider, his mouth open in indecision. He panted under the stress. He looked at Turd again, then swung Nick's laser pistol toward him. Turd saw his intention and turned to meet the threat.

"You fucking little weasel!"

The laser chirped as Fred shot him in the stomach. The pistol was still set to needle beam, so the bolt only made a tiny hole, but Ferguson pulled the trigger three times; Murdoch jerked in shock as each beam struck home. Before he could pull his own trigger, Nick was moving. He covered the ten feet between them in three steps and launched himself; Turd collapsed under a flying tackle with Nick on top. Nick ripped the pistol out of his hand and slugged him in the face with it.

At the same moment, Harvey Farrington leaped to his feet with excitement and bumped the desk with his thigh; the .44 roared explosively, recoiling halfway across the room. Monica screamed and so did Harvey, though the bullet barely grazed his shirt; Henry Farrington stared at the smoking pistol for a brief second, then dived for it, spilling his vinegar.

Nick spun to face Henry just as he came up with the weapon, and ducked as Henry fired. The .44 was heavy and Henry's aim was poor—the slug snapped past Nick's left cheek and exploded in the wall behind him, but the Ru-Hawk's recoil slammed the gun back into Henry's forehead and knocked him out cold. Nick got slowly to his feet, his heart beating hard, and motioned to Ferguson with his head.

"Keep an eye on Murdoch. If he wakes up and tries anything, shoot him in the eye."

Wide-eyed and trembling, Ferguson nodded and hurried forward to stand over Turd. Nick advanced a few steps and picked up the .44; Henry lay moaning, a trickle of blood spreading from his forehead. Harvey Farrington had dropped back into his chair, shaking like a leaf. Piss dribbled onto the floor.

Monica had stopped screaming and was now sobbing. Nick walked over and put an arm around her.

"Settle down, your Honor."

"Is it true? About Misery?"

"I'm afraid so. Your friends are very thorough."

She clung to his hand, tears streaming from her eyes. "You don't understand, Nick! It isn't what you think!"

"Oh, I think the evidence is very clear." His eyes bored into hers. "You're a corrupt judge. Bought and paid for."

"But—"

Nick spun as motion caught his eye. The door to Henry Farrington's office had opened and a small boy came out. He took a few steps into the room and stopped, staring at all the people with wide, innocent eyes. He looked about eight years old, tall and straight, with dark curly hair and chocolate skin.

"I heard a gun!" he said.

Monica spun toward the voice. "Charley!"

The child's eyes lit with excitement. "Mommy!"

He raced past Henry Farrington and into Monica's arms. She swooped him up in a desperate hug, turning in a circle. Nick stared in utter astonishment.

Monica, still holding her son, saw Nick's expression and blinked away her tears.

"They were holding Charley hostage," she explained, "ever since he was a baby. I had no choice."

Nick was still digesting that when a third door swung open as if kicked. A new voice bellowed through the room.

"Everybody *freeze!* U.F. Marshal!"

Guns drawn, Marshal Milligan strode into the office, followed by Murray and Beech.

* * *

The paramedics took Turd Murdoch to the hospital in Government Annex. Russ Murray left to search the rest of the top floor, including the Farringtons' private quarters. Both Farringtons sat on the floor with hands E-cuffed behind them, and Milligan lectured Nick Walker sternly.

"I thought you were in the Star Marines!" he bellowed.

"Yes, sir, I was."

"Didn't they teach you anything about teamwork?"

"Yes, sir!"

"Unit cohesion, deployment in depth, covering fire?"

"Yes, sir!"

"Then what the *fuck* were you thinking! You don't walk into a situation like this without backup! We had to scramble to get here when we did, and then we went the wrong way because I thought you were going into the lockup!"

"Sorry, Marshal. It won't happen again."

"It better not!"

As Milligan glared at him Nick felt like a raw recruit again. After a moment Milligan's expression softened a little.

"Anyway, it's a good thing we did go into the lockup. We found Tarpington in there, nekkid as a jay-hawk and spread out to dry."

Nick's blood ran cold. He'd forgot all about Tarpington.

"Is he...?"

"Alive. Barely. They damn near skinned him, but I think they were saving him until they had you. Then they could eliminate you both at once."

"Where is he now?"

"On his way to the hospital. He'll be all right in a few days. He's been knocked around some, but he's tough for such a pretty boy."

Nick sagged slightly, his cold fear turning to numb relief.

Milligan turned to look at the prisoners, who glared sullenly back at him.

"What are we charging these people with?"

"Everything," Nick said. "Kidnapping, rape, murder, sabotage, conspiracy, and a whole list of corporate offenses. It'll take me a week to write it all up."

Milligan nodded. "And who runs this place in their absence? The Outer Worlds can't afford any interruptions in water shipments."

"If you'll authorize the space fare, I can have Carmen Castillo-Bernal here in three days. She can oversee operations until the courts sort it all out."

"All right. I'll see if I can scare up a judge on Mars to grant her power of attorney until a receiver can be appointed."

"I can do that," Monica said from a few feet away. She was seated on a divan, holding her son in her arms. Charley had fallen asleep.

Milligan shook his head. "I don't know about that. Seems like you have a few charges pending against you as well."

Monica gently disentangled from the boy and stood up. She looked from one man to the other, conflict in her eyes.

"After you hear my story, maybe you'll think about withdrawing that complaint."

Milligan raised an eyebrow at Nick. Nick turned to Monica.

"Let's hear it."

"Remember I told you I came out here for love? I wasn't completely honest about that. My husband wasn't dead when I got here. Mark and I had an apartment in the Village for about six months. Then I got bored and decided to get a job. I applied at Farrington and they hired me in their legal department."

She fought back a surge of emotion as she explained.

"What I didn't know was that the whole bunch was racist. Both Farringtons and Cramer too. They called me names, started harassing me, and finally Henry started raping me. They said if I told anyone they would kill Mark. By then I was already aware of three suspicious deaths due to 'mining accidents', so I knew they weren't bluffing.

"Then...I got pregnant. I knew it wasn't Mark's because we had agreed not to have a family on Ceres, and he used birth control. So Mark found out, and I had to tell him what was going on. He went ballistic, of course, and confronted Henry Farrington. The next day..." She stopped, her lungs seizing, and began to sob.

"Mining accident?"

She nodded. A moment later she was able to continue.

"When Charley was born, Henry took him. He said I could visit him once a month, but I could see him more often if I wanted to 'cooperate'."

"Sounds like you were already cooperating."

"That's what I thought, but they had other plans. They wanted their own judge, someone they could control. I said okay—and the next thing I knew, Judge Boxner was dead. In a matter of days I was appointed to the bench and...well, you know the rest."

Nick stared at her in wonder. He still had a ton of questions, but most of them could wait. He glanced at Milligan.

"What do you think, Marshal? Tarpington hasn't filed that complaint yet."

The old man cleared his throat with a rumble.

"I think this all needs to be documented and the Martian Judiciary needs to review it." He grimaced. "But it all fits with what we know and suspect, so I'm inclined to believe it. For the time being, I don't see why Judge Maynard can't remain on the bench on a provisional basis."

Monica tried to smile but failed as fresh tears arrived.

"Thank you!" she whispered.

"However..." Milligan gazed at her sternly. "...the first thing you should probably do is revisit any tainted cases where people are still locked up and start turning people loose. Even if you were under duress, you've harmed a lot of people. The quicker you correct that the better, and it may help your case when all this comes under review."

Monica nodded weakly. "Of course I will."

Milligan turned away. Nick put an arm around her and kissed her on the cheek. He pressed his face into her thick hair and whispered in her ear.

"So all that stuff about being horny...was that Cramer's idea, too?"

"No!" She pointed to Henry Farrington, sitting on the floor. "Do you think I would sleep with *him* if I had a choice? After I became judge he moved on to other women. I recovered from the rapes and started to have normal desires again. But— well, you know...microbes."

Marshal Milligan conferred with Beech and Murray, then returned to Nick.

"Looks like you have things under control here, so I'm going to take the judge home—assuming you're done with her. I'm an old man and I haven't had my dinner yet."

Nick nodded. "Nothing pending that can't wait." He glanced at Monica, who looked totally wrung out. "I'll stop in later to check on you. Don't go anywhere."

"You don't have to worry, Nick. I just want to get Charley out of here. Maybe we can have a decent life after this."

Suddenly his eyes narrowed.

"How did you get out of lockup?"

"Turd Murdoch broke us out. He murdered the night man."

"Zima?"

"No. A man named Williams."

Nick and Milligan exchanged glances. One more charge against Murdoch.

"Go ahead and call that Castillo woman," Milligan said. "Tell her to get on the next ship headed this way. We have to keep this operation running or those outer colonies will dry up."

"I'll call her tonight."

"Tomorrow I want you to draw up a list of suspects and charges. We may need to import some help, but I want every son of a bitch arrested who had anything to do with this mess. As soon as Gary Fraites gets back from Mars, he's gonna want the information."

"What about Tarpington?"

"He's too junior for this." Milligan nodded toward Monica. "And she'll have to recuse herself; she may still face charges of her own. This will have to go to Mars for trial, and it's gonna be a hell of a scandal."

Chapter 31

Nick turned back to gaze at his prisoners. Murray stood over them like guard a dog. Fred Ferguson, no longer armed, stood to one side like a lost pup, shifty and nervous.

"Did anybody bring a scoop shovel?" Nick asked no one in particular. "I see an awful lot of shit stacked on the floor."

Russ Murray snickered. "Ain't that a hoot? Especially since the Turd is already gone."

"Marshal Milligan said you guys went into the lockup. Any sign of Nikki Green?"

"No, but we haven't searched the whole thing yet. We did find another woman, though, in the same room with Tarpington. I have no idea who she is, but she was in pretty bad shape."

Nick's face heated with anger and he glared at the twins on the floor.

"You know what? You better get these bastards out of here before I decide to violate their constitutional rights."

Murray grinned, his eyes gleaming with admiration.

"Where we gonna put 'em? If we lock 'em up here someone will probably turn them loose."

"Take them to System Springs. I'll call Zima and tell him you're coming."

Murray nodded and began hauling the prisoners to their feet. Henry Farrington, still bleeding from the forehead, scowled angrily; his brother, looking dazed, seemed unaware of what was going on. Nick wondered if his mind had finally snapped.

"What about me?" Fred Ferguson looked at Nick hopefully.

"You don't belong with this crowd," Nick told him, "but you're still under arrest for killing Misery Allen."

Fred's face fell. "You said helping you would make up for that."

"I said it *might* help—but you still have to stand trial. Tell the prosecutors what you told me and testify against the guy who ordered the hit. You did a good thing here tonight, Fred. Don't fuck it up by doing something stupid."

Ferguson, looking despondent, pursed his lips and nodded.

"What're you gonna do?" Murray asked as he prepared to herd the Farringtons toward the door.

"I'm going to try to find Cramer. He left just before you guys got here."

"What's his involvement in all this?"

"I don't know exactly, but I do know he's up to his eyes in it. I'll see you back at the shed."

"What about this guy?" Murray nodded at Ferguson.

"I'll hang on to him. He works here, so he can help me find my way around."

Murray eyed Ferguson with contempt. "Don't turn your back on him."

*

Nick called Milo Zima as soon as the deputies left with the prisoners. He arranged for private cells for both Farringtons and asked Zima to send as many armed men as he could spare over to the Farrington facility. They were facing a security problem that could turn serious if it wasn't handled speedily; with only four U.F. Marshals on the asteroid, and roughly two hundred armed Farrington prison guards...well, the math was pretty clear.

Nick finished the call and turned to Ferguson. "Ready to shave some time off your sentence?"

Fred gulped. "What do you mean?"

"You said you're a plumber here. You should know this place like the back of your hand."

"Yeah, I do."

"Good. I need a tour guide."

With Fred at his side, Nick entered the Farringtons' private quarters. Beech had already searched them but Nick wanted to see for himself. He was impressed with the size of the suites each man lived in, if not exactly the style in which they lived. Harvey's suite was cluttered, messy, filled with an assortment of expensive toys that bordered on the eccentric—working models of space ships, maglev trains, and scientific novelties filled one entire room; by contrast there were racks of old paper books, some of them centuries out of date; a holographic entertainment suite that must have cost a million terros...and a computer system that tied in to an observatory on the surface of Ceres. All in all, it looked like the playhouse of a very rich twelve year-old nerd.

Henry's suite was very different. His quarters were neat, tidy, and clean; he seemed interested in religion, with tomes of ancient Greek and Hebrew scripture and a holo-reader with a library of contemporary religious material. But the room next door was decorated with holo-porn posters that left nothing to the imagination. With a flick of a controller an entire wall sprang to life depicting sex acts of the most brutal and disturbing nature. Nick watched in disgust for ten or fifteen seconds before shutting it off.

"What a sick fuck!" Fred Ferguson breathed.

Nick turned in surprise—he'd almost forgotten that Fred was there.

"Did you know about any of this?"

"No. I haven't been in this room."

"But you've been in this suite?"

"Yeah, once. He had trouble with his water supply a few months back and I fixed it for him."

"Any idea where the kid's room is?" *I hope Charley never came in here!*

"Yeah, I'll show you."

Fred led the way into an adjoining apartment, a small one. Charley's room was a small bedroom with very few decorations and only a few toys. The bed was made and everything was in order, as if a maid had just left.

"Did you see anyone else in here? A young black woman?"

"No. I was only here once, and there were no women around."

Nick compressed his lips. He had hoped that Henry was holding Nikki Green nearby for his personal entertainment; as bad as that sounded, the alternative might be much worse. He sighed in disappointment.

"Okay, let's go into the lockup."

* * *

They returned to Harvey's office and exited through the same door Cramer had used when he left. This led to a private elevator that only had one button. Nick pushed it and they started down.

"What's on these other floors?" he asked Ferguson. "Two through six."

"Just offices, maybe some document storage. Nothing else."

Nick nodded and fingered his .44. His pulse quickened a little as he anticipated what might lie ahead.

"When we get into the lockup, you stay behind me. If anyone challenges us, be ready to hit the floor."

Fred's eyes widened and he gulped. "You think there might be trouble?"

"Maybe, maybe not. Just be prepared."

The lift stopped abruptly and the door opened. Nick looked out onto a long, dark tunnel that stretched fifty yards into the distance, from the office building to the prison. A dim light every two hundred feet provided the only illumination, and as he stepped out of the lift it felt as if he was walking into an ancient coal mine. The tunnel was unfinished—the floor was starcrete, but the top and sides were just bare rock. It looked like the perfect place for an ambush, so long and dark that he couldn't tell if there were cross tunnels or cutouts; anyone could be waiting down there.

Nick drew his .44.

Fred stayed ten feet behind, breathing heavily. Nick's own heart was beating in his ears. He moved steadily forward, eyes narrowed, watching for any sign of movement. His leather heels rang on the hard floor and echoed back at him from the far end. He hadn't felt this exposed in a long time.

But they encountered no hiding places and reached the other end without incident. The tunnel ended at a flight of steps, and Nick moved up them slowly, gun ready. At the top of the steps he saw another corridor and picked up a whiff of human excrement. They had reached the prison.

Just yards ahead they encountered a window with a brightly lit room behind it. Nick stared through the window at the accoutrements of torture, saw splotches of blood on the floor and walls; saw the generator with alligator clips, the crossbeam with suspended cables for dangling prisoners...but no one was in the room.

"What's this place?" he asked Fred in a low voice.

"Interrogation."

Nick turned on him. "Interrogation! It looks like a torture chamber!"

"Well...that's what they called it."

"Have you ever seen it being used?"

"Yeah. There's almost always someone in there."

"Male or female?"

Fred cleared his throat, as if reluctant to answer. "They fuck women in there. Can we keep going now? That place gives me the creeps."

Nick nodded. Score one for Fred...maybe. Unless the room gave Fred a guilty conscience.

They continued down the corridor.

They came to a T and stopped. Here they saw women's cells, dozens of them, stretching away to the left. To the right appeared to be offices, interview rooms, and the main entrance to the cellblock. Light from an office window glowed into the corridor but Nick didn't see any personnel. To his left the cellblock was dark; he heard women snoring lightly, and a few others moaning in their sleep. He put his head together with Fred Ferguson, talking in low tones.

"What I don't need right now is attention, and if we go past those cells there's a chance someone will wake up and start making noise. I need to know where someone might stash a prisoner that no one knows about; do you know of any dungeons or isolation cells where they might be holding a woman illegally?"

Fred shrugged. "There are several isolation cells in different parts of the prison, but most of them are in the men's lockup. The only one on this cellblock is the one we just passed."

Nick frowned. "Are you sure?"

"Marshal, I've been all over this place for years, and the only place I've ever seen a woman like you're talking about is in that one cell. I've seen a lot of different women in there, but never anywhere else."

"Isn't it possible they hold women in the men's lockup?"

"Sure, it's possible. I'm just telling you what I've seen, and I've never seen any women over there. Except..."

"Except what?"

"Sometimes they put female prisoners in with the male prisoners for a few hours. I think the male prisoners bribe the guards for doing it."

Nick felt a wave of despair. If Nikki Green was in the building, he needed to find her...*before* Stan Cramer learned that his partners were under arrest. Cramer had said he had something to "take care of"; what that meant Nick could only guess, but under the circumstances it sounded ominous. Nick had mentioned Nikki Green's name, and if Cramer felt threatened by Nick's interest, she could be in serious danger. Goddammit, he *had* to find her!

But he needed help.

With a sigh of resignation, he turned to the right and marched down the corridor toward the lighted window. When he reached it he saw a guard sitting at a desk with his feet kicked up onto the corner of the desk, eyes closed, a concert headset plugged into his ears. Still gripping the .44, Nick shoved the door open and kicked the guard's feet off the desk; the sudden shift of balance almost dragged the man out of his chair. He jerked erect with a startled look and a shout, then his eyes focused on the cannon in Nick's hand and he gulped in fear.

"On your feet," Nick told him. "Up against the wall."

Shaking with fear, the guard stumbled upright. Nick shoved his face against the wall and relieved him of his sidearm, then stepped back.

"What the hell is going on?" the guard panted. "Who the hell are you?"

"U.F. Marshal. Hands behind your back."

"What for?"

Nick placed a hand on the back of his head and slammed his forehead into the wall. "Because I said so. Now *do* it!"

The guard obeyed and Nick cuffed him with his own E-cuffs. Holstering the .44, he searched the man and then shoved him back into the chair.

"What's your name?"

"Spencer."

"How many guards are working tonight?"

"Three. Me and two others."

"That's all? Three men for the whole building?"

"No, just this cellblock. There's maybe a dozen on the other wing."

"All right. Where are your buddies?"

"Making the rounds. What the fuck is this about? Why are you cuffing me? I haven't done anything!"

"This facility is now under Federation control. Your employers have been arrested, and unless you want to share a cell with them, just do what you're told until we get everything sorted out."

Spencer looked shaken. "What the hell did you arrest them for?"

"If you have to ask, maybe I should arrest you, too. Sit there and shut up."

Shaken and confused, Spencer glanced from Nick to Fred Ferguson.

"You under arrest, too? What the hell did you do?"

Nick tapped him on the forehead.

"I told you to shut up. I'll ask the questions."

"All right! I'm shutting."

"Have you seen Stan Cramer this evening?"

"Yeah. Why?"

"What time was that?"

"Thirty, forty minutes ago."

"Did he talk to you?"

"No. He just walked by."

"Walked by? Which way was he going?"

"Out." Spencer inclined his head toward the main entrance. "He was leaving the building."

"Did you see which way he went?"

"Yeah, he left the building."

Nick sighed in frustration.

"*After* he left the goddamn building, which way did he go?"

"I dunno. I didn't look out. Ask the guy at the gate."

Nick had left the "guy at the gate" E-cuffed on the floor of the guard shack. He stepped into the corridor and called Murray.

"When you left the prison, was anyone in the guard shack?"

"Didn't see anyone."

"Okay. Looks like Cramer has left the Farrington facility. He could be anywhere, so pass the word to be on the lookout. I don't think he knows yet that we've arrested the Farringtons, but he does know I was on to him, so he might be looking to eliminate witnesses. We need to find the bastard as quick as possible."

"Got it. I'll tell Beech and Zima."

"Where are you now?"

"System Springs."

"Good. As soon as I'm done here I'm going there next. Wait for me."

Nick disconnected and peered down the corridor—he didn't want to be taken by surprise before help arrived. At the moment everything was dark and quiet. He turned back to Spencer.

"Do you know David Tarpington?"

Spencer reacted as if he'd been slapped. He sucked in his breath and his eyes grew wide. Sweat beaded on his forehead.

"Yeah."

"Were you here when he got here this afternoon?"

Spencer swallowed, blinking rapidly. He didn't answer right away.

"Tarpington is still alive," Nick told him, "so when I talk to him, your story had better match his."

Spencer's eyes watered and he looked ready to cry. He only nodded.

"You *were* here?"

"Yes."

"Did you put him in that torture room?"

"No!"

"Did you strip him naked and string him up?"

"No!"

"Did you wire up his dick with electricity and turn on the juice?" Nick still didn't know what had been done to Tarpington, but Milligan had made it sound pretty bad, so he used his imagination. It seemed to be working. "Did you skin him like—"

"No! *No!*"

"—a goddamn *raccoon?*"

"*NO!!* I didn't do any of that! I would *never* do that to David. I love him. I've been in love with him for a long time. I would never hurt him."

Nick stopped, startled. It hadn't occurred to him that Spencer might be gay. The man was sobbing in his chair, broken, as if he'd just lost a family member. Nick was inclined to believe he really was in love with Tarpington.

"Tell me what happened. And don't leave anything out."

* * *

Zima's people arrived twenty minutes later, thirteen armed men. They were a rough looking lot, men you wouldn't want to insult in a bar, but none of them had that felonious look in their eyes that was so prevalent among men on Ceres. Nick met them outside and briefed them.

"Eventually we're going to take control of the whole prison, but right now you're just going to occupy the women's cellblock. Nobody gets in or out without U.F. Marshal authority. If anyone tries, you have authorization to use deadly force. I have one guard in custody and there are a couple more roaming around somewhere, so when they show up just disarm them and stick them in a cell. We'll be getting more men in a few hours, and this thing will all be over in a couple of days. So dig in and be prepared for anything."

Nick took them into the building and placed them at strategic points. He placed three in the office building with orders to keep everyone out. That done, he collected Fred Ferguson and headed back to System Springs.

Chapter 32

Sunday, August 11, 0440 (CC) — System Springs - Ceres

Milo Zima had placed the Farrington twins in the same cells recently occupied by Fred Ferguson and Monica Maynard, at opposite ends of the lockup. Nick found both men looking dejected and subdued. Harvey seemed somewhat recovered from his shock; his jaw was rotating full speed and his grunting had gone into overdrive.

Uh! Uh! Uh! Uh!

His pants were soaked in urine and he no longer looked arrogant or condescending; rather, his eyes shifted rapidly from point to point like a trapped animal.

Nick stared at him a moment and concluded that he was in no shape for interrogation. Although it might be fun, it would net nothing, because the man was bordering insanity, and time was short. He moved on to the other cell where Henry Farrington waited.

Henry also looked stunned at his sudden reversal of fortune, but his eyes were clear. He glared at Nick with pure hatred, but the sneer was gone. An adhesive bandage covered the cut in his forehead. Nick pulled up a chair and sat outside the cell, gazing at him. Russ Murray stood nearby with a handheld recording device.

"Anything you want to talk about, Henry?"

Henry looked up with barely concealed fury.

"No. We didn't do anything wrong. You have nothing on us."

Nick and Murray exchanged glances; Murray shook his head in amazement.

"Nothing?" Nick said. "Are you that out of touch with reality? Even before I start interviewing victims I have enough on you for forty life sentences. When you go to trial it'll take an hour to read the charges, and when the jury comes back with the verdicts it'll take twice that long. The trial will last a year, at least."

"It wasn't us. It was Cramer."

"Cramer! Was it Cramer who raped Monica, killed her husband, and held her son hostage? Was it Cramer who framed Jessica Garner, killed her husband, and tortured her for two years? Was it Cramer who—"

"Yes. *Yes!* He was behind all that. This whole thing was his idea. It was his operation from the beginning. We were just the front men, the public face."

Surprised at this sudden admission, Nick leaned forward encouragingly.

"So how did it play out? How did it all get started?"

Henry grimaced. "My brother and I were down on our luck. We'd failed in business three or four times and were looking for a new opportunity. Cramer came to us with a plan, and we went for it. He would put up the money and we would run the operation. He was the senior partner; it was a three-way split, with Cramer owning fifty-two percent. He gave us twenty-four percent each."

"So even if you opposed him you didn't have enough juice to reverse him."

"Exactly."

"And you went for that?"

"Sure. It was a good deal. We had nothing, and this was a gold mine. Cramer is good at business, and he served as our attorney."

"Where did he get his capital? Was he already wealthy?"

Henry shook his head. "He was legal counsel for some little church in SoCal. The church had millions, and Stan had signatory power over their bank account. Over a period of time he diverted several million terros into his own private account in SiriusBank—"

"Sirius!"

Henry glanced up. "Stan was born in Missibama; he's a Sirian citizen."

"Go on."

"Well...when he had enough stashed away to use for investment, he approached us about coming to Ceres."

"Why Ceres? Why pick the asshole of the Solar System to start a business?"

Henry shrugged. "Stan's a lawyer. He said the rock is populated by criminals and nobody pays much attention, because the water supply is too important to the Outer Worlds. He said the Federation would look the other way."

"How did you guys know Cramer? If you were down on your luck, why would he hang out with a pair of losers?"

"We were members of the church I told you about. He knew us by reputation."

"As losers?"

Henry scowled angrily. "As businessmen! He knew we were ambitious and wanted to make a success at something."

"But he made himself senior partner so you couldn't fuck it up for him."

"I...guess you could put it that way."

Nick smiled. "I just did. Okay, so your brother came to Ceres and tried to purchase Agua Solar, but they wouldn't sell. What happened then?"

"Stan told us they would probably refuse to sell, but we should make the offer anyway. He was right—they refused the offer."

"And you did what?"

"Nothing. We went on with our lives. Stan told us to be patient; he gave us money to live on. Nothing happened for a year or so, and we were thinking it was all over, then Stan called one day and told us to meet him on Mars. We were going to make the offer again."

"And this time the offer was accepted?"

"Yes."

"What made the difference the second time?"

"Agua Solar was crashing. Their stock had gone to shit and the government was on their back for safety violations. Their back was against the wall, so they took the offer."

"For nine cents on the terro."

"Something like that."

"Why did their stock go south? Did you have anything to do with that?"

"*I* didn't. Neither did Harvey. We were in California then. I know there were some accidents—"

Nick sneered. "Can you say 'sabotage'?"

Henry inclined his head. "I don't know if it was sabotage. I heard rumors, but I never asked any questions. I didn't want to know."

"So Cramer was responsible for all the death and destruction that befell Agua Solar during that period?"

"I can't confirm that. All I know is that Harvey and I had nothing to do with it."

Nick was silent for a moment, evaluating the story. Henry's brow was furrowed in what passed for sincerity. Nick suspected much of what he was hearing was the truth, but had no illusions that Henry was telling him the whole story, or feeling repentant for his own misdeeds.

"Did you rape Monica Maynard?"

"I had sex with Monica. I never raped anybody."

"You told me earlier tonight that you don't fuck...black women. That was a lie?"

Henry scowled. "I'm not proud of it, but she's a sexy bitch. I couldn't help myself."

"Did she initiate it, or did you?"

"She did. I just didn't resist her."

"Why would a happily married woman initiate a sexual adventure with someone like you?"

"Who said she was married?"

Nick frowned. "What?"

"Monica wasn't married. Her husband was dead."

"After you killed him. 'Mining accident', wasn't it?"

Farrington stared at him as if he were crazy. "He was dead before she ever got here! He was killed in a bar fight three days after he landed on Ceres."

"Bullshit! Why would Monica travel all the way out here if he was dead?"

Henry Farrington sighed in frustration. "Nobody knew who the guy was. He had just arrived and didn't even have a job yet. Nobody contacted Monica because nobody had ever heard of her."

"If that's true, then how do you know all those details?"

"Monica told me. Once she arrived and found out what happened, she put all the pieces together herself."

Nick didn't believe him, but this was going nowhere; he moved on.

"So your relationship with her was one hundred percent consensual?"

"Yes. If anyone was reluctant, it was me."

"But you held her son hostage."

"Charley is my son, too. Monica had visiting rights."

Nick's eyebrows rose. "*Visiting* rights? Was there a custody hearing?"

Farrington shook his head. "She could see him whenever she wanted. It was a mutual arrangement. Her schedule was too hectic to raise a kid."

Nick's lips compressed into a grim line. Henry was lying through his teeth.

"Tell me about Jessica Garner."

Henry glanced up. "That bitch attacked me with a stylus. I pressed charges. That's all."

"But once she was locked up *in your facility,* you raped her twice a week."

"I never raped anybody. She sent word that she was sorry and wanted to make it up to me. She offered me sex as penance, and I took it." He shrugged. "Why wouldn't I? She's a beautiful woman."

"What did Nikki Green offer you?"

"I had nothing to do with Nikki Green. She was Cramer's toy."

Nick sat silent a moment, his blood chilling. "*Was* Cramer's toy?"

Farrington locked eyes with him, and understood.

"As far as I know, she's still alive."

"Where?"

"I don't know. Ask St—"

"*Where*, goddammit!"

"*I don't know!* Ask Stan."

Centerville - Ceres

It was nearly three in the morning when Nick arrived at the hospital. David Tarpington was under sedation and couldn't talk to him. Turd Murdoch had undergone surgery for his laser wounds and was also out cold. Due to the hour, Shirley Chin was off duty, so there was no reason for Nick to remain at the hospital. He walked back out to his E-car and drove on over to Centerville.

Dead on his feet, he took the lift up to the fourth floor. He debated knocking on Monica's door, but decided against it. She and Charley were probably asleep, and his investigation could wait four or five hours. Instead he went into his own room, changed clothes, and washed up (he would have used the shower but didn't trust it; he might never use that shower again). He made a pot of coffee and sat at the table trying to think what he should do next.

Probably the smartest move was to get a few hours' sleep, but that option didn't seem feasible at the moment. Stan Cramer was loose on Ceres, and if he didn't yet know that the U.F. Marshal had shut down Farrington Industries, he would before long. Nick already considered him a threat to potential witnesses and victims such as Jessica Garner...

Oh, God! Oh God!

Nick had mentioned Jessica Garner's name in Monica's chambers, in Cramer's presence. In doing so he had violated the promise he'd made to Jessica, to keep her name out of his investigation. He'd felt safe when he did so, thinking Cramer would be locked up minutes later, but now he was free and at large. Even though Nick didn't believe everything Henry Farrington had told him, he was convinced that Cramer was a dangerous man, in more ways than one; not only was he a force to be reckoned with in the business world, he was also capable of extreme violence.

Nick turned off the coffee pot, grabbed his gunbelt, and bolted out of the room.

Ceres North - Ceres

Because of the hour, the artificial light had been turned off. Every habitat on Ceres was dark as a tomb, save for night lights spaced at intervals along the streets and walkways. As Nick followed a winding stone path to Jessica Garner's apartment, the air was still; his heels rang against the stone and echoed back to him from nearby buildings. It was an eerie feeling, as if someone were lying in wait for him in the shadows. His heart pumped and his throat turned dry.

He drew his gun.

Jessica Garner's apartment faced a rock wall not fifty yards away; in that respect, it was the least desirable location in the habitat. Nick mounted the stairs to the balcony that fronted the apartment, stepping slowly to keep the noise down, eyes and ears alert for danger. Maybe it was fatigue, or an overblown sense of drama, but his scalp tingled as he drew closer. He paused at the top step, gripping the railing with his left hand, looking right and left. The balcony was dimly lit, but no one was in sight. Nick turned left toward Jessica's door, walking softly now, almost on tip-toe. For some reason his heart was racing, as if this were to be an inevitable showdown. He breathed deeply to fight the adrenaline.

He reached Jessica's door...and stopped.

It stood open several inches. A light burned inside. Nick's heart sank.

He swallowed hard, took another deep breath, and keeping to one side, nudged the door all the way open with the barrel of his gun. He stared for a moment, taking everything in. After a moment he stepped inside; one step, two. He stopped. The furniture was overturned, some of it broken. Fragments of glass and broken knick-knacks littered the floor. A laser shot had burned a hole in the wall near the ceiling...and a laser pistol lay on the floor. Nick's tongue traced his upper lip as he took another few steps, expecting to find a body. But there was none.

He searched the kitchen, the bedroom, and the bath, but...

Jessica Garner was gone.

Chapter 33

Government Annex - Ceres

Nick was dead on his feet when he got back to the U.F. Marshal's office, but his mind was racing and he couldn't seem to slow it down. He had a desperate feeling that time was running out for Nikki Green, and now Jessica Garner as well. Garner had lived quietly for two years in her apartment, and tonight, just hours after Nick's raid on Farrington Industries, she was missing? That was no coincidence.

Stan Cramer had said he had "something to take care of"; Nick had feared that "something" might be Nikki Green, and maybe it was, but Jessica's sudden disappearance, with signs of violence, was doubly foreboding. He hadn't met Nikki Green yet, but according to Jessica she had taken Jessica's place in the torture cell, which meant they had a great deal in common. In Stan Cramer's mind, they might represent a threat too serious to ignore, in which case they must both be eliminated.

Nick sat back in his desk chair and closed his eyes for a moment, resting his body while his mind did its own thing. His body felt numb, but he was too tired to sleep.

When Cramer left Harvey Farrington's office, everything had been under control from his point of view—Nick was a prisoner and Murdoch had orders to kill him. Why, then, would he choose that moment to dispose of the women? With Nick out of the way, everything should have been going his way.

But according to Henry, Cramer was the real brains behind Farrington Industries. With fifty-two percent of the business he was making millions, yet his name did not appear on any of the documentation Nick had seen. Cramer was clearly smarter than the Farringtons—those two, for all their arrogance, were about as bright as the sun when seen from Ceres...a Christmas tree bulb. As a lawyer, Cramer probably knew the operation would eventually crash and burn, and when it did, the Farringtons would be left to take the fall while he, Cramer, took his money and disappeared.

He was also smart enough to know that killing Nick wouldn't solve his problems. Once the U.F. Marshal—*any* U.F. Marshal—zeroed in on the criminal aspects of the operation, it was over. Thirteen years of crime and corruption had created too much wreckage, left too many witnesses, for it just to go away. Killing Nick might buy him a few hours, but apparently he hadn't even been willing to take that chance—he had skipped immediately, leaving his "partners" in blissful ignorance.

So where was he now? Where would he go?

And what were his plans for those two women?

Nick sat up and rubbed his eyes. He debated making a pot of coffee, but decided against it; he was already wired and caffeine would only make it worse. Instead, he would take care of first things first.

* * *

It was shortly after five in the morning when he walked into the Government Annex hospital. The artificial light outside had been increased slightly to simulate dawn and life was beginning to stir on Ceres. The asteroid was coming awake for another day.

David Tarpington was awake, though still sedated. He peered at Nick through a swathe of bandages that covered much of his face and body. In spite of his condition, he managed a feeble grin.

Nick took his hand.

"David, I'm so sorry! I should never have sent you in there alone."

Tarpington attempted a shrug. "I agreed to it."

"Can you tell me what happened?"

Speaking slowly, his speech slightly slurred, he gave Nick a thumbnail account of finding a woman in the torture chamber and his own capture.

"I don't know who the woman was," he finished. "She never came through the court. I would have recognized her."

"Who did this to you?"

Tarpington's eyes closed for a moment and Nick thought he had dozed off. The heart monitor beside the bed began to beep a little faster as the eyes opened again.

"The person who slugged me was Henry Farrington. After that I don't remember much."

Nick spent thirty minutes with Tarpington, then headed for the basement, hoping to find Shirley Chin. She had just arrived and was slipping into her lab coat. Her eyes were bright from just waking up. She peered at him with something less than enthusiasm as he stepped into her office.

"You never came back last night," she said.

"No. Things came up. Sorry."

She stood over her desk, rearranging papers, clearly ill at ease.

"I wasn't sure if you worked on Sunday," he said.

She shrugged. "Nothing much else to do."

"Did you have something to report?"

She picked up an autopsy report. "Misery Allen's death was due to hyperthermia. She was boiled alive."

Nick stared at her, feeling numb. He hadn't thought of Misery for several hours, and the mention of her name depressed him. He didn't answer right away.

Shirley Chin raised her eyes to meet his.

"I'm willing to testify," she said.

Nick blinked. "You are?"

She nodded. "If you can guarantee my safety, I'll testify. But not on Ceres. Get me off this rock. Get me to Mars or Terra first."

Nick pulled out a chair and sat down. Shirley Chin remained standing.

"Tell me what you will testify to. What do you know?"

"Everything you were asking me about. Falsification of death certs, phony diagnoses. Terror and intimidation."

"How did they intimidate you? What do they have on you?"

"They don't have anything on me. They simply told me that I would end up in a torture cell if I didn't cooperate. They didn't need any more than that."

"Who told you that?"

"Stan Cramer."

"You didn't report this?"

Her laugh was a harsh bark. "Who would I report it to? Marshal Milligan? Until you showed up he only had three men, himself included. Farrington runs the whole rock, including the courthouse! Half the men on this asteroid work for Farrington, and every one of them is a threat to my life. You say Cramer is locked up and that's great, but as long as Farrington Industries exists my life is in danger. That's why you have to get me off Ceres before I'll say another word."

Nick's eyes narrowed. "The Farringtons have been arrested. Within three days the operation will be under Federation receivership. We're probably going to arrest and prosecute everyone who works in the lockup, and hundreds more as well. The investigation will go on for months, maybe years."

She sat down suddenly, her eyes wide.

"What about Turd Murdoch? He's one of their most dangerous employees."

"He's upstairs right now recovering from laser wounds. He won't be going anywhere for a while."

Staring at him in disbelief, she closed her mouth and swallowed hopefully.

"You mean it's really over?"

Nick grimaced. "Almost. Unfortunately, Stan Cramer got away. He's at large right now—"

"*What!*" She leaped out of her chair, wringing her hands. "You *bastard!* If he knows I've talked to you—"

"He doesn't. And he won't. He's on the run. He knows it's over and he's trying to save his own skin."

"Oh, thanks a lot! Killing me will help him do that!"

"Look, Doctor Chin—"

She shook her head, waving her arms. "Get out of my office! Don't come back until you have *everybody* in custody. Maybe I'll talk to you then. *Maybe.*"

Nick sat there a moment staring at her. Clearly she was too distraught to cooperate any further. He stood up.

"Okay. I'll come back after I find him."

He started for the door, then turned back.

"Do you have any idea where I might look for him?"

"*No!* I'm not his friend! Why would I know anything about him?" The look in her eyes was very close to panic. She pointed at the door. "Get out, please! Just go!"

Defeated, Nick nodded and left.

*

Nick walked back to his office and sat down at his desk. Milligan wasn't in yet and, since it was Sunday, Nick had no idea if he would be. He hadn't even been on Ceres a week, so he didn't know who took days off or when...if they ever did. As Shirley Chin had said, there didn't appear to be much to do on the asteroid except work or drink in a bar somewhere.

Nick placed a call to Carmen Castillo-Bernal on Mars, told her she was needed to take over Farrington immediately, and spent ten minutes assuring her that it wasn't a joke. Between sobs of gratitude, she thanked him profusely and promised to be on the next ship headed for Ceres. Nick disconnected, but ten minutes later she called him back with an itinerary; she already had her passage booked—she would be arriving on Thursday.

Again Nick disconnected, then pulled up the Airlock Authority on his computer to check docking schedules for arrivals so he could meet her when she arrived. As he scanned the arrivals column, he noticed the departures column right next to it, and his heart suddenly thundered in his chest...

FSS *Aurora* was scheduled to depart Ceres in four hours, destination Mars. There wouldn't be another departure for four days.

Nick glanced at his watch—it was almost six o'clock. He grabbed his porta-phone and started punching in numbers, but at that moment the front door opened and Russ Murray came in, followed by Sandy Beech. They stared at him in surprise.

"You look like hell, Walker. Didn't you get any sleep?"

Nick stood up and shook his head. "I started to, but—" He quickly filled them in on Jessica Garner's disappearance and his conclusions about Stan Cramer's flight. "Henry Farrington said he's a Sirian citizen. I'm betting that's where he'll go, if he can get off the asteroid. Most likely he already has his money in SiriusBank, so all he has to do is get away."

Both men stared at him thoughtfully.

"So why do you think the women are in danger?" Beech asked.

"Nikki Green hasn't been seen in two years, so I just want to locate her. But Jessica Garner is suddenly missing, too, and I can't think of anyone else who might have taken her. From what I saw in her apartment, she definitely didn't go willingly."

"But why would Cramer kill her?"

"She's a witness."

"So is Judge Maynard and the Farringtons and a lot of other people. Once he gets to Sirius none of them can hurt him, so why would he take the time to kill just one witness?"

Nick stood swaying with fatigue, his mind grinding to a halt. He shook his head dully.

"I dunno. I just feel like she's in danger. And...it's my fault."

Murray glanced at Beech. "Walker is right about the *Aurora*. We need to make sure Cramer doesn't leave on that ship." He turned to Nick. "But he could also get off the rock by heading to another asteroid. We need to check the jalopy departures, too."

Nick frowned. "If Cramer left the rock in a jalopy, how would that help him? If he wanted to get to Sirius he would have to leave from Mars or Terra, and the only way to get to either one of those would mean leaving Ceres in a passenger ship." He blinked in confusion. "Wouldn't it?"

"*If* he's trying to get to Sirius. At this point, that's just a theory."

"But—"

"Get some sleep, Walker. You're dead on your feet. Sandy and I will cover the exits for the next few hours. We'll call you if we need help."

Nick dropped into his chair, a hand on his forehead. "Oh, God! I *am* beat."

"You've had a long day. And a longer night. Go sack out. We won't let the bastard get away."

Centerville - Ceres

Full simulated daylight had been switched on by the time Nick arrived at the hotel. People were out and about, on their way to work or play. Nick entered the hotel lobby and headed for the lift, too weary to take the stairs. As he passed through the center lobby he saw Marshal Milligan talking to a group of people. At second glance he recognized Rev. Sledge and his two daughters. Puzzled, Nick detoured slightly and joined them.

"Marshal Milligan. What's going on? What are you doing here?"

Milligan peered narrowly at him. "I was just heading out to breakfast. I live on the third floor."

Nick felt stupid. It had never occurred to him to ask where Milligan lived, but it seemed everyone else in local government lived in the hotel so it only made sense that Milligan did too. He smiled weakly.

Rev. Sledge stuck out his hand to Nick.

"Marshal Walker, I'm glad we ran into you. We're about to board the ship for Mars, but I wanted to thank you once again for rescuing my children. God knows what might have become of them if you hadn't been there."

Nick accepted the man's hand and nodded. He still thought Sledge was a fool, but saw no point rubbing it in. Martha and Mary, looking lovely but subdued, also thanked him.

"Just doing my job," he said mechanically. "Glad it worked out the way it did." He chewed his lip briefly. "And...I hope neither of you will ever return to the asteroids. It just isn't safe."

"You don't need to worry, Marshal," Sledge replied. "I think we've all come to the same conclusion."

Nick excused himself and continued on to the lift. At least those girls were safe...but what about Jessica and Nikki? He still had no idea where they were, but was convinced they were still in danger. Stepping into the lift, he yawned, grateful that Murray and Beech had taken over the search. He had to get some sleep, at least for a few hours. He pushed the button for his floor and leaned against the elevator wall, closing his eyes briefly. That bed was going to feel awfully good.

The elevator jerked to a stop and he straightened up. The door slid open and he stared in surprise at the small figure huddled against the wall. His heart hammered with a surge of adrenaline as he stepped into the corridor and knelt in front of the child. It was Monica's son, Charley.

He was covered with blood.

Chapter 34

Nick's scalp tingled as he looked up and down the corridor. No one was in sight. He put his hands on Charley's shoulders and looked into his eyes. The boy had been crying and looked dazed; his shoulders twitched as he sniffled.

"Charley? Are you okay? Are you hurt?"

Charley shook his head, staring at Nick with listless eyes. A tear trickled down his cheek.

"What happened? Where did all this blood come from?"

Charley turned and looked down the corridor, toward the door to Monica's suite. For just a moment he didn't answer, then fresh tears appeared and the trickle became a flood.

"Mommy..."

"Jesus Christ!"

Nick stood abruptly, his fatigue vanishing. A few quick strides brought him to Monica's door, which faced the door to his own room. Monica's door stood ajar, and Nick drew his laser pistol. His own door was still closed, and he quickly unlocked it. Motioning the boy toward him, he pushed him gently inside.

"Charley, stay in here until I come for you. Okay? Don't open the door for anybody!"

Before the boy could answer Nick secured the door and locked it. He stepped up to Monica's door, noting a smear of blood on the handle. He listened for a moment, but all was quiet. Pistol ready, he nudged the door aside and peered into the suite. Everything seemed in order at first glance, no obvious signs of violence. Nothing overturned, nothing shattered. He stepped inside and swept the living room with his gun. He saw no one, but a pool of blood stained the white carpet near the bedroom door. His heart thundered faster, and he crossed the room quickly, shoving open the bedroom door.

Monica lay on the floor at the foot of her bed. She was wearing a bathrobe, also white, also bloodstained. At first he thought she was dead, but her eyes flickered and she lifted her head weakly.

"Nick..."

Nick shoved his gun into its holster and hurried forward. As he started to kneel beside her, he saw alarm in her eyes—she was looking past him.

"...look out!"

Nick spun around barely in time to see a male figure looming over him, but not fast enough to avoid the attack. He raised his elbow to deflect the heavy porcelain lamp that was headed his way, but it shattered against his skull with only slightly diminished force. He collapsed onto his left side, head spinning but still conscious; his right hand reached for his laser pistol again, but a sharp-toed leather shoe kicked it out of his hand and he found himself staring up into the grim face of Stanley Cramer. Cramer was holding a laser pistol of his own, and it was aimed straight at Nick's eye.

"I believe you have another weapon, Marshal," Cramer said coldly. "Give it to me...slowly."

Nick squinted and shook his head against a wave of dizziness. He rolled slowly onto his back.

"You're cooked, Cramer. You might as well give it up. You'll never get off the asteroid."

Cramer smiled in his quiet, unassuming manner.

"I believe I will get off the asteroid. And you're going to help me."

"Like hell I will."

"Give me the other gun. Or I'll shoot the niggo again."

Nick's eyes narrowed. He glanced at Monica, whose eyes were dull with pain. She was gasping, her expression hopeless. Weakly, she laid her head on the carpet. Nick reached for the .44 and drew it out of the holster with his finger tips. Cramer bent over and took it, raising his eyebrows in surprise.

"That is one heavy weapon!" he said in admiration.

"Yeah. Big enough to decapitate five or six crooked lawyers with a single shot."

Cramer smiled and stepped back. He took a moment to pop the cylinder on the .44 and dump out the bullets, then tossed the gun onto the bed.

"It won't hurt anyone now. Get up."

Cramer stood well back as Nick struggled to his feet, keeping him covered with the pistol. Nick shook his head to clear it, swayed once or twice, and stabilized, his mind racing.

"Why did you shoot Monica? What did she ever do to you?"

"She betrayed me."

"Did she, now? I thought she worked for you. I thought she was on your payroll."

Cramer smiled from behind his dark glasses, his teeth small and uneven.

"Exactly. But when push came to shove, she decided to save her own ass."

"Isn't that what you did to the Farringtons? Abandon them to save your own ass?"

"Those worthless twits! They don't have three brain cells between them. Why should I care what happens to them?"

Nick shrugged. "Good point. They aren't very bright, are they? They took *you* at face value." He glanced down at Monica, who appeared to have passed out. Her breathing was shallow and irregular. "Before we go any further, Cramer, if you want my help you're going to have to get her some help. If you just let her die, then I won't lift a finger for you."

"Marshal, the only reason you're alive right now is because I need you. If you refuse, then I might as well kill you where you stand."

Nick shrugged. "You have that option, but killing a U.F. Marshal is an automatic death sentence. Have you ever seen what happens in a vacuum chamber?"

Cramer's cheek twitched. "They have to catch me first."

"That's right, they do. But they have the exits covered, so they will. You said yourself that you need my help to get away."

Cramer grimaced. He glanced at the woman bleeding on the floor.

"So you're suggesting we call in the medics for her? Then you'll help me?"

"It's the only way I'll do it."

"Right. So let's see...we just stand here like this while the medics come, and when they leave they won't say a word to anyone about the man with the gun holding a U.F. Marshal at bay? You and I will continue our chat and no one will be the wiser?" He shook his head grimly. "You're a fucking idiot, Walker."

Nick smiled. "Oh, I don't know. I'm not the one who stole three corporations, murdered dozens of people, and got himself cornered by the U.F. Marshals. Who's the real idiot?"

"Let's move into the other room. It stinks in here."

"If she dies, you're cooked."

"In the other room! *Now!*"

With a last glance at Monica, Nick preceded Cramer into the living room, stepping around the blood on the floor. His eyes scanned the suite as he walked slowly toward the kitchen. Apparently Monica had been cooking when Cramer arrived—the smell of breakfast hung in the air; the coffee smelled especially good.

"That's far enough. Take a chair."

Nick turned—Cramer was still ten feet behind him, pistol in hand. He was pointing at the dining table. Nick pulled out a chair and sank into it.

"You and I can move this conversation somewhere else, Cramer. Call the medics...we don't have to be here when they arrive."

"We're going to talk now."

"I'm not listening." Nick placed both hands over his ears, closed his eyes, and began to babble, comedian style.

"Yadayadayadayadayada—"

Cramer banged a fist on the table. Angrily.

"Stop it!"

Nick opened his eyes and lowered his hands. Cramer's hand was shaking.

"Okay, here it is—Airlock Authority has been alerted. You can't get on a passenger ship even with me as a hostage...and even if you did, the authorities on Mars will be waiting for you. There's no other way to get to Sirius without first going to either Mars or Terra."

Cramer's eyebrows lifted. "Sirius? Who said anything about Sirius?"

"Henry Farrington told me you're a Sirian citizen. I'm guessing you've moved all your money to SiriusBank, and since the Federation exiles criminals to Sirius—or used to— there is no extradition treaty that would send you back."

Cramer's lip curled at the edge. "You're smarter than I gave you credit for. Well done, Marshal!"

Nick spread his hands. "Makes no difference. You'll never make it to Sirius. With or without me."

"Oh, but I will. Because I'm not taking a passenger ship."

Nick frowned. "You're not?"

"No." Cramer chuckled. "Not as smart as you think you are, badge boy. I'm taking a water freighter."

"A *water* freighter? To Sirius?"

"No, you fucking idiot! To Titan."

Nick stared in utter disbelief. All his theories tumbled down around his ears.

"How will that help you? There's no passenger service from Titan to Sirius any more than—"

"Why are you so fixated on passenger ships? Once I get to Titan I'll hop a freighter for Sirius."

"A freighter...to Sirius...from *Titan?*"

"That's right. The Outer Worlds buy half their grain and beef directly from Sirius, which produces more meat and produce than North and South America combined."

Nick shook his head numbly. His fatigue was flooding back in. "I didn't know that. Even so, how do you plan to get away with it? If you slip the net here, every world in the Federation will be alerted and on the lookout for you."

"That's where you come in, Walker. Once we get to Titan I'll make for the Sirian Consulate, and you'll be my hostage if anyone tries to stop me."

Nick shrugged. "Then you'll be a prisoner in the consulate. Unless you're extremely lucky and there's a Sirian starship in orbit when you get there. How often do those ships arrive?"

Cramer frowned. "Don't concern yourself with any of that. I have it worked out, and I have contacts who will help me. Your main concern is to get me off Ceres."

Nick laughed. "And how in the name of crap am I going to do that?"

"We'll leave the hotel together, with me as your prisoner. Only you'll take me to one of the B Terminals while your friends are watching the A Terminals."

Nick stared blankly. "With you as my prisoner."

"That's right."

"With your hands E-cuffed behind your back."

"I never said that. I'll be armed, you won't. We'll avoid people as much as possible, and you'll take me directly to the B Terminal."

"And why would I cooperate with that plan?"

Cramer smiled cruelly.

"Because your niggo friend isn't getting medical attention until I'm on board a ship."

Chapter 35

Nick rubbed his face with both hands to get the blood flowing. He looked up at Cramer with red-rimmed eyes.

"Okay, let's say I decide to go along with this—"

"You don't have much choice."

"I haven't slept for nearly thirty hours. Can I at least have a cup of coffee before we start?"

Cramer considered for a moment, then nodded. "Sure, why not. I could use one myself."

He walked past Nick into the kitchen, still holding the pistol. Without turning his back on Nick, he pulled down a pair of cups and took them to the table, then returned with the coffee pot and filled them.

"Where are Nikki Green and Jessica Garner?" Nick asked.

Cramer glanced at him in surprise. "Why would I know that?"

"Because you broke into Mrs. Garner's apartment last night and kidnapped her."

Cramer returned the coffee pot to the warmer. "Who said so?"

"Aw, Christ, Cramer! You've already admitted to enough crimes to keep your bones in storage for several centuries, so why deny this? If it wasn't you, then who was it? The Farringtons are in custody, Turd Murdoch is in the hospital, and nobody has bothered Mrs. Garner for two years, yet suddenly last night she goes missing? Who else could it be?"

Cramer pulled out a chair and sat down, the gun resting on his knee. He sipped his coffee.

"Why would I kidnap Jessica Garner? I just want to get off the rock."

"Maybe you figured to use her as a hostage. Now you've got me, so you don't need her anymore." Nick sipped his coffee. It had been sitting awhile, was bitter, and scalding hot.

"You have a theory for everything, don't you?" Cramer shook his head. "Okay, you're right. I don't really need the bitch now. I kept her on ice for two years just in case, but you make a better hostage."

Nick eyed Cramer narrowly. "You kept her on ice? Is that why Farrington furnished her apartment and paid for her groceries? As a bargaining chip in case you got caught?"

"Sure, why not. No criminal enterprise lasts forever. No matter how good you are, or how carefully you plan, everything eventually gets uncovered. If you don't recognize that going in, then you're a goddamn fool."

"Like the Farringtons?"

Cramer dipped his head. "Case in point."

"You always knew you'd get caught?"

"Always. I figured we might last three to five years, max. I paid off the right people, finagled my own judge, killed whoever had to be killed, and damned if it didn't work for nearly thirteen years!"

Nick's eyes were wide with wonder. "I suppose it didn't hurt that the Outer Worlds depended on your company for survival."

"That was probably what did it." Cramer smiled, relaxing a little. "But I always knew someone would come along who would smell a tripod rat. What was it that tipped you off?"

Nick sipped more coffee. "Some of the felons you hired to run your prison enjoyed their work a little too much. I spotted prisoner abuse and went looking for that. I had no idea about the rest."

"Um. Always a weak link." Cramer shrugged. "Anyway, I figured you were trouble the minute I heard you stood up to Turd Murdoch. So I sent Fred Ferguson to eliminate you."

Nick peered at him bleakly. "So you admit to killing Misery Allen?"

"Not intentionally. The shower was meant for you." Cramer scowled. "Don't you ever bathe?"

"Yeah, every Saturday night. So where is Jessica now? You never told me."

Cramer took off his glasses and laid them on the table. His own eyes looked as red and bleary as Nick's.

"She's safe, right here in the hotel. After we're gone she'll come out. You don't need to worry about her."

"And Nikki Green?"

"With the Garner woman."

"And where did you keep her for the last two years? No one in the prison remembers seeing her."

Cramer stared at him a moment, then smiled faintly, as if with a fond memory.

"She was in my apartment most of that time. Hottest thing I ever laid my hands on."

"You didn't beat her? Torture her?"

Cramer shook his head. "That's Henry's idea of fun, not mine. You don't take a beautiful work of art and scar it up. You treat it gently, preserve it, and then you can enjoy it again and again, forever."

Nick drained his coffee cup. "I need one more cup if I'm gonna save your worthless ass." He stood up. "You want another?"

Cramer's gun came up, but the question was innocent enough. He nodded.

"Okay. So you're going to do it?"

Nick walked to the coffee pot and carried it back to the table.

"Only because I don't think it will work," he said, pouring coffee into Cramer's cup. He poised the pot over his own cup, but held it while he finished the thought. "We might make it off of Ceres, but I seriously don't think you'll ever get on board a Sirian starship. The Titan authorities will get you."

Cramer smiled. "I guess we'll find out, won't we?"

"I guess we will."

Nick smashed the coffee pot down over Cramer's head, shattering the glass and drenching him with near-boiling liquid. Cramer screamed in agony. Nick grabbed his gun hand and slammed it onto the edge of the table, breaking his wrist; the gun chirped loudly as a bolt of light slammed into the floor, then the gun skittered across the carpet.

Still screaming, Cramer bolted out of the chair to escape the scalding coffee that still soaked his hair and shirt. His good hand floundered about his head, trying to brush away the pain, but Nick put a knee into his spine and forced him to the floor, hauled both arms behind his back, and E-cuffed him. He stood back, breathing hard, trembling like a leaf. It was over, at last. He had the bastard.

He picked up Cramer's weapon and hurried into the bedroom, where he knelt over Monica. She was still alive, but drifting in and out of consciousness.

"Monica! Hang on, I'm calling for help right now."

"Cramer?" she mumbled.

"In custody. He's done for."

"What about...Charley?"

"In my room. He's safe. Just hang on, don't let go."

* * *

Marshal Milligan was still having breakfast in the hotel lobby when Nick reached him by pocket phone. He arrived three minutes later, right behind the medical team. As Monica Maynard was wheeled away on a gurney, they stood over Stanley Cramer, boiled and bedraggled, and gazed at him with contempt in their eyes.

"So you got him," Milligan grunted.

"Actually, he was waiting for me. Made it a whole lot easier."

"Did he admit to—"

"Pretty much everything. The only thing I don't know at this point is where he's holding Nikki Green and Jessica Garner, but he did say they're alive and in good shape."

"You believe him? He's a pretty accomplished liar."

Nick shrugged. "I don't see why he would lie about that. We already have more on him than he can ever explain away."

Milligan grunted again. "You know, you could save the Federation a whole bunch of taxpayer money if you just pushed this fuck out an airlock."

Nick stared at Milligan in surprise. Milligan returned the gaze.

"You have a streak of the vigilante in you, Walker. You seem to enjoy hurting people."

Nick let his breath out slowly, not sure whether to be offended.

"Only people who hurt other people," he said. "After what he did to Misery Allen? This is only a fraction of what she suffered."

"Well..." Milligan gazed at the prisoner again. "Maybe he deserves the airlock."

Nick nodded slowly, his pulse picking up speed—the idea was intriguing. "I guess I could do that. You wouldn't tell anyone, would you, sir?"

"Who would I tell? I'll be retiring soon."

Cramer, whimpering in pain, sat with his head down. If he heard them, he didn't acknowledge it.

"On second thought," Nick said, "I think maybe I won't. I hate injustice, and I hate people who practice injustice. When I get the chance to make people like that suffer, I want them to *really* suffer. Throwing him out an airlock is too quick. I enjoy hurting people too much to let them off that easy."

Milligan shrugged. "Have it your way. Do you want to take him in, or shall I?"

Nick considered briefly. "You take him, Marshal. I need to check on Charley. He's waiting in my hotel room."

"Okay. See you back at the office."

* * *

Nick unlocked his room and stepped inside. Charley was sitting at his kitchen table, eating a granola bar he'd found in the pantry. To Nick's surprise, he was no longer covered in blood—his face had been washed and he was wearing Nick's own bathrobe, though it was much too big for him.

The boy looked around with wide eyes. "Is my mommy okay?"

Nick nodded and crossed the room to stand next to him. "She's on her way to the hospital. Charley...what happened to your clothes? Did you clean yourself up?"

Still chewing the granola bar, Charley shook his head. "Aunt Nikki did."

"What? Who—"

Nick spun around. Someone had jerked the .44 out of his holster from behind. His eyes widened as he saw Jessica Garner standing six feet away, the .44 aimed squarely at his chest.

"You swore you wouldn't tell anyone I talked to you!" she cried, tears running down her cheeks. "You betrayed my confidence!"

Nick sighed wearily and raised both hands to appease her.

"They were already in custody," he explained. "It was part of an interrogation."

"If they were in custody, then how do you explain what happened to me last night?"

"Cramer got away. As soon as I realized you were in danger I went to your place, but I was too late."

"Where is he now?"

"Back in custody, and I promise you he won't get loose again."

Jessica Garner stared at him with half-crazed eyes, the gun trembling in her hand.

"How do I know I can trust you?"

"Who else are you going to trust? I'll tell you this much—you can leave Ceres now. The U.F. Marshal will pay for your passage to Mars, if that's what you want."

The gun trembled harder. She didn't answer.

"That gun isn't loaded," Nick told her. "Pull the trigger if you don't believe me."

She stared at him for another irrational moment, then popped the cylinder to check for herself. She sagged slightly as she saw the six empty chambers, then handed the gun back to him. She backed across the room and sat down on the edge of the bed.

"How did you get in here? I locked the door when I put Charley inside."

"Cramer owns this whole rock. I think he has a key to everything."

Nick frowned. "He put you in my room? Why?"

"He said he had business with the judge. He said to wait for him."

"Why didn't you make a break for it after he left?"

She shuddered. "If he saw me, he'd kill me. And he said he'd kill the child if I didn't wait for him." She put her hands over her face and began to tremble.

"Where's Nikki Green? Cramer said you two were together."

As if on cue, the bathroom door slid open and a figure appeared. Nick had never met Nikki Green but would have recognized her anywhere—two years in captivity had done nothing to erase her vid-star looks. She gazed warily at him as she strode slowly across the carpet. Her eyes were clear, but troubled; a permanent crease was etched into her perfect forehead, a sure sign of long-term stress.

"Nikki Green?" he asked.

She nodded. "You must be Nick Walker."

"Yes, Ma'am. United Federation Marshal. I've been looking for you."

She stopped six feet in front of him. "I heard Stan talking about you."

Nick studied her closely. "Were you tortured?"

"For a few days. Stan actually rescued me. He saw what they were doing and made them stop before any permanent damage was done. I guess I owe that bastard my life."

"You don't seem terribly fond of him."

She laughed, low and bitter. "A slave well treated is still a slave. No, I hate him with all my heart. He said he was going to take me to Sirius. Is it true that slavery is legal there?"

Nick shrugged. "I've never been to Sirius. I have no idea."

She closed her eyes dramatically. "*Please* tell me you won't let him get away again!"

"I promise. Are you willing to testify against him?"

"Yes! I'll testify against him, and Henry, and Silva, and the judge, and Turd Murdoch, and just about everybody else who ever worked over there."

Nick glanced at Charley, who was just finishing his second granola bar. The boy stared back with innocent eyes. Nick looked at the two women again.

"Would either of you be interested in some breakfast?" He smiled. "I'm buying."

END

About the Author

John Bowers discovered his love of writing in the seventh grade. He began his first novel at age 13 and before he graduated high school, he wrote four more. Today he is the author of three popular science fiction series: the Starport series; the Nick Walker, U.F. Marshal series; and the Fighter Queen saga. Bowers is married and lives in California with his wife and two cats. Now retired, he is a computer programmer by profession, but a *Born Novelist* by birth.

Made in the USA
Middletown, DE
28 June 2024

56360611R00186